D1345198

TOUCH THE SILENCE

Recent Titles by Gloria Cook

The Pengarron Series

PENGARRON LAND
PENGARRON PRIDE
PENGARRON'S CHLDREN
PENGARRON DYNASTY *

KILGARTHEN
ROSCARROCK
ROSEMERRYN
TREVALLION

LISTENING TO THE QUIET *

TOUCH THE SILENCE *

* *available from Severn House*

To Val Vivian with many thanks

Chapter One

The way the dogs were barking spoke of a stranger's approach to the back door being barred. Emilia Rowse grabbed her mackintosh and pulled on her boots to investigate.

Dashing the first few yards over the flagstones, she froze at the cause of the disturbance. A figure in a shabby dark greatcoat and billycock hat was in the yard, trapped inside a huddle of territorial Jack Russells, and with darkness only an hour away and more rain imminent, the shadows were making him appear outlandish and looming. He was the tallest man Emilia had ever seen, with unattended grey hair and a long beard, and in a single moment she thought of wizards and Fagin and the Russian mad monk Rasputin. She wished she had brought the shotgun with her.

Alone except for her employer's senile grandmother, she allowed the dogs to carry on agitating and growling around the stranger. 'What do you want?'

He swept off his hat. 'Pardon me, miss. My name is Archie Rothwell. Would it be possible to speak to the farmer, Mr Alec Harvey?'

'Why do you want to speak to him?'

'I asked in the village for work, in return for a little food and hopefully shelter. The landlady of the public house suggested I enquire here.'

Emilia moved closer and could see he was younger than she had first thought, perhaps in his mid-thirties. His hair, which reached his shoulders, was in fact a sandy colour, and not scruffy, merely tangled by the sharp wind. His eyes had a startling brightness and were of a deep greenish hue. His voice was the most surprising, mellow and refined and she had heard every word clearly above the din of the dogs.

He did not change his bare expression, and this kept Emilia resolved to caution. The farm was the largest in the parish and had once had a workforce of seventeen, but with the war relentlessly robbing it, and the nearby village of Hennaford, of young men, workers were sorely needed. Except during the busiest periods of spring and harvest, when the aged, the housewives and children helped out, there was now only Emilia herself, her father, the cowman, and the youngest Harvey brother, Ben, currently chopping logs for the winter store; but she was sure Alec Harvey, who was in Truro on business, wouldn't want this kind of labourer – a tramp, even though he wasn't the usual rough kind.

'I don't think you'll find what you're looking for here. You'll have to try elsewhere.'

The stranger replaced his hat, again without emotion. 'I'm sorry to have troubled you. Perhaps you would be good enough to call off the dogs so I can leave.'

He brought his other arm forward from the folds of his coat, and Emilia noticed he had a stout walking stick. She was afraid he was about to lash out at the dogs, but he made to turn, wobbled, fought to keep his balance, then with a cry of alarm fell sideways, like a felled log, on to the muddy cobbles.

The dogs leapt towards him, snarling, and Emilia shouted at them to get away. They obeyed, but maintained their fretful pacing at a distance. Her dilemma now was whether to help the stranger up or to hold her space. 'Are you hurt? I'm sorry about that.'

There was something defensive and self-sufficient about the man, so she watched, ready to spring forward to his aid, while he gripped the horse trough and levered himself upright. Using the stone side as a prop, he rubbed his knee and elbow and shook dirt off his coat.

Then he fastened his extraordinary, vibrant eyes on her. 'Good day to you, miss.'

Emilia noticed that except for where the mud had soiled his clothes they were clean, and she was close enough to detect no impure smells on him. When she saw his laborious forward-tilting steps, the way he had to lean on his stick, the flames of guilt flushed her cheeks and she dashed on ahead and faced him. He could be a war veteran, a wounded hero – an officer by the way he had spoken – and she had treated him with contempt. Had sent him away with the wind strengthening, a further threat to his frail stability, its raw fingers parting his hair and wrapping it forward under his chin as if making a scarf of empty comfort. The air was growing heavier and for a moment was strangely hollow, then a dense bone-chilling mist swept down over everything, the advance of a heavy shower. He wouldn't get far before receiving a thorough drenching. 'Look, perhaps you could come back another time. Or if you'd like to shelter a while in the barn, I'll fetch you some food.'

He looked up from the ground for a moment. 'Don't bother yourself, miss. I have enough for my needs today. Goodbye.'

She moved out of his way, keeping the dogs behind her until he disappeared. It was hard to say if he had been offended, resigned or hurt by her behaviour, but she kept his quiet dignity in mind while hurrying back to work, which she was later than usual in getting on with.

She was preparing a tea tray when the door of the kitchen was suddenly opened, making her splash boiling water over the scrubbed-white pine table. 'Ohh!'

'Sorry I startled you, Em.' Ben Harvey smiled in from the cold stone floor of the back kitchen, where he was discarding his grimy boots and rough work coat.

Emilia swept the heavy iron, copper-spouted kettle back on top of the range and wiped up the spillage. 'Are you sure Dad didn't see you come in?' She could hear the lowing of the twenty-strong herd – the mainstay of the farm – and her father whistling to the sheepdog helping to drive them into the milking shed. 'He'll be expecting you. I'm going to be late getting out there. Will you explain?'

'I saw Edwin taking out his pipe.' With his quick, energetic actions Ben was there, stretching out his arms to her. Unspared of height, he had an athletic control of his lean, wide-shouldered body, a confident lift to his head, all in perfect association with his strong dark features. 'And Alec's not back yet, we can make the most of it.'

Even though the war had swept away many former attitudes, and the shortage of servants meant good ones were now prized, Emilia's lifelong friendship with Ben meant she had always been looked on at Ford Farm as more than a skivvy. Their romance was a recent development. Alec Harvey did not seem to mind, but Emilia thought that perhaps he didn't expect it to be permanent. Her father, who had ordered that she and Ben no longer spend time alone, had welcomed it, but with reservation, for next month, when Ben reached the age of eighteen, he was to follow his two other older brothers, one now dead, into the Army. Emilia still marvelled that Ben, who stirred the hopes of the village girls and those in superior places, was now hers.

Their first kiss had been accidental. While sweeping out the barn together in preparation for the threshing, the simple act of her tripping over one of the cats and him catching her round the waist, and them laughing as always over such an occurrence, had broken their usual cosiness. They had shared many sibling-type hugs, but this one had ended in an off-balanced kiss, the brotherly touch of Ben's lips landing not on her cheek but firmly on her lips.

In that moment, all they had taken for granted about each other had been swept away in a startling new reality, an awakening of physical attraction. Dazed, staring eye to eye, rather than retreat, they had explored the riot of sensations and emotions stirred up in them with a tentative kiss, and this had provoked an immediate unquenchable enthusiasm to hold and cling, to taste and try, while unleashing the powerful hope to experience more. Amazed at not discovering this before, both had felt their being together was meant to be.

Emilia glanced at the clock. Time was speeding away and she had work in the dairy and then the Harveys' supper to prepare, but she went straight to Ben. The instant his arms were about her she forgot about the stranger. She kept her eyes closed when their eager, intense kiss ended and rested her face against his neck.

The glow of the oil lamps had set their images in the window, showing their innocence, their early maturity at having to work eighteen-hour days, of coping with shortages of almost every kind and the constant fear of news of family deaths, all mingling with their iron will to carry on without complaint or self-pity.

Ben gazed at her reflection. Admiring her. Wondering about her. Emilia had been born two days later than himself, yet often seemed a generation older. Full of good sense, was what people said about her. Sometimes she had a quiet way, other times her manner was direct and resolute, and when she got angry, people were in no doubt about it. She had a measure of stateliness, which could make her seem a little mystifying, yet she was practical and unfussy, wearing her thick rich-brown hair in a single plait and working in trousers, not bothering with corsets – how soft and warm and stimulating her natural shape felt in his arms.

She had first been brought to the farm as an infant, and had worked there since leaving school. She had shared every important moment of his life, as his comforter, his source of calm and wisdom. He knew he relied on her. A little too much. Perhaps it would have been better if they had stayed chums, she being the sister he had never had, and he had not fallen in love with her. A stupid dreadful thought! These new intimate memories of Em would help get him through whatever he was to face after his officer training.

The first angry spits of rain distorted their likenesses on the glass. Emilia traced the firm angle of his jaw, his skin cold and tense from being outside since dawn, the dark stubble needing a second attention from a razor. She felt his body give a mysterious tremble. She knew Ben better than anyone, yet there were so many new things to discover about him, and so little time left in which to do it.

She eased herself away from him. 'I mustn't delay a minute longer taking in your gran's tea, my love.' Emilia's voice had a soothing notable rhythm, pointing to the careful attention she was willing to give others. 'It's a wonder she's not woken from her nap by now and calling for it.'

Ben reclaimed his coat and boots, but lingered long enough to take in the overflowing basket of laundry on the settle, the afternoon's collection of muddy eggs waiting to be taken to the washhouse and dealt with, the breakfast dishes not yet put away on the cluttered dresser, the crumbs of bread and cheese his grandmother had made around her armchair while eating her midday meal. The cats were clustered asleep on the wool rug, whose floral pattern was confused by lost fur of more than a day's standing. 'Alec's hoping to employ some more hands today. It's time he got a new housekeeper. You shouldn't have to keep doing so much by yourself, darling. And you'll have another stormy walk home tonight.'

'I get through,' Emilia said, matter-of-fact about her workload, which had increased greatly a year ago when the kitchen maid had suddenly, and inexplicably, left. Tragedy had followed almost at once when Alec's wife, Lucy, died in miscarriage, and the housekeeper, whom Lucy had brought with her to the marriage, also deserted the farm. Emilia was touched by Ben's concern. His thoughtfulness was one of the reasons she loved him. She did not mind the burden of caring for his 83-year-old grandmother, even with her incessant humming and meaningless chatter, and the necessity of cleaning up after her occasional 'accident'. Every time she looked at Mrs Harvey, her gaze had been refreshed by trusting, smiling eyes. 'Someone was here not long ago looking for work. I suggested he come back.'

'An odd-looking fellow, limping on both feet? I saw the back of him when I was bringing in the wood cart. Can't see what use he'd be.'

'He didn't go back to the village then. The first thing he did was to offer his name, so he probably was genuine. I made him fall over – I feel awful about that. He could have managed in the garden and done a few jobs about the yard.'

Emilia picked up the tea tray but dropped it down again. 'What on earth was that?' The wind had been howling round the corners of the house all day, but she had heard a peculiar caterwauling.

'Probably one of the dogs investigating something it shouldn't, you know what Pip's like.'

The abnormal noise came again, longer, higher-pitched. 'Sounds like an animal in pain.' Emilia joined Ben at the stable door, peering out across the lower half.

They listened. The cows were quiet, all would be feeding. The rain was being blown in a slant, hitting the numerous buildings ranged around the yard in wicked spatters, hisses, drummings, clinkings. They could hear loud tricklings of water seeping along gulleys and whooshing down drains, and the wind thrashing through the trees at the perimeter hedges and its distant roar as it battered the woods across the field at the back of the sprawling property. The only movements were leaves and stalks of straw being hurled about before disappearing or gathering in corners. The larger inner yard was partitioned off by a medium-height stone wall and anything amiss in there could not be seen.

Once more the unnatural wail pitched through the murky October air. Emilia grabbed Ben's arm. 'What is it?' It sounded like the pain and terror in her nightmares of her brother, Billy, maimed or dying in a mud-filled Flanders trench, reaching out vainly for her. He was with Ben's surviving brother, Tristan, and according to the previously agreed coded words in his last letter, the fighting was soon to intensify again.

A horrifying thought sent her dashing back into the kitchen and towards the door that led to the front of the house.

'What's wrong?' Ben tore after her.

'I need to made sure your gran's safe! I haven't looked in on her all afternoon.'

The sitting-room door was ajar. Emilia burst in to where she had left Mrs Harvey in her winged armchair, beside a protected fire, feet up on a stool, covered with a plaid blanket.

The old lady was not there. Her lace shawl was on the carpet, apparently having slipped off her shoulders, the blanket lay heaped in front of the chair.

Mrs Harvey was unable to climb the stairs unaided, and Emilia skidded up and down the long tiled passage, searching the dining room, the small parlour, the old play room, Alec Harvey's den, even the cupboard under the stairs, where Mrs Harvey had on one occasion shut herself in. All were empty. Then she saw the key of the front door was in the lock, instead of hanging on its high hook, a precaution to protect Mrs Harvey, who was inclined to wander off. The grandfather clock chimed three forty-five, accusing Emilia of being over an hour late in checking on her charge.

'Oh, dear Lord, Ben, it must have been your gran we heard! If we don't find her and she gets as far as the woods or the ford . . .' The ford was at the bottom of the hill, a short distance down the lane, and it was deep enough today for a person to drown in. The narrow stone bridge that ran along the side of the hedge for pedestrians was muddy and slippery.

Ben followed her out through the short vestibule and the porch. In the steady chilly downpour, they stared into the rapidly fading light for any sign of the old lady. Pray God, she was trying to find her way back in.

'Mrs Harvey! Mrs Harvey!'

'Grandma! Grandma!'

Emilia shook Ben's arm, warning him to keep still and listen.

'You search round here,' Ben whispered, lest he drown out his grandmother's voice or fumblings. 'I'll look through the yards and outhouses. Don't forget the shed. Grandma liked her gardening in the old days.'

There was a loud drawn-out screech, an unearthly sound. Emilia's heart jerked in fright.

Then they both saw her. Mrs Harvey was staggering on all fours in one of the neglected flower beds, her clothes so lagged in mud as to be camouflage, her white hair hanging down about her stricken face in rats' tails. With a feeble lift of her head she cried out, like a frightened, bewildered child.

'Oh, dear God! It'll be all right, Lottie!' Emilia screamed the name the old lady was most apt to respond to. 'We're coming for you.'

'Grandma! Grandma!' Ben shouted, in the most terrifying moments of his life. Haring down the gravel path and across the large rectangular quagmire of lawn, he reached her first. Even with his strong arms he found it difficult to lift his grandmother up, for she was tall and plump and struggling against him.

'Quick, carry her inside!' Emilia reached them. 'We must get her warm and dry.'

Lottie Harvey's mental condition meant she understood nothing of normal everyday life. Childlike, easily alarmed, sometimes impatient, she occasionally hit out at those attending to her, pinching them, trying to bite. Although weak, exhausted and shivering, out of sheer panic she smashed a muddied hand into Ben's face and pushed against it. Sobbing and muttering, she was trying to get to Emilia.

Emilia clamped hold of Lottie's slippery hands. Ben blinked frantically as earth and tiny stones scratched his eyes. He took a step forward, slipped and fell on one knee. Yelled out in pain and frustration. Lottie screamed in terror, her hands torn from Emilia's grasp.

'It's no good, Ben! Let her go. Let her come to me, I'll lead her inside.'

He obeyed. It took their combined strength to hoist Lottie to her feet. 'Lottie, it's Em. Come inside with me and Ben and get warm by the fire. You'd like that, eh?'

Registering Emilia's voice, Lottie became calmer, allowing her waist to be held and her hand taken, then to be moved, her steps faltering, towards the house. Rubbing at the searing pain in his eyes, Ben got up, shaking his leg to unlock the hurt in his knee.

The door had slammed shut. Bending her head against the opposing might of the wind, Emilia strove to get Lottie inside and finally safe and secure. She prayed Lottie hadn't been outside long enough to have got chilled through with the risk of succumbing to pneumonia. Ben stumbled on ahead and groped for the door handle.

As she was coaxing Lottie over the doorstep, the fuming skies released an even heavier deluge of bitter rain. Emilia led Lottie down the passage, unaware of her own discomfort but horribly conscious of Lottie's wet spongy arms, the folds of her torn dress sticking to her wobbly legs, her feet in ripped stockings only able to shuffle while leaving a mucky-dishwater trail. Her pearls were tangled in her cameo brooch, her skin grazed, nose running, mouth dribbling. She was reduced to a dirty, aged urchin, her flesh shrunk by more than age.

In the sitting room Emilia ordered Ben to push a sofa, a buttoned-back piece, up close to the hearth. Panting, drops of water stinging her eyes, Emilia eased Lottie down on it, sat beside her and cradled her against her body. Lottie flopped her head on to her shoulder. She was stunned and shocked, breathing raggedly and shuddering violently from the effects of the cold, the wet and her ordeal.

'What now?' Ben gasped, still blinking and trying to rid his eyes of grit with one of Lottie's handkerchiefs. With his back to the moulded mantelpiece, he stared amazed at the dishevelled spectacle of his grandmother – an unknown sight that horrified him. Coming from upper-middle-class stock, as Harvey wives had for the last century, she had never suffered this much discomfort and distress before. This should never have happened.

Emilia motioned for him to pick up the shawl and the blanket and pass them to her. She wrapped the shawl round Lottie's shoulders, wiping her face with an edge of soft lace, and covered the rest of her with the blanket. Lottie whimpered. Emilia used tender words until she fell quiet with only the occasional nervous gulp. Ben sat close on Lottie's other side, spreading his arm across her back, resting his hand on Emilia's shoulder. 'It's all right, Grandma. Em will look after you.'

Emilia felt Lottie's trembling fingers seizing her shirt. 'I'm afraid she's not going to let me leave her, Ben. Can you fetch me the things I'll need to give her a wash, and her night-clothes and slippers? Her shoes must be out there somewhere. I might as well get her ready for bed now.' Emilia recognized a certain smell. 'Oh, and some clean underwear. I'll take your gran through to the kitchen and watch her to see if she needs the doctor. You get changed as quickly as you can, Ben, and wash out your eyes before you join Dad.'

'What about you, Em?' He gave her dripping plait a gentle tug before making for the door. 'Grandma's covered you in mud.'

'Oh, fetch an extra towel and find me something to wear, anything will do. Ben, why was the front door unlocked? No one's come or gone by it for ages.'

He let out a deep sigh. 'It could only have been my absent-minded brother. As if life isn't already difficult enough. Alec's taking his time about this business in town. I'll have something to say to him when he finally gets back.'

Chapter Two

Emilia was helping Lottie to sip hot milk laced with rum when Alec Harvey sprinted into the kitchen. Soaked from the journey home, his hat hanging from one hand and Lottie's mud-caked shoes dangling from the other, he was making puddles on the tiles. 'Emilia! How is she? Ben's just told me what happened. Do you think I should send for the doctor?'

'I'm sure Mrs Harvey's going to be fine,' Emilia replied, smoothing at Lottie's long white hair, now washed, combed and drying over a towel round her shoulders. 'She's only had a bad fright really, and you know how she hates Dr Holloway fussing over her. I'm so sorry about this. It was all my fault.'

He nodded at his grandmother's shoes. 'What shall I do with these?'

'Just drop them down. I'll see to them in a while.'

'Yes, yes, it's nice,' Lottie muttered, taking a last noisy sip of the flavoured milk and puckering her lips in Emilia's direction. Emilia brought her face close so Lottie could kiss her. Then she kissed and stroked Lottie's soft, wrinkled cheek; so thankful she had not been hurt or lost. Emilia couldn't move away yet for Lottie was seeking the comfort of her hand.

Alec responded to the rapport between Emilia and his grandmother by shrugging off the tension. Without due thought he placed the shoes on the end of the table and threw his outdoor things over the back of the settle, wetting the pile of dry laundry. His undisciplined ways, a deliberate development since he had inherited the farm, had often brought quick and bitter complaints from his late wife. Emilia, however, never gave him as much as a chiding look. She had no idea how much this meant to him: to be able to feel at ease in his home, where every day of his childhood he had been subjected to ridicule and shame and rejection over an incomprehensible disorder that made him barely able to read or write, His father, a hard, unfeeling man, had agreed with his schoolmasters' accusations, that he was being lazy and was a liar.

He crouched at the other side of his grandmother's armchair. 'What were you thinking of, Grandma, eh? Giving our dear Emilia a fright like that. We're going to have to keep a closer eye on you, aren't we?' He tucked her shawl in snugly round her stout waist, but Lottie kept her gaze on Emilia.

'You're so good for Grandma, Emilia. I don't want you blaming yourself for her wandering off.' Alec reached across in front of Lottie and pressed a light hand on Emilia's shoulder. 'I don't sleep well, you see, and have a habit of wandering about at night. Last night I got a bad feeling about Tristan. I was afraid for him. I opened the door to send out the protection I'd prayed to be all around him, and I forgot to lock it again.' Tristan was his and Ben's surviving brother. Henry, the second eldest, a university graduate with a promising career in science, had perished at Neuve Chapelle, in 1915.

'I understand, but I don't think we can go on like this.'

Lottie prattled, 'Pigs at a wedding. Two at a time. Can't you see them? Never, never mind.' Then she slipped into a little world of her own, humming a low indefinable tune, and Emilia was able to get up. She made a start on the supper, a meatless dish to be cooked in yesterday's beef gravy, already heating on the range. She would be leaving for her home, one of the many small cottages Alec owned in Hennaford, even later than usual this evening.

'I agree, and we won't be.'

He rose and lit a cigarette, and Emilia followed his solid figure, clad in good cloth and riding boots. He was a gentleman farmer, who rode an ageing mare now nearly all the country's horses had been commandeered for war service. His hair, which habitually strayed into untidiness, was coal-black like Ben's, and he held a similar soft grey gaze, but while Ben shone with openness and energy, Alec, although equal in strength and diligence, often seemed withdrawn, and he could be vague and evasive. Occasionally he was sharp with Ben, and Emilia had narrowed this down to impatience with business matters. Would they exchange hard words over his excursion to Truro today?

Emilia had noticed he was always civil, kind even to women. She had marvelled at his patience with the highly-strung Lucy, whom she had never liked and who had given her a tough time, and who, so devout to her own class observances, had often treated Alec with disrespect because, Emilia had assumed, he disregarded them. He shunned many things of the usual order, insisting most people call him by his first name, as if he wanted to be seen as unique, a rebel perhaps. Emilia, so new to the wonders of love, had formed the habit of comparing every man to Ben, and it struck her then how Alec had often seemed lonely, although he was a little more open without Lucy's overbearing presence. Perhaps his patience with Lucy had been more of an indifference. Perhaps—

With a jolt she realized she was staring at him and he was steadily regarding her. She bent her head over the cutting board. 'You've managed to get more help then, Alec?'

'I have, and not before time according to Ben. I've just had him ranting at me about you doing too much – as if I didn't agree with him.' The hint of rancour made her glance at Alec. 'I've engaged someone to live in and take over the housework, as from tomorrow.'

'Good,' Emilia said, with a frankness that would have made Ben laugh if he had heard it.

Alec's sternness vanished in a slow smile. 'I'm glad you're pleased. A Miss Tilda Lawry will be arriving in the morning. I approached her at the suggestion of one of the persons I had lunch with at the Red Lion. Miss Lawry was his parlour maid – she can turn her hand to anything, apparently. You know how things are with the government continually urging the well-off to release their servants for work more suited to the war effort – people don't want to appear unpatriotic,' he added with typical cynicism.

'She sounds perfect.' Emilia dabbed her eyes, watering from chopping onions. 'I'll be pleased to have more time to get on with my usual work. Did Ben tell you about the man who turned up asking for work this afternoon?'

'He did, and if this man reappears I'll consider him.' Tapping ash into the brass fender, Alec came up close to her. 'Ben's pleased you're going to be living here from now on.'

'What?' Emilia dropped the chopping knife. Even living in the same house as Ben would not compensate for the loss of her little bit of freedom, to rarely see her mother or Honor Burrows, her closest friend.

'You do see it's the obvious answer, Emilia? Grandma needs you. You're the only one she really responds to.'

'Yes, but I can't live here, my father wouldn't allow it.'

'Edwin's already agreed, even to you staying tonight so you can watch over Grandma, seeing what she's just been through. You can sleep in Grandma's room, then move into one of the bedrooms tomorrow. Tilda Lawry's a committed Anglican and she's in her forties, so there'll be no raising of moral eyebrows.'

Emilia vented her indignation – how dare he take her for granted. 'Alec, I don't want to live here.'

'Is that so, Emilia?' A play of ironic amusement chased away the weariness scoring his strong brow, making him seem a more youthful twenty-eight years. 'I've noticed how you've always liked the farm, how you've made the dairy your own. I'm not going to keep you here a prisoner twenty-four hours a day, my dear. Tilda Lawry can help to attend to Grandma. Your mother and your quiet little friend can come here at any time. Sound better?'

'I should have liked to have been asked about these arrangements before they were made.' She wiped her hands and banged a pan of dripping down on the hob. 'I suppose I'll just have to get on with it.'

'I'd be pleased if you would, Emilia. I apologize for taking the liberty, but as you've said yourself, we couldn't go on as we have been. I forgot to ask Ben just now: did he call on Ursula today?'

'He did. I'm afraid she and Jonny weren't there.' As she set the onions sizzling, Emilia heard Alec's sigh of discontent. Ursula was Tristan's wife. Alec was concerned for his five-year-old nephew, Jonathan. It was common knowledge that Ursula had taken a lover shortly after Tristan's last leave. 'I'll go to Ford House myself tomorrow.'

When Emilia turned back, Alec was staring at the cardigan she was wearing. Fetched for her by Ben, it was of fine wool, a delicate design, softer against her skin than the flannel things she normally wore. 'Is something wrong?'

'It was Lucy's. I thought her people had taken all her things away after the funeral.'

Reminded of his bereavement, Emilia reddened in shame. She shouldn't have shown her ire just now. All Alec had done was to make a reasonable arrangement, and this was a time when sacrifices should be made eagerly. 'I'm sorry. Ben said these clothes belonged to your mother.'

'The dress does. You wear it well.'

'Do you want me to take this off?' She fingered the pretty mother-of-pearl buttons on the cardigan.

He nodded. 'Some of my mother's things are stored in the metal trunk in the boxroom. Help yourself to anything you'd like and keep it. You should find something for tonight. Edwin will bring your own things over tomorrow.'

'Thank you. Alec, don't you think, I mean, would you like me to pass on anything I don't want to a charity, for the war effort?'

'Do whatever you think's best. This house needs a woman for that sort of thing.' He stared down at the paving beneath his feet for some moments, seemingly grim and sorrowful, and lonely again. Before heading outside, he said, 'I really need you to be here, Emilia.'

Lottie lay under her coral-pink quilt, lulled to sleep by unhurried hugs and gentle songs. She was snoring, although not obtrusively. In case her breathing turned harsh, indicating infection, Emilia remained alert, stretched out on a couch in the spacious room at the front of the farmhouse, which had seen a lot of fine upgrading throughout the reign of Queen Victoria.

Although she was only moving a mile away from home, Emilia was experiencing the sort of thrill as if actually breaking out into the world. She was excited now at the additional nearness to Ben – his room overlooked the yards, next to Alec's, who had moved out of the principal bedroom on Lucy's death.

It was comfortable here, surrounded by softly falling drapes, thick carpet and delicately shaped walnut furniture. Her own tiny bedroom had bare floorboards, rag rugs and a steeply sloping ceiling. Now she had access to a porcelain-furnished bathroom. There was the wonder of radiators in addition to fireplaces in every room, although the necessary economies meant only the sitting room, Lottie's bedroom and the kitchen range were regularly lit.

She was wearing an ivory-coloured satin nightgown and negligée of Dorothea Harvey's, the bodice of both a luxury of pleated lace. It made her feel – she searched her mind for the right word – sensual. Dorothea Harvey had been stylish and poised, and like Emilia herself, tall and slender and femininely shaped. Knowing she had little chance of sleep, Emilia looked over the clothes she had set aside for herself. She had chosen something for all likely occasions. Fashion was plainer and hems were higher than in Edwardian times, but the service of a sewing needle and removal of fripperies would turn them into acceptable wear.

She drifted off to sleep. And dreamt of years gone by. Of Ben and Billy and Honor and herself. Playing in the meadows, the streams and the woods. Ben's games. Ben had a wild and vivid imagination. The mind of a hero. He, the natural leader as Ivanhoe, King Arthur, Robin Hood. Billy, although five years older, his faithful liegeman. She and Honor, helpless maidens, running or hiding from witches, dragons, or Prince John's men. Rescued again and again.

Then she was rescuing Ben from a furnace, a bottomless pit. Billy had already fallen in.

She was wakened by her own cries. Sitting up, she pushed back her heavy hair, which was making her scalp burn. She prayed feverishly for Billy's safety, then whispered, 'Please God, I know it's selfish, but don't let Ben join the fighting.' Heaven already had Henry Harvey and five other young men and a V.A.D. nurse from Hennaford.

She didn't want to have to wonder several times a day, as she did about Billy, if Ben was still alive. If he was frightened or suffering. Billy was certainly enduring terrible deprivations at the Western Front. For three years the war had been raging on land, sea and in the air, and Ben was eager to get through his officer's training with the Sussex regiment that had accepted him, and then past his next birthday to join the thick of the fighting, and not be, as he termed it, stuck at home worrying and waiting with the women. During the times the conflict seemed to be heading in the allied powers' favour, instead of being heartened, Ben had expressed concern he would miss out.

Ben's outlook on war was like most young men's: that to fight and maybe die for his country – probably die, so tragically high were the casualty lists – was ennobling, proof of his loyalty, his courage, his manhood. 'It's what I was born for,' he would declare. 'No, it isn't,' she wanted to plead. 'You were placed on earth to love me, to marry me and give me babies, and to farm this quiet acreage of countryside.' She kept it to the back of her mind that Ben's ambition was not to stay working at the farm on a generous allowance from Alec, but to become a professional soldier.

She checked Lottie was as peaceful as she appeared. Then to while away the remaining hours till first light, she planned the next day. Lottie tended to be a late riser, so she should be able to slip away to prepare the lamps, build up the fires, fetch in the logs and join the men for the milking. The separating, the first stage of the butter and cream making, a long process, was her specific job. Then she would cook the men's breakfasts before Lottie demanded attention. She hoped to get some tidying done before Tilda Lawry's arrival. Perhaps she ought to creep about now with a duster.

The door opened in a whisper and she held her breath. Ben came in, a dressing gown over his pyjamas.

He held up his hands to forestall her protest. 'It's not what you think, Em. It's my eyes, they're hurting so much. Will you bathe them for me?'

His pain and discomfort made her dash to him. 'Oh, Ben, with everything else going on, I forgot all about your poor eyes. We'll have to creep down to the kitchen.'

There were two flights of stairs in the house, and they crept down those at the front to avoid Alec's room. The water in the kettle was still warm. She fetched a glass bowl and cotton wool from the floor-to-ceiling cupboard next to the range. When he was sitting at the table, she placed a towel over his shoulders. Bringing the lamp close, she could see his eyes were enflamed and swollen, the left eye bloodshot and weeping. Holding the bowl up to his right cheek, she trickled water from the inner corner of his eye to wash it out. She didn't stop until Ben said it felt soothed.

'The other one hurts the most. Feels like it's been stabbed with a red-hot drill,' he groaned, turning the chair round. She repeated her ministrations. 'Still feels like there's grit in it.'

'Put your head on the table.' He moved again, placing a hand on her waist. She pulled down the lower lid of his eye and saw a particle of grit in the bloodied seepings. 'You really need a doctor to look at this.'

'I can't wait till then. Do something, Em.'

She fetched a clean hanky and, twisting a corner, she used the pointed edge as a lever. Ben winced. 'Keep still, Ben.'

'I'm trying to. Hurry up, I'm in agony.'

She repeated the probing. The particle moved. She wiped it out of his eye.

He yowled like a savage, pushing her away and rubbing at the site of intense pain. Blood-stained tears gushed down his cheek. 'God in heaven, what did you do to me?'

'Shush, Ben! You'll wake the others. I'm sorry, it had to be done. Stop rubbing it. Let me bathe it again. It should stop hurting soon.'

He allowed her to irrigate his eye until the water ran clear. She gave him the hanky to mop his face. Ben was brawnier than most youths his age, but now he seemed small and hunched, wistful and pathetic.

'Oh, Ben, if you find this so terrible, how will you cope in the trenches?' With compassion and anxiety, she enclosed him in her arms. 'I'm so sorry, my poor love. I feel awful for neglecting you.'

Ben clung to her, then moved position so his legs were either side of hers. He dragged her head down and kissed her fiercely. Emilia leaned into him. When he began to move his hands inside the negligée, she allowed him to continue.

He got up, ignoring the pain in his left eye and the stinging moisture leaking from it. He pulled at the ties of the negligée, and when the glossy material parted he took a close lingering look at her womanly contours, revealed in fine detail in the nightgown. 'You're perfect, Em. You'll get cold here. Let's slip into the sitting room and cuddle up on the sofa.'

How she wanted to, but duty and common sense took priority. 'I must go back to your gran, Ben.'

'I'll come with you. The couch is large enough for two.'

'But your Gran's in the room. It doesn't seem right.'

'Even if she wakes, she won't know what we're doing. Em, we're going to get married. It doesn't matter if we do anything now, you know what I mean . . .'

Although Emilia was kept away when the bull served the cows, it was inevitable that she knew what few other girls her age did, the details of the act of physical union. She wouldn't countenance doing anything of the kind with someone close by. 'Not now, Ben. We need to talk about it first.'

He searched her expression. 'You do want me, Em?'

'Yes, Ben, of course, but it's not going to be easy to find the right place.'

'You do love me?'

'Yes, I love you.'

The floorboards in the room overhead creaked, making the dark varnished beams close above Ben's head seem to press down on them both.

'Bloody Alec,' Ben swore. 'Why can't he rest like normal people?'

'I must go, Ben. He mustn't see me like this.' Emilia wrapped the negligée in tight.

Ben placed a fiercer hold on her. 'Swear you'll meet me alone the very first chance we get.'

His plea reminded her of the old days, when Ben made her and Billy and Honor swear allegiance to him. He took such an undertaking seriously. 'I swear, Ben. With this woman coming tomorrow, we should get the chance quite soon. Now we must go. I'll tidy up here in the morning.'

Thinking if Alec came down he would use the back stairs, she hastened to the front flight, only to be confronted by him halfway in descent, still dressed.

'Is everything all right, Emilia?' He kept his gaze on her face.

Feeling exposed and foolish, and guilty, as if she'd been discovered doing something wrong, she looked down at the bottom step. 'I've had to bathe Ben's eyes. He needs to see the doctor.'

'I'll see he does. Thank you, Emilia.' He moved against the banisters so she could pass him by with plenty of space. Then he added, 'What would we do without you?'

Chapter Three

'Post for you, sir.' Billy Rowse beavered into an officer's dugout, just one tiny section of the miles of trenches of warfare hewn out of the Belgian soil.

Lieutenant Tristan Harvey glanced up from the official diary where he was filling in the details of the deaths of two of his men, one from sniper fire while inching his way along a communication trench, the other had been buried alive under an avalanche of mud and slime from a shell blast near his position when on stand-to at dawn. These sort of incidents were accounting for as many losses of life among the British Army as its frequent direct assaults on the German front lines.

'Thank you, Corporal. At ease.'

Billy handed over a collection of letters. 'Took eleven days to catch up with us this time, sir. September twenty-fourth, my post's dated. Not bad, eh? I got a parcel from my mum and dad with a tin of biscuits in it – here, sir.' Apologetic over his dirty hands, due to the frantic rescue attempt of his dead comrade, the rebuilding of the blasted-out area, and the scarcity of water for washing, he offered Tristan a couple of plain biscuits wrapped inside a used envelope. Tristan thanked him and motioned for him to sit on the camp bed. Billy's cheery voice grew unsure. 'And I got a letter from Em. Says she and Ben are courting.'

Tristan knew what Billy was thinking. Did he approve? 'Well, good for Ben. I've got a letter from him too, bearing the same news, no doubt. I suppose it was inevitable, it's hard to imagine one without the other. Ben's always thought himself the strong one, but Emilia could always keep him in line.'

The dugout shook as an incoming shell exploded only yards away. It was part of German tactics never to allow British troops well back from their front lines any peace. Particles of earth and clay rained down over the two men and the field furnishings. Candle flames flickered and Tristan shot up a hand to steady the lantern hanging near his head. Both men snatched at their breath. Although used to the constant boom-boom-boom of enemy and friendly artillery, its significance today made them particularly tense. It was the start of another 'big push', and short hours ago, along the front lines the battle order had been given, the whistles had blown. Men just like themselves, perhaps men from another section of the 'Shiny Sixth', of the Duke of Cornwall's Light Infantry, attached to the 14th Infantry Brigade, had joined soldiers of the many other battalions in the offensive to capture the Passchendaele ridge. Somewhere out there thousands of ordinary men like them had and were sacrificing their lives. A fact. Another fact, one they accepted, was that their turn to make a direct assault would come.

The two men shut out the thought that either, or both of them, were likely soon to become the subject of a sorrowful letter or a black-edged telegram. Fighting the ravages of cold, the lice and the rats, the need to somehow keep dry in the infernal, never-ending rain, and the aching loneliness of separation from their loved ones, was enough for their minds to dwell on. Right now, they were glad to be in this pseudo-shelter, out of the bone-shivering, skin-withering, teeming rain.

Yesterday had been a rest day in their billet two miles away, the cellar of a café for Billy, one of its small basic bedrooms for Tristan, and they were now a little energized. When not on trench duty, they trained in mock battle, practising with live ammunition, so were feeling some confidence about their ability to fight.

Billy was tapping his fingers on his knees and banging his heels together. A constant fidgeter, short, agile and boyish, able to nip anywhere with stealth, he had earned his nick-name, Nipper, from his training days. A ready volunteer, he had told Tristan on the first day of their arrival here that he felt up to anything thanks to his childhood games with Ben, and later, he had said thinking of those times was helping him get through the daily miseries.

It had been Billy's determination and trustworthiness, rather than any residual notion of boyhood bravado, that had made Tristan take him along on an intelligence-gathering mission and, on another occasion, send him out with three privates to capture a shell crater in no man's land, a small but important advancement towards enemy lines. Any time now he expected Billy, on his recommendation, to be promoted to sergeant.

'Mr Harvey won't mind, Em being a dairymaid?' Billy asked, watching his superior anxiously, although he had never known him to look down on anyone.

'Definitely not. From Ben's letters to me, Emilia has been a mainstay on the farm for quite some time.' Tristan lit a cigarette, hungry for the nicotine. He shared his brothers' dark colouring and grey eyes, but wasn't handsome like Ben, or impressive in stature like Alec. Tristan was hushed and simplistic, and this despite the necessary adaptation of having to scrub out his own worries, and his hopes and memories of comfort. His calm made men of all ranks seek his company and his counsel, to help dispel, among the usual fears of death and mutilation, that their personalities had not yet been swallowed up forever. 'You'd have to go a long way to find someone with as much strength of character as your sister. I remember her skidding across the yard as a little girl, skinning her forearms until the blood ran, and she got up and carried on as if nothing had happened.'

'All the blokes want to meet her.' Billy took a family photograph, taken in a Truro studio prior to his embarkation, out of the few personal effects in his tunic. He gazed in awe at his sister's image. Emilia had dressed up for the occasion, demure and poised in the obligatory manner, yet smiling her warm, restive smile. 'I don't really know how to explain about Em sometimes. She's always made me feel safe, like she can make everything wherever she is all right.'

A sudden cheer went up outside. 'One of ours,' Billy glanced up at the claustrophobic roofing, referring to an aeroplane outside of the Royal Flying Corps. 'Hope he hits the right spot.'

Tristan was pondering Billy's description. Safe? When was the last time he had heard that word? Emilia Rowse was hard-working and loyal, and passionate where her affections lay – the qualities of a good wife. He turned over the letter in his hands that bore his wife's writing. Would it contain mostly information about Jonathan, and while expressing her hopes for his safety, as for a time long standing, not a single loving message from herself? Where had all her devotion for him gone? His letters to Ben and Alec seeking reassurance about Ursula had been met with just that, reassurance, mentioning that she was living quietly and they were looking after her, but he remained unconvinced. Alec had always been protective towards his younger brothers and might have dictated that Ben write what he thought was best for a man facing combat daily.

Billy sprang up. He had lingered long enough. The lieutenant's batman soon would be bringing in his lunch. 'I got a letter from Honor Burrows too, sir. She supports everyone she knows by keeping in touch, but I'm hoping she's a bit sweet on me.' When he stepped outside, his bashful expression changed into one of tight resignation while he tied his rubber groundsheet over his shoulders for added protection against the pitiless weather.

A chill spread all the way through Tristan as he recognized an ominously familiar rustle. A huge rat leapt on to his desk and dashed towards the biscuits Billy had given him. 'Bastard!' Crashing down his fist, Tristan crushed the thief's head with one blow.

Leaping up in disgust, he flung the dark-brown corpse outside by its long, tapering tail. He was used to rats on the farm, but the home-bred variety were docile in comparison to the evil-looking creatures he came across here. They were too used to gorging on dead horseflesh – and fallen soldiers, even those who were alive and wounded if they didn't have the strength to fight them off.

The rat lay on the mud-lagged duckboard. Feeling sick, Tristan washed off his bloodied hand with drinking water from an old petrol can; to do so in one of the pools of death-contaminated water was a sure way to disease. A huddle of men, lined up with mess tins for their helping of bread, and offal, potatoes and onions cooked over a wire grid, were grinning at the spectacle that had suddenly broken the awful tension.

'Well done, sir. He was a particularly big bugger,' a private said, whipping out a pencil and scrap of paper from somewhere. Private Leslie Jory, a muscular, redheaded builder's mate, the section joker and the most accomplished maker of foul oaths, led the huddle into whispers.

'Are you writing a book, Jory?' Tristan said, the smell of food making his guts agitate further.

Private Jory stood to attention. 'Sir?'

Tristan glared at the mangled corpse. 'Put my name down, five bob says the rat's every bit of fifteen inches.'

'Yes, sir!'

Tristan returned to the dugout to murmurs of him being, 'A bloody good bloke.' 'The best.' 'Nothing's left of that rat's skull. God help the Fritz what he gets his hands on.'

Drinking the tea but ignoring the meal brought into him, Tristan finished his report. He put aside the letter from Ursula, not wanting to become depressed by the expected lack of her affection. Then he opened it, needing to hear news about his son. The letter was headed by the address of Ford House, the property, the only legacy, left him by his father. Ursula had never complained about living there in the disparaging way Lucy had about the farm. Ursula had rarely complained about anything, but he had always known she preferred town life and had moved in with her parents at the end of each of his leaves. Her explanation for remaining home after his last leave, thirteen months ago, had been that she no longer got along with her mother; not unlikely, her mother was a sharp-tongued, uncompromising snob.

The letter was all about Jonathan, ending with, 'Your loving wife, Ursula.' Loving? Not measured against their romantic courtship and the early passion they had shared as husband and wife.

Ben's letter, enthusiastically prosed, contained the news about his newfound love for Emilia. What was Ben thinking of, forming a romantic attachment when he'd soon be leaving home to learn how to fight? What was Alec thinking of by allowing it? But after their father's early death from cancer, Alec had been a quiet guide rather than a disapproving father figure to Ben. The letter went on to say they were still finding it a struggle at the farm. Damn your jealousy over that scullery maid, Lucy Harvey! Tristan's thoughts were savage. It was you who couldn't get enough sex, not Alec. Sex – the lack of it – surely that wasn't what was the matter with Ursula? He couldn't bear to think about it anymore.

There was a kind letter from the rector. The final envelope bore an unfamiliar hand. There was no return address given. Tristan studied the postmark. Truro. It read:

> Dear Lieutenant Harvey,
>
> I'm sorry to have to inform you of this but I have the impression your brothers have not written to you about the appalling fact that your wife has been having an illicit affair for several months. It's with a man called Bruce Ashley. Your wife met him in the mayor's chamber during a function to raise funds for the war. Ashley is a hanger-on, one of those fellows with good looks who turn up out of nowhere and who prey on lonely or gullible women.

Tristan read no more, except to look for a signature. 'From a well-wisher.' He believed every word of the insidious, heartless communication. He had the reason for Ursula's coolness. Unfaithfulness. She had fallen out of love with him and attached herself to another man. While she hadn't been cold or unresponsive towards him during his last leave, she had been unsettled, anxious and lonely. Ripe to be swept away by some handsome lounge lizard.

He had to get back home immediately! But it was impossible. There were at least a dozen other men higher than him on the list for leave. There was nothing he could do about his marriage; he was helpless here so far away. He could write to Ursula, but it was unlikely to be of any use if she was in love with this man. He was plunged into his worst nightmare: not dying or being horrifically injured or becoming insane, but of losing the woman he had thought of as his lifeblood.

He had experienced many horrors and fears in this war, but he had never hated the enemy. Now his sense of rejection made him hate with a force he would never have thought possible. He hated the man who had stolen his wife, desecrated his family, possibly his home, the reasons that had kept him hoping to survive and look towards a new future. Hate, and the desire for retribution seeped into his soul and for one terrible moment it took him over completely. Ursula had cast him off, and while part of him was desperate to win her back, another part of him wanted to retaliate in kind. *Leave me and be damned!* But if she did, he might lose Jonny for ever too. And if this Bruce Ashley bastard character deserted them, what would happen to them?

Rent by worry, grief, hurt and anger, he tore the letter to shreds. He took refuge in fury. Fury against the 'well-wisher'. Fury against the war. But he forced himself to dissolve it. He had to, for the sake of the men under his command, when at any moment they might have to face the greatest danger. Ben's and Alec's silence on the matter? Right or wrong of them? He'd think about that later, when the despair in his soul had dissipated a little. He clung to the hope of Alec's protective nature.

The field telephone rang. Burying his emotions, he listened to the colonel's voice and filled in a different page of the war diary. He took a moment to empty his mind, he would not allow others to bear the cost of his distress. Then he put on his greatcoat and peaked cap and went outside under the sadistic grey emptying skies and called the NCOs, including Billy Rowse, together.

'Tell the men that when darkness begins to fall we'll be moving up to the first line. This is it. We'll be leading the assault on the German positions tomorrow morning.'

It was bitingly cold when a nervous dawn began to steal through the dust and smoke of the night's bombardment.

'Stand to! Stand to!'

As they followed the hated dawn ritual of standing up to the parapets, rifles at the ready in case of sudden man-to-man attack, Tristan's section waited for the battle orders. There was a sharp exchange of strafe and artillery power. Unnatural noises and colours, 'whizz-bangs', 'coal boxes' creating clouds of choking black smoke. The tense marking of time was broken with forbidden talk and the direness of false gaiety.

'All the best, old mate.'

'Hope they keep me dinner warm.'

Minutes earlier, handshakes had been given all round and last letters written to loved ones. Goodbyes were now being said inside heads, and pleas to God to be allowed to live through this day, or at least, to enable the supplicant to act with honour. There was another deafening explosion and the men were peppered with debris. Nerves were pared to fine slivers. Each man knew the odds were almost non-existent of getting close enough to take out an enemy machine-gun post, of achieving much towards the main objective of crippling the German army and breaking through to the Flemish coast to capture the enemy naval bases.

Tristan received a nod from the captain. He moved up and down the ranks, a word of encouragement for each man. A blast momentarily halted the tormented burst of activity in removing greatcoats and leather jerkins, rolling them up and leaving them in any dry place – movement in combat must not be hampered. Gas masks were already in place round necks. The occasional trembling hand ensured an already fixed bayonet was secure. Rigid glances were exchanged. Throats that had turned dry were wetted by unworkable swallows. Here and there came a coarse oath.

Tristan returned to the captain. 'The men are all ready, sir.'

Pistol in hand, Tristan stationed himself in front of a ladder. He was going to be one of the first to go over. He found himself standing next to Billy Rowse. He didn't take his eyes off the ladder but he did press a hand to Billy's shoulder. 'See you back here, Billy.'

'A certainty, sir.'

Whistles shrilled. Hearts hammered. Nerves were severed, fragmented.

'*Over! Over! Over! Over!*' Tristan wasn't sure if he or the sergeant was shouting.

He mounted the ladder and was then climbing and edging through chewed-up barbed wire and skew-whiff posts. Somewhere a Highland regiment was being piped into battle. Dodging mounds of slush and rubble, an iron wheel and a heap of something – he didn't want to consider what – he began his run. 'Follow me, then spread out! Keep running. Keep running.'

Running soon proved to be impossible in the mire. Men were walking, even crawling, some floundering, already in danger from death by drowning.

'Keep going! Keep going!' His words referred to the gruesome orders that no soldier must assist another who fell during an assault. His eyes fixed ahead, he darted and squelched on over the hellish landscape, through the explosions and flashes and rat-tats of machine-gun fire, whistling, whipping, skimming, scudding all around him.

A soldier was suddenly immediately in front of him. The soldier was hit by strafe, his arms flailing outwards. Tristan leapt over him before he was flat on the ground.

The ground was ripped open yards away on his right and those running there at that moment disappeared. Tristan felt their blood and matter and mud spatter all over him. Ducking and tacking around ever increasing wreckage and craters and the fallen, he kept running and shouting to the men, any men, for he was now among those from other battalions.

He came across a Lewis gunner staggering on shredded legs, trying still to carry his heavy weapon with only one arm left, his carrying party scattered dead like grain plucked off an ear of wheat. A brave lot. They didn't usually go over the top until support was required. Tristan whirled round. 'You there! Are you capable of firing this gun?'

'Didn't do too badly in training, sir,' a soldier, hazy in the hail of grit and fragments, shouted back.

'Rowse! Billy, take it off this soldier. I'll get you a carrying party.'

The Lewis gunner keeled over. Before Billy hefted the gun on to his own shoulder, he took a second to look at his anonymous dying comrade. 'R.I.P.,' Billy muttered before striding forward to find an advantageous setting-up position.

Soldiers, who were to be Billy's loaders, were picking up the magazines and spare parts. 'Keep going,' Tristan shouted at them. There was a shell crater on higher ground. The machine gun could be mounted on its ridge, a suitable place to fire on the enemy positions.

Tristan left them. He kept going by believing, like all the others, that he wouldn't die. His pistol empty, he reloaded without stopping. For an instant the air was clear and he saw he was wading through a stretch of mud up to his knees; framed by a few devastated trees it might have once been a meadow. He'd never see the meadows and trees of Ford Farm again, never see his son enjoying their delights – if Ursula did not take him away from them. He and his men and all these others were solid in their duty, but they wouldn't live long enough, in the necessary numbers, to get behind and eliminate the network of German ferro-concrete machine-gun posts, which were defiant to anything except a direct hit from a heavy shell.

'This is for you, Jonny,' he shouted, plunging onwards.

The sky in front of him was raining lead balls. He halted, arm up protecting his face, feeling the little demons thud into him. A shell exploded somewhere and he felt himself being thrown backwards and the red-hot incisions of steel casing. Then he felt nothing at all.

Billy scrambled to set the machine gun up on its tripod. He pulled the butt against his shoulder, digging his feet into the tacky clay to stop himself sliding down into the pit. He fired off the first magazine and his number one loaded a fresh one. After each round he retargeted. If he fired incessantly, the German machine gunners would mark his position and he and his mates would be done for.

Billy raised his face a fraction to resight the gun and a single bullet passed through his head.

Chapter Four

Emilia was waiting for Ben in the washhouse, where everyone cleaned up after outdoor work. He was on his way after mucking out the stables and feeding the pigs, and she was daring to steal a quick kiss with him. Seeing her peeping out the window, he quickened his confident strides, then paused and beckoned to her. Her father must be stationed at the back door, waiting for her.

She took a step outside and sniffed the air, still and heavy now the wind had dropped. Filtering through the usual whiffs of animals, fowls and their manure was the seductive delicious smell of hot food.

'Tilda Lawry's here already,' Ben said, reaching her. 'See there? And joy of joy, she's cooked our breakfast.'

A modest-sized woman in a grey calf-length dress, a starched apron and white frilled cap was on the flagstones, her posture straight and unruffled, waving them inside. She had sprucely brushed ginger hair and close freckles, gleaming red cheeks and a cheery smile.

Emilia likened her to a contented pussycat, glad to see that the woman she was relinquishing the kitchen to appeared to have no first-day nerves, that there was not likely to be a clash of personalities. Lifting her hand to return the salute, she said, 'How did I miss her arriving?'

Ben laughed and tugged her plait. 'For once, your all-seeing eye has let you down. Alec slipped off a while ago, obviously to meet the horse-cab. Don't know why he couldn't just say so. Why does he have to be so damned mysterious?'

'Well, he's always deep in thought, isn't he?'

While she and Ben walked together, Emilia swept her eyes over the house, which she had always admired for its two entirely different characters. Here at the back, its late eighteenth-century origins were plain. Thick uneven walls and windows deep-cut, many and small and variously shaped. Indiscriminate additions had formed quirky projections and fascinating recesses, promising secrets and delights within – some of hers and Ben's childhood hiding places. If Tilda Lawry had noticed the fine Victorian facings at the front of the rambling building, and that the farmstead was in good order, hopefully she wouldn't think too badly of her because of the neglect and chaos inside.

She turned her attention to Ben's bloodshot, puffy eyes. 'Are they still hurting?'

'Just a bit sore now, thanks to you.'

Emilia wasn't convinced. Ben usually made light of injuries and was likely to be feeling embarrassed about the fuss he had made last night. 'You'll make sure you see the doctor, Ben? Your eyesight's too precious to neglect.'

'Alec's arranging it.' He lowered his voice. 'You just concentrate on when and where we can be alone, Em.'

They had reached the back door, and Tilda Lawry dropped a small curtsey, more in a friendly than a subservient way. 'Come on in, young Mr Harvey, and you, Miss Emilia. Breakfast's all ready to be put on the table. Mr Harvey, Mrs Harvey and Mr Rowse are waiting for you to join them. I'm Tilda, as you must have guessed. Pleased to meet you both. I remember seeing you, sir, when you was a little boy at the market with your father, always was a longshanks! Going to turn into a rough old day again, and I'm going to see that you're not sent out in it feeling empty. I'll have your crib bag packed full. Come on then, wash your hands and all you've got to do is sit yourselves down.'

Before he followed the women inside, Ben gingerly touched a hanky to his left eye, careful to rearrange his expression afterward to hide his pain and discomfort.

Lottie had been placed at the table in her dressing gown

and slippers, next to Emilia's chair. 'I had no trouble bringing her down with Mr Harvey being here, but she's waiting for you, Miss Emilia,' Tilda said.

'Good morning, Mrs Harvey.' Emilia held the hands reaching out to her.

In his substantial chair at the head of the table, Alec was gazing into space. Emilia greeted him, but only for Tilda's benefit: there was no point in speaking to Alec when he was this remote. Ben had once remarked, 'He goes off somewhere inside his head to plan and scheme.' She had not thought of Alec as a schemer, until his prearrangement of her life last night.

She kissed her father, who seemed diffident about the form, then she asked him how her mother was.

'Well, she's missing you, maid, but that can't be helped. She's coming up tomorrow, she and little Honor. I'll bring your things later on.' Edwin shot a hard look at Ben, then treated Emilia to one of the same. 'Took your time coming in, didn't you?'

'Did we?' She pretended innocence.

'You sleep well, Em?' Edwin asked now in a soft, fatherly way. A small, stooped man, with full side-whiskers, he had aged radically by years of hard outdoor work.

She lied that she had. It seemed the farmhouse wasn't a place to find peace or rest. Long into the dark its oldest timbers had shuddered in time with the wind. Ben had stayed downstairs after her embarrassed escape from Alec. During a need to slip to the bathroom, she had paused on the landing and listened to their voices. It had mainly been Ben's voice, then she had realized he was reading aloud from a newspaper, about the war and local news, with the occasional comment from Alec. A strange thing to do in the dead of night, and an effort for Ben with his hurting eyes. When Ben had finally retired he had coughed and paced about his room for nearly an hour. Alec, it seemed had stayed up all night. There were sounds of him going up into the attics and moving things about in the boxroom and the room between Lottie's and his late brother's.

Emilia waited in contained appreciation for her food to be put in front of her. Tilda Lawry's presence would mean the return of much of her former freedom; she had always preferred to be outside. She was served porridge and boiled eggs and expertly sliced toast. All the while, Tilda talked gaily about the conditions she found here, like having hot piped water, at a rate that Emilia's mother would call 'nineteen to the dozen'.

Then Tilda sat down, nodded at Alec and bowed her head.

Emilia had to lean past Lottie and prod Alec out of his reverie. It took a moment to realize what was required of him, then he issued a careless blessing over the food.

Ben tucked in straightaway, joking, 'Proper food at last.'

'I'm sure Miss Emilia is a good cook. Her butter's the best I've ever tasted.' Tilda winked at Emilia while plying him with more helpings.

'We wouldn't have coped without her these last few months,' Alec said, his gaze on Emilia as she tucked a tea towel around Lottie's neck.

'A beauty, a beauty,' Lottie was nodding her head.

'Absolutely right, Grandma.' Alec stroked her deep-veined hand, as if agreeing to the subject fleetingly in her mind. He was still looking at Emilia.

Sitting at the foot of the table, Ben noticed where his brother's admiration was directed. He blurted out to Tilda. 'Em and I are walking out.'

'Do you know, I thought as much. You looked a pair of happy little souls coming across the yard just now, even though you're both a mite young. Mr Rowse, you must be pleased, eh?'

Edwin looked uncomfortable at being singled out. He ran a thick finger round the neck of his collarless shirt. 'As long as everything's kept above board.'

'Of course it will be, Edwin,' Alec said, as if he too was taking the moral high ground.

Angry at being spoken about like this, Emilia produced a disapproving noise in her throat. She helped Lottie finish her porridge, then poured her a cup of tea.

Ben saw she had isolated herself from everyone but his grandmother, and he was maddened at his brother's hypocrisy. Alec wasn't living as a celibate widower. There was an address in Truro he sometimes visited on a Saturday night, or after business on market day. 'When am I to see Dr Holloway?' he growled down the length of the table.

'I've sent him a message, via the postman. I saw him in the lane, no letters for us today,' Alec replied. Everyone, except Tilda, totted up that it was two weeks since a letter had arrived from Tristan; the same applied in the case of Billy Rowse. While postal communications remained difficult their anxieties were kept at a similar level. 'I've asked for Dr Holloway to call late this morning, so stay near the stead until then. Edwin and I will take feed to the herd.'

'That suits me.' With the two men out of the way, and Tilda Lawry here to help keep an eye on his grandmother, he and Emilia might get the chance to slip away together.

'Perhaps I should ask the doctor to take a look at Mrs Harvey, seeing as he's going to be here anyway, Alec?' Emilia saw the lift of Tilda's eyebrows. 'Mr Harvey?'

'I'd be grateful if you would, Emilia.' He smiled at her, then turned to the housekeeper. 'We don't bother with formality here, Tilda. I've got one brother dead and another at the Front. Fighting for freedom of every kind is the way I see it. Take your time settling in. Thank you for breakfast.'

The men fetched their canvas crib bags and left the women to clear the table.

'Alec's different to what I'm sure you'd expect to find in a boss, Tilda,' Emilia said, carrying a stack of dishes to the back kitchen. Tilda had used a lot more crockery and utensils to produce the meal than she had ever bothered with before.

Tilda was filling the sink with hot water. 'Always was different to most folk. It was the talk of the town when he married Miss Lucy Pollard.'

'Did you happen to know her? It must be a sad time of the year for the Pollard family. She was their only child, wasn't she?' Emilia picked up a dishcloth but Tilda took it from her.

'You leave this to me and concentrate on Mrs Harvey. Dear old soul, isn't she? Can see how much she likes you, but then I can see you're a pleasant little soul yourself, and I'm a good judge of character. As for Miss Lucy, I saw her on the times she dined, before and after her marriage, with my former employers, the Rules of Stratton Terrace. The mistress told me that Mrs Pollard had said to her that she was grateful the Almighty hadn't given her a son for the war to take away from her too. I was well placed with the Rules, but 'tis some relief to be offered this post. I was brought up not far from Hennaford, in Marazanvose, and it'll be nice to be back in the country again.'

Emilia was hoping for more revelations about Alec or Lucy Harvey, but she was glad Tilda was not a gossiper. She now knew who one of the persons was Alec had dined with yesterday: Mr Ernest Rule, the Harveys' lawyer. 'I hope you'll like it here, it must be awful to be suddenly uprooted. Sorry about the state of the house. You'll find it a bit bare. I thought it best to pack a lot of stuff away.'

'No need for you to apologize. I can see how things have been for you. I'm only happy when I'm busy, I'll soon put this place to rights.

Emilia had already brought Lottie's clothes downstairs to the sitting room and she prepared to take her through to get her dressed. Her curiosity now centred on the new housekeeper. 'Do you have any family, Tilda?'

'Last cousin I had, from up-country, fell at the Somme, God rest him.' She paused with a washed plate in her capable hands, as if seeing this cousin in some far-off place. Happy, sorrowful, and then resigned.

'I'm sorry. I'm so glad you're here. You're going to be a God-send, Tilda.'

'Well,' Tilda passed her a perky look. 'According to Mr Harvey, there's an angel here already.'

It was twenty-four hours since Lottie had wandered off, and Emilia made sure she was safely napping before she moved her things into the bedroom Alec had allocated her. Although she had been given no say about this either, she couldn't help feeling an interloper, for this had been Henry Harvey's room. She paid silent homage to the ordinary, studious young man, who, try as she might, she remembered little about. It troubled her that she had forgotten him already, especially when he, against expectation, and to the pride of his brothers and the county, was a posthumous recipient of the Military Cross. Alec never mentioned him, but perhaps he was thinking of Henry sometimes when he cut himself off. And Lucy? Did he recall her piercing voice, or her demands over finicky detail? Or her beauty of the classical kind, and the way she had floated regally about the house, and how, when holding at-homes or a dinner party, she would metamorphose into a sparkling, sweetly responsive hostess with a siren-like appeal. Emilia had liked to watch and admire her then. Before yesterday she had given Alec little thought. Why was staying under his roof changing that?

The room was on a corner of the house and from the front windows she could see all the way down the hill to the ford. The side window overlooked the kitchen garden and out across the fields. Nestled near the woods was Ford House, where Tristan's adulterous wife lived in virtual seclusion after being shunned by her own family. The woods made Emilia wonder about the tramp; others of his kind had sought shelter there. With times being hard and drunkenness almost a national problem, more and more men, unfit for regimental service, were becoming homeless. Was alcohol a problem with Archie Rothwell? From what she had seen of him, she thought not.

Tilda, who had taken over the best accommodation in the attics, had aired the room but it still felt bleak and unwelcoming. Until Tilda's duster and polish had brought everything to a satisfying shine, small bare patches in the dust on the washstand, dressing table and mantelpiece had pointed to where some of Henry's things had been removed; during Alec's wanderings last night, Emilia assumed. Reverently, she had packed up the rest of Henry's typically masculine possessions – lead soldiers, stamp and mineral collections, taking them down to the den as Alec had instructed. His clothes she put in the boxroom, and found that a lot of items, including furniture, were missing from there since she'd delved into Dorothea Harvey's trunk.

'I'll put these on the bed for you, Em.' Ben brought in a small dented suitcase, a large box and a carpet-bag – the things inside them the sum of her belongings. 'It's strange knowing Henry will never use this room again, even though, unlike Tris and I, he'd never been interested in the farm.' Ben made a boyishly wicked face. 'Pity I've got to pass Alec's room to get to yours. He'll probably lay a trap for me every night.'

She smiled with mock demureness and started unpacking the box. She found what she was looking for, a photograph of herself, Ben, Billy and Honor taken at Rowlands Fair in Truro during peace time; all, except Billy, still at school at the time. 'I don't suppose Alec will mind if we sit together alone downstairs. He won't think we require a chaperon, I'm sure.'

'Think you know Alec well, do you?'

'Don't get jealous, Ben. It's you I love, never forget it,' she laughed.

'He's brightened up in the twenty-four hours since you've moved in. Rare for him to change so fast. He can brood on something for months.'

Tilda could be heard heading towards them. Emilia said, loud enough for her to hear, 'What did the doctor say about your eyes, Ben? Sorry I've had no time to ask you till now.'

'He hummed and hawed for ages. Waste of time! Said to keep bathing them and gave me these drops, and an eye patch if I think I need it.'

He took a small brown bottle out of his trouser pocket and handed it to her. She prised off the lid and sniffed the lip of the glass. 'Smells like antiseptic and dead flowers. I'll make sure you do as he says. Your right eye looks less anguished but the left's gone a bit cloudy. Does it hurt much?'

'Like merry hell when the cold gets to it.'

'Well, wear the eye patch. The doctor expects it to clear though?'

'Of course. He says if it's still bothering me after a few days he'll send me to a consultant.'

Tilda bustled in with an armful of lace runners. 'I've found these in a drawer. Thought they'd pretty up your room, Miss Em.'

'Thank you, Tilda.'

'Right then.' Tilda made straight for the door. She winked at Emilia. 'All's quiet. See the pair of you downstairs in a few minutes.'

'She's going to be a gem,' Ben said, as he and Emilia closed in on each other to take advantage of the housekeeper's kind discretion.

After putting Lottie to bed, Emilia, although unsure if she was expected to stay down with the two men, went to her room, feeling more comfortable about it being hers now. She changed into one of her newly acquired skirts and a lawn blouse – such a soft rippling feeling against her skin. She put on a pair of dark-blue suede shoes with high heels. How delighted she was to find Dorothea Harvey's feet had been the same size – she had always wanted a pair of elegant shoes. Freeing her rope of hair, she shook its sweeping waves loose about her shoulders. Parading in front of the mirror of the handsome wardrobe, she felt graceful and feminine, something she had not bothered about before.

There was a tap on the door. Assuming it was Tilda, she called out, 'Come in.'

Alec opened the door but stayed in the doorway. She had not seen him since breakfast – the 'drenching' of a sick cow had kept him away from the supper table. 'I knew you'd come round to my way of thinking,' he said. Some sort of satisfaction was clear in his frank expression.

Emilia had never been insolent, but she took a moment to reply. This might be Alec's house but this was her room, and she continued with the last of her unpacking. 'If you've come about your gran, the doctor said she's fine. Her heart's as strong as a lion's, and apart from her mind, he's never seen a patient of her age as healthy as she is.'

'Thank you, I hope Grandma lives for ever.' He added something low and soft. Emilia thought it sounded like, 'Angel.'

'I'm sorry,' he went on, 'But could I get something I'd forgotten on top of the wardrobe?'

'Of course.'

She stood back, watching as he reached up and took down a thick parcel, wrapped in crumpled brown paper and tied with string. It was addressed to Alec, the ink smudged. She was close enough to know he had drunk his evening glass, or two, of whisky, and he also smelled of something pleasant and indefinable. Himself, she guessed. Then she was ashamed of taking in such intimate details about him.

'The things that were in Henry's kitbag and his tunic pockets when he died,' he explained. 'Did you know they even sent back his uniform, complete with blood stains? I buried it in Long Meadow, Henry's favourite place, and said a few words over it. It was the saddest thing I've ever done.'

He was gazing at her, moisture glistening along the rims of his eyes, and Emilia felt privileged he had shared this sorrowful memory with her. 'No, I didn't know that. How terrible for you, Alec.'

He returned to the doorway. 'So, your mother and Honor Burrows are coming to tea tomorrow? You and Tilda must entertain them in the sitting room. Grandma will enjoy the extra company. Pity Honor's a frail little thing, she could have been working here long ago.'

'Honor would like to, but that snobbish old aunt of hers won't allow it, which it ridiculous because they badly need the money. Pity she doesn't die off and let Honor lead her own life.' Emilia dashed a hand to her mouth. 'I didn't mean that. And it's unlucky to wish someone dead.'

Alec opened out the palms of his hands and shrugged. 'Some people don't deserve long lives. Is Florence Burrows mean to Honor then?'

'She stifles her, I call that mean. Wants Honor to marry a gentleman, but no gentleman is likely to consider her with the fact she lives in a decaying house and she's got nothing settled on her. I think she would have been happy with Isaac Annear. Florence Burrows took a high and mighty stance just because he was a carpenter! She may have educated Honor herself but Honor grew up with us village children. She won't be happy unless she marries someone she feels comfortable with.'

'It's all academic now.' Isaac Annear had been killed shortly after Henry. 'You feel comfortable with Ben, though, Emilia?'

'Of course, besides, Ben's not a snob.'

'Well, I agree that one should marry someone they're suited to in temperament, position shouldn't necessarily count. I find your honesty and opinions refreshing, Emilia. We must talk more. Thank you for allowing me to disturb you.'

Chapter Five

'Well, look at you, decked out like a lady fair.' Dolly Rowse walked around Emilia in a circle, her stout fingers flicking at the crêpe de Chine embroidered dress she was wearing. 'Where did you get this from? And the shoes?'

While Emilia explained, she took her mother's and Honor Burrows's coats then ushered them into the sitting room.

'It was a strange thing for Alec to do, giving you his mother's clothes.' As she frowned, Dolly's dull, old-fashioned, wide-brimmed hat, which she had refused to relinquish, dipped over her forbidding brow.

'Doesn't this dress suit me?' Emilia used a questioning gesture to gain Honor's opinion. Honor always told the truth.

'You look lovely, Em,' Honor said, smiling and taking the end of the sofa next to Lottie's chair. She leaned forward and greeted the old lady. Lottie stared back at her, as if with suspicion, then craned her long neck and appeared anxious until she recognized Emilia among the strangers.

'I didn't say it didn't suit you, Em. I said, it was a strange thing for Alec to do. He's your employer, after all,' Dolly persisted. Before the outbreak of the hostilities, although always alarmingly candid, she had been jolly and tolerant, a hair-netted housewife, wearing an apron all day long and content to 'do' for the rector's wife. Now she wore the pinched and blanched face of a worried mother, the risk of a tragic fate for her son making her choose to resent what she saw as her daughter's defection to live in here. Dolly was as keen as Honor's aunt for people to 'know their place'. She greeted Lottie in a humble way. It should be remembered Mrs

Charlotte Harvey was the lady of this grand farmhouse, even if her mind no longer functioned properly.

'And Ben, my young man, is his brother.' Emilia hid her disappointment and banked down the desire to rush upstairs and change into her own simple church-going dress. She had only wanted to look nice, not play at being a lady. 'Why shouldn't I wear his late mother's clothes?'

'Now you're living under the same roof as your young man and his brother, they'll soon find out your tongue can be as tart as an unsweetened gooseberry, Emilia Rowse.'

'I wonder who I got that off.' Emilia would usually have kissed her mother by now but she kept her distance.

'Did you say just now that we're having cake?' Dolly asked. 'How did this Tilda manage that then?'

'Tilda can make a feast out of a few supplies. She says the word "shortage" means "a challenge" to her. The sponge we're having looks as light as duck's down, but then, of course, there's always fresh eggs here. And I have kept the larder well stocked with preserves. Well, make yourself comfy, Mum. Have you heard from Billy?'

'If I had, maid, the letter would've been out of my handbag by now. Lieutenant Harvey will look after him.' Dolly noticed a photograph of Tristan in his dress uniform on the piano, where a collection of sepia Harveys were gathered importantly together, and she stared at it as if imploring his image to do exactly what she hourly prayed for, to keep her son safe. She finally perched on the edge of a seat, and never having been in the finer part of the house before, absorbed the surroundings. Emilia waited for her opinion, wanting her to like her new home.

'Very nice, very plush. Flock wallpaper. Wouldn't look right on our walls, but wouldn't it be lovely to have anyway? Look at the size of that mantelpiece, all scrolls and beadings, and a skeletal clock, how fancy. The rectory is dismal in comparison. I'm always cleaning the damp off the walls. Mrs Harvey looks elegant this afternoon. Takes me back to the days when both she and the world were sane.'

For her mother's and Honor's visit, Emilia had taken pleasure in dressing Lottie in some of the well-designed clothes she had worn for soirées and charity gatherings up until five years ago, before her mind had lapsed into senility. As if something of her earlier days had returned to her, Lottie sat up straight in her chair, smiling serenely, humming intermittently.

'This is nice,' Dolly said, fidgeting with her handbag when Tilda joined them, minus her cap and apron. Her mother's self-consciousness made Emilia want to give her that missed kiss. After an initial reserve, due to Dolly's stiffness, the two older women entered a conversation about domestic things.

Emilia gave Lottie her tea and a slice of the golden jam and cream sponge. She sat on a footstool near Lottie's feet and allowed her, humming without a break now, to fiddle with her hair, while she talked to Honor. Honor had brought her knitting, and her steel needles click-clicked into it between the delicate sips and nibbles she took.

Emilia looked at her with fondness. If anyone should be labelled an angel it was Honor. Her white-blonde hair shone in delicate Empire curls, her pale skin was flawless, her blue eyes like velvet, her expression tender and trusting. She was femininity at its sweetness, guileless and faithful. The princess in Ben's games. Honor was not frail, as Alec and others thought, but she appeared so, and Emilia, Ben and Billy had always sought to protect her. She lived on the north side of the main road that divided the village. Her aunt, the widow of a high-ranking police officer, a martyr to her reduced circumstances – rumoured to be due to her husband's philanderings – tolerated her friendship with Emilia owing to Emilia's close connection with the Harveys.

'Alec's said that any time one of the horses isn't needed for working, I can use the trap to take Mrs Harvey out. You must come with us, Honor,' Emilia said. 'One day, if I can stretch the time, we could go into Truro.'

'Wouldn't we look grand?' Honor said in her soft voice, casting off a khaki sock. She and her aunt collected all the

Red Cross village contributions for the fighting forces, and the less fortunate.

'Well, you and Mrs Harvey will,' Emilia joked. 'Have another piece of sponge.'

'No, thank you. Save some for Ben.'

'Don't worry, Tilda will see to that. Wish I could send a fruit cake to Billy. Don't know when we'll be able to get the ingredients again.'

'He knows you're always thinking of him.'

'Wish we'd hear from him. I'll give Mum a letter to post to him on the way home. Wonder what he'll make of me living here.'

Honor looked at her in an insightful way. 'You're obviously not finding it disagreeable.'

The humming behind Emilia had stopped and her hair, now pulled out of its ribbon, came to rest in a cloud of waves on her shoulders. She glanced round at Lottie. The old lady had fallen asleep. 'Come upstairs with me, Honor, while I change before feeding the hens.'

'You'll come here often to see me, Honor?' Emilia said, tucking an old shirt of Billy's into her trousers.

'Of course.' Honor was sitting on the bed, admiring the views from the windows. 'Em, Aunt Florence is selling off more furniture to make ends meet. Things are obviously worse than she'll admit. The house may have to go next.'

'What will you do, Honor?' This new concern for her friend added to the heavy weight Emilia already carried worrying about Billy. 'I pray to God it doesn't mean you'll have to move away.'

Honor gazed down at the bed quilt. 'Do you think Alec will want to marry again?'

'I suppose. From what I've gathered he's always wanted his own family. Why do you ask? Oh, I see.' Honor marrying Alec would solve her and her aunt's financial troubles. Emilia didn't like the idea of anyone, except, perhaps for Honor, becoming her next mistress. Then the thought of the small-minded Florence Burrows moving into the farm filled her with revulsion. She felt a strange possessiveness for Ford Farm. 'Do you like Alec in that way?'

'Oh, no. He's so . . . sort of manly, isn't he? I mean, oh, I don't know really. What do I know about men? I quite liked Isaac Annear, I thought it would be interesting to watch furniture being made. Isaac was about the same age as Alec. I think I'd prefer someone nearer my own age.'

Emilia fell quiet while rebinding her hair. Honor had always admired Ben. He would have been the ideal candidate to rescue her from this real life predicament. 'Well, whatever you do, Honor, don't marry someone just to please your aunt. It will be hard to get a good price for the house in the present circumstances, but if your aunt does sell up, perhaps she could rent something off Alec. Hopefully there would be enough funds to keep you both for a few years. Have you ever thought about Billy? He would be good for you. He won't need much of a nudge in your direction, he mentions you in all his letters. He's got no money, of course, but Mr Best's keeping his job for him at the nursery. Billy's a dedicated gardener, and a cottage goes with the job.' She turned round from the mirror. 'You remember all the fun the four of us used to have?'

'I remember Billy in my prayers everyday, Em.' Honor looked suddenly confident in her serene, acquiescent way. 'Getting myself a job would help ease things at home. I'm going to look for one and Aunt Florence will just have to accept it. I'm pleased things aren't so hectic for you now, but you must still watch that you don't allow yourself to get worn out. I've noticed how both Ben and Alec tend to take advantage of you.'

'Not in ways that I mind, Honor.' Emilia's eyes sparkled. 'I'm going to walk back with you and Mum as far as the ford. Ben will be down there, keeping out of sight. We've arranged a quick meeting.'

'Em! What if you're seen together? You know what people will say about you.'

'Ben and I are going to marry one day, Honor. Anyway,

what does it matter?' Emilia was suddenly impatient. 'If I was to lose my reputation, the gossips might as well be telling the truth. Don't look at me like that, Honor. Ben's going away soon, and I haven't the notion for doing only what's right and proper.'

'But you don't intend to . . .' Honor lowered her voice to the barest whisper and blushed, '. . . indulge in married love, do you? Say you don't, Em! What if you have a baby? That's what happens, you know. You should be thinking of getting married as soon as possible. I'm sure your father and Alec would give their consent. Yes, yes.' Honor nodded, as if seeking to reassure her worries about this. 'You must take the wisest course, Em. You'd be a properly respected widow if Ben were to—'

'Don't say that! Don't even think it.' Emilia reached out a work-roughened hand and tenderly touched Honor's alarmed face. 'Whatever happens, Ben will come back to me, and Billy's coming back to start a future with you. They have to. We must believe they will.'

Emilia waved goodbye to Dolly and Honor at a spot where the lane forked off in two directions, one leading to Hennaford, the other, around an immediate bend, uphill to Ford House, eventually another route to the main road, just inside the village boundary. Eager to slip back across the bridge and into the field where Ben would be, Emilia was startled to see Alec blocking her way.

'I thought you might be here about now.' His expression was stone-cold. 'I may need your support, and Ben's. Stay here, Emilia, while I fetch him.'

'Alec – ' Emilia started following him – 'what's this all about?'

'Just do as I say.' Something severe and grave in his tone made her obey. Speculating about the reason behind his mysterious behaviour, she stared down at the fast-moving muddied waters of the ford, which emerged from the field through an unseen shute under the bridge, and after passing across the lane it carried on, wider and stony-bottomed, in sight for about five hundred yards, between two other fields.

Moments later, Ben was staring at her, equally baffled, as Alec headed off for Ford House.

'He's ordered that we wait here for ten minutes then follow him and stay outside the gate,' Ben said. 'Alec wouldn't say what it's about. I've never seen him looking so deadly serious.'

'For a moment I thought he'd come to tick me off for being here to meet you. Well, we'd better do what he wants, at least we can be alone for a while.'

They kissed and stayed arm in arm. Emilia homed in on the vivid redness spreading down from under Ben's eye patch to his cheekbone. She was about to say he should see the doctor again, but he said, 'Listen, darling, I've been in the woods turning our old camp into a comfortable place for us to be together. All we need now is the chance to be alone for a reasonable length of time. Do you think Honor will cover for you?'

'I'm not sure. You know how she hates lying.'

'You'll just have to convince her then!'

'There's no need to raise your voice at me, Ben. Is your eye troubling you?'

'It's tender, nothing more. I'm only wearing this silly patch to be sensible. Sorry, Em, for snapping at you.'

He turned his head away. Shortly before Alec had called him from where he was concealed beyond the field gate, he had been rubbing around his eye, muttering and swearing in pain and frustration. It still felt as if the particle of grit was stabbing into it. He had blinked and blinked, and wiped thick discoloured moisture away with the clean handkerchief Emilia had given him after breakfast. Then he had looked down at the waterlogged ground. He could see as usual with the right eye, but there was a hazy patch, the size of a pea, blocking his vision on the left. It just had to clear. He would not be allowed to take up the commission promised to him if it didn't. He had to serve. It's what he desired with all his heart and mind – even before Emilia, at this moment. One day soon someone would be handing him a white feather.

Alec let himself into his brother's house using the key Tristan had entrusted to him. Ursula Harvey had good reason to keep her doors locked. Some of the villagers had walked in before and vilified her over her unfaithfulness to her well-liked and highly respected husband. His popularity and Henry's war decoration were the reasons why the Harvey family had not been written off socially.

Alec crept into the parlour. Ursula was there alone, with a tea tray set for one, working on a square of embroidery beside a docile fire. In a decorous high-necked blouse and plain skirt covering her ankles, and singing softly to herself, she made a perfect wifely picture. But, just as Lucy had been, her best function as a wife had turned out to be merely decorative. Here was a prepossessing, dark-haired woman with prized white skin, beautiful on the outside, but treacherous and selfish within. Many times he had implored her to give up her lover, to consider Jonathan's feelings, if not Tristan's. Tristan, who loved her so much, had fought back tears, perceiving, Alec believed, that she no longer loved him, when saying goodbye to her on his last leave.

As if sensing some ominous presence, Ursula sprang up, blood appearing on her finger where she pricked it on the needle. 'God in heaven, Alec! How dare you walk in like this? What do you want?'

'Where's my nephew?' His voice was abrasive.

He looked as cold as ice, but Ursula, although depending on him and Ben to bring provisions, and knowing Alec could be inflexible and persistent on matters that were deepest to him, parried in a stringent manner. 'Whatever you've come for, keep your voice down. Jonny's having a nap.'

'I'm not here to waste my breath. Jonny's too old for a nap, isn't he? Is he unwell?'

'He has a slight cold, that's all. Now say what you must, then go.'

Alec moved up to within an inch of her. 'I understand it's you who's going, Ursula. Out of this house and out of Hennaford for good, having planned with your lover to run off together and take my brother's child with you.'

'How . . . ?' Ursula's delicate narrow fingers flew to her breast.

'Did you think I'd not find out? You didn't try to hide your affair, not with the number of visits you've made to Bruce Ashley's lodgings in Truro, and you and he thought you were being clever. Not so. While Ashley was promising his landlady all manner of rewards to be discreet about your plans, I was paying her to inform on you both. I also know you're four months pregnant. I'm afraid I can't stand back and allow you to just go off with Jonny, to deprive Tristan of his son. I'm here to ask you to allow me to take him with me to live at the farm. I have two honest, reliable women living at the farm now. Jonny will be well cared for.'

'But you can't expect me to leave Jonny behind.' Ursula backed away from him, swept out hands of appeal. 'I was about to write to Tris. Explain that it wouldn't be the last he'd see of Jonny.'

'And tell him what? That you're about to go off with a cad, a ne'er-do-well, and plunge his son into an improper, unacceptable life. Ashley hasn't got a job, Ursula. He'll never amount to anything, and I know for a fact he damaged his own kneecap to get out of service to his country. Do you really want to swap Tris, the loving father that he is, for a man like that? Jonny used to be gregarious, but he's grown reserved and anxious because he's being shunned by his grandparents and that's something you're responsible for. Don't you think it's time you put Jonny first?'

Having her inflexibility suddenly whipped away, her promised joy threatened, Ursula paled but fought back. 'It's not that easy, Alec. Think what it would do to Jonny to be without me.'

'Think what it would do to him if your life with Ashley goes to form. Could you bear to see him running away from Ashley's debtors? There's a certain syndicate in Truro who are not above strong-arm tactics, about to call in his loans.'

Ursula shook her head, as if to stop herself from absorbing the truth of his arguments. 'Bruce has said there's some people he's got to settle up with before we go.'

'Do you really believe that, Ursula? Don't you think it would be better if you were the one who Jonny saw occasionally?' Alec was grim, sighing, for the whole thing was such a mess and he was hating this.

'I can't do it. I can't leave Jonny behind.' She sank down into her chair, her head bent over, and started weeping through her hands.

Alec felt little pity for her. Ursula might mean now to reunite Jonny with Tristan later, but the risk of Tristan never seeing his son again was too great. He had promised Tristan he'd look after Jonny and he would use any means to do it. 'Then perhaps I should inform the police about the part Bruce Ashley played in Lucy's death.'

Ursula's head shot up. 'But Lucy made him help her.'

'Yes, she did, because his behaviour made it easy for her. She told me all about it, how his extortion of an old man's life savings led to her blackmailing him into finding out a particular address for her. How she made him take her there, and afterwards drop her back to the farm under the guise of a cabbie. His crime cost me the life of my child and I'll always hate him for that. He should be rotting away in gaol for what he did. I don't want Jonny near that man. How can you?'

Ursula stopped crying and glared at Alec as if she wanted to hurt him. 'You're just an embittered hypocrite, Alec. You were never faithful to Lucy.'

'Lucy and I never declared we were in love. Now let's get back to Jonny.' He lowered himself in front of Ursula. 'If you want, I'll help you. Give Ashley up and let me look after Jonny for a while. Go away and have your baby; you can tell Jonny you are to do war work. Tris loves you, I'm sure he'd forgive you. You know it's only fair, don't you, Ursula? Make your decision. Is it to be Ashley or Jonny and Tris?'

*   *   *

Emilia and Ben watched, astonished, as Alec carried Jonathan Harvey, robust and dark, peeking out nervously from his woollen balaclava, through the gate. Alec had a suitcase in his other hand, which he passed to Ben. Ursula brought up the rear, her face an immobile mask.

'Wave goodbye to Mummy, Jonny,' Alec said, with a false jaunty smile. 'Uncle Ben and Emilia are here to walk with us to the farm.'

'Mummy, don't leave without me.' Jonathan started to weep and, looking over Alec's shoulder, he held his arms out to Ursula.

'We should go quickly,' Alec ordered Ben and Emilia. He strode off down the hill.

Ben glared at Ursula, then grabbing Emilia's arm, marched after his brother. Emilia glanced back and saw Ursula crumple to her knees, then with her arms stretched out after them begin to wail.

Jonathan struggled and sobbed until the sounds of his mother's lamenting had been left behind. 'It's going to be all right, old chap.' Alec pressed the boy's face gently against his shoulder. 'Mummy has to go away, but she knows you'll be happy with us until Daddy gets back.'

'Alec, is Ursula going away with a certain person?' Ben asked.

Alec whispered so Jonathan could not hear. 'Yes, and she's carrying his child. I managed to reason with her not to take Jonny with her.'

'She was terribly upset,' Emilia said. A short time ago she would have believed the woman had got what she deserved, but the echo of her suffering made it harder to be self-righteous.

'I offered her a way out but she's made her choice.' Alec walked on, trying to ignore the acid chewing away at his insides.

Chapter Six

Tristan was walking away from Ford Farm, in the opposite direction of the ford. The lane tapered to a mere cart's breadth and it was hard to avoid the overhang of sopping foliage and tangled dead brambles on the hedgerows, and the banks of mud thrown out by farm conveyances and traps and the rare motorized vehicle. Inevitably, there was mud under his boots. Always, always he could not get away from thick, cloying mud. A sea of the foul-tasting muck seemed to be clogging up his lungs. If ever there was an end to this war, he didn't know if he could bring himself to return to farming where there would be mud to contend with throughout the long winter months and whenever it rained.

A comfortable desk job, perhaps writing for a living was tempting. Ursula had urged him to sell Ford House, get a loan from the bank if need be, and set himself up in a business. He had been content to help run the farm with Alec; one of his tasks had been to see to written matters because of Alec's humiliating condition. *He had been content.* Perhaps he had also been boring and dull, and this was why Ursula had turned to another man.

He passed the turning that led off to Druzel Farm, and was reminded of the son from there who had died of trench fever. His name? His name? He should know his name – Tristan was the same age as the poor unfortunate. And here was a lonely dwelling – he couldn't remember who lived there. Wayside Cot. Alec owned it, didn't he? It seemed empty, deserted.

He took a left fork. This way led to the parish church, where it hid itself, among the ancient yews and oaks, in aloof aloneness from the village. Here and there the lane fell away into sharp ditches filled with murky brown water. Miniature trenches. He shuddered. Trees were arching over him, the twigs of the lowest branches curving upwards, like beckoning fingers. Ben had named this stretch of lane Devil's Arch, and he and his playmates had dashed under the trees calling out a sacred oath, of Ben's invention, for protection. Tristan half expected to see his tearaway younger brother as a little boy in knee britches come hurtling towards him, whooping and issuing bloodcurdling threats to some imaginary enemy. So reckless Ben had been in his games, never a week had gone by without him coming home covered in scratches and bruises, his clothes ripped, or his boots reduced to tatters. Pray God, if the time came for him to suffer in the trenches he acted sensibly in them. Those God-deserted, abominable, man-made creations.

The tunnel of trees seemed to be going on for ever. It was getting darker. Colder. Why was he walking away from home? He wanted to go home so much. To see Jonathan. To see if he could wrench Ursula away from her lover, to see if she could love him again, and he love her as he did before.

Billy Rowse was coming towards him. Tristan broke into a run, ready to shake the corporal's hand. 'You got back in one piece too! Well done, Billy. Have you anything to report?'

Billy didn't stop, or stand to attention and salute. Billy didn't see him. He was staring at nothing. He walked straight past him. No – *he walked straight through him.*

Tristan's body gave a violent shiver. Billy had felt as cold as death.

The rest of his section was marching towards him. What a brave sound their boots made on the dull ground. The captain was at the front, baton under his arm, head up. Well turned-out. Proud. But there was a blur under his cap instead of his face. None of the men had faces. A shiver of fear and revulsion raced up Tristan's spine. He leaned into the hedge to give them room to pass. They did so with the speed of a whizzing shell and the slowness of a cortège. He watched them disappear, not under Devil's Arch, but into a mire of mud. *Dear God in heaven!* He snapped his eyes shut.

Then he was in the churchyard, a lonely half mile further on along the lane and he was looking down at Lucy's grave. Thin slate. Alec had chosen slate so thin and brittle for her headstone it looked as if the merest puff of wind would disintegrate it. *Lucy Jemima Harvey. Beloved wife of . . .* Alec had omitted his name. *Also their infant son.* But Lucy had not given birth. The child had perished with her in the fifth month of her pregnancy. Above anything in the world Alec had wanted a son. How sad, how terrible, he had had a son and lost him.

'Tristan.'

'Ursula?'

'No. It's me, Emilia. You shouldn't be here, Tristan.'

He couldn't see Emilia. There was only her voice, soft and caring, with its soothing intonation. 'Emilia, where are you?'

'You have to go back to look after Billy. You must go back. Go back, Tristan.'

He opened his eyes. He was lying on his side with his face on his arm. He coughed on the mud that was in his mouth. Looking up, he saw only greyness and looming shadows.

He opened his eyes again, and guessed more hours had passed. There was a smoky darkness now, but only for a second. His heart jerked in pain and fright as the darkness was lit up by flashes and darts of fire. Then he became aware of the continuous roar of heavy artillery and the shattering raps of machine guns. He tried to put his hands over his ears. He'd go mad if he didn't stop the noise echoing round and round inside his head. But he couldn't move his arms. *Jesus, Lord God. I'm injured.*

Now came the terrible sense of wetness underneath him and the rain pelting down on him. And pain. Pain like he'd never known before. Burning pain and thumping pain in every part of him. He couldn't see any barbed wire, only a stretch of hideously pock-marked terrain. Must be in no man's land, where he had fallen in the early morning. A star shell lit up the sky and the land.

What was that close by? A bush? No. It was a body. Lots of bodies. A tableau of heads and limbs hanging at strange angles, with the embellishment of a single upright rifle. There was a large lump. A mound of earth? In the next shocking spiral of light he made out the remains of a headless horse. It was rotting, been there for some time, but he had not noticed it in the attack. He grinned. It was incomprehensible but he found it funny, an interesting difference to Ben's tales of a headless rider on a horse. *God, I'm going mad. At least I've got some company, even if it's dead.*

A weight was pressing in on his back and another weight was crushing his chest. His lungs were packing up. *I'm dying. Bloody, bloody fool, why did I ever hope to survive this hell?*

Best to get out of it. Leave all the pain behind. His body was screaming in agony but the torture in his mind was a thousand times worse. Then he saw Jonathan's face. His handsome little dark-haired boy, who'd wanted to come here with him, be brave with him. 'Don't be afraid, Daddy.' Jonny's last words to him.

He shouldn't just lie here. He would drown soon if he didn't move. He had a reason to try to get to safety, a son to live for, a son's freedom to fight for. Providence had dictated so far that he hadn't been blown to smithereens and he must get up, get back, get himself patched up so he could take another crack at Fritz. Grunting with the effort to keep his head up, he tried to move his arms again. In the eerie illumination of a Very light, he saw his arms were moving, he just couldn't feel them with the weight of mud that was clinging to them. Probably the same thing figured for his legs. Somehow he rolled and got up on to his forearms, then started the long process to raise himself on to his knees. A pain-filled process, every movement telling him where bits of metal were embedded in his flesh and bones. It would be impossible to walk. His left ankle was pierced through, shrapnel sticking out of it. He must crawl back to his front line, but which way? For

God's sake, which way? He nearly gave way to a rush of panic.

The outline of a Lewis gun tilting skywards made him feel he should know something about it. Billy Rowse! Billy could be anywhere by now but he had to check. Every moment as he squirmed over the mud was a nerve-jarring event. Sharp objects ripped into him, further tattering his uniform, halting him until the tears of pain and frustration and dreadful isolation subsided. He had to keep moving and he dare not fall on his face – if he passed out he'd inhale the filth and die. He yelled out as he nearly careered over the edge of something. It was the shell crater and it was filling up with a deadly porridge-thick brew of mud. A body was head downwards in it. A wounded soldier who had crawled into it to wait for help only to drown? Or was it Billy? He felt about for the machine gun, touched something anomalous and recoiled. Hair, that's what it was, and underneath it was a cold rigid head with a gaping hole from front to back. He pushed the body over and stared into the face, waiting for the next flash of war so he could see if he knew who it belonged to.

Next moment he saw that the stiff open eyelids and astonished expression belonged to Billy Rowse. 'Oh, God, oh, God.' Searching inside Billy's shirt, he ripped off his identity disk. Winding the evidence of just one more insignificant death in High Command's grand scheme round his wrist, he crawled away through the carnival of fantastically monstrous sights and sounds.

He heard something. Lower, indistinguishable noises. Was that a voice? 'Don't shoot, don't shoot.' His own voice sounded small and pathetic, like Jonathan's after a bad dream.

His shoulders were grabbed and he was being hauled along at what seemed breakneck speed. He was falling, falling. He couldn't bear the spinning sensation, the stabbings and piercings and bumpings of pain. The greyness was coming back and was mercifully overtaken by the darkness.

Chapter Seven

Alec thought he was imagining things. He was up on a ladder, finishing off the thatching of a fern rick, which would be used for animal bedding, and he had a good view over most of his property. Wayside Cot was empty but he was sure he had seen smoke coming out of its chimney. The last tenant, a hostile old man with dirty habits, had died of liver disease during the summer, and Alec hadn't found the time to renovate the two up, two down building to rent it out again. He hammered in the last 'broach' – a stick of stout blackthorn – into one head of the rick, to hold the reeds of wheat straw in place. When he looked up again, smoke was definitely coming out of Wayside Cot's chimney.

'Blasted tramps!' He jumped to the ground, and after fetching a shotgun, called one of the Jack Russells to him. An excellent guard dog, Pip was smaller than the others Alec had bred – he was an intimidating white, black and tan, rough-coated creature inclined to baring his teeth, and so cantankerous at times he was not allowed in the house.

Emilia had come outside with Jonathan after coaxing him to join her in helping Alec with the last job to secure the rick, to join the broaches together with noir ropes. With Alec and herself up on ladders, the boy was to go back and forth between them with the long ropes attached to a tall bamboo, and thus the bedding would be threaded down and kept dry all winter. She eyed the shotgun and her employer's no-nonsense demeanour. 'What's up, Alec? Where are you going?'

'I've a little matter to attend to, Emilia. You and Jonny can play at something until I get back, shan't be long.'

Jonathan shot after him. 'Uncle Alec, come back!'

Alec lowered himself down, cradled the boy on his knee and stemmed his anxious tears. 'There's nothing for you to worry about, Jonny, I promise you.'

'But you're going off to war! I don't want anyone else to leave. Mummy's gone, and my daddy might not come back. Lots of people have gone away and they're never coming back. They're dead, like Auntie Lucy.'

While Emilia watched in fascination at his tenderness, Alec kissed Jonathan and pulled his little tweed cap firmly down to his pert ears. 'I know there's been some terrible sadness, Jonny, and we can't pretend not to be worried about your daddy, but I promise you that I'm never ever going to leave here. Nor is Emilia.' He glanced up at her. 'Are you?'

'I've got no plans to go away, Jonny,' she reassured the boy. The shadow of war lay over her future with Ben, so there was no point in mentioning she was to become a soldier's wife.

After promising Jonathan he'd teach him how to play chess, Alec was on his way. He let Pip run on ahead down the lane and bound into the tiny wreck of Wayside Cot's front garden. Pip was sniffing and growling round at the back when Alec caught up with him. Ordering Pip back, pushing the door open on its creaking hinges, Alec cocked the shotgun, which he had not loaded, and strode inside. He kept a grip on the two cartridges, just in case.

His former tenant had used all the inside doors for firewood and he could see straight through the small mistreated kitchen into the living room, and slumped beside the hearth, his back against the wall, was a man in dark clothing. The tramp who had turned up at the farm a few days ago, from Emilia's description. He was trembling, probably an alcoholic gone too long without a drink.

'You're trespassing. Out!'

Pip shot up beside Alec and snarled, showing all of his sharp teeth.

The tramp brought his head up as if it was an effort to

move. He was damp with sweat and had a high colour. 'M-my apologies, sir. I presume you are Mr Harvey, the owner of Ford Farm. I'm Archie Rothwell—'

'I don't want none of your fancy talk. I just want you off my property.'

Archie Rothwell's hand shook as he reached for his bedroll and stick. His breathing was harsh and gurgling. 'If you'd . . . just allow . . . a minute.'

Alec moved back to give him room. The blaze he had built from a mess of sticks was almost out. Why had the man, who no doubt had been banking on remaining undiscovered, not gathered enough wood to last him the night ahead? Alec looked down at his crippled feet. They were clad in quality leather, worn down at odd angles by his disability. 'Do you need a hand?'

Archie Rothwell nodded.

Alec 'broke' the shotgun, then crooking an arm under the other man's armpit yanked him upwards. Archie Rothwell used the dust-laden wooden shelf over the fireplace to keep his balance, and although not quite straight, he towered over Alec. Alec passed him the stick. There was no smell of drink on him. As Emilia had remarked, he was clean and tidy. Given his obvious fall from a higher living, the long hair and beard suggested he was hiding from something, most likely his true identity. Alec considered reporting him to the constable, but if he was, as Emilia had wondered, down on his luck after military service, that seemed a bit harsh. Pip was getting impatient and darted off outside to sniff about. He sensed no danger from the stranger and that would do for Alec, for now.

'Sometimes I feel so cold, you see,' Archie Rothwell said.

'Why do you feel so cold?'

'My ship was sunk, a destroyer, at Jutland. Nearly all hands lost. I was in the water a long, long time. I'm sorry I troubled you, I'll be on my way again.'

'You're obviously well bred, I take it you had a high rank. How come you to this sort of life?'

'By choice, Mr Harvey. I am all alone in the world. I can

prove who I am. You may look at the documents and photographs I have on my person, and in light of your interest in me, if you were to give me some work, and I am looking for regular work through the winter, you'd be in my everlasting gratitude.' Archie Rothwell offered Alec the leather wallet with gilt edgings that he took out of his inside breast pocket. 'You'll find references in there too from various employers over the last year.'

Alec drew the contents out of the wallet. He glanced at a small photograph of Archie Rothwell in officer's uniform but did not unfold the papers. Alec felt himself blushing. 'Tell me what these say?'

Before answering, Archie Rothwell found it necessary to clear his throat, which brought on a fresh outbreak of sweating and shivering. 'I was the commander of my ship. Afterwards, I was medically discharged.'

'Have you no home at all?'

'There was nowhere for me to go after I was discharged from the nursing home. I did not want to live on charity. I prefer my own company and as a sailor I'm not used to staying in one place.'

'Where did you start out?'

'From Lincolnshire, Mr Harvey.'

'You have travelled a long way.'

Archie Rothwell eased his balance and winced. 'I've got an infection in my foot. If I could just be allowed to stay a little longer to rest it . . .'

Alec had the welfare of three women, his younger brother and nephew to measure, but he considered the request. There were tragic reports of men coming home from battle to find they no longer had a home, perhaps abandoned by a wife like Ursula, their money spent. Rejection, desertion, injury and shock could make even the most level-headed of high-ranking officers turn away from normal life. 'Where were you today before you found your way in here?'

'Washing dishes in a hotel in Truro. I found it too noisy, too intrusive. I liked the quietness of this area when I passed through this way a few days ago and decided to return. I was actually making my way to Ford Farm when the pain and the shivers got too much.'

'I've heard enough. I'm prepared to take you to the farm and see about doing something for your foot. You obviously have a cold too. You can bed down for the night in the hay house, but I'll be ordering my dog to keep an eye on you. You're welcome to a hot meal, but as for work and shelter, I'll have to think about it. Is this agreeable to you?'

Archie Rothwell leaned back against the wall and expelled a long breath. 'God bless you, sir.'

Ben and Alec were in the den. While Alec trod the polished planks, making all the necessary business decisions and adding up figures swiftly in his head, Ben was sitting behind the desk compiling or adding to lists, making out receipts for goods or stock to be sold and filling out government forms. Alec was able to sign cheques and this he did. They finished quickly, for they were efficient at this hated part of farm life; then they relaxed as they usually did, with a glass of whisky.

'So, have you decided what to do about this Rothwell character?' Ben rubbed at his tense brow, careful to avoid the tender area of his left eye. The papers you asked me to read seemed all in order.'

Alec lit his third cigarette in fifteen minutes. The frustration of not being able to attend to his own business always made him edgy. 'Well, I can hardly turn him out, he hasn't even got one good foot to walk on. I had to practically carry him here. Tilda took him some hot salted water and bandages but he insisted on seeing to his feet himself. She's made him onion soup for his chest. She was nervous of him at first then seemed quite taken with him, you know how women can get silly about down-on-their-luck sorts. Emilia was pleased to see him again. Jonny stared at him as children do. Rothwell seemed unhappy about that, but no one likes being stared at. I suppose he could be useful in the garden, peeling vegetables, doing light jobs about the yard. On his request, we'll keep his naval service between us on the farm. He says people ask such morbid questions. What do you think about it?'

'I think we should definitely give him a go. Hate to think people would shun me if I went a bit dippy because of my service.'

'You think he's got mental problems?'

'Well, no, but battle fatigue, yes. I spoke to him briefly when I collected his plate and mug – seems a reasonable fellow, a bit eccentric, I suppose. He was well wrapped up on the bales, with plenty of pillows, and a flask of hot cocoa standing by, thanks to Tilda and Em. The cats like him, Snowy was curled up on his legs. Had his boots off, they stank to high heaven from the infection. Perhaps we could find something else for him, or Honor from her Red Cross collections.'

'Seems the fellow's already settled here in our minds. I believe he's genuine, he's made a great sacrifice and we can't allow him to go on sinking down.'

Ben poured himself another drink and topped up Alec's glass. 'You didn't pay a visit to your usual rendezvous on Saturday night.'

At last Alec allowed himself to recline in front of the fireplace. The room took on a different ambience for him now. It was a man's room, half-panelled in rich dark oak, sparingly furnished with well-used leather. It was his retreat, only spoiled for him when he became aware of the shelves lined with his father's books, or when there was business to get through. 'I shall call on Eugenie again soon, but only to tell her our association has to end. Now I've taken on the responsibility of Jonny, he'll come first.'

'Won't you miss Mrs Bawden's services?'

'If you must put it that way, yes. I shall miss her company and friendship even more.'

'You were going to marry her once, before Lucy dazzled you. Now Eugenie Bawden's a widow, why not consider her again? It would solve a lot of problems.'

'I didn't love Eugenie before and I don't love her now. She's content to live on her husband's bequest, and she certainly wouldn't care for life as a farmer's wife with the way things are.'

Ben was thoughtful. 'Are you saying you'd only consider marrying again if you were to fall in love? I know you didn't love Lucy. What man could?'

'I would certainly have to trust and respect a woman before I go down that road again.' Alec stubbed out his cigarette and tossed it into the log basket with more effort than was required. 'Ben, could you not talk about Lucy in that way.'

Ben viewed his brother with wryness. Lucy had treated everyone either with disinterest or contempt. She and Alec had quarrelled often, she had struck him frequently, but he wouldn't allow a word against her. Strange loyalties, he kept. Their bedroom life had been good, apparently. When he had realized the significance of the noises coming from the now empty master bedroom, he had been amazed at the regularity of their intimacy. After Lucy's death, Alec had swung from despair to anger, to bitterness to disregard. This was the first time he had mentioned her to him in ages.

'I thought I'd slip away with Emilia for an hour tomorrow afternoon,' Ben said, as if issuing a challenge. 'She didn't get away at all yesterday. It was Sunday and she should have had her half day off. She is entitled to it.'

'Of course she is. It's fine by me,' Alec replied, gazing at Ben's troubled eye. 'Edwin might not agree.'

'He won't know what Emilia's doing unless someone tells him. Anyway, he shouldn't be so damned small-minded! I'm not playing with Emilia's affections. We should be able to have more time to ourselves. We rarely get the chance for even a quiet word. If she hasn't got Jonny clinging to her, then Grandma needs her attention or she's working like a skivvy.'

'I said, it was fine by me, Ben. I understand.' Alec got up and peeped out between the curtains. 'We're in for a few more wet and windy days. I don't know where you could go in weather like this.'

'I've got plans.'

'Which I don't want to hear about.' Alec went to the door. 'I'm going up to see if Jonny's settled down. He's getting a little used to being here, I think. Tilda said he ate all his meals today. He enjoyed setting up the chess set with me and learning the moves, he's a bright child. Your eye, Ben. You don't complain about it, but it obviously isn't healing. I've been to see Dr Holloway. He's arranged an emergency appointment for you, the day after tomorrow, with a Mr Preston at his clinic, at the infirmary.'

'There's no need. It will right itself in time.'

'Ben, you can't see out of it properly. You're walking into things. Both I and Emilia have noticed it.'

'I can see perfectly well! I'm being clumsy because there's too much to do and not enough people to do it, and I object to you talking to Emilia about me in secret. I'll see this bloke, then I'll stay on in Truro and call in at the shops for the things I'll need to take with me to the military college. I know when I've gone it will mean even more extra work for you and Edwin, but you're going to have to get used to it. Archie Rothwell's limited services may be of help. You could take on some prisoners of war or approach the Land Army. Lucy's not here to object to other women about the place any more.'

'I'm considering several options. Ben, why are you being aggressive towards me? We've always got along fine until recently. Are you nervous about leaving home? Worried about the training? Afraid of the fighting? Or is there something else?'

Ben looked away. He had no right to be offhand with Alec, who, since their parents' deaths, had filled that terrible void, mainly with patience and paternal concern. 'There's nothing. Life's hardly wonderful, is it?'

Emilia listened outside Jonathan's bedroom, which was between hers and Lottie's, for sounds of him being awake and fretting for his mother. After Emilia had read him a story and he had said his prayers, he had insisted she close the door when she left. Emilia had smiled to herself: Alec would be pleased his confidence was growing. He was marvellous with Jonathan. The boy was beginning to lose his understandable shyness and suspicion following the abrupt wrench of his mother's desertion. He had responded to Alec's interest and affection with a chuckle while they had finished the rick. Alec would have made a good father. It seemed sadder, the sudden loss of his baby while Lucy had been shopping at Truro. Emilia grinned at thoughts of Ben's clumsy attempts to impress Jonathan. He was a serious child, with no interest in games that involved a grown-up pretending he was a puppy, or a big bad wolf or an aeroplane. Jonathan had stunned everyone by telling them how an aeroplane could actually fly.

Alec crept up close to her and whispered, 'Is he asleep?'

'I think so.'

'We should take a look. I'll never forget that first night when we found him huddled in the corner sobbing without making a sound. It still chills me.' It was something Alec had done on many occasions after receiving his father's denunciations. 'Did you leave the lantern on?'

'Yes, up safely out of reach.'

Setting his face in concentration, Alec slowly opened the door. 'He's not in bed!'

He and Emilia pushed through the door together and both sighed with relief. Jonathan was stretched out on the hearth rug, with a bundle of letters in his hands. 'Hello, Uncle Alec, Emilia,' he said, as if this was not an unusual occurrence.

It was not the first time Emilia was struck as how adult he sounded. 'You should be sleeping, young man.'

'What have you got there, old chap?' Alec was all smiles as he got down on the floor with the boy.

'Letters from my daddy. Mummy put them in with my toys. This one says, "How's my little hero?" That's me.' Jonathan pointed to himself. '"Tell him, I'm sure he's grown an inch or two since I last wrote." I think I have, Uncle Alec. I'm getting big. What do you think?'

'You can read, Jonny?' Alec gasped, glancing up at Emilia.

'Of course. I can read all the small words, and I know the

big ones in Daddy's letters off by heart. Mummy taught me. She's taught me many things. How to grow seeds. How to make toast. She was going to teach me how to paint with oils.' Jonathan suddenly clung to Alec's neck. 'Make her come back, Uncle Alec. She said she never could. I miss her so much. I want her back.'

While Jonathan sobbed, Alec wrapped him up tight. 'Your mother had to go away. I'm sorry, but there was nothing I could do about it. You have me and Uncle Ben and Emilia now. You like Tilda, she makes you nice things to eat, doesn't she? And you like Great-grandma. She makes you laugh, remember? Perhaps tomorrow there will be a letter from your daddy. Emilia will take you out to the lane and look for the postman. You'll do that, won't you, Emilia?'

'Of course, I will.' Emilia came close and, reaching down, stroked Jonathan's silky dark hair. She was struck at how attentive a mother Ursula had been. 'Then we'll find lots of interesting things to do.'

Jonathan stretched out a hand to her, and Emilia clasped it and knelt beside him and Alec.

'Don't worry, Jonny,' Alec repeated his pledge of earlier in the day. 'Uncle Ben has to go away soon, but Emilia and I will always be here.'

Chapter Eight

'This is better than being in a draughty hideout in the woods, isn't it, darling,' Ben said, as he locked the back door of Ford House behind him and Emilia.

'A place all of our own for a little while.' Emilia took off her gloves and rubbed her hands. This autumn seemed colder than any previous one, but each succeeding season since the war seemed harsher, with less sun, less colour. They had slipped here under the threat of a shower of rain, and added to the chilliness of the house was a sense of brooding loneliness and sorrow. If Tristan stepped foot inside here again he would be bringing more sorrows with him, for a letter had been sent from his brothers informing him of the reason his son was now residing at the farm. 'Wish we could light a fire.'

'I'll make you warm.' Ben smiled with gentle humour.

This was her Ben. Tender and loving. To hide her fearfulness at his having to leave her soon, perhaps forever, she didn't wait until they went through into the sitting room to kiss him. Ben's eagerness was the same, then he smiled into her eyes and took her hand.

'I expect there'll be some sherry in the sideboard.' He was speaking like a host. Emilia could tell he was as nervous and shaky with the anticipation of what might happen as she was.

She settled herself in the chair beside the hearth, noticing the signs of things being removed – small personal things, she supposed. Crumpled on the sewing table was a piece of embroidery, spattered with tiny red spots, a needle hanging down from a short length of silk. She picked up the square of pale blue satin and flattened it out on her lap. The spots were obviously blood. Ursula had abandoned this in much the same way as she had her marriage. 'I suppose Ursula will have written to Tristan by now.'

Ben was pouring the sherry and she put the embroidery back in its place. He was sombre for a moment. 'She was quite a good sort, really. I was fond of her until she made Tris a cuckold.'

Emilia took the glass he brought her. 'I've only tasted sherry before at the farm, when Alec opened a bottle last Christmas Day.'

Ben knelt in front of her. 'I promise to give you everything after we're married and have our own home. One day you might find yourself a colonel's wife, perhaps out in India, then we'll settle back in England, two old dears together. Like the sound of that, darling?'

'I haven't thought much about being an Army wife, leaving Hennaford and the farm.' She felt a strange sense of disappointment at the prospect of leaving her present life. 'But wherever you are, Ben, that's where I want to be.'

Ben clinked his glass against hers. 'A toast to our future then, Mr and Mrs Ben Harvey. Wait a minute.' He took her glass away and held her hand. 'I haven't done this properly yet. Emilia, darling, will you marry me?'

She kissed his lips. 'Yes, Ben, of course.'

Ben pulled her to her feet. A long time passed in which they showered each other with devotion. 'I should have a ring for you,' he said.

'A ring's not important. Only you and I and our love matters.'

They finished the sherry and tasted the sweet liquid on each other's lips.

'Why don't we go upstairs?' he breathed against her face.

She looked straight into his eyes. 'All right.'

From Tristan Harvey's bedroom window, Emilia looked out across the fields all the way to Ford Farm. How quickly things could change. A week ago, Lottie's wanderings had led to her sleeping at the farm. There were two new workers there now, and Jonathan. Ursula had left, giving her and Ben a place where they could consummate their love. A week, in which thousands of men would have lost their lives. Fate could take a loved one away in a single moment. Would fate deprive her of Ben?

'You're not worrying about Grandma, are you?' Ben noticed the direction of her gaze.

'Of course not. I was just thinking . . .'

'If you've changed your mind, I'll understand, Em.' He put his arms around her from behind, placed a peck on the back of her neck. 'Although I'd be terribly disappointed.'

'No, it's not that.' She turned in his arms, rested her face against him. 'It's nothing at all.'

'Let's just concentrate on us.'

Emilia tried to imagine they were the only two people in the world, but while they were discarding their coats she became aware of the open wardrobe doors and the pulled-out drawers – the signs of Ursula's careless packing. 'We'll tidy everything before we go. I'm sure Alec means to see the house is in order before Tristan's next leave.'

'Forget the others, Em.'

At his mild scolding, Emilia looked up at Ben's gorgeous face. He brushed her hair back with his fingertips and kissed the tender skin at her temples. Their lips met and without all the usual restraints to stop them, they began exploring, yearning for new experiences. Tenderness and adoration rapidly flamed into pressing desire.

His breathing coming fast, Ben began undoing the buttons on her cardigan. His anxious fingers wouldn't work and he pushed the cardigan down off her arms. 'Sorry, darling, I didn't expect to feel so eager.'

Emilia saw to the buttons of her blouse and stepped out of her skirt, then took off more clothes.

Ben wrested off his jumper, his sight rooted on her body, shaped in wondrous femininity in just her chemise.

Her insides fluttering, Emilia glanced at the screen, longing for the sanctuary behind it. To bare all for the first time, even with Ben, was a little too much, too sudden. Perhaps there was a dressing gown of Tristan's in the wardrobe she could put on.

Ben had got his shirt and vest off before he noticed her, frozen and tense. He swept back the covers on the bed. 'Darling, get in as you are.'

She lay down on the cold linen sheets that smelled faintly of Ursula's delicate perfume, and pulled the bedcovers up to her shoulders. When naked, Ben leapt in beside her, sought her lips immediately, freed her from the covers and set about examining every impression of her body.

He hoisted her chemise up and lay over her. He was shaking, his breathing loud and harsh. 'Help me, Em. I'm afraid I might hurt you. I can't stop. I'll die if we don't soon . . .'

To Emilia, he was the vulnerable one now. All her love for him welled up inside her, but she had no notion how to help him. 'I don't know what to do, Ben.'

Then he was hurting her. She bit her lip to prevent herself crying out.

'I'm sorry, darling. Please be patient. I . . . oh, my love, my love.'

Emilia cried out and clutched his back. It felt as if he was tearing her apart inside. She tried to concentrate on Ben's love, caring only that he was getting enjoyment from her. Then he adjusted his position, and the pain turned to discomfort and she was able to put her arms around his neck and respond to his kisses. She was willing to wait, subdued and sacrificial, until it was over. Then a tiny thrill of pleasure came from somewhere deep within her. Then another. She couldn't locate exactly where the points of pleasure were inside her, all she was aware of was that they were joining together and spreading out in tiny waves of delight. When she felt she might join in with Ben, he shuddered, groaned in ecstasy and fell still.

He kissed her again and again before rolling away on to his back and bringing his arm up across his brow, panting. Emilia turned on her side to him. Tears were on his flushed cheeks. He felt for her hand. 'That was the most fantastic experience of my life.' He took his arm away and looked at her. 'I'm sorry, darling. Forgive my selfishness. I know that it wasn't good for you. You are all right though? It wasn't too awful, was it?'

'It was wonderful, Ben, because it was with you.' She caressed his damp face, then laid a hand over his heart. It was thudding wildly. As long as his heart was beating, as long as he was alive, she didn't care about her own pain and discomfort. And there was the hope of more enjoyment and fulfilment for herself next time.

He faced her and held her against him, stroking her hair and giving her gentle kisses. 'We're as one now, Em, like it says in the marriage service. Don't worry if anything's happened – a baby. I want us to get married before I go overseas anyway. I want to take as much of you with me as I can. We'll convince Edwin to give us his blessing, even if it means telling him what we've done. Em, you're quiet, what are thinking?'

'That I'm blessed to have you love me.'

'Honestly?'

She raised herself up and with feather-light fingertips wiped his tears away. 'Honestly, Ben.' She had the clearest look at his hurt eye. He moved his head slightly, as if he must to gain direct access to her gaze, something she had noticed him doing before, to her and others and objects he was about to touch. There was something wrong with his eye. She wouldn't mention it now. She didn't want anything to spoil this special afternoon.

'How are you . . . you know, down . . . ?' he asked.

'I'll live.' She laughed.

He became serious. 'You're so much stronger than I am, Em.'

'Am I now? Then I have you in my power, Ben Harvey.'

'You always have had, Emilia Rowse.'

Emilia pulled off her boots outside the back door of the farm. Ben was about to open it and she knocked his arm down.

'Don't, Ben. We shouldn't go inside together.' Her face was on fire.

'Edwin's not likely to be there, and I'm tired of us having to avoid each other.'

'I can't help thinking that people will know what we've done just by looking at us.'

'How can they possibly tell?'

'I don't know! They just might.'

'There's nothing for it but to face them, Em. If you run off somewhere else immediately they probably will make certain deductions.'

'Well, just make sure you act naturally.' Making love to her had empowered him somehow. He seemed more mature, more confident and flushed with pride. 'Take that huge smile off your face, Ben.'

'Don't be such a silly. I'm bound to be happy after spending time with the woman I love.'

They stepped inside together. Tilda was lifting a pie out of the oven and only turned her head towards them to smile. Jonathan was stooping to the kitchen floor, winding up a mechanical toy. 'Look what Uncle Alec's found for me, Emilia. It was his once. Emilia, watch Great-grandma, she enjoys this.'

Alec appeared from the walk-in larder, where he had been hanging up a brace of pheasants. Glad there was no emphasis on herself, Emilia admired the tin dog, which, when wound up walked on its four short legs. Jonathan stood beside her to watch the toy. 'See, I've laid out a piece of string, to time how fast the dog gets to it.'

Ben swung round to speak to Alec and knocked Jonathan off his feet. He fell with force, striking his ear on the table leg. He was shrieking and screaming, holding on to his ear. The toy was sent bouncing along the floor. Lottie's bleats of delight turned to frightened wails.

'Jonny!' Alec raced to him. 'Oh, no!'

'Ben,' Emilia gasped in disbelief and horror. 'Didn't you see him there?'

'No! I'm sorry. I thought he was further away.' He reached out to pat Jonathan's back – he was now up in Alec's arms, but Alec steered him away.

'For goodness sake, have more care, will you? You'd have to be blind not to have seen him.'

Emilia forgot Jonathan's distress and Lottie's need for comfort as a terrible truth hit her. 'Oh, my God, that's it, isn't it? You can't see properly, Ben, because you're blind!'

Chapter Nine

Ben looked up and looked down and looked straight ahead, obeying the instructions of Mr Preston, the optical consultant. He submitted to a thorough examination. Mr Preston, white-coated, as thin and bony as he was impersonal and serious, a wearer of big round spectacles and dangerously crisp collars, disappeared into another room with a bundle of notes and X-rays.

Hemmed in alone in the small bare, pale-green room, with the alarming raw smell of antiseptic thick in his nose, Ben wondered if the consultant had gone off to study his findings, to get a second opinion, or was simply a sadistic rotter to leave him to wait and wait for his final diagnosis.

Ben had not mentioned his blindness. Mr Preston had, in a terse manner, as if aggrieved about his silence on the matter. 'But it will clear?' Ben had asked, willing the consultant to say it would. 'It's only a little dark spot on my eye. Surely, it need not prevent me from serving our country? It's all I've been waiting to do for the last three years.'

Mr Preston had made a dismissive grunt, as if conveying it was his turn to keep silent.

Ben felt the high walls were folding in on him. 'Please, God, let me do my service. Don't make me stay at home like some coward or a conchy. I couldn't bear that. All my life I've wanted to be a soldier. I'd still be in the cadet corps if it wasn't for the shortage of workers on the farm. Please do something, even now . . . please.'

The door opened. In came Mr Preston, minus his white coat. A good or a bad sign? Mr Preston resumed his seat at the desk, and took a moment to smooth at the knife-edge creases of the trousers of his severe dark suit. He looked at Ben and Ben recoiled at the teeth-exposing grin the consultant now displayed. 'Mr Harvey – Ben, I'm afraid it's bad news, as I'm sure you must have expected. The grit that punctured the delicate tissue of your left eye has, sadly, resulted in you losing half of your vision there. If the offending matter had been removed by a doctor, without a doubt there would have been a good chance of saving your sight. Whoever attended to you did so most clumsily. There's nothing I can do to reverse the damage. You must take heart in the fact that this tragedy happened as a result of you performing an act of rescue.'

Ben felt as if he was being swallowed up by something monstrous and unholy. He would rather be standing in front of enemy lines, facing certain death, than this. 'So I'm blind – partially blind. Tell me it need not stop me from doing my duty to fight. I've lost one brother in this war, and even as we speak, my other brother might be dying or already dead. I need to avenge Henry. I need to support Tristan if he still lives. It won't matter, will it, that I can't see as well as I should? Your other senses improve greatly when you lose one, don't they? I will adapt. I already have. I'm beginning to instinctively correct my limited vision.'

Echoes of Jonathan's screams until his ear had stopped hurting, memory of how he'd clung to Alec or Emilia for the rest of the day, made Ben shiver. Emilia had been loving and sympathetic, of course, but then, it seemed to him, she had given a strange secretive smile. He knew what that smile meant – she was hoping his injury was permanent and would keep him safely at home, to fight the war by producing crops in the fields he had walked past alone on the way here. It was important to keep the country fed, people sometimes said. Not to him it wasn't. Anyone could work the land. Not everyone was as willing as he to face death and danger.

'A colleague of mine is on the premises, Ben.' Mr Preston persisted with his horsey smile. 'He's an Army medical man.

I'm positive that he will pass the same judgement as I, that you are medically unfit for service.' Ben let out a cry of despair. 'But he's willing to examine you. I can take it you are agreeable to the idea?'

'Yes, yes, please.' Ben clung to this last hope. 'Will he examine me today?'

'He's on the other side of the door. I'll call him in.'

Alec was waiting in the trap just inside the high bleak walls of the infirmary. He watched Ben trail his overcoat through the puddles, his hat off, head down, oblivious to the comings and goings of ambulances, patients and medical staff. There were various uniforms of His Majesty's services. It was raining steadily, fittingly gloomy for Ben's day of reckoning.

'Dear Lord, why did this have to happen?' Alec asked the leaden skies. Ben would be feeling drained, empty, blank, rejected, worthless. A horrible debilitating combination. Alec knew it intimately. Only the ownership of the farm and the responsibility of raising his youngest brother had kept him from succumbing to drink, opiates, or madness to escape his own despair. Now that Ben was suffering the same way a heavy touch of the bleakness and desolation settled on him. He jumped down off the trap. Ben had not seen him and was about to turn off down Infirmary Hill.

Ben leapt when he felt a hand on his shoulder. Still staring down, he recognized his brother's boots. It was market day, and Alec should be at the market, selling and buying stock. 'What are you doing here?'

'I couldn't let you face this alone, Ben. I can see it's what we'd feared. I'll take you straight home.'

'You can see? How bloody damned wonderful for you!' Ben cuffed Alec's hand off him. 'Well I'll never know what it is to have two good eyes again. I'd rather you take me for a drink.'

'You know it's illegal to buy another a drink nowadays.'

'Then I'll buy my own. I won't be needing the money for anything more important, will I?'

'I'm so sorry, Ben. We'll go to the Red Lion. Get on the trap.'

During the short negotiation of Truro's busy streets it seemed every other man was kitted out in uniform. Men on leave from their training, as indicated by their smartness and proud bearing, and men who had 'done their bit', haggard and old beyond their years, some displaying the aftermath of injuries; badges of honour. All warriors. Heroes. A stand outside a newsagent declared: 'OUTSTANDING BRAVERY IN FLANDERS MUD'. Ben's head sunk to his chest. He'd never be a part of the allied powers, never train, never fight, never become a prisoner of war. He would rather be certain of death on foreign soil than face the long years ahead of incapacity and non-achievement. He was a failure before he had done anything with his life.

Alec kept glancing at him. 'They can manage at home without us for a few hours. Honor and the Burrows woman arrived just after you left, offering to pitch in on the farm. Believe it or not, Florence Burrows is practical and helpful. She's pitching in with Tilda, and Honor's helping Emilia and Archie unload mangolds.'

'Yes, who'd have believed it?' Ben's tone was pure bitterness and sarcasm. 'The woman who believes she's the lady of Hennaford acting as a skivvy, and me a fallen soldier, although not on a battlefield but in a bloody garden!'

Alec pulled on the rein to direct the nag down St Mary's Street to the back of the hotel, where he would leave the trap, and the cathedral came fully into view. Ben let out an angry snarl. His heart felt as if it was being ripped out of his body. Short years ago, as a schoolboy, he had helped put the protective sandbags in place round the towering building. Now the only way he could protect his country was to wallow on his knees in prayer – and that didn't work!

'Ben—'

'You can't say anything to make me feel better, Alec, so keep your mouth shut! A liability, that's what I'd be. A danger to myself and the men I'd have had serving under me. A liability, even in the ranks. That's it, plain and simple. It's what the Army medic that Mr Preston called in told me.'

The two men climbed down on to the wet pavement. A groom, the only one employed at the hotel now, waited patiently to ask if they wanted the nag stalled. 'I know how you must be feeling, Ben, but we have important work to do for the country as farmers,' Alec said.

'I knew you'd bring up that pathetic excuse!' Ben was in no mood to keep his voice low and passers-by stared at them. 'You've never wanted to fight, admit it! You don't know how I'm feeling because you're a bloody coward, Alec. A whore-shagging, two-faced coward! You don't know the meaning of pride and honour.'

'Is that what you think of me?' Alec waved the astonished groom away, hurt and betrayal plain on his face. 'Get back on the trap. We're going home.'

Ben had nothing left inside himself to care. He took several steps away. 'I'll go home when I'm ready. I'd rather walk back alone anyway.'

'Have it your own way, but you were wildly unfair. I'd have gone with Henry and Tris, but someone had to run the farm and as its owner it was my responsibility, as you yourself were then. Don't you think I'd like to put on a uniform and kill every bastard German for butchering Henry, for putting Tris through all kinds of hell? Well, I can't go out there any more than you can. I can't read or write properly, remember? I'd also be a liability. I couldn't read an order or fill in a report, something as basic as that! How do you think that affects my pride and honour, Ben? You should have mentioned that you couldn't see days ago, something might have been done about it then. You've either cost yourself your dream by keeping it a secret or it was just a terrible accident, but it wasn't my fault!'

Ben was left steeped in despair and resentment as Alec leapt up on the trap and ordered the nag, in furious tones, to walk on. People they knew had witnessed their quarrel, overheard the details of both of their weaknesses. Alec's days of bluffing his way through business transactions in the town and market-place, until Ben or their legal representative read the small print, was over.

The wind was often channelled unkindly down this street and an icy draught made Ben's eye water and smart. 'To hell with you, Alec. At least you've got the farm, at least you're your own man.' Stuffing his hands in his pockets, something he had never done before, for he had always hated slovenliness, he stalked off.

Emilia took Archie Rothwell's midday meal out to him, where he was perched on the rear of the unloaded cart. He had been invited inside, but, as always, had politely refused. He had Snowy, a scraggy white barn moggy, hugged to his chest and was stroking him with his long, lean fingers. Man and cat had the same colour eyes, but while Snowy's were usually fierce and predatory, Archie Rothwell's were clear and watchful, as if he had long ago fortified himself to never reveal much about his inner person. Pip, who had made friends with him on the first night's watch in the hay house, was up on the cart, his muzzle pushed into the crook of his arm. The three had slept each subsequent night together.

'Thank you, Miss Emilia.' His cold had cleared and his speech was back to being rich and precise.

'Animals like you, Archie.'

He nodded, reluctant to speak, as always.

Emilia felt she still owed amends over her treatment of him the first day he had come here. 'How are your feet? You never complain, but we'd hate to think they needed a doctor's attention and you felt you couldn't say so.'

'They're comfortable, thanks to all of you here, and these boots Miss Honor kindly procured for me.'

'You're aware of the worry about Ben's eye?'

'Yes. I hope there won't be great sorrow for him.' His gaze was soft, sympathetic, but drifting away.

Emilia glanced anxiously towards the lane, hoping to see Ben arriving home, then she left Archie to his privacy.

Indoors, she found it strange to have Florence Burrows wait on her, wearing an apron previously worn by the maid-of-all-work whose services she had long been forced to dispense with. She thanked Florence for the mug of tea and plate of bread and cheese that was placed in front of her. The woman always had an expression of disciplined composure on her heavy oblique features. Her silvery hair was tastefully groomed, but her habit of tight-lacing had produced a figure that was aggressively thrust forward. The ballooning effect was completed by a spreading posterior and generous hips.

'Be careful to keep those thick gloves and your hat on, Honor, dear,' Florence said, serving her niece tea in a cup and saucer. 'And don't look into the wind, or you'll end up looking like Emilia.'

'How do I look? Like some shrivelled-up old witch?' Emilia demanded.

Florence studied her as if she was something received on approval from a shop inferior to what she was used to. 'You are attractive in a pink-skinned, healthy kind of way, Emilia. You have a pleasing deportment and a good shape. Your hair needs urgent attention, but it gives you a wild, pre-Raphaelite look that many men would be fascinated by. I am keen for Honor to keep the desired pale looks of a lady, that was all I meant.'

Emilia turned her hands over and decided she was proud of their coarseness. 'I didn't ever expect to receive a compliment from you, Mrs Burrows.'

'I give credit where credit is due, Emilia.' Florence's intention to float down on to Alec's carver chair was spoiled by a swift ungainly rise, for his penknife was on the seat, having slipped out of his pocket. She hid its presence behind the large blue milk jug and carried on as if nothing discomforting had happened. 'Did you know you're talked about as a desirable bride more than any other local girl? It's not surprising that Mr Benjamin Harvey is besotted with you.'

''Tis more than that.' Tilda joined them by taking a seat on the form. 'Young Mr Ben and Miss Em are in love. They're engaged.'

Emilia glared at Florence while waiting for some disparaging remark to be made about foolish marriages. Her mouth opened in shock and she shot a look of wonder at Honor when Florence rejoined with, 'Do accept my congratulations, Emilia. Your place is at the farm.' Then she was suspicious of the woman's sentiments. Was it a ruse to aid her in the ensnarement of Alec as a husband for Honor? It had been plain from Florence's coquettish behaviour and her meaningful phrases to Alec before he left, that she was undertaking her ambition in earnest. How two-faced! To look down on the behaviour of others but to ruthlessly set about trying to marry off her niece so she could live in comfort. It was a good thing Honor wasn't disturbed by it – she had said, while transferring mangolds into the clamp from the cart, that she didn't expect Alec, who obviously had a lot on his mind, to even notice her.

'Thank you, Mrs Burrows,' Emilia said with all the stateliness of preceding Harvey wives. She checked on Lottie, and was satisfied to see the old lady was content in her armchair, winding up a ball of khaki wool. Lottie was making a poor job of it but it would be just about knittable. 'Where's Jonny? He was disappointed there was no letter from his father again, then he got upset because he couldn't go to Truro with Alec. He's not sulking, is he?' Jonathan was unsure of Archie and she hoped he wasn't staying indoors because Alec and Ben were not there.

'He's in the schoolroom.' At Emilia's puzzled frown, Florence explained. 'The playroom. He didn't recognize me at first and took me for a schoolmistress – I suppose I do have that sort of officious air about me – and I asked him if he wanted to play at being in school. I can't bear little boys running about and making all manner of noises, and I could see he is a bright child. Tilda fetched some paper from the den, and I set him some lessons. Jonathan's will to learn is voracious. He's kept me busier at marking his work and setting him more than I've been about my tasks in the house.'

'He's cleverer than even Alec thought,' Emilia smiled. 'It's very good of you, Mrs Burrows.'

Florence was suddenly up and on her feet. 'Off you go now, girls, to the kitchen garden and fetch some vegetables. Tilda and I have much to do in here. And Honor, be very sure you keep away from that tramp.' She stared in an interrogatory manner at Emilia. 'We don't know his history, do we?'

Emilia ignored her probing. She swallowed the last of her cheese on her feet, but held on to the mug Florence tried to wrench from her until she'd drank the last drop. 'Before I go out, Mrs Burrows, I must take Mrs Harvey to the lavatory. Unless you'd like to do it?'

Florence turned an unladylike shade of red.

It was mid-afternoon, Honor and Florence had left, and Emilia and Jonathan were scattering grain for the hens when Alec returned. She grabbed Jonathan's hand and ran towards the trap. 'Where is he? Is it the worst then?'

'I'm afraid so, Emilia.' Alec hauled Jonathan up beside him and put the reins into his hands. 'Take us to the trap house, old chap.' He inspected the boy's hurt ear; it would stay swollen and bruised for days.

'Is Uncle Ben's eye dead?' Jonathan said, twitching the reins too softly for the old mare to obey.

'It's one way of putting it, I suppose, Jonny,' Alec sighed. 'What have you been doing this morning?' He looked down at Emilia. Her thoughts were on Ben and the suffering he must be going through. Going through without her. 'Jonny seems chirpy. Emilia?'

'What? Oh, yes, he is. Where's Ben now?'

'He'll come home when he's ready,' Alec said, his imposing features tightening, a tiny nerve contracting in his neck.

'What happened to Uncle Ben's eye?' Jonathan fixed the sort of penetrating gaze on his uncle that preceded a barrage of inquisitiveness. 'Did it happen in the war? Did he have an accident? Does it hurt like my ear hurts?'

'What a lot of questions.' Alec laughed, but he looked grim.

'Your ear's going to get better, Jonny, but Uncle Ben's eye is not. I don't think it would be a good idea to mention Uncle Ben's poorly eye to him. It might upset him.'

'I see. I've got lots to show you, Uncle Alec. Put me down and I'll fetch it for you.'

'Must be important, I can hardly wait.' Alec sounded impressed as Jonathan ran off indoors.

'Talk about an old head on young shoulders,' Emilia said. 'It's a pity Tristan can't see him now.'

Alec jumped down beside her. 'God above, how I wish he was here now. Were Honor and her aunt of much help?'

Emilia met his concerned grey gaze. 'Actually, they were. Mrs Burrows now sees it as her duty to come over two or three times a week, and, in her words, put her shoulder to the wheel. Tilda didn't seem to mind her ordering her about. She was cold towards Archie, but that's only to be expected with someone like her.' Archie had whispered something under his breath when Florence had sauntered past him on her way home. His expression had stayed bland, but Emilia had the impression he would not tolerate any insults from her.

'She won't accept payment for hers and Honor's help, but we can help them in return by supplying them with produce. I'm glad of anything which eases your life, Emilia. You're my greatest asset, you know that, don't you?'

'Thank you, Alec.' She was pleased by his remarks, then she remembered her worries. 'Just how upset is Ben? Do you think he's angry with me for the way I blurted it out about his eye yesterday? He was awfully quiet afterwards.'

'It's likely, but he's not thinking straight. It's best to let him come to terms with it in his own time. I'm afraid we might be in for a rough ride, Emilia. There couldn't have been a bigger blow to Ben. He's a dreamer, an adventurer, he's always seen himself as a pioneer. He was deeply, almost romantically, in love with the idea of joining the fighting. After Henry's death, it's going to be his greatest loss, and I don't think he'll ever be the same again.'

The day dragged on and Emilia watched from the upstairs

windows or out in the lane for signs of Ben. She walked as far as the church with Jonathan, hoping to meet him on his expected route home. They climbed the tallest hedges and every field gate, scanning the parts of the road where the twisting lanes allowed visibility. On the way back they stopped off at the rectory to tell her mother the grim news about Ben's eye. With every passing moment Emilia grew more worried, admonishing herself for not realizing long before that the incident with Lottie had left him partially blinded. He must have been so scared at the infirmary, so disillusioned, so bereft and lonely.

When she and Jonathan were back outside the farm they heard a sombre whistling – no one displayed cheerfulness nowadays – coming up the hill. 'It's the postman. The second post!' Jonathan dashed away in excitement.

'He might be on his way somewhere else, Jonny,' she shouted after him, not wanting to see his bold little face crestfallen again today.

'There's one from my daddy among this lot!' Jonathan was waving a fistful of letters up in the air in a manner of victory, when he reappeared moments later.

Emilia waited at the farm entrance for the postman, a portly, dim-faced individual, who was inclined to be forgetful, to appear on his bicycle. 'Hello, Mr Crewes. Have you delivered anything at home from Billy?'

'Sorry, m'dear.' Hector Crewes doffed his cap and brought his creaking machine, which his bulk overflowed indiscriminately, to a halt. He rubbed his nose. 'Your Billy's probably got his eye on a French maiden or two. Must get on. Where'm I going next? Oh, yes, the rectory. Cheerio!'

Emilia caught up with Jonathan. He had climbed up on the granite wall of the inner yard, and was in the process of reading one of the letters. 'You mustn't do that, it's naughty, Jonny. It's addressed to your uncles. Give it to me.'

'Shan't. And it's addressed to my mummy. She isn't here, so it's mine.' Jonathan handed over the other letters.

Emilia couldn't think of an argument against his reasoning;

Alec had arranged for Ford House's post to be delivered to the farm. 'Is your daddy all right? Does he say anything about my brother, Billy?'

'It's quite old,' Jonathan said sadly, folding the letter. 'It's dated October twelfth. That's four weeks ago. Mummy had a letter before she left, dated after Daddy wrote this one. This must have got lost somewhere. Do you think my mummy will write to me?'

So melancholy was his tone she looked up from scanning the writing on the other letters; they all appeared to be on business. 'She might, when she gets settled.'

'She wouldn't say where she was going. Do you think she's gone to fight the war with Daddy?'

'No, I shouldn't think so.'

'Emilia . . .'

'Yes, Jonny?'

'I wish they were both here.'

'I know, my love.'

'My mummy's gone, my daddy could be dead and Uncle Ben's eye is hurt forever. Why is everything so bad?'

'It's the war.' She hugged him, needing his warmth as much as he needed her comfort.

'If it's ever over, will things get better, Em?'

It sounded so much like Ben, as a boy, calling her 'Em' that she choked back her tears. 'I hope so, Jonny. We must hope so.'

In the begrudging light of a cold silvery moon, Alec was sitting on Ben's bed, his hand resting on the pillows. He was concentrating on Ben, willing him away from all harm and to come home safe. And repentant. He was hoping Ben would come to feel bad about the way he had unjustly and publicly ostracized him in Truro. It was terrible, what had happened to Ben, but it didn't excuse his insolence, his reproach, his callousness. His vicious change of character. Ben had made him look more than a fool. It was going to be humiliating to face even his genuine business alliances again.

God, he prayed, *except for Tristan and Eugenie, am I fated never to find true acceptance for who and what I am? My parents were ashamed of me. Before Grandma became senile she wasn't sure what to make of me. Henry was too interested in his books to notice me. Is there no one else? If only Emilia was free. She's everything Lucy wasn't, but even she might be horrified if she knew the truth about me.*

A shawl over her nightdress, Emilia crept into Ben's room. Sleep was futile and she needed to be where his things were. He was there on the bed! Her heart leapt in relief, then she saw it was the broader muscled outline of Alec in the semi-darkness. He had his back to her. She made to steal away.

Alec detected the soft lavender fragrance she had bathed in. 'Come in, Emilia,' he said, looking over his shoulder, not feeling so wretchedly lonely now.

She took half a dozen steps on to the mat, uncaring about the wrongfulness of remaining here alone with him. 'I just wanted to . . .'

'I understand. I used to go to Henry's room like this before we received word that he'd been killed, willing him to live. I'd pray that if the worst happened it would be over quickly. At least I had the comfort of knowing he didn't suffer. Ben cried when he read the letters from Henry's commanding officer and his batman. There were letters too from the chaplain and the officers he had made friends with. Kind, informative letters, in which we could piece together Henry's last moments. It didn't need any imagination to realize he must have been terribly disfigured by the blast that killed him and his group of men. They were holding on to their position, enabling others to retreat safely. I can't picture him dead like that, thank God. Thinking of Ben now, all I can see is his expressions of gentleness or his bravado, with two good eyes.'

Alec shivered and Emilia went closer to him.

'But the way he looked at me when we parted – it was as if he despised me. I think perhaps he has done for some time.'

'You're wrong, Alec. Ben holds nothing but the highest regard for you.'

'Who knows what goes on inside another's head? Ben will be looking for someone to blame for his pain and humiliation. It's better that it's me, I suppose.'

'Blame? Why should he blame anyone at all? Losing his sight was an accident.'

'I left the front door unlocked.'

'But that was only a moment of forgetfulness. You might as well say he could blame your gran for wandering out through the door, or me for not checking on her earlier. Surely Ben will understand no one did anything to hurt him deliberately.'

Alec got up. She could make out the way the strong angles of his face were steeped in hurt and sorrow. 'People can think bitter and twisted thoughts when the thing they covet most is wrenched away from them, and then it can affect everything they do.'

She could not make out if he was making a philosophical statement, admitting something personal or giving her a warning, but he was adding to her fears for Ben. 'I'm scared he'll do something reckless, like going off and trying to join up elsewhere.'

'No regiment would consider him. I thank God it's obvious he's blind, at least *he* won't get any accusations of being a coward.'

His last words were harsh and discordant. How he must be suffering for Ben. Such care and concern he lavished always on those dearest to him. 'It must be hard for you. You've already lost so much and still have Tristan to fear for. Alec, if Ben's not back first thing tomorrow, you will go and search for him? Or will you let me do it? You have a cousin living on the Newquay coast, don't you? It's possible Ben could have gone to her.'

'If he's not back by midday tomorrow, I'll ride into town and track him down. I think it's unlikely he'll go to Winifred's. She's a war widow, and in his present mood he'll feel too disgraced to face her. You must stay here, Emilia. I know my young brother. He'll be ashamed to have a woman, even you, come looking for him. He might not easily forgive such an event.'

Alec went to the window and gazed up at the desolate sky. 'They're all out there somewhere. Ben, Tristan, Billy. If we try hard, perhaps in some way we'll be able to reach them. Come here, Emilia, we'll pray for their safe return.'

She joined him, and as she closed her eyes he placed his arm over her shoulders. Instantly she felt his warmth and his strength and soon afterward their union of minds, as they pleaded through time, space and silence for protection of those they loved.

Chapter Ten

Ben was staggering along Malpas Road. He had slept in a hedge on the outskirts of the village of Malpas, not far from Truro's town centre, which he was now heading back to, barely aware of the coming of the tidal Truro River, only yards away from him. He smelled of liquor, due to finding a pub where the landlord paid little vigilance to the stiff licensing laws. And he smelled of urine, having taken no care when fronting a tree on the bank minutes earlier. He tripped and fell, dangerously near the water's edge.

He stared down at the green estuary waters, high on a spring tide. One quick splash and he could put himself out of his misery. But he wasn't a coward. Somehow, he would face life with only one good eye. At all costs he must keep his honour and self-respect, hold fast to the family's good name. He must keep faith with Henry, not let Tristan down.

His mind filled with thoughts of Alec and Emilia: the brother who owned the farm – who would own him for the rest of his life if he didn't break out on his own; the girl he had intended to make his wife in between his officer training. Edwin wouldn't give his consent after this, unless she was pregnant from their assignation in Tristan's house. Emilia, the strong-minded, wise, resourceful, lovely girl he loved. But who, it had occurred to him during his tortured musings since leaving the infirmary, had advised Alec not to call in Dr Holloway to attend his grandmother, and if the doctor had come that day, his sight could have been saved. She had neglected to wash out his eyes until he'd had to beg her, and then, according to Mr Preston, had torn the grit out of his eye so clumsily it had created the lasting damage.

Could Emilia have done it on purpose to keep him at home with her? No. He couldn't believe that – she loved him, she knew how much doing his service had mattered to him. But perhaps . . . A tide of despair and depression dug their claws into him once more.

There was a mysterious noise heading his way. A chugging, brum-brum sort of noise. A Zeppelin? His head fuzzy, he looked up. The sky was empty, only tainted by miserable dark grey clouds. Had the sky ever been blue? All life seemed to had lost its colour since the war began – even he, in his hopes to lead daring raids against the German might, had seen everything in multiple shades of gloom. The chugging stopped. Perhaps it had been inside his head. That would figure with the way it was aching and pounding. Pounding, pounding, pounding; it was how Tris had described the noise of the artillery. What he would give now to be able to speak to his good-hearted brother.

He heard approaching footsteps. 'I say, you there! Have you had a mishap?' It was a man's voice, a young voice, a toff's voice.

'Bugger off!' Ben bawled, adding another expletive with a threat in it. He did not bother to look up to see who had hailed him.

'Come away, Julian. It's only a tramp.' A refined female voice.

'No, Polly, look at his suit. He's one of us. He might be ill.' Ben felt a prod on his shoulder. 'Are you in need of assistance, old chap?'

Ben had a peculiar urge to giggle and he did just that, not caring how offensive it sounded. Finally, he faced his Good Samaritan. The man was of weedy build, with skin as white and as thin as paper. His lips were bluish and dark shadows formed rings under his eyes. A ghoulish sort of face, only there was nothing threatening about it. 'Yes, friend, you can fetch me a bloody good drink.'

'Ben Harvey! Haven't seen you in ages. It's Julian Andrews, don't you remember me?'

Ben's head was spinning and he tried to focus on the other youth's face. 'Andrews? There was a chap in my class called Andrews. He had a heart condition. Good heavens, it is you! Help me up, Andrews.' Ben remembered his soiled state and was flooded with horror and shame. 'Oh, damn it, I'm afraid I'm far from being at my best. Had a drop too much yesterday. I'll understand if you leave me here.'

'Wouldn't hear of it.' Ben detected the awed note in Julian Andrews's voice. His escapades at school had always rendered this effect on his weakling former classmate. 'You must have a good reason to be like this. I'm with my sister, Mrs Polly Hetherton. Come along with us, Harvey. We'll take you to our house at Kenwyn and have you sorted out in a jiffy.'

Galvanized into hope of regaining his composure and restoring some of his honour, Ben got upright under his own strength. Julian Andrews was in dinner dress and he explained that he and his sister were returning from an overnight stay at a residence in Malpas. As Julian introduced him to his sister, who was looking out of the back window of a convertible bespoke motor car, Ben stood at a respectful distance, swearing he'd never allow himself to get in this sort of disgraceful condition again. Mrs Polly Hetherton was a marble-skinned, fair-haired lady of grace, clad in chic black, about a decade older than Julian. She was gazing at him as if faintly amused.

'I can't thank you enough for stopping, Mrs Hetherton.' Ben was blushing in embarrassment and misery, for he was in the company of a distinguished war widow. He had seen Mrs Hetherton's photograph both in the *Western Morning News* and *The Times*, taken after her husband's memorial service in Truro Cathedral. Captain Hugh Hetherton had died of wounds received at Monchy-le-Preux. Ben would never get a posthumous Victoria Cross like the captain, or a similar epitaph. *The county pays tribute to a valiant hero.* 'I'm like this because I learned only yesterday that my eye has been blinded to a degree that denies me my right to fight in the war.'

Polly Hetherton inclined her velvet and feathered head. 'You have something in common with Julian then, Mr Harvey. I fully understand your grief, the knowledge is worse than the debilitation. Would you mind cranking the handle before hopping in next to Vosper?'

The chauffeur, tiny in a buff uniform, appeared as old as the river, squinting inside horn-rimmed spectacles. Ben glanced at Julian. Of course, his weak heart prevented him from this simple task. Julian accepted this with dignity and got in beside his sister. Turning round on the plush upholstery of the front passenger seat, answering his saviours' questions politely, Ben noted how, despite his scrawny build, Julian keep his demeanour upright. He was holding on to his self-esteem. He had been like this throughout every wretched year at school, even though he had been mocked and bullied over his disability, and even though he knew he wasn't expected to live far beyond thirty. Julian Andrews was a truly brave man.

Ben vowed he would do his utmost to emulate the boy whose bullies he himself had taken to task more than once. He must do something immediately. Putting on a confident expression, he spoke of the farm. 'We're terribly understaffed. I think after I've freshened up and eaten the meal you've so kindly offered me, I'll scour the streets for some suitable unemployed men. It's something I've been intending to do for some time, but I rarely get the chance to leave the property.' It was something Alec had done occasionally with no results; he must better that.

'Good for you, Harvey. Polly and I will put our thinking caps on. We might know of someone, eh, old girl?

'Yes, Julian, dear.' Polly Hetherton answered her brother's excited suggestion as they motored up Pydar Street.

'A day of new opportunity,' Ben said, trying to work up a little of Julian's enthusiasm.

A unit of soldiers was marching down the hill. Polly ordered Vosper to slow the car down and she and Julian waved and shouted patriotic encouragements to them. Ben sat up straight and saluted until they were out of sight. Then he crumpled in a heap and wept the most wretched tears of his life.

Chapter Eleven

Emilia's continuing vigil was rewarded with a sight that turned her blood to ice, even though the boy approaching the house might be the bearer of good news. She met him halfway down the gravel path.

The spotty-faced, gawky youth pulled off his cap. 'I've brought a letter for a Mr Alec Harvey.'

Emilia took the white envelope from him and glanced at the elegant script that spelled out Alec's name. 'Who's it from?'

'A lady, Mrs Bawden. I deliver groceries to her in Truro, she asked me to bring it out here.'

Her heart quickened in hope. Ben had mentioned a Mrs Bawden before as 'a very close friend of Alec's'. She might be sending news about Ben. 'Just a minute.' Emilia raced into Alec's den and snatched up a coin from a pile on the desk; Alec had a habit of leaving loose change on its corner. All of yesterday's correspondence was there too, unopened. She gave the threepenny piece to the delivery boy and she was soon racing to Long Meadow, where Alec was clearing ditches.

He saw her haring towards him. She must be bringing news about Ben, but for a moment, he imagined she was hurrying to be with him. She looked so lovely and vital, with that wonderful touch of primitiveness that was hers. He wanted to hold out his arms and have her run into them.

He rushed to meet her. She thrust the letter into his hand. 'This has just come, from a Mrs Bawden. It could be about Ben. Read it!'

Alec shied away from the letter. He had two reasons not to want to open the envelope in front of Emilia. The contents might be intimate, and he'd hate for her to discover his weakness. 'It might not be about Ben.'

'But you have to read it to find out.' His reaction was inexplicable and frustrating. Didn't he care about Ben in the way he confessed he did? 'Open it, Alec, please.'

Alec glanced at his hands. It was not unlikely Ben had gone to Eugenie for shelter and this was to inform him he was there. 'I've got muck all over them. You open it.'

Emilia tore the envelope open and pulled out the sheet of white paper inside. There was half a page of scrupulously fine writing. She held it up to his eyes. 'Does it say anything about Ben?'

'I-it's . . . I . . .'

'What's the matter? Is it bad news? Has something happened to him?' The police would have come to the house if something tragic had happened to Ben, but was he in some kind of trouble? Why had Alec turned scarlet? She had never seen him looking so distraught. She felt near to hysteria. 'What is it, Alec? For goodness sake, tell me!'

'I . . . don't know. You read it, Emilia.' He drove the letter back at her.

'What?'

'Just read it!' He turned away with an angry tortured sigh. 'I can't.'

She didn't wait for further explanation. 'It's an address in Falmouth Road. It says, "My dear Alec, I do hope you have changed your mind by now. Please come and see me again soon. With fondest regards, Eugenie."'

Emilia's disappointment that there was no news about Ben gave her no time to wonder about the brief contents. Alec kept his back to her. She walked round him. 'I'm sorry. I've come on a false errand but I had to know.'

His fierce, dark expression, while staring into nothing, took her unawares. He seemed to be harbouring all kinds of fury. She reached out and touched him. 'Alec, are you all right?'

He did not answer, just looked at her, keeping that same dreadful stare.

'You are going to look for Ben after lunch? Alec, why don't you answer me? What's wrong?'

'Nothing.' He snatched the letter out of her hand, making her leap away from him. 'Go back, Emilia.'

'I don't understand. I've upset you in some way. I was worried about Ben. Well, if that's how you feel!'

She stalked off, but he caught hold of her. He wasn't hurting her arm but it was a tight, relentless grip. She put her hand over his to prise his fingers off her. Their eyes clashed. She had no idea why he was behaving in such a peculiar way, but she'd smack his face if necessary to get away from him. The man she loved, his vulnerable younger brother, was wandering about, the Lord only knew where, feeling the worst wretchedness of his life, and Alec was behaving as if he was incensed about the whole matter.

He tossed the letter away as if it was something deadly, and the hurt and despair in his action made her understand the reason. 'Oh, Alec, you can't read, can you?'

He let her go and turned his hands into rigid fists. 'I'm not stupid! It's just that I can't see the words right or write them down to make much sense.'

She had never seen anyone so close to tears and so frantic to hold them back, so filled with emotional agony. 'You're the last man I'd call stupid, Alec. You're greatly respected in all circles. You're a wonderful uncle to Jonny. You're good and kind and committed to those you care about. I'm sorry, I didn't mean to humiliate you.'

His turbulence eased, he unlocked the tension throughout his body. 'Lucy enjoyed taunting me about it. My father beat me over it, he made my life hell. My teachers never attempted to work out why I couldn't apply myself to my lessons, they refused to listen when I tried to explain. It's hard to shake off something like that.' He gave another long discouraged sigh and raked a hand through his hair. 'Forgive me, Emilia. I've no right to be thinking about myself. I wish the letter had been good news about Ben. If anything was to happen to him . . . Tris probably won't come back, and I'd only have Jonny left – and you. I mean, I can always count on you, Emilia?'

She wanted to reach out and comfort him. He had so many responsibilities and, it seemed, few friends to confide in. 'Of course you can, Alec. I swear.'

He looked down at the crumpled letter. 'I can trust you never to reveal my problem?' He could do nothing about those who already knew his shame but he was desperate it would never be known in Hennaford.

'On my life. You can always talk to me, Alec, if you want to, about anything at all.'

'Thank you. I'd be glad to do that, Emilia.'

She waited a moment, not wanting him to feel she could dismiss him quickly from her thoughts. 'Ben will come home, won't he?'

With the backs of his fingers Alec smoothed back the hair loosened from her plait in her run. His hand came to rest close to her neck. 'Of course he will. He hasn't lost everything. His life is at the farm. Where you are, Emilia. I envy him that.'

'Uncle Alec! Everyone! Come and look!' Jonathan came tearing into the kitchen, creating havoc as the Jack Russells, led by Pip, piled in after him, barking madly. Alec paused in putting on his riding coat for the search in Truro. Emilia was about to lead Lottie into the sitting room but left her in her armchair.

Hope made her blurt out. 'Jonny, is it Ben?'

'He's back, in a grand motor car left parked in the lane, with a big boy and a beautiful lady,' Jonathan said, grinning importantly at gaining the grown-ups' attention, including Tilda's. 'And there's other people with them too.'

'My word,' Lottie chuckled. 'I was only saying the other day . . . a little bit of silence . . . it wouldn't hurt.'

'Will you watch Mrs Harvey for me, please?' Emilia asked Tilda. She was out of the back door before Alec got his wits to move.

She flew up to a pair of roughly dressed men, obviously related by their swarthy complexions and stocky stamp. Shuffling their feet by the pump, they greeted her civilly. There was no sign of Ben. She was desperate to see him. Then reasoning he would have taken the 'big boy' and 'beautiful lady' to the front door, she backtracked and tore round the side of the house.

He was there. Immaculately turned out, his hair newly barbered, his shoulders proud, chin up. She caught her breath at his confident, handsome, smiling face. He stepped away from the boy and the lady with him, holding his arms out to her.

'Ben! Oh, Ben, thank God you're back safe.' She cared nothing for the refined strangers in brogues and veiled hat, or if anyone from the kitchen had followed her and was watching. She ran straight into Ben's arms. He swept her off her feet and their lips were meeting before she was on terra firma again. 'I've been so worried about you, darling. Are you terribly upset? I've been so afraid for you. I'm so sorry about your eye. But please don't ever go off and leave me again.'

Ben squeezed her until she had no breath left. 'You can explain what you mean by that later,' he said. Emilia was puzzled by his firmly spoken words but she was too joyful to give it any thought. He kept a possessive hold on her hand while Alec and Jonathan approached them. He made the introductions between his family and friends, describing Emilia as his fiancée.

Alec was already acquainted with the lady. 'It's good to see you again after all this time, Polly. And it was good of you and your brother to bring Ben home.'

'It was kind of you to pass on your sympathy, via Eugenie, after Hugh's death, Alec,' said Polly Hetherton, fluttering a gloved hand. 'You have a fine house. It was an unexpected sight after wringing ourselves through these quaint little country paths.'

Emilia was trying to tame her wayward hair. She felt shabby in the brother and sister's presence, although her only care was not to let Ben down. 'Charmed, Miss Rowse,' Julian said with quiet chivalry. 'You're even lovelier than Ben's description of you.'

'I've brought some workers for the farm, Alec,' Ben said, a chary gaze on his brother. Alec's rigidity meant he had not forgotten his disrespect of yesterday. 'Brothers, Cyril and Albie Trewin. I thought—'

'So I saw.' Alec broke Ben off in cool tones. 'I've already been approached by those individuals and refused them work. They're vagrants. Untrustworthy.'

'They've told me about that and your opinions of them,' Ben replied, narrowing his eyes. 'But in view of what I'm about to say I'm sure you'll reconsider. Julian has contacts with the police, and they've given me a good character of both men. The reasons for their homelessness are as equally honest as those for the other man you've allowed to lodge here. I'm confident the Trewins are good workers. I thought they could live in Wayside Cot. It needs attention, but they won't mind bedding down with Rothwell for a couple of nights.'

Emilia looked at Alec for his reaction. His expression was unreadable. He said, with the charm of a host, 'We'll talk about it later. Perhaps Mrs Hetherton and Mr Andrews would care to step inside for tea or sherry.'

'I've already invited them in,' Ben said, as if he hadn't a care in the world. He spied Tilda peeping round the corner. 'Tilda, would you bring out a mug of tea to the men, then place some extra towels in the washhouse so they can clean up please?'

Emilia was growing uneasy over the chilly atmosphere between Ben and Alec. She was delighted about Ben's positive undertaking, but she understood Alec's resentment over the manner in which he was giving orders.

She saw someone coming around from the yard. 'Here's Dad.' She thought it best to unhook her hand from Ben's.

Her smile was wiped off her face.

She moved away from the gathering. Her father was walking towards her as if on drunken feet, and clinging to him was her mother, dressed in black and weeping. Honor was bringing up the rear in slow reverential steps.

'No! No!'

In that moment the world closed in and lost all its meaning for Emilia. She shook her head. She didn't want to witness the macabre march of her parents and her best friend. Her knees buckled and she fell to the ground, her hands up to her face. 'Billy! Oh, dear God, not Billy!'

Alec intimated to Tilda that she should take Jonathan away. He waited for Ben, who had turned ashen and frozen, to go to Emilia. But Ben suddenly veered away and was hurrying down the garden path. Alec called after him but he didn't stop. He could only express his apologies for his brother's behaviour to Julian Andrews and Polly Hetherton with an expression of hopelessness.

'We'll go after Ben,' Julian said in a hushed tone. 'And then we will take our leave.'

'We can see . . . our condolences.' Polly motioned towards the grieving family, then she took Julian's arm and they walked away.

'Come along, Emilia.' Alec lowered himself down to her. 'You have to be strong, my love, for your mother's sake. Get up now, I'll help you. I'm so sorry about Billy. Here's your parents and Honor. I'll leave you with them.'

'No, stay.' She felt out of control and could not stand up on her own. She clung to his body, shaking, weeping, moaning Billy's name.

Edwin took her from Alec, and holding Dolly too, the three of them gave way to the chasm of their grief.

Alec and Honor stood aside. She wiped her eyes with a hanky. 'I happened to be at the cottage when the telegram arrived. It said that Billy was killed in action. By the date, it happened eight days ago.'

'There should be a letter on the way about it from Tristan,' Alec whispered. The Rowses would find out the details then about Billy's death. An arctic chill invaded Alec's heart. Was Tristan still alive? As soon as he could get away he'd go to

Ford House to see if a telegram had been delivered there.

Emilia's face was resting on Edwin's shoulder. 'Where's Ben?' she appealed to Alec through her sobs.

Alec was at a loss to explain. 'He's escorting his friends to their car.'

'Are you saying he couldn't be bothered to stay here with me?' Her tears grew more desolate. How could Ben desert her when she needed him most?

'That boy hasn't got as much backbone as he'd like everyone to believe,' Edwin snarled, his eyes wet, stroking the heads of his womenfolk. 'Sorry, boss, but I call that behaviour damned shallow and callous.'

'Ben's going through a crisis of his own,' Honor said, feeling the need to point this out. Ben was her childhood hero. She could never bring herself to believe he'd ever merit Edwin's description.

'Doesn't compare. The loss of some of your eyesight for a life.' Edwin swallowed his grief. 'Can I take them inside, Alec?'

'Of course. Give me a moment and I'll open the front door. Use the sitting room, and please stay, the three of you, for as long as you need to.'

Chapter Twelve

More greyness. Strange, Tristan thought, heaven should be ablaze with colour, sparkling with countless gems and lit by the Shining Presence. A sharp pain piercing his shoulder told him he wasn't dead. Not yet.

'Decided to join us at last, Lieutenant Harvey? Sorry about that, just removed a sliver of metal working itself out of you there.'

'What? Who are you?' Tristan was aware of the dry croak his voice made, and instead of the sulphurous putrid stench, other sour-sickly odours. Moans of delirium and wretched groans of pain reached his befuddled brain. Something moist and tepid was wiped across his brow. Then something blissfully warm was pushed between his lips, wetting his raw throat. His sight cleared slowly and he found himself looking into the sallow, rubbery face of a ward orderly. He was thickset and heavy-footed but thankfully light-handed. 'God forgive me, but you're ugly.'

'Charming,' the orderly replied, taking no offence and finishing off with wash bowl and shaving gear. 'You're in 24 General, sir. You were on the dangerously ill list for days but started coming round in the small hours this morning. Regular pincushion, you were. Too dangerous to move you, and we like to move casualties on quick with a push like this going on. The surgeon got all the lead balls out, but you'll have shrapnel popping out of you in strange places for weeks. The name's Maynard Lucas. You may remember me, we spoke when your second-lieutenant, God rest him, was stretchered in here a month ago. We've got a rush on, so you won't get much rest today. The doctor'll likely say you're fit to travel now, so you'll be on your way home this evening. Must go, 'fraid I've got to get on. Good luck, sir.'

'Wait! How did I get here? And please, tell me the score. I mean, my ankle looked crocked. Have I still got a foot? And I need to know who else survived in my section.'

With an air of good-humoured reluctance Maynard Lucas came back. 'Everything's intact, sir. Your ankle's a nasty wound – the surgeon was in two minds. Could end up with a limp. As for your men, 'fraid I couldn't say about that. You was fetched in by a returning recce party, so we're told, couldn't say by who exactly.'

Tristan glanced down the bed and saw the shape of his foot under the blanket. 'Thank God, but the cost, the cost.' He wept silently for Billy Rowse and the other thousands dead.

'Look, I'm not bad enough for a blighty,' Tristan protested to the sister, who got busy with the usual observations: pulse, temperature and examination for tell-tale signs of gas gangrene on his numerous dressings. 'And I've taken up a bed for far too long. I can rest in my billet until I'm fit enough to resume active service.'

'The doctor thinks otherwise,' the Sister said, hardly giving him eye contact. Tristan fancied she had long ago developed a necessary self-protective callousness, but every now and then she offered a queer little smile. She was small and nondescript, but exuded power and efficiency, instilling a much longed-for confidence to the patients temporarily in her care. 'You'll be seeing the inside of another hospital ward for some time yet.'

'I suppose my wife has been informed of my injuries?'

'A telegram has been sent to England. We've managed to get hold of your batman. He's brought you another uniform and left a note. Good luck.'

Good luck? Why did people keep wishing the impossible? There had been no good luck for his section. His batman had listed the survivors; barely into double figures.

The twenty-five other officers in the ward were all strangers to him, and after an insipid meal which made him feel sick after every mouthful, he talked Maynard Lucas into wheeling him to the enlisted mens' ward. There was no one he knew among the crowded rows of suffering Tommies.

He sat with a private, whose boyish face reminded him of Ben, while he died of a haemorrhage. As more casualties were crammed into the field hospital, he accompanied another private, paralysed from the waist down, to the Red Cross ambulance.

Private James Worth, of a Lancashire battalion, stared at him, during spells of consciousness, throughout the bumpy journey. Tristan talked to him and smiled at him. He held his hand. And shortly after they had been unloaded at the railway station, with no padre free for the task, he prayed the last words over young James Worth as he gasped his final frantic breath from pneumonia. Briefly, he had been the boy's closest friend and mentor and link with the world of the living. Tristan had prayed James would live. Now he would write to his parents and tell them how well their nineteen-year-old son had died.

Before covering the silent body he touched it. To stop himself from spinning out of control in the constant discordance of noise and crazed activity. Tristan held on to the silence of tragic meaningless, until he was wrenched away.

How many friends had he made and lost in these last three years? Friends of a few weeks, six months at the most. Eight, ten, twelve among the officers. It wasn't wise to make friends. The grief was almost too much when they died. Yet he was a man who desired companionship, someone with whom to share his hopes and fears. God willing, if the ship he was to board wasn't sunk by a U-boat or German aeroplane, he would be back on British soil before daybreak, and after the medics were finished with him, he would be with his son again. Perhaps Ursula could be persuaded to bring Jonathan to visit him. But perhaps somewhere in all the confusion on this foreign soil, a letter was waiting for him bearing the news he was dreading, that she had left him and taken their son with her. He had survived for Jonathan; it would be unbearable to learn he had lost him.

Shattered, nauseous, tormented by his aches and agonies, he made to close his eyes and shut off all thoughts until the rail journey was over. But a soldier with a boy's face – they all seemed to have boy's faces – desperate and pain-ridden, was watching him. How the lower ranks watched the officers, to gain confidence, to settle their fears. It drove some officers mad.

Tristan conjured up a calm smile. 'You want to speak to me, private?'

Chapter Thirteen

Honor and her aunt were eating a meal of ham and bread and butter, the food accepted by Florence, with red-faced grace, from Ford Farm. There was no coal and only enough sticks to keep one unsatisfactory fire alight, so the women were in their kitchen, wearing extra cardigans and shawls to keep warm. With no funds to pay a gardener, Florence, with some relief, was allowing a villager to keep the ground at the back and front planted in vegetables, for rent in kind, so they also had vegetable soup.

The room was dank and fusty, the walls damp with condensation. Most of each week it was inhabited by a wooden clothes horse drying laundry, and Florence held to an unbreakable belief that opening even a crack of window between autumn and spring would lead to dangerous chest infections. Honor was increasingly finding her home a miserable place to live in and she longed for a more companionable atmosphere, like she found at Ford Farm – had found there before the news of Billy's Rowse's death and the subsequent events.

Bracken House, so named by Florence when she had taken up residence fifteen years ago, was the largest in Hennaford after Ford House, a square, four-bedroomed dwelling, in sore need of fresh paint and repairs to the roof and walls and front gate. Not far from Tremore Farm, the house had once housed the stewards of the long-dismantled Tremore estate, much of which had been acquired by Silas Harvey, Alec's grandfather.

Having no appetite, Honor was trailing her spoon through the watery soup – all hers and her aunt's food had to be eked out.

'You're not being fair, Aunt,' she said with forced calm, in answer to the near-hysterical lecture she was receiving. 'I can't see what I can do to make Alec Harvey interested in me. He's got too many other things on his mind and I'm no sort of vamp.'

'You're not trying hard enough to get him to notice you.' Florence banged her hand down on the table. Her heated breath was enough to threaten the air around her to burst into flame. 'When we're at Ford Farm you spend all your time with that wretched girl.'

'Emilia's in mourning, Aunt. She needs my support.' And Emilia was less wretched company despite her terrible grief.

'That girl doesn't need anyone, she's as strong-willed as General Haig, impossible to shift from her own ideas. She's mourning in an undignified manner, of course! Either rushing about like a frenzied hare or silent to the point of rudeness. She's successfully harnessed Ben Harvey but now she's treating him to a cold shoulder. What on earth is he supposed to have done? No, don't bother to tell me I wouldn't understand, because that certainly would be the case. And another thing about her, it would be more fitting if she put some space between herself and that tramp.'

'Archie Rothwell seems a harmless character.' Honor truly believed this. Emilia had told her, in confidence, about the casual labourer's tragic naval past. He was civil and respectful, and, she took it for granted, intelligent and from a good background. She felt he would become less distant in time. He had won Jonathan over by his empathy with the animals, and occasionally indulged in short serious chats with the boy on thought-provoking topics.

Florence thumped her fist down this time, making the last of her fine crockery rattle. She was shaking, her breath coming in uncontrolled shreds. 'Never mind them! Do you want to see us turned out on the streets, girl? Even if I sold this house the proceeds wouldn't be enough to settle our debts. Look around you: all our best pieces of furniture, all our valuables are gone. Our only hope is for you to marry a rich man. The Harveys have always been well placed and Alec Harvey must have profited from his wife's death. Lucy Pollard had a splendid trust fund settled on her, apparently.'

Honor knew her aunt was exasperated over her lack of cooperation and she was afraid her aunt would have an attack of some kind, but she couldn't offer the comfort she was seeking. 'I'm sorry, Aunt, but your scheme isn't going to work and you're going to have to accept it. Alec Harvey can't be flattered or fooled into a second marriage. Lucy Pollard wasn't a suitable wife for him and neither would I be. In fact, if he likes anyone, it's Emilia.'

'Oh, and don't I know it!' Florence scraped out her chair and stamped up and down on her inhospitable time-dulled linoleum. 'His admiration for her earthy and beguiling ways is evident in his every manner. He's gentleman enough to stand aside at the moment while she's still attached to his brother, but I believe if the rift grows between Ben and that girl, he won't dally in putting a claim on her. Then our cause will be completely lost! You must work hard to get those two reunited. You're close to both of them, they'd listen to you.'

'Then what?' Honor fixed her sight on the raving woman. She wanted to rush to her and soothe her but knew her aunt was more likely to lash out in this current mood than to accept consoling. 'Please Aunt, you really should calm down. You'll make yourself ill.'

Florence swallowed hard and noisily but regained only a little control. She was panic-stricken, imagining the degradation of eviction, the humiliation. The workhouse. 'Well, we mustn't give up, we just mustn't. Alec seems to like women who aren't afraid of work, you've already showed him you are willing in that direction. I can think of another way for you to grow closer to him, to show him you have some pleasing feminine attributes. We need to move quickly, Alec's planning to take his nephew up to London soon to see the boy's father in hospital. You must get yourself invited to stay overnight at the farm, Honor. We must do something to make you look older, and think of how you can be witty and entertaining.'

'Aunt Florence, I don't want to do this. I won't.' Honor had never disobeyed or stood up to the woman who had taken her in as an orphaned infant, but now her mind was set. 'Don't you see, it's mercenary. It's dishonourable. It's horrible. And I'll certainly have no part in playing a whore for you. You should have let me take a job ages ago.'

'Why, you ungrateful—' Florence stood stock-still and started to weep – the distraught weeping of someone suddenly faced with a multitude of unpalatable truths about herself. 'Oh, forgive me. I had no right to ask you to do such a thing. I've been doing a lot of things wrong these last few years. But if I had allowed you to work, Honor, what could you have done? You'd never have earned enough to solve our troubles. Your uncle always took care of money matters and since his death we've been living off his savings. I'm so frightened, Honor. I don't know what to do.'

Honor couldn't bear to watch her aunt wilt and fold. She went to her and as she gave comfort, she became the stronger one. 'You've brought me up to believe we're better than most of the others in the village, but we're not, are we? Even Archie Rothwell is better than us because he seeks nothing unless he's earned it honestly. Perhaps life will take an easier turn now we've faced facts. Try not to give way to despair, Aunt. Alec Harvey's a good man, and if necessary I'll throw the pair of us on his mercy. Emilia wouldn't stand by and see us suffer and, as we've agreed, she does have a lot of influence with him.'

Chapter Fourteen

Emilia was in Wayside Cot, putting linen on the beds for the two men Ben had hired. It had taken a fortnight to complete the renovations, the rebuilding of the single chimney, the making of a workable kitchen and the creation of new doors, all undertaken by the farmhands themselves.

In between her usual duties Emilia had worked here, scrubbing, disinfecting and fashioning comforts. It was where she could be alone, away from the noise and bustle and the sympathetic expressions and abnormally soft speech people used at times of a bereavement. It was somewhere away from Ben.

After emerging from the initial shock of Billy's death, she had felt sorry for Cyril Trewin and his younger, retarded brother, Albie, in the same way as she had Archie Rothwell. Cyril, unfit for service after surviving the sinking of a merchant ship in the English Channel, was inclined to be suspicious and defensive, as if always expecting to be reprimanded or cast out. Not surprising, after coming home to find Albie being ill-treated by his employer, a greengrocer in Calenick Street, and his protest leading to them being evicted from Albie's room above the business. One of the few people whom Cyril trusted was Ben, who monitored his and Albie's progress at the farm with encouragement, but it galled Emilia how Ben treated the Trewins as if he was their commanding officer.

When Alec had witnessed the brothers' worth as labourers, he had made amends for his previous contempt by furnishing the cottage with good items from his attics, and also adding to the clothes Florence Burrows had brought them from Red

Cross donations. All this kept Emilia's mind off her double grief, of losing both Billy and her respect for Ben.

In Albie's midget-sized bedroom, she laid out his meagre possessions, a creased photograph of his stick-thin mother, a grubby comb and a tattered comic book. On a nail protruding from a beam of the low, sloping ceiling, she put up a colourful picture of the farm, which Jonathan had drawn for him. She would have added something of Billy's, but she couldn't bear to part with any of his things.

Tonight, Albie would sleep here and Cyril in the next room, and Archie would return to the hay house. He had adamantly refused to share it with them, saying he would move on if he couldn't be alone. Not wanting to lose him, Alec had offered him the washhouse floor, and he had risen each morning with his things stowed away before anyone wanted use of it. Emilia had waited anxiously for antagonism to spring up between the workers, but Cyril Trewin's comment on Archie's desire for isolation had been: 'War does strange things to a bloke. If he wants to be alone, who am I to criticize?' Relations between Ben and Alec had remained frosty, but in her grief, Emilia had given it little care.

The stairs descended into the narrow living room and she pattered down to build up the fire she'd lit on her arrival. Ben was there, his head touching the rough black beams. Her body froze and her heart exploded with a multiplicity of emotions.

Ben surveyed the straight set of her mouth, her fiery eyes and taut posture. 'I've had enough of you avoiding me, so I've come here to talk, to find out if we still have a future together. Where Alec can't interfere, or put words into your mouth, and assume you need protecting from me.'

'I've needed time to myself, Ben.' She saw his hurt, some of it justified, but she couldn't get it out of her mind how he had deserted her. She headed towards the fire to build it up, but he blocked the way.

'Two whole weeks?'

'Yes.'

'And?'

'Please, Ben, I'm not in the mood for this.' She dropped her eyes to the split logs she intended to pile on the dying blaze.

'Too bad, because neither of us are leaving until we've talked openly and sensibly.'

She took in his dark, brooding stare. 'All right, go ahead.'

'We might as well sit.' He jerked his head at his brother's contribution of seats – a rocker bearing a flat cushion and two padded chairs.

'No. I don't want to. I have to keep busy.' She was frowning, edging towards the kitchen, endeavouring to fill her thoughts with mundane things. If she opened her heart to Ben she would have to face again that Billy was dead and lying somewhere in a foreign land, perhaps not decently buried. And she might say something terrible to Ben, for there were times she wanted to lash out at him over his thoughtlessness. She had never felt vengeful or out of control of her feelings before and it frightened her.

He placed himself in her path, using his hands to emphasize his next words. 'Have you no kind word for me any more, Em? How long are you going to act like this?'

'Ben, I . . .' She gave a tremendous sigh, tears stinging her eyes. 'I can't think past that day, when my parents arrived . . . I'm sorry.'

'Let me have my say then. Will you listen?'

She looked into his eyes, the one dark and beautiful, the other marred with a permanent milky spot, both full of sorrow. She couldn't deny him. Nodding grimly, she sank down on the nearest of the padded chairs, leaning forward with her arms pressed against her body.

Ben moved the chair's twin to where he could face her, close up. 'You think me selfish and heartless for staying out all night when it was confirmed I was blinded, and then for running out on you when Edwin came with the news about Billy, don't you? I accept that I deserve your contempt, and that all I've lost means little in comparison to Billy being dead. Oh, God, Em, how can I make you understand? You're usually so sensitive to what's on my mind. When I saw Edwin and Dolly hobbling towards you, with the spirit wiped out of them, and I saw your reaction, I felt all of your grief. I swear I did. But I couldn't stand the shame of being only half a man while Billy had fought and died for his country, for my freedom.

'I came back to you almost at once, but Alec insisted I allow you and your parents time to be alone. Hasn't he explained this to you? Let me make it up to you, Em. I'm trying to be a man. You think I should be more like Alec, don't you? Alec, who stays with everyone – even Lucy at the end, even though she cursed him to her last breath.'

Emilia watched in a strange fascination, as if from a distance, as huge, sorrowful, silent tears glistened down his face and dripped off his chin. Everything seemed unreal or larger than usual or to be working in slow motion. She knew this was the numbness of bereavement and that she was clinging to it, afraid to feel its next instalments, of anger or an anguish she couldn't bear. 'I've wanted to speak to you, Ben, but you and I, us . . . it hasn't seemed important.' She knew her words were hurting him, this man she loved, but, God forgive her, she was afraid to care, about him or anyone or anything else until she was ready to.

Ben closed his eyes for a moment, hoping to see her awful expression had tempered when he looked at her again. He was disappointed. 'That was a horrible thing to say, Em. Look, I'm trying to understand you. I thought you might have talked to me after Tristan's letter about Billy's death. I acknowledge that I've acted weaker than I'd ever thought possible, but I swear to you, if I'd been with Billy and I'd seen the bullet coming that had killed him I would have sacrificed my life for his. I've said this to Edwin – I think he's forgiven me.' He waited expectantly for her to respond, willing her to become his dear, reliable Em again.

'Dad's always said that a man who can cry real tears and admit he's afraid or weak shows true strength and courage.' Emilia was aware of the pain of keeping her arms clenched so tightly. She gazed at them and untwisted them, but it was as if they were not hers.

'And?' Ben grasped her hands before she could entwine them again. He couldn't bear her remoteness or the dreadful dignity she was maintaining – she had cried every day in the last fortnight but always in private.

'I still love you, Ben, if that's what you're hoping to hear.' She raised her chin and it brought her face a breath away from his.

'Of course it is,' he said impatiently. 'We've made love. It's important to me that you did it with me out of love. So, do you forgive me? Admire me again? Think me shallow? All kinds of a bastard? What? For heaven's sake, Em, I have to know. Please don't be cruel. It's been a bloody terrible time for me too.'

Emilia looked at him for a long time. 'Tell me this, Ben. Were you put out that day because Billy's dying stole your limelight?'

He dropped her hands, gulping as if her question had been a physical blow. 'What? How can you think such a thing?'

'Because I know you. You've got a hard question for me too, haven't you?'

'Very well, if you don't want to make this easy, there's something I need to know. Did you want my eye to be blinded?'

She moved until her back was against the chair. 'That's a childish idea. What put that into your head?'

'Childish?' He sited a denigrating edge in his voice. 'Not what, Em, *who*! Mr Preston, the consultant. He said the appropriate attention would have saved my sight.'

'You think I did something to deliberately hurt you? I suppose I can see how you might think like that; it's the usual reaction to blame someone else when something devastating's happened. The answer is no, Ben. I'd never do anything to hurt you and not once did it occur to me to do something that would stop you joining the war. I know how much a military career meant to you. Do you believe me?'

'Oh yes, I believe you.' Flinging aside the chair, he stormed towards the front door. 'Your honesty was only one of the things I used to admire about you, but I can't accept its brutality right now. So you think me superficial and begrudging? Well, here's my honesty for you. I didn't receive the news of Billy's death as it being his moment of glory – that happened the instant he signed up to fight. I was filled with an aching sorrow at losing one of my closest friends, and an acute loss that I'd never see him again. Your estimation of me, Emilia, couldn't have hurt me more than if you'd thrown me a white feather.'

He was lifting the wobbly iron latch and she shot to her feet. 'Ben, don't go. I shouldn't have said that about you and Billy. I've never lost anyone as close before and I've been feeling hurt and I wanted to hurt you back. And about you being childish. I'm sorry, it was me who's been childish.'

He came back to her. 'Swear to me that the thought didn't pass through your mind even for a second.'

The blood drained from her face. She grabbed his arms. 'I can't, but I haven't been thinking straight.'

He put his hands on her shoulders and she felt his grip tighten. 'Strange, isn't it? We never hurt each other once as children but suddenly we're childish and being hurtful.'

'We're going through bad times, Ben. The worst in our lives.'

'And it isn't going to get any easier for me because my sight will never come back. Billy's dead but his memory is always going to be revered, and one day in the future your memories of him will lose their terrible sadness. I'm supposed to be the man you loved, yet not once in two weeks have you allowed me to offer you a grain of comfort. But you've let Alec ply you with tender words and understanding. It was his arm you took at Billy's memorial service – you walked down the aisle in the church in front of the whole village, shunning me. You understood him quickly enough when he admitted he was wrong about the Trewins, the men he'd chosen to leave rotting on the bloody damned streets!'

Emilia knew that if she wasn't feeling so dead inside she would acknowledge that his rising anger was justified, but she merely stared at him and didn't interrupt.

'You've refused a dinner invitation of Julian's because you said you didn't feel like socializing, yet you've agreed to consider an offer from Alec to take you, Grandma and Jonathan to visit our cousin Winifred, because he says the sea air will do you good! You've quickly got fed up with the boy Harvey, but you like and respect the man Harvey, don't you, Emilia? Well, you just be careful of what kind of good my brother's planning for you. He's had a mistress in Truro for years, a woman called Bawden. Why do you think the last maid left the farm so suddenly? It was because Alec couldn't keep his hands off her. Lucy found out and threatened to write to the girl's parents. You think Alec's the sun and the moon, don't you? But he can't even read. He's just as useless and human as the rest of us.'

'I know Alec can't read or write properly,' Emilia said coldly. 'He's told me.'

'He's told you his great secret? Why? Just how close are you to him? Is he bedding you already? Is that why you don't want me any more? Is it, is it?' Ben pushed her back against the banisters of the stairs.

'Alec's never tried to get me into bed, and if it's true what you've said about him, I don't care. I'm not in the least bit interested in him! I only care about Billy. You're selfish and double-faced, Ben Harvey. You can't say you love me if all that you want is to make me see things your way. Why do you feel the need to belittle your own brother, who cares for you so deeply? You're right about one thing, Ben. You are a boy. A vindictive little boy. Even Jonny wouldn't behave like this.'

He let her go. Stood back and studied her as if she was something nauseating. Emilia put her hands to the painful places where he had squeezed her. She said nothing. Only returned his thunderous stare.

'You're the heartless one, Emilia Rowse. From now on, damn well keep out away from me.'

It was getting dark when she realized she had stayed too long in Wayside Cot. Her quarrel with Ben and all the terrible things they had said seemed to have happened in a faraway dream. She was chilled to the marrow, the fire was almost out and she set to work to rebuild the blaze, not wanting the Trewins to come home on their first night to a cold house. When at last the feeble flames had been coaxed to life she pulled on her coat.

Out in the lane, as if finally emerging from some soporific state, she became fully aware the daylight had gone. She was overwhelmed with stark, cold fear. 'Dear God, what have I done?'

She ran over the muddy ground and up the hill at a furious rate. She had to see Ben alone. It was imperative to make him understand how sorry she was for the way she had treated him. She had foolishly and unfeelingly allowed their love to become degraded and dishonoured. She had accepted his brother's comfort and rejected his. She had ignored his hurt and suffering, and allowed him to leave her in anger and distress. But Ben would never lose his kind and loving ways. Surely he would forgive her?

Chapter Fifteen

From out in the lane Emilia could hear Lottie shrieking. She hurtled into the sitting room to find Lottie up on her feet, struggling against Tilda.

'Thank goodness you're back, Miss Em,' Tilda gasped. Her face was scratched and her cap had been knocked off. Emilia was appalled to see Lottie was clutching strands of her ginger hair. A bowl of water and a flannel had been tipped over on to the floor. A china soap dish lay broken in half. 'Mrs Harvey's wet herself, but when I tried to give her a wash and change her clothes she went berserk.'

'Lottie! Lottie, dear, it's Em. Calm down. It's going to be all right. I'm sorry about this, Tilda. You can let her go, I'll see to her now.'

It was Lottie who had Tilda in her clawing grasp and it took a further struggle for the housekeeper to free herself. 'What an afternoon! First a telegram arrives and I was feared to the bottom of my soul what news was in it. I'd just asked Albie to run to the fields with it when Mr Ben comes home in a terrible rage and shouts at the pair of us like we're something unholy. I've been rushed off my feet. I don't mind that, but I didn't expect to act as a nursemaid when I came here.'

'I really am sorry, Tilda.' Emilia had got Lottie motionless but she was still in a fractious mood. From her dash up the lane and now with Lottie pulling her about, her hair fell in long coppery tangles. 'I promise I'll never leave Mrs Harvey for such a long time again. Do you know what was in the telegram?'

'Yes,' Tilda righted her dress and replaced her cap, thrusting in strands of tortured hair. 'It was from Mr Tristan, putting off Mr Alec's and Master Jonathan's visit to him. He's being moved to another hospital and having an operation on his ankle, by some special surgeon. And he's been made up to captain.'

There was the sound of running feet. 'I've fetched Uncle Ben!' Jonathan shouted out in the passage.

With her hopes dashed of seeing Ben alone, Emilia put on a smiling face to greet him.

At the same instant he and Jonathan raced into the room, Lottie picked up a photograph from the piano and threw it at the window.

'Grandma, no!' Ben was too late. The glass broke with a loud smash, chinkling on to the flower beds outside while splinters flew on to the carpet and shot out in all directions. The company was dazed, all except for Lottie, who, after folding her arms and emitting a loud, 'Humph,' flopped down in her chair.

Emilia glanced from face to face. Lottie had settled herself. Jonathan was staring at his great-grandmother, his mouth opened wide, clearly amused. Redder than before in the face, Tilda was holding a quivering hand to her panting bosom. Ben's good looks were corrupted by a fury that Emilia knew he wasn't going to contain and he was glaring at her in a way that made her heart dive.

'Tilda, take Jonathan out of the room and make sure he doesn't return in here until *she* – ' he stabbed a finger towards Emilia – 'has cleared up the glass and the rest of this damned mess.'

'Please don't shout at me, Ben. You'll upset your gran,' Emilia cautioned, after the housekeeper and the boy had gone. She edged closer to Lottie.

'How dare you use my grandmother to deflect your sloth and selfishness. You're responsible for all of this.'

Emilia was unprepared for his swiftness. Suddenly he was dragging her halfway across the room. She tried to resist but he kept her in a vice-like hold. His breath hit her face in icy blasts. 'This is the second time you've neglected to look after my grandmother properly. Remember you're only a worker here, a servant. Why aren't you in the milking shed with those of us who are prepared to work? You think you can shirk your duties because you're my brother's favourite. And you think your grief over Billy runs deeper than anyone else's. There's nothing special about you. The country's full of grieving sisters, and widows and fatherless children and mothers without sons, but they're all getting on with their lives, not moping about in a self-pitying drama. Either you see to your own work from now on or you can bloody well find yourself another job.'

She tried to place loving hands on him, but his terrible grip meant she couldn't reach out, couldn't move. 'Ben, listen, let me explain.'

'You can't explain away your contempt towards your duties as far as I'm concerned. Do you understand?'

Her resolve to apologize, to show him her love again began to evaporate. 'Yes, Ben, I think I do. Your bitterness comes from the first time I neglected your grandmother.' She tried to push him away from her. 'But it wasn't my fault your eye was blinded. Won't you ever believe me?'

The eyes which had once radiated care and gentleness were like sharded ice. 'To think I'd trusted you, relied on you, needed you. To think I loved you and wanted you for my lifelong mate. One way or another you took my sight from me and everything I'd ever valued. I'll never ever forgive you for that. And I'll never give you the chance to treat me like dirt again as you did this afternoon.'

He pushed her then, making her stagger away several steps, her back hitting a bureau, its hard edge stopping her from toppling to the floor. He came at her again, seeming to enjoy her discomfort, her shock, her pain. It would have been unbelievable before, but Emilia knew he wanted her to be afraid. She loathed him then. She drew herself up to her fullest height. 'One disappointment, Ben Harvey, that's all you've had, but how quickly you've abandoned all the upright codes you'd sworn to always live by.'

He laughed, a horrible, grim, mocking sound. 'Don't you like it, Emilia, that I don't need you any more? That I'm going my own way from now on? It will please Alec, leave the way clear for him to get to you. A word of warning. He's got a lot of good in him, but you don't know him like I do.' Ben gave a look of prurient derision up and down her body. 'And he doesn't know you as well as I do. You're a fine one to talk about honour.'

Emilia was thanking God she hadn't become pregnant during that one encounter with him. 'You're detestable and pathetic. I can't imagine why I never saw you as you really are, why I ever felt anything for you. I'm grateful I stayed away too long from your grandmother this time, because if all this hadn't happened I was going to tell you how sorry I was for the last two weeks, to beg your forgiveness. I would have come grovelling to you for nothing. That might have been the biggest mistake of my life.'

'Believe me, girl, you haven't made it yet.'

'Are you threatening me?'

'You've never been frightened of anything, have you, Emilia? Perhaps it's time you were.'

'If you won't agree to anything I suggest, then I want what's rightfully mine on my birthday tomorrow.' Ben's voice had been raised against Alec for some time. They were in the stables, grooming the workhorses at the end of the day's work. 'I want the money Father left me.'

'It isn't yours by right until you come of age,' Alec replied, looking over the hooves of the handsome great beast he was checking for signs of needing the farrier's attention.

Ben left the other horse to come close to his brother, his fists curled in frustration. When Alec wouldn't join in a quarrel he was at his most intransigent. 'Under the conditions of his will, as my guardian, you can sign it over to me at your discretion.'

'You're seriously asking me to hand you over five thousand pounds just like that? Not on your life.'

'I don't want to have to go on asking you for every penny for the next three years. I hate the fact that you own me body and soul. I'm a man, I want to be treated like one. I deserve more than an allowance for all the bloody hard work I do on your property, every waking hour. I don't see that I'm asking too much.'

Moments ticked by. Alec completed the ministrations on the plough horse. Ben knew by Alec's stubborn silence that he wasn't going to win . 'Please, Alec. You're usually willing to at least compromise when we disagree.'

'Yes, I am. You choose to forget that I'm normally lenient with you.' Leaning now against the outside of the stable doors, Alec lit a cigarette and took two slow puffs. He spoke tight, grim words. 'I'd be willing to release five hundred, but if you squander it, don't waste my time asking for more. You wouldn't even get the swill for the pigs out of me.'

'Suits me. You can wager your soul you'll never be able to accuse me of squandering a penny. I may have been denied my first dreams but I mean to make something of myself. You just see where I am in ten years' time.' Ben stomped away, swivelled round and mouthed over his shoulder. 'I'm off to Julian's, don't expect me back until morning.'

'Wait there, Ben Harvey.' Alec tossed the cigarette in front of Ben's next step. 'You may have finished with me, but there's plenty I want to say to you. About Emilia.'

All the while she was giving Lottie a bath and putting her to bed, Emilia heard Ben's quarrelsome voice. When she went downstairs all had gone quiet. Tilda, still looking roughed-up and on edge, glanced up from patching a work jumper of Ben's. 'Mr Harvey wants to see you in the den,' she said in a small voice.

'What sort of mood is he in?'

'I really couldn't say.' Tilda kept her head bent over her sewing. 'Emilia, I'm sorry about you and Mr Ben falling out, but sometimes it doesn't do to overstep the mark, if you understand what I mean. Perhaps it's for the best.'

'Oh yes, Tilda, it most certainly is.'

Just before knocking on the door of the den, Emilia realized she had forgotten to tidy her hair. She didn't care. Offended by Tilda's inference that she wasn't good enough for Ben, angered by Ben's unjust remarks and his menace, she didn't wait for permission to enter. If there was any truth in Ben's assertions about Alec having designs on her, he had just better keep himself in line.

She was surprised to find Alec so deep in thought he was unaware of her presence. The fragrance of Scotch lay pleasantly on the air, a low measure of the dark-amber liquid in the glass near his motionless hand. 'You wanted to see me, Alec?'

'Oh, Emilia.' Coming out of his trance, he came round the desk to her. 'Yes, sit down. How are things now? You've had a tough time lately. Can I get you a drop of brandy or something?'

'I thought you'd be angry with me.' Her gaze followed him to the drinks table.

'I'd prefer it if you didn't leave Grandma for quite so long, but I don't agree with the manner in which Ben took you to task over it. Jonny told me all about it, with a childlike glee, I might add. It's the first sort of excitement he's seen in a while. I've put Ben straight about it, I won't tolerate him upsetting you. Well, there was no harm done in the end, except to you and Ben and your future together. I'm sorry about that, I hope you both sort things out.'

His kindness, which she had taken for granted until earlier today, made her wary of him. 'Are you forgetting that Tilda was badly shaken up and a window was broken? You must take the cost out of my wages. Was the photograph damaged?'

'Tilda will be fine by tomorrow and don't worry about the window. The shutters will do for the night and there's plenty of spare glass in the garden shed. Cyril will fit the new pane in tomorrow. The photograph landed on an evergreen and was undamaged.' He brought the glass of brandy to her for she had not moved. 'Go on, take a sip.'

She sipped because she wanted to. She relished the burn on her lips, the strong taste on her tongue, the soothing heat in her throat and the calming warmth that flooded her stomach. Since news of Billy's death, she'd felt only icy emptiness there. 'Can I ask what you and Ben were quarrelling about?' She was sure Ben had objected to Alec's reprimand, but why had the clash lasted so long?

Alec put a gentle hand under her elbow and led her to his chair at the hearth, then he made himself comfortable in the one opposite. 'His friend, Julian Andrews. He's suggested to Ben that he'd like to help out here with the paperwork. Ben wanted him to come two or three times a week. I didn't agree. He's brought enough strangers here.' Alec took no pains to hide his impatience.

'You think Ben's told him about your problem?'

'No. It was Andrews's suggestion from the start – well, he can do his charity work elsewhere. But Ben did throw my weakness at me. He said he was fed up doing the correspondence and accounts. Suddenly, Emilia – ' Alec floated one large, rough hand in a gesture of hurt astonishment – 'I've always been lazy and I didn't pay enough attention to my lessons. Do you know something, I've met men broken by their experiences in the war, but this business with Ben, I just can't get to grips with it. I've never seen anyone so bitter. He's even against the arrangements I'm making to take on a boy and a girl from the workhouse.'

'Why should he object to that?'

'No idea, unless it's just to nettle me.' Alec gazed searchingly into her eyes. 'Why don't I suggest to Ben he takes you, Grandma and Jonny to our cousin, Winifred's? It could help you to become reconciled. Now Tristan's put off mine and Jonny's visit to him, you could all go in a day or two. What do you think, my dear?'

Emilia used her brandy glass to look through and covertly study Alec's relaxed body. It was the only time she had seen him this restful, smiling without a break. His long legs were stretched out across the rug, his feet nearly touching hers. He kept studying her ruffled mane, in between looking straight into her eyes, and occasionally dropping his eyes to her lips. Was he up to anything? How much of Ben's claims about him were true? To have a mistress wasn't unusual, especially in an unhappy marriage. She understood Mrs Bawden, the letter writer's, brief message to Alec now. Then there was the matter of the dismissed maid. She remembered Maudie giggling and loitering about Alec, and Lucy stalking outside one summer evening to 'get that trollop away from my husband!' Had Alec taken advantage of the maid's friendliness? She, herself, had never suspected him of doing so. It seemed more likely Ben's spite had been born out of jealousy over Alec's caring attitude. Alec cared enough to want to see her and Ben reunited. Hardly the course of a man who'd prefer to see them apart for his own ends.

'After the terrible things Ben said to me on two separate occasions today,' Emilia said with conviction, 'I don't think he'd want to go as far as the ford in my company. Nor I his.' It would take a long time for her to forgive his despicable accusations and brutality. Perhaps she never would after what he'd implied she was for making love with him in Ford House.

She watched Alec for his response. He appeared to be saddened. 'It's a great shame how things have turned out for you both. I'll arrange the visit to Newquay as we'd previously planned, it will be an overnight stay. It will make up for Jonny's disappointment at not see his father until a later date.'

There had not been a definite agreement over her going to Newquay with him, but she let him continue, happy about the arrangement. A break away from Ben would be welcome.

'The poor little chap is convinced Tris will be able to get Ursula to come back. I'm hoping Tris will want to stay here with us when he's discharged from the hospital – he can share Jonny's room. He'll have lots of sympathetic company, then when or if he returns to his battalion he'll be the stronger for it, and Jonny will have happy memories of his father being here with him. Another drink, Emilia?'

Emilia knew she should leave. Tilda was probably counting the minutes she was spending here alone with Alec, but there was something she wanted to ask him. 'No, thank you. Alec, can I mention something to you?'

'Anything you like, my dear.' His smiles grew even softer.

'Well.' She leaned forward, growing pink because she knew she was speaking out of turn. 'It's looking increasingly likely that Florence Burrows will have to sell her house. You know how difficult things are for her and Honor, don't you? I was wondering if you might think about . . .'

'Buying the house?'

'Yes. I'm so worried about Honor. If Mrs Burrows can't get her married off as the answer to their financial ruin, I'd hate to think what it will mean for Honor.' Emilia blushed until her face and neck burned, 'You're aware of what the woman's up to when she comes here, aren't you?'

'No, my dear, I can't say I've given her much thought, except to be grateful for her help. I'm afraid her situation is more desperate than she's been leading Honor to believe. She doesn't own the house. She's renting it off what remains of the Tremore Estate.'

'What? That lying old so-and-so! When she can no longer scrape up the rent she and Honor will be homeless. My mother wouldn't hesitate to take Honor in, but she wouldn't fancy having Florence Burrows too. There's only the farm left now, a few fields and the woodland, isn't there? I know Dick Buzza's been managing it for someone all these years, and he's never done a proper job of it. My mother's said he's looking to retire, to live with his daughter at Idless. Do you know who Florence Burrows's landlord is?'

'The property's changed hands many times in the fifty-odd years since the manor fell down.' Alec stretched himself out even more, as if settling himself for a long cosy chat. 'The current owner is a fellow I know. He intends to go off to live in India and has put the farm and Bracken House on the market.'

Emilia braved another outrageous suggestion by working up her first smile in over two weeks. 'Couldn't you buy it? You'd be Honor's landlord. You wouldn't see her homeless, I'm sure.'

'It's good to know you have a high opinion of me, Emilia. I don't mind confiding in you that I'm in the process of buying the Tremore property. Of course I wouldn't see any friend of yours without a roof over her head. The Burrowses may live there rent-free providing there's a proper understanding they work for me in return. I'm thinking of installing Ben at the farm. It would give him something to build on, be his own boss, as it were, and with the farm situated on the other side of the village, it will be easier for you, Emilia, now it looks as if things will never improve between you.'

Putting a hand to her breast, Emilia sighed with relief over Honor's more settled future, and while she found it in her heart to be glad for Ben, if he remained difficult, it would be good if he wasn't so close. 'Would you mind if I told Honor her biggest worry will soon be over?'

'I'm afraid I must ask you to wait until the legalities are signed. Then you may tell her as soon as you like.'

'Thank you, Alec, and thank you for confiding in me.' She stood up to go but instead fixed her eyes on him, mesmerized by his soft grey gaze. It was as if she was seeing his hushed face for the first time, its extraordinary strength, and fineness and nobility. His mouth was wide and fully masculine, his jaw line firm, his eyes fascinating, with bright enticing depths. It was easy to understand why Lucy Pollard, a fickle, social-climber by reputation, had settled for him when she, apparently, could have ensnared a titled gentleman with much more wealth, land and prestige.

'Stay Emilia, let's talk some more.'

She hesitated. He smiled, slow, encouraging, and motioned that he would pour her another drink. She stayed.

Chapter Sixteen

Tristan was staring at the ceiling of the officer's hospital in a quiet part of south London. The medical staff insisted the ceiling wasn't grey, but it was how he saw it. Depression. That was what he had, apparently, the reason for him expecting everything to be grey, wanting everything to be grey. Grey was dreary, but it was safe somehow, non-committal. White meant purity and there was no purity anymore. Black meant death, the silence of all silences. All other colours held no meaning for him. Grey was commonplace. Commonplace stopped him from going mad. Like the chap in the next bed had last night.

'A visitor for you, Captain Harvey.'

Tristan felt no threat from the mediocre man, of average build, of no notable features, in an ordinary grey mackintosh. The nurse, thankfully, was an ordinary-looking sort with dull hair – he'd have hated it if she had glossy tresses and was wearing lipstick. She addressed the man in the sort of hushed efficient tones that indicated her priority was her patient's welfare, for which Tristan was comforted. 'Just ten minutes. The captain is to be kept quiet.'

'You have news for me, Mr Smith?' The man had a nice everyday name.

Mr Smith fetched himself a chair, placed it close to the bed and sat down. He employed his toneless voice. 'How's the ankle, Captain?'

'Might be strong enough for me to walk without a limp eventually, so they say.' Tristan's brain fogged over. 'Captain? When did that happen?'

'You were promoted just before you arrived here. You've been through a lot, it'll come back to you. Now to business.' Mr Smith tapped the large brown envelope he had brought, then he shielded it with a small pale hand, as if it might be a matter of national importance. 'The details are all down in here. You can read it later but I'll give it to you straight, 'tis my way and usually best appreciated, I find. I've made extensive inquiries. Even went down to the West Country myself. Your wife and the gentleman in question boarded a midday train at Truro railway station on October sixth. They bought tickets for Bristol and that's where they got off. They took lodgings near the docks the same day, left after a week without paying the rent. I'm afraid I could find no trace of them after that. 'Tis possible they've made their way overseas, despite the dangers. I've done the usual surveillance on the lady's relatives and came up with nothing. Of the gentleman, I couldn't find out anything about him. He's obviously an expert at covering his tracks,' Mr Smith concluded with a sunbeam smile, as if he had been clever and deserved congratulations.

'Bristol? I thought they'd have gone further than that, but I suppose they didn't have much money. They must be somewhere, Mr Smith. You must know something more.' Tristan sat up quickly and foolishly from the pillows, causing pains to shoot and stab at various parts of his body. The dreadful news in Ben's redirected letter that Ursula had left him for this Bruce Ashley character, that she was pregnant, was harder to bear than the physical or mental consequences of the fighting. Surely fate owed him more knowledge of her whereabouts? She was his wife. He needed answers to all the whys. Part of him wanted to know if she was all right. 'People don't just vanish into thin air, especially a woman as striking as Mrs Harvey. Are you absolutely sure you've checked every possibility? What am I to tell my son when I see him?'

'You have my word, sir.' Mr Smith glanced sideways at the nurse, who was hurrying back. 'I tried all forms of travel in and out of the city and all types of accommodation. I even ventured into the less savoury areas. Ladies are sometimes abandoned . . . and they have to make a living somehow.'

'How dare you!' In a rash movement that made his head spin revoltingly, Tristan snatched the envelope, buried himself down in the bed, curled up and hugged the envelope to his chest. Not that for Ursula, please, God. 'You've been paid. Go now, please. I'll think of something else.'

'I've very sorry, sir. Goodbye. Good luck.'

'I'll punch the next bastard who wishes me that.'

The nurse pressed the backs of her fingers to his brow and read his pulse. 'Now, now, Captain Harvey, you've got yourself into a fine state. I'll put the screens around your bed. You are to have a long sleep.'

'Are they grey?'

'Is what grey?'

'The screens?'

'I suppose you could call them a shade of grey.'

'I certainly could.'

Chapter Seventeen

'Is it much further now? How old is Cousin Winifred's girl? Do you think I'll be able to play on the beach? Can we come again after today? Is that the Atlantic Ocean? We're high up. How deep is the water? Daddy and I could come and stay here, couldn't we? Tilda says sea air's good for you. It will be good for Daddy when he's con-con-convesling or something.'

Jonathan's questions went on and on, and Alec, driving the trap into Watergate Bay, on the outskirts of Newquay, on the north coast, answered them with patience and a sense of fun.

Emilia sat in the back with Lottie, whom she had wrapped up in all her furs, pointing things out to her as they had passed through tiny winter-bleak hamlets and villages. Lottie nodded like a marionette, replying, 'Yes, yes, yes,' to everything.

Having journeyed only as far as Truro before, and the occasional trip, as a child, to the seaside at Perranporth, when she, Billy and her parents had walked the three and a half miles there and back, Emilia enjoyed every minute of the long, rough ride. In her own finer clothes, she allowed herself to feel a little grand, and rested and soothed. Her mother was attending to her dairy work at the farm and there was nothing for her to worry about.

After descending a long hill where they looked down on a long, wide expanse of golden sand and craggy rock with headlands in the distance, climbing again past the grand-looking Watergate Hotel, then travelling along a short track and a gravelled carriageway, the party arrived at Roskerne. A solitary house, imposing and well maintained, fifty feet up on the cliff, it was a fine example of classical Victoriana.

Emilia gazed out across the dark-blue waters, which stretched as far as the eye could see up coast and down. Gigantic waves were forming a long way out from the shore, rising in frothy white crests and charging the long strip of pale golden sand with thunderous gusto. She had never seen a more exhilarating sight.

There was a light touch on her hand. 'We've arrived, Emilia. Would you like to get down?'

She returned Alec's smile. 'Oh, yes, of course. Isn't the sea beautiful? It's so much better than I remembered.' It was strange to be helped to alight as if she were a lady, usually she would have jumped down, but it was good to feel cared for. 'I'll help with your gran.'

Rounding the trap, she became aware of the wind tugging at her hat, and her hair – more carefully arranged in a twist today, and she became aware of half a dozen females, including a small girl, in attendance at the front door. It was easy to pick out Alec's widowed cousin, Mrs Winifred Stockley, from a family group in a photograph at Ford Farm.

Winifred Stockley was about Alec's age. She wore black from neck to lower-calf without gloom and had a swan-like grace. There were two nondescript middle-aged servants and the other lady, an advanced version of Winifred Stockley, and sister to Lottie, though with no resemblance, was introduced as Great-Aunt Clarissa. The girl, the same age as Jonathan, was as fair as her mother, and as Emilia was to learn, every bit as precocious. The children were whisked away to the nursery.

'Alec, Grandma, how lovely you could come.' Winifred Stockley sparkled with charm. Emilia liked her immediately. 'And you must be Miss Emilia Rowse. Alec told me all about you at a luncheon in Truro recently. He says you will be keen to explore the cliffs. You must feel free to wander as you will until dinner tonight. I will attend to Grandma.'

Emilia was denied the unpacking of hers and Lottie's

overnight bags, and found herself in the drawing room, the grandest room she had ever been in, and packed close with furniture in rich woods, many beneath fringed, embroidered covers, and masses of pictures and ornamentation in the typical Victorian manner. Rather than take in the lavishments, she looked out of the window at the sea, and listened, as did the great-aunt, while Alec and Winifred caught up on family news. The lone man in the room, taking part in a ceremony of drinking tea and eating plain biscuits, Alec was unimposing and gracious.

'So it's at least another three weeks until Tris will be able to travel home?' Winifred was saying. 'Such a shame you haven't been able to go up yet. I hate to think of him being all alone. How Jonny's grown since the last photograph Tris sent me of him. Has either received any word from Ursula?'

'No, none at all.' With satisfaction, Alec glanced at Emilia – she was reading Tristan's letters to him now. 'But she might have sent poor Tris something out there, of course, and it hasn't been redirected yet.'

'It's all so sad. And there's been sadness for you too, Miss Rowse, or may I call you Emilia? Do accept my condolences on the tragic loss of your brother.'

Feeling the whole room had its eye on her, Emilia was forced to cleared her throat. 'Thank you, Mrs Stockley. Please accept mine in the case of your husband.'

'Your brother and Major Stockley weren't far from each other on the Ypres Salient, you know we have a special source of empathy. It seems every family in the land has been bereaved by this terrible war. Do take off for a stroll any time you care to, Emilia,' Winifred ended kindly. 'Jonny and Vera Rose will be down on the beach with the maid by now, but don't feel you have to join them.'

'Thank you, yes, I'd like to take a stroll.'

'Be careful not to get lost, my dear.' Alec escorted her to the door. 'You'll need to borrow a pair of boots from the cloakroom.'

There were less than half a dozen properties in the bay and

apart from the children, squealing excitedly while running about on the beach with the maid, no one else about. After waving to them she wandered along the narrow cliff path, spongy grass on one side, breathtaking perilous drops on the other. She inhaled the tangy air, so full of salty flavour, and so different to what she was used to every day. She didn't find it difficult to empty her mind of all things disagreeable.

From the exposed parts where she was buffeted by the force of the elements, the path occasionally took short turns into sheltered hollows. After about a mile, in one of these little sanctuaries, she took a small piece of her own work, as intricate as lace, out of her coat pocket. A heart shape, a symbol of love, fashioned in corn. This was to have been her birthday gift to Ben. How could it have been that she had not celebrated the occasion with him? She had mulled over and over every loving word and act they had shared, and every bitter reproach. Before they had fallen in love she had expected them to remain friends for life. It was still a shock to realize how quickly her feelings for him had changed, how Ben's misfortune had changed him. Her mother had deliberated that their youthfulness was to blame.

Whatever the reason, her life, her future with Ben was over. She threw the corn heart-shape as far as she could and watched it spin, its lightness borne on the wind, until it hit granite many, many feet below.

She moved on from the hollow. She would not stay and brood and pander to regrets. She had this gift of a little precious time to herself, after almost three years of continuous drudgery. Yet that wasn't how she saw her life at Ford Farm. There was something satisfying in being part of the cycle of nature and creation, of birth and rebirth. In one of the rector's harvest sermons he had mentioned that working the land was more a spiritual activity than toil. It was true for her, it did feed her spirit. She didn't want to do anything else nor could she imagine being anywhere else. And it had to be Ford Farm, the same fields and valleys and moors and streams where she had roamed as a child. Had it been Ben she had always wanted or only him as the reason to stay there? Strange, she had felt she had loved him so much, but now her heart resented him for never wanting to stay forever at the farm.

She had caught him unawares in the den yesterday and he had bawled at her to get out, hastily covering up what had looked like documents he was signing. No matter. Her place at the farm was secure. Alec said so.

Her next thought about Alec was so mercenary, so unlike anything she had ever imagined herself capable of, she gagged on the sea air. Her father had worked at the farm all his working life, but her only guaranteed permanent connection there could be with Alec. She scolded herself for being covetous, even if it had only been for an instant, of having the same shameful thoughts as Florence Burrows for Honor, to seek to tie herself to a man for her own ends.

She stared out to sea, and it was as if she was looking into her own soul. She bowed her head in shame, for Billy no longer had body or breath, or a mind in which to make plans or cherish hopes. The waters went on and on, seemingly forever, a never-ending unknown world. Was Billy in such a place? Lost and alone? Billy, who had sacrificed his goodness to die in pride and honour. Was she lacking those same admirable regards?

Oh, God, I don't know. I didn't mean to think of something so wicked.

She retraced her steps at a run, only slowing down when reason came drifting back. 'We're only human,' Billy used to say.

No, not *used to*. He was saying it now. She had heard his voice as plainly as she could hear the ocean. He was here, with her. She had heard stories of dead soldiers leading their wounded comrades to safety in subsequent battles, or keeping them company through long, pain-filled hours until rescue came. The part of them that was left on earth until their final duty was done.

'Billy?'

He was there, feet away on the cliff path. Billy, as he always had been, ordinary and kind, not a scrap of mud on his uniform, a reddish mark in the middle of his brow indicating his fatal wound. 'We give what we can, Em. Don't ask more of yourself.'

He was only there a moment but it seemed an age. The sense of peace he had brought stayed with her. Now she could go back and get on with her life. 'Thank you, Billy. I'm not confused any more.'

She would never speak of this tiny pocket of eternity she had shared with Billy, it was personal and precious and theirs alone.

Soon she was looking down on the unmistakeable figure of Alec. The children had gone. He was alone on the shore. Completely still. Where did he go in his thoughts? Was she included in them at this very moment? Did she want to be? Really want to be?

With slow careful steps she approached him, hoping he'd remain unaware of her so she could study him in his contemplation. As expected, his eyes were closed, the long dark lashes resting above his high-set cheekbones. Such a powerful face, and dignified and splendid. His mouth sensuous and gentle, his hair ruffled by the wind. She could stay here all day and not tire of looking at him.

Then he was looking at her, with the softly formed smile he always gave her. He stretched his arms as if waking up. 'I could dream forever in a place like this.'

'Is that what you were doing, dreaming?'

'It's something I've had to do, to enable me to go on. Have you been relaxing, Emilia?'

'Mostly. Then I thought about Billy, imagining him lost in a vast space somewhere and I panicked, but I know he's all right, that I'll see him again one day. You used to come here every summer as a child, didn't you? You must have had such fun with your cousin. I'm pleased you've had some happy times, Alec.'

He gazed at her in a searching way. 'Think me sad, do you, Emilia?'

'Sometimes you seem sad and lonely.'

'Sometimes I am, but never when you're near.'

'I'm glad of that.' Shy now, for their relationship seemed to be steering towards something different, an intimate level, one neither of them was pulling back from, she gave her attention to the next surge of breakers. 'There's some driftwood coming in.'

Alec waded into the water and retrieved a plank of painted timber; valuable firewood. 'It hasn't been in the sea long. See? No barnacles, no decay. I'm afraid it's likely part of a blown-up ship.'

'How terrible. There's more.' They gathered in all the tragic harvest, carrying the timber, much of it jagged, back from the tide line, working side by side in the same way as a few weeks ago when reaping and fetching in the crops from his fields.

'Oh, what would your mother think of me, treating her clothes like this?' she said, rubbing off debris with her wet gloves and picking out splinters from her fur-collared coat. 'I suppose we must think about getting back.'

'Yes, we must.' He gentled away strands of hair that had escaped her hat. 'In a minute.'

Long moments passed in which they gazed at each other.

'Have you brought a gown to wear for dinner, Emilia? We don't usually bother to change, but Great-Aunt Clarissa and I thought we'd make the effort as we have company.' Having bid herself entrance into the room Emilia was sharing with Lottie, Winifred Stockley did not wait for an answer. 'Come with me. I've just the thing for you. It's the colour of claret with black lace over the bodice, and it will sit well on your figure. And of course it's a special occasion.'

'It is?' Bewildered, wearing her negligée after taking a bath, Emilia followed her hostess – who had been amused at her bedraggled state from the beachcombing – to an impressive double room.

'Tomorrow's your birthday. Or had you forgotten? Alec mentioned it to me.'

'I've not given it a thought this year,' Emilia said doubtfully.

'Oh, it will only be a quiet little affair. Just something to cheer us all up, and don't you think we need it with so much sorrow in our hearts? The best way for us to stand firm at home is not to allow our spirits to be dragged down, don't you agree?' Winifred pointed to a gown hanging over the door of her wardrobe. Silk orchids of the same claret colour cascaded down over one shoulder strap. 'Do you like it? I wore this on my honeymoon to New York.'

Emilia touched the stunning material. 'Alec kindly gave me some of his mother's clothes, but I've never dressed up in my life.'

'Let's get you ready then. You'll enthrall him.' Winifred tilted her head to one side. 'You do want to, don't you?'

Emilia ignored the meaning in Winifred's question. She was suddenly afraid, because she did want Alec to notice her in a seductive feminine way, and it wasn't right so soon after recent events, and certainly not wise. She must remember he was her employer. To become involved with him harked at all manner of risks. 'The dress is gorgeous, but don't you think the neckline's too low? My mother would be horrified.'

'Oh, Emilia, dear, how starved you are of feminine niceties. I think your mother would be proud of you. After tonight, as proud as she possibly could be.'

An hour later Emilia showed off her corseted, coiffured self to Lottie in the drawing room, where she was drinking sherry with Great-Aunt Clarissa. 'Do you recognize me, Mrs Harvey? Look, I've even got a feather in my hair, and Mrs Stockley's loaned me a pearl choker.'

'Little bud, little bud.' Lottie nodded her head, smiling at her widest and happiest. She no longer recognized her sister, but had enjoyed all the attention lavished on her throughout the day, and at once held out her hand to Emilia.

'Who's blossomed into a beautiful woman, Grandma.'

Emilia's heart stopped, then began again at a furious rate.

While enduring Winifred's titivations, many of which she had thought unnecessary, she had wondered every moment how Alec would find her. She turned to him in what she hoped was a graceful swing. Her heart thudded to a halt again. She had seen him in his dinner suit before, but she had never considered then if he made a handsome image. Now here he was, astonishingly good-looking, his smile full of masculine appeal and dangerous somehow. He seemed to be drinking her in. The exhilaration of viewing the sea was wildly outmatched by the sensations his attention was giving her.

'It took me a ridiculously short time to turn your little mainstay into this stunning creature, Alec.' Winifred appeared, sophisticated, demure, in a more up-to-date black gown. 'But, of course, Emilia was lovely to begin with.'

'I totally agree, Winnie.' Alec kept his eyes on Emilia. 'My dear, may I wish you a happy birthday for tomorrow? I've brought you a little present. I've shown it to Edwin and he's agreed that you may have it.'

He held out a long narrow box. It could only contain jewellery. 'I . . . thank you, Alec.'

Alec pressed the box into her hand. He kissed her cheek and then the other. He whispered, 'For all you mean to me.'

'Get a move on, Miss Rowse,' Great-Aunt Clarissa drawled. She was apt to be undignified and boisterous, and was indeed a little inebriated. 'Don't keep us in suspense.'

Her hands fluttering in excitement. Emilia lifted off the lid. 'Oh! Oh!'

'How clever of you, Alec, to find something so exquisite. But you never do anything without the deepest thought, do you?' Winifred was peering over his arm, at the delicately fashioned wristwatch nestling on a bed of red satin in Emilia's hands. 'I'm envious to the point of bursting.'

Emilia was staring at Alec. 'It's the most wonderful thing I've ever seen. I think I'm going to cry.'

'The one thing we're always battling against at the farm is time, Emilia,' Alec said. 'I thought I'd give you something to tell it by.'

'I think you'd better escort her to a chair, Alec,' Great-Aunt Clarissa observed. 'The poor girl is quite overwhelmed.'

'Emilia's not the sort to get overwhelmed, Great-Aunt. She's strong and wise and resourceful.'

'Em looks overwhelmed to me.' Jonathan skipped into the room with Vera Rose, to say goodnight.

Emilia felt Alec's hand under her forearm and she was borne along to a sofa. She never took her eyes off him while he fastened the watch around her wrist, despite having Jonathan leaning over her lap. Alec was sitting close enough to touch her body. Emilia was sure her father had not realized the value of the watch, that it had diamonds set around the superb face.

'It's beautiful, but I'll only wear it on special occasions.'

'We'll have lots of those,' he whispered.

The children were put to bed, and after a meal of roast duck, the duck supplied by Alec, the adults returned to the drawing room. Great-Aunt Clarissa, who had downed a greedy amount of wine, thumped out a tune on the piano. The jolly melody was in keeping with the tone of the evening. Alec asked Winifred to dance with him. He laughed uproariously when he saw Emilia's wry face. 'What?'

'I've never imagined you dancing before.'

'Such a sober-sides, am I? Well, I'll dance with you afterwards and see how many other misconceptions about me I can eliminate.'

On the sofa beside Lottie, who was waving her index fingers in time with the music, Emilia clapped her hands, laughing as Alec and Winifred whirled around the room to a polka. Then he was in front of her, bowing low, taking her to the middle of the carpet. One hand grazing the small of her back, the other warm and pressing around her fingers, he seemed to be holding her unnecessarily close as they spun out the same circuit again and again.

The wine was kept flowing. The company were invited to nibble on a box of exotic chocolates, which, to Alec's query at how they were acquired, Winifred merely winked in reply.

Almost oblivious to the three ladies, Emilia gazed at her watch and gazed at Alec. He kept her exclusively in his sight.

At ten o'clock, Great-Aunt Clarissa announced she and Lottie should retire. 'We're done for, aren't we, sister? Can't expect any more from such old bones, but ye Gods, we've had a splendid evening.'

Emilia made to say a reluctant goodnight and take Lottie upstairs.

'You stay were you are. I'll put Grandma to bed, then I'll retire to do a little reading,' Winifred insisted, ringing for the maid for assistance. 'You and Alec must stay down for at least another hour or two – it is your holiday. Before we go up, Alec, I want to make a suggestion about Grandma and Jonny. You have so much to do at home, why not let them come to us? Grandma's equally as comfortable with me as she is with Emilia, and Jonny would be company for Vera Rose.'

Before Alec could answer, Emilia blurted out, 'No, please don't take Mrs Harvey away from us. She's no trouble to me, I enjoy looking after her. And Jon—' Emilia dropped her eyes. 'I'm sorry, I've spoken out of turn. I beg your forgiveness.'

'Emilia's right.' Alec, who was close beside her, made a dismissive motion with his hand. 'We wouldn't dream of relinquishing either of them. They both belong at the farm, in Jonny's case, until Tris is home for good.'

Winifred surveyed the couple and nodded. 'I understand. Goodnight to you both.'

'I've got a big mouth,' Emilia said when they were alone. 'I hope I didn't offend Mrs Stockley and your great-aunt, they've been so kind to me.'

Alec was looking at her mouth as if he had a warm opinion of it. 'My lovely outspoken angel, of course they're not offended. Winnie thinks you're quite perfect and if Great-Aunt Clarissa didn't like you she'd simply say so.'

'Do you know, I think you'd let me get away with anything.'

'And why not? What shall we do now?'

'Well, I know it sounds silly, but we've got to leave here

first thing tomorrow and won't get a chance to look at the sea again, and as I've drunk too much wine, could we take a breath of fresh air?'

'Excellent idea. We'll wrap up and walk to the end of the garden.'

The war conditions forbade use of lights after dark and an indifferent moon was casting a lacklustre path of silver all the way to the horizon, but neither needed an excuse to aid the other's wary steps by linking arms in the darkness. They listened to the steady roll of the ocean for long silent minutes. When they were rocked on their feet by a sudden blast of the bitingly cold wind, Alec suggested they shelter in the summer-house.

'Emilia?'

'Yes?'

'I've got something else to give you for your birthday.' His voice was suddenly grave and she tried to read his expression in the meagre light of the moon. He placed a piece of paper into her hand. 'Edwin asked me to pass this on to you. It arrived a few days ago. He didn't have the heart to do it himself.'

'Is it from Billy?' Seeing him so recently made tears of wonder rather than grief well up in her heart.

'Yes, it is. You can read it by the light of my cigarette lighter.'

Sharing the padded seat of a garden bench, he held her in a comforting embrace. Wanting Alec to share this with her, she unfolded the last message her brother had written to her, and read aloud. 'My dear Em, I'm writing this birthday greeting early, to make sure you get it on time. I wish I could be there to see you become a woman and I wish I could give you a little something, but here's my blessing for you, dear one. Be happy in all things, in all ways. Until my next letter, or,' she faltered, 'or until we meet again. Your loving brother, Billy.' Billy had chosen to appear to her on the day before her birthday. Had he known it was going to be a special time?

Alec was stroking her neck. 'Try not be too sad, Emilia, darling.'

'I'm not. It's something to treasure, Billy's gift to me. It sounded as if he knew he was going to die, Alec.'

'He couldn't have known for certain, except that he loved you and wanted to wish you all the happiness you deserve.'

She kissed the letter, folded the paper and dried her eyes. She knew from a letter of Tristan's that Billy had received her letter about hers and Ben's courtship. Billy had thought her happiness was going to be with Ben. Or had he known it was to be with someone else?

Alec closed the lighter and they were in the enveloping warmth of almost total darkness. 'Do you want to go in?'

She rested her head against his shoulder. 'I wish we could stay like this for ever.'

'We could stay together for ever.' He lifted her face to his. 'Do you want to?'

'Yes, I think I want to.' She sought the lips she knew were questing hers in the darkness. The contact was delicious, exquisite beyond measure and she let out a terrific inner sigh.

Alec kissed her softly, hardly able to contain his elation at her response to his question. The day had gone better than his hopes, he thinking he might only have made a tentative approach to her. Whatever the reasons were for Emilia seeming to want him as much as he wanted her, he did not care. Pray God, she would have no regrets in the morning.

Emilia liked the feel of his mouth, the tender way he was gliding it over hers, slowly at first, then pressing harder, searching, probing. This was different to what she was used to. It was a deep, shocking kiss, and the knowledge that he was fully experienced in the ways of making love excited her, made her eager for him in a way that surpassed all previous desires.

She pulled off her hat, pressed into him and took his mouth again. She became urgent and awkward. 'Hush now,' he whispered. 'Leave this to me.'

He threw the padded cushions down on the tiled floor and

spread his overcoat over them. Lying there in his arms, she sank into the pleasures of his many and varied kisses, his devastating gentleness and finely discriminating overtures, until at exactly the right moment, he made the move that enabled her to do every blissful thing to him that he was doing to her.

Chapter Eighteen

Honor went to Ford Farm that same day to get away from Florence. Her aunt's anxiety was making her snap and complain about everything. She was hoping Ben would be in the yard. He was, mucking out the horses.

His hardy limbs moving in liquid, subconscious motion, he was making short work with the shovel. He was lost in thought, obviously far from the stables, perhaps imagining he was fighting on some foreign field, taking part in a great victory for hearth and homeland. No, that wasn't it. He was smiling round the eyes, enjoying his reflection, his handsome face straight, not incited and intense. He paused before making the journey with the wheelbarrow to the dung heap. There was definitely a passion of some kind going on inside his head and he was either enjoying a replay or the prospect of it. Had he taken up with a new woman? She hoped not.

From the corner of his good eye he saw her. A melody of tenderness and concord. A warmness flooded his heart. He cherished the way Honor made him feel good about himself. He liked the uninterrupted adoration she paid him. This lovely, harmless girl, who had commiserated with him over the loss of his sight, over all he had lost, even Emilia, as soon as she'd been given the chance. He hadn't wanted to talk about Emilia. Honor had respected that.

He came to stand at a small distance from her – there'd be a ripe smell on him. 'You're always a welcome sight, Honor.'

'I fancied some company, even though Em isn't here. Aren't you missing her, just a tiny bit, Ben? I miss us all being friends.'

'I'm afraid we can never go back to how things were.'

She silently implored him to reconsider. Saw it was hopeless. Nevertheless, gave him an encouraging smile. 'I know.'

'I wish I had time to take a walk with you but I'm afraid I've got lots to do today. Go in and talk to Tilda. Mrs Rowse has gone on to the rectory and she's lost with just Edwin and Archie about the place.'

'Well, I'll do that then. Let you get on.' Honor disguised her disappointment with false enthusiasm. She would like to have spent a few minutes more with Ben, for old times' sake.

Ben sensed her loneliness and searched through his day's schedule. Sadly, there wasn't another second he could spare, he had an important appointment in Truro immediately after this. 'We should get together sometime, Honor. Meet up for afternoon tea in town; let's make it soon. After all, you're my friend as much as Emilia's, and despite everything, she'd not see it as disloyalty on your part.'

'I'd really like that, Ben. And no, Em wouldn't.'

Having something to look forward to at last, Honor slipped away to the kitchen. Tilda, who had embarked on an extra-large baking session in the strangely quiet room, was pleased to see her. Honor talked her into letting her tackle the overflowing laundry basket, and a contented, industrious morning was spent at either end of the vast table.

Honor's hands were aching when she relinquished the heavy hot irons to go home for lunch, but she was satisfied that her efforts had meant less drudgery for Tilda. Putting her coat, hat and gloves on, she thought about how, much earlier, Ben had charged through the house, had taken a bath, before bidding her and Tilda a swift goodbye and going out by the front door. He'd looked so gorgeous in his suit and smelled so divine, the only explanation could be that he was off to see a woman. This, and the dismal thought of facing the miseries of Aunt Florence, made the lowering sky look all the more sullen.

To save Tilda the trouble, she braved the yard again to deposit a shirt of Archie Rothwell's in the hay house. She looked around. Where was his bed? It had been made up in a draught-proof spot, an old mattress and blankets on bales of hay. She'd have to go back and ask where the secretive casual labourer was sleeping now. Then she saw the mattress was rolled up and tied with string, standing in a corner.

There was the scurry of violent movement. A rat shot into view, followed hotly by Pip, barking loudly. The dog caught the rat in its jaws and with a rapid twist broke its neck. Honor shrieked and leapt back. Pip let the rat plunge to the dusty ground. 'Take it outside! Go on, you dreadful little dog.'

The dog eyed Honor as if enjoying a malicious game. Then it picked up the rat in its teeth and spilled it at her feet. Honor screamed and rushed backwards. She hit a bale of hay, was off-balanced and sent tumbling down. Afraid the rat might next end up on her lap, she used the shirt as a shield. 'You beast! Get away from me and take that disgusting creature with you. Tilda! Tilda, I need your help.'

'Miss Honor, hold fast, I'm coming.' It was Archie Rothwell's voice.

Honor sucked in her breath until he reached her on his strange tripping steps. The tenor of his voice carried authority while he ordered the Jack Russell outside. Using a two-pronged fork, he edged the rat's body out after it. Honor regained her feet and tried to regain her decorum, but she was shaken up and dropped on to a bale to wait for her thumping heart to settle.

Archie Rothwell returned. 'Are you all right, Miss Honor?'

'Yes, thank you, Mr Rothwell, I am now. I do feel silly. Oh, I brought this shirt in for you but couldn't find a place to put it. I'm afraid it's got rather crumpled.'

After a moment in which to ensure his balance, he took the shirt from her and packed it into the bag slung over his shoulder. 'I'm grateful to you. If you'll excuse me, I must get on.'

Honor shot up. Her eyes excited and narrowed, she was about to let rip of a kind unknown to her before. 'No, I'll not excuse you, Mr Rothwell. It's obvious you're leaving and doing so while Mr Harvey is away and Ben has gone out.

Why are you treating the people who have befriended you in such an underhand way?'

Archie Rothwell used his vivid green eyes to peer all around the barn as if trying to escape from something, before bringing them back to meet Honor's indignant stare. 'I've left Mr Harvey a letter explaining my reasons. I don't like goodbyes and I don't like a fuss.'

With no one here in charge, Honor felt she should say something more. 'Are you leaving because the workhouse children are due here soon? Would it be too many people about for you?'

'Your observations are correct, Miss Burrows.'

Honor marvelled that his tone, as always, was polite and calm, but feeling now that he was deceitful, she wondered if this was a deliberate cultivation.

He added, 'And when one stays in a place too long people start asking questions.'

'That's your own fault.'

'I beg your pardon?'

'Mr Rothwell, if you don't want people to wonder about you, then I suggest you do something to make yourself less conspicuous?'

He surprised her by seeming amused and it took some of the gauntness off his troubled expression. His long fingers touched his copious beard and tumbling hair. 'I found it warmer the first winter after . . .' In another rapid change of mood he swallowed hard, and as if in panic, twisted to face the doors. 'I'm sorry, I have to go.'

He rocked on his unstable feet and Honor had to move quickly, grabbing at his greatcoat to prevent him plummeting to the ground. For a time he seemed stunned, then thanked her in a barely audible voice. Silence. Either he didn't know what else to say or he wasn't going to speak any more. She understood how Emilia had felt the first day he had come to the farm. There was something vulnerable and achingly sorrowful about him. She revalued him again. Even though he was roughly twice her age, she felt protective towards this mystifying stranger, who fought so hard to remain an outsider.

Honor released her grip, retreated to give him the space he desired. 'Please don't go like this, Mr Rothwell. It's a cowardly and unkind thing to do, and I would prefer to think you are neither a coward or unkind. At least talk to Mr Harvey or Ben first. Why don't you sit down? You look overcome.'

He gave a short bewildered nod, then shuffled to the bale of hay she had used, clutching his stick as if it was a lifeline. He said nothing, just looked somewhere above her head.

'Why not let me help you make up your bed?' She persisted because, watching his almost boyish discomfort, she felt him worth the bother. 'You ought not to go right now. I heard you coughing when I arrived, you're getting another cold. Colds are sweeping through the village at the moment. If you were to become ill, wouldn't it be better to be among people who care about you?'

He glanced at her, then looked away. He sighed. It was hard to tell what his feelings were.

'I doubt if you've been treated as well or had your privacy respected as much anywhere else you may have worked. Am I right?'

Silence.

She searched her mind but couldn't think of anything else to add. This was awful. Another second and she would leave and let him to do as he willed.

As she turned away, he gave a strange strangled cry, like an echo of anxiety, of terrible suffering. She swung back. He appeared to be fighting something trapped in the fathoms of his soul.

'Trust me, Archie, or at least try to. I only want to help.'

His leaden expression gave a little. He released the white-knuckled grip on his stick. His penetrating gaze was on her suddenly, in such a way that Honor coloured hotly. He was, after all, an elder and a former naval officer of high rank. From her usual manner and her looks he must see her a mere child, and she was now expecting a reprimand over her impertinence.

He said in the softest of ways, 'You're right in all you've said, Miss Burrows. I don't suppose you happen to have a pair of scissors with you, so I can trim my beard?'

He wasn't actually smiling, but Honor felt he was from somewhere within his deepest self. Bursting with relief and triumph, she cleared her throat to forestall a little shriek of joy. Em could argue people into good sense in a trice; this was the first time she had achieved something similar. 'I do have a pair in my handbag. They're small but sharp enough for the job.'

'I don't know how I'm going to manage with my hair.' He tugged at the luxurious length clinging to his neck.

'I'll do it for you.' If Em could pluck a chicken and gut a rabbit, she was sure she'd not be squeamish about cutting a man's hair.

'No. It's kind of you but I couldn't ask you to. It would make you late getting home.'

She was ready with the scissors. 'I don't mind, honestly. You're the right height there for me, you'll only have to turn your head from side to side.'

He relinquished his bag, produced a comb from an inside pocket and turned the collar of his greatcoat down. When close to him and lifting the first sandy lock, she fought down the reappearance of her natural shyness. After the first cut, in which she had three inches of his hair tingling her fingers, she grew confident, snipping and shaping, calling on her memory of the close-cropped effect Ben's barber made for him. From time to time she glanced into Archie's face but he was keeping his expression detached. Speculation abounded in Hennaford about this man. There were many theories about him: an ex-serviceman suffering from shell shock; a disgraced gentleman in exile; an eccentric scholar; an escapee from a 'loony bin'. She and Emilia had discussed his likely full story many times. Honor was burning to know all about him. Her simplest question: did he miss the sea?

Using her hands to sweep off the snippets clinging to his coat, she moved in front of him and started tentatively on his beard, trimming around the lean outline of his jaw, giving his moustache a neat line. He closed his eyes for this, perhaps, so she thought, to allow her no passage into whatever he was so set on concealing.

When she stepped back to survey her handiwork, and he unlocked his eyelids, she hid a gasp of wonder. He was transformed. She had considered him old enough to be her father, but now he looked about Alec's age. And while she had never thought of a man as being beautiful, it was how his eyes were now. Vibrantly green like burning emeralds in the lantern light, and, before his hauntedness returned a moment later, extraordinarily soft and serene. She experienced a surge of victory, certain that for a while, at least, she had breached his torment and given him comfort.

She rooted about in her handbag for a mirror. 'Would you like to take a look?'

'I don't think so. It's been a long time since I saw myself.' He used his fingers to feel the difference she had made. 'I'll have to be even more careful now to avoid a cold. The cough comes and goes. I'm very grateful for your kindness, Miss Honor. I shall stay here at Ford Farm, at least throughout the winter. Could I ask you to keep my intention to leave today in confidence?'

'Of course. You'd better keep the scissors.' She was overcome with sadness. What had made him want to wander aimlessly, to insist he sleep at a distance from all others? And despite some unexplained optimism on Emilia's part for her and her aunt's prospects, she was overcome with gloom about their fate. 'No one's future is certain, Mr Rothwell. I must go before I get caught in a shower.'

She looked into his eyes. He was considering her as if with sympathy, as if he knew she had some crushing worries. He gave her a brief smile, the first smile he had given anyone here. She smiled back.

She got as far as the ford when rain lashed into the front of her body. Clutching her hat, she made to hurry over the bridge. Her foot slipped on the mud-slimed surface and she grabbed at the wet hedge to steady herself. Unable to get a firm purchase on the saturated foliage or bare twigs, it seemed she was fighting with something unyielding and hostile before she plunged into the ford. She screamed in fright, and then in pain as her side hit the slab of granite, before ending up in two feet of freezing cold water.

Then, although badly shaken, she was screaming in fury. And she swore for the very first time – she had overheard some choice language from Cyril Trewin, and she used every word in outrage and frustration. Somehow, she hauled herself out of the churning water. Dripping and tender where she'd hit her side – a magnificent bruise would come up there – she ripped off her gloves and hat and threw them on the ground. Kicked at the hat, wanting to destroy it.

Lifting up her face to the teeming rain, she shouted to anything that cared to listen, 'Damn and bleddy and bugger and all the rest of it! I've had enough! Can life get any worse?'

She decided to go back to the farm and borrow some dry clothes of Emilia's. It struck her then how funny her outburst would seem when she related it to her friend. How Em would laugh when she heard what she'd bawled out in the worst temper of her life. 'Perhaps I'm not so different to you, after all, Em.'

Honor bent to retrieve her battered hat and thought she was dreaming to see a grand carriage-built motor car heading down the hill towards her. It was brought to a stop and Ben jumped out from the back seat.

'Honor! What happened? Are you hurt?' Within seconds she was being lifted up and hurried into the vehicle. 'Julian, give her your rug.'

Ben got in beside her and covered her with the rug. He placed his overcoat round her shoulders, keeping his arm around her. 'Don't worry, my love, we'll take you home. I'm going over your way as it happens. You've met my friend, Julian Andrews, haven't you? Julian, this is Miss Honor Burrows.'

Honor glanced at the nattily dressed young man she had

been seated next to. 'I saw you at the farm the day Emilia learned of her brother's death. It's good of you to stop, Mr Andrews. I hope I'm not making you wet.'

'Not at all. I'm only glad we happened upon you in your predicament, Miss Burrows. Vosper, drive on.' Julian tapped on the chauffeur's shoulder, for he was partially deaf. 'I think there's a medicinal drop of brandy in here somewhere.'

'No, thank you,' Honor said, bracing herself for the bump, the swoosh of water and the rise across the ford. Ben was caressing her shoulder in a comforting manner.

'It's time something was done about that bridge,' Ben said. He was using a different intonation in his voice now – public schoolboy, like his friend's. 'It's too narrow and it becomes slippery and dangerous.'

They had turned off on to the main road that passed through Hennaford. There was the shop and the tiny concrete square where the village pump was and, set back from it, at irregular angles, were rows of small, thatched cottages and single dwellings; one the home of Edwin and Dolly Rowse. If the fierce shower of rain had not been keeping people indoors, many would have rushed out to stare at the unusual sight of the 'posh' motor car. Ben directed Vosper to turn left at the next junction.

When they were navigating the narrow twists and turns of Back Lane, Honor said, 'You came along at the right moment, I'd have caught my death.' She was shivering – even her underclothes were drenched and clammy.

Ben hugged her tighter.

They arrived at Bracken House and he escorted her inside. Florence was not there. It was likely she had taken herself off to take tea in the cheerier surroundings of the schoolmaster's wife's sitting room. Ben stoked the fire that had been banked in inside the old cooking slab. 'I'll fetch some more wood inside for you.'

'We haven't any,' Honor sighed.

Ben couldn't have felt more shocked and sorry if he'd heard the roof had blown off. Honor was the lady in distress of his old games, the last person who should suffer deprivation. 'You should have mentioned this to me, Honor. I'll bring a cart-load over for you later today, I promise.'

'Thanks, Ben. I'd better change out of these wet things.' She handed him Julian Andrews's rug. Now she was standing in front of the fire trying vainly to warm herself, she felt she was about to cry and cry. She thanked heaven her aunt was out – she would have fawned over Ben, travelling as he was in the sort of splendour she had always craved.

Ben heard the tremble in her voice. 'Oh, sweetheart, what's wrong? It's more than taking a tumble into the ford, isn't it? You haven't been yourself for ages.' He'd had no need to ask – the fine complement of Florence Burrows's personal furnishings was sadly diminished.

'I can't put things right, Ben. I'm just useless.'

'You'd never be that, you're my little princess, remember?'

'I should be tough and capable, like Em. She'd have stood up to my aunt and not pretended she was something she wasn't. We're just two ordinary people, not a cut above anyone else. We'll become homeless any given moment and I don't know what to do.' She rammed her fists against her face. 'I don't know what to do, Ben! I want to be brave, but I'm not. I'm scared.'

Ben reached for her, stroking her hair, soft and fine and fragrant despite its dampness. 'There's nothing wrong in being human, Honor.' And needful and vulnerable. She felt child-like and fragile to hold in comparison to Emilia.

It seemed a lifetime since he had touched and kissed Emilia, and, although he loathed to admit it, she had left him with a terrible loneliness. He missed her warmth and love. But she had turned against him without pity when he'd needed her most. She couldn't have loved him as much as he had loved her. During their first crisis as sweethearts, as lovers, the loss of his Army career had meant more to him than she had. She had seen his weaknesses and resented them. Emilia was tough and capable – he didn't want a woman who was stronger in will and spirit than himself.

'You've always trusted me, haven't you, Honor?'

It felt so good to feel safe for a while. So good that it was Ben holding her. She leaned into him, never wanting him to let her go. 'Yes, Ben.'

'Do you believe me if I promise to make everything right for you?'

She raised her face to his. His tone, his expression was determined and confident. 'How could you do that?'

He angled his limited sight in the dim light and saw her candour and softness, saw her hope. This was what he needed now – someone who relied on him, who was devoted to him.

She saw the Ben of old, kind and caring and fun. The boy who had ripped up his own shirt to bind a bad cut on Billy Rowse's leg, who had shared his treats out equally with his gang, who would never hurt an animal or allow a wounded or sick one to suffer. Strong, courageous, assertive Ben. Handsome, masculine, desirable Ben. Part of her had always adored him as the man he was. Pray God he had only been with Julian Andrews all morning. She hoped he would kiss her.

Should he kiss her? If he did, would he steal the belief she had in him? She was keeping her face tilted upwards, closing her eyes. He kissed her. With care and tenderness. He sensed no unease in her. She returned his gentle, steady pressure with devotion, a commitment that spoke of indissoluble loyalty. She really did trust him. This sweet girl would never misread him, deny him, or turn against him. She would never hurt him. And he would never experience the terrible need to hurt her as he had Emilia, who had brought out the best in him, and the worst.

Honor forgot she had ever had worries as she concentrated on Ben and the glorious answer to her question as to how he could make everything right for her.

He released her as gently as he had held her. 'Tell your aunt I'll be back later to speak to her. Now I'm going to ask you something, Honor. I want you to stay away from the farm for the next few days.'

* * *

'What an absolute little pearl,' Julian said, when Ben rejoined him. The rain had stopped and a watery sun was peeping out of the sulky clouds. 'Do you think I'd stand a chance with her?'

'You and Honor? Sorry, old man, I've already laid a claim on her.'

'So soon after Emilia? Is that wise?'

'To line up the perfect wife for myself, yes, I do.'

'Well, good for you, pity for me. Miss Honor Burrows seems the quiet, gentle sort I could cope with.' Julian's voice fell away. He touched his feeble chest over where his defective heart lay. 'This and my boyish looks have meant I'm overlooked. I know I have little attraction for a woman, except my wealth, but I'd have liked a wife and children in the few years I've got left to enjoy them. I can't be vigorous in the bedroom department, of course, but Miss Burrows doesn't look as if she'd expect too much.'

Ben gave Julian a sideways glance. 'So you've made heavenly contact then?'

Julian grunted. 'Two bob's worth in a back alley the first time and not at all satisfying.' Then he grinned, 'There's a certain address I know, old chap, where one can seek a bit of comfort. There's other activities to excite the blood too. Liquor, gambling, ways past the shortages, if you get my meaning.'

'Sounds just the place, Julian.' The motor car chugged smoothly on.

'Have you by any chance . . . ?'

'Of course.'

'Same sort of assignation as I?'

'Nothing like that.' The motor car rounded a tight bend and made the short distance to Tremore Farm and parked in the lane, which was straight and comfortably wide here, with a crossroads in sight and a small woodland beyond. The two young men got out.

Ben had spoken just now with emotion. 'Surely not with Emilia? She seems a jolly decent sort of girl to me.'

'It was with her, Julian. It happened once and we were in love.' Ben stared down at the animal-fouled road. 'I can trust you not to mention it?'

'Absolutely.' Julian was thoughtful. 'Ben, why don't you try to win her back?'

'Too much has happened between us.' There was no track leading to the farmstead, it stretched back from a low granite wall that was overrun with dead weeds. Ben cast his attention over the dejected huddle of buildings. 'This is the property I intend to make my own. All the land from Bracken House and what you can see from here will be mine. The woods have little commercial value, but beyond the trees lies the ruins of the old manor house. I intend to make use of its timber and stone.'

An aging collie was lying down in the middle of the entrance, much of its long whiskery coat matted with mud. It trailed its head off its front paws, sniffed the air, showing its blindness from cataracts, then dropped its head down, disinterested and unbothered.

'Hello, Sully, I haven't seen you in ages.' Ben stroked the collie's head. In this simple act of friendliness he was washed through with the comforting sense that he belonged here, had been predestined to own this place. 'We have something in common, only yours was caused by nature.' His moments of bliss were stolen by the harsh recollection of the girl he would never forgive for his disablement.

'Are you sure you want this place, Ben?' Julian called from where he was staying put so as not to further soil his expensive leather shoes. 'It doesn't look much in comparison to Ford Farm. It's only about half its size, isn't it? It all seems pretty bleak, the house a leaky draught-ridden hovel.'

Ben rose up, tall and straight and commanding, dazzling his friend by his air of deadly intent. 'It's exactly what I want. A challenge. The Ministry's been on to Buzza, the manager, for ages to build up its production. It's one reason why the owner wants rid of it: he can't be bothered with the harassment. I'll help win the war by doubling the yields from these fields next year, I swear. I've got enough money to buy Tremore and put in good healthy stock. And I'll add to my holdings, you see if I don't! My brother might own one half of Hennaford, well, I'm going to own the other.'

Chapter Nineteen

On the second evening after the return from Roskerne, Emilia was packing for Alec and Jonathan, who were to take the early morning train next day up to London, to visit Tristan.

This was the first time she had entered Alec's bedroom since Tilda had taken over the cleaning. She chewed her nail, wondering how she could have become involved so quickly with the brother of her former fiancé, and become engaged again.

She stroked the pillow where Alec's head should have lain last night, then picked it up and hugged it against her body. She loved him. Why else had she allowed him to steal into her bedroom last night and not leave again until just before dawn? She loved him and she had everything she wanted.

The cases finished, she carried Archie's supper out to him, marvelling again at the pleasant change in his appearance rendered by Honor's unexpected skill with a pair of scissors. She asked him if Honor had mentioned when she was coming over again, and he answered he did not know. She said good-night to her father, and then to the Trewin brothers, on their way home to Wayside Cot carrying their meal, a pail of rabbit stew.

Alec was late for the supper table, having been suddenly called into Truro by Mr Rule, about the business of the Tremore property, according to the hand-delivered letter she had read to him. She ate with Lottie, Tilda and Ben. There was the minimum of polite conversation. Once or twice she noticed Ben staring at her in a strange manner, but at least he didn't seem so hostile. She was not looking forward to his reaction when it was disclosed, after the London trip, how close she was now to Alec.

'Something's cheered him up,' Tilda whispered to her, while dishing out the steamed treacle pudding and thick golden cream.

'Here you are, Ben.' Emilia passed his helping to him.

'Thank you, Emilia.' He gave her the merest smile, and the change to 'Emilia from 'Em' reflected the loss of their friendship.

'Jonny's so excited he'll have trouble dropping off to sleep tonight. He was drawing a picture for his daddy when I left his room.' Emilia kept up the conversational tone.

'It will be good to see Tris again,' Ben said.

Alec suddenly crashed through the door, causing a draught to rush like a malevolent phantom around the kitchen. He fixed his eyes on Ben. A steady, unflinching glare, and it was so full of hurt and anger that Emilia's first reaction was to run to him.

'Emilia, you and Tilda take Grandma and leave the room. I need to speak to my brother alone,' he said in the deadliest tone.

Ben leaned back in his chair, casual, unperturbed. 'Yes, we do need to talk man to man, Alec. Shall we go to the den?'

'If you were a man, Benjamin Harvey,' came Alec's blistering reply, 'I'd insist on us going outside and I'd give you a well deserved thrashing.'

'What's he done?' Emilia looked from Alec and stared at Ben.

'I've only taken control of my own affairs, Emilia,' Ben replied, flicking his hands in a manner to show he thought his brother's wrath was of no consequence to him. 'Alec's had them in his hands far too long. It's none of your business but you might as well hear this, it will affect you.'

'I'll take Mrs Harvey out of the room,' Tilda said nervously.

'No, stay, Tilda. I guarantee there will be no unpleasantness on my part, and Alec is too considerate to make a scene in front of you. There's going to be some changes here, from this very minute actually, and as you're part of the establishment here too, you might as well know now.'

'What's going on, Ben?' Emilia demanded. 'Are you leaving? Is this what it's all about?'

'I shouldn't be surprised you'd cotton on to part of the situation at once.' Ben smiled at her – to Emilia it was a smarmy smile. 'How Alec admires your astuteness, and I can predict he's going to rely on it more and more in the future.'

Emilia glanced at Alec. The rigidity throughout his whole body grew more pronounced. Tilda took hold of her hand.

'Sit down, ladies,' he said, 'and listen to the tale of my brother's betrayal. I'm sure it will disgust you both as much as it does me.'

They obeyed, but he remained standing, his hands splayed out on the table, leaning towards his brother. His features growing more and more contentious. 'Go on, Ben, spit out what you want to crow about. You have centre stage.'

'I don't see it as a betrayal, Alec.' Ben's eyes parried with Alec's, the milkiness of the blinded left side glowing unnaturally. 'I've always wanted to strike out on my own, you know that, and as soldiering is out of the question, I decided I'd like to own the Tremore estate rather than just be your manager there.'

'And you've achieved what you want by two despicable acts,' Alec cut in. 'Taking advantage of the fact that I can't read. I'd have not known about them until it suited you, you stinking Judas, if Ernest Rule hadn't been examining recent transactions of mine.'

'Making that tiny alteration to sign for my own money was merely a matter of taking what's mine, when I want it.' Ben made a jeering dismissive gesture. 'And then I made a more appealing offer for the Tremore estate? So what? That's business.'

'I can still stop the cheque!'

Ben was unruffled and unrepentant. 'Why do that? You might as well get me out of the way. And you wouldn't want

Tris to come home to a major upset in the family, would you? Then there's Honor to consider.'

'What's Honor got to do with this?' Emilia was advancing on Ben with the desire to smack the sickening smugness off his face.

He looked straight at her. 'We're engaged. I'm going to give her the stability she's never had. Her aunt's happy with the prospect.'

Emilia's eyes expanded, she was struck speechless.

'Well done, Ben, it's obvious you'd have made an excellent soldier,' Alec spat. 'A more honest and trustworthy officer would have been difficult to find.'

'There was no need to say that!' Ben leapt to his feet. His fleetness brought him almost eye to eye with Alec.

'Oh, isn't there?' Alec hissed into his face. 'You didn't make an honourable deal with the Tremore estate, you did it solely to hurt me. To gain some form of juvenile one-upmanship. You may have your money, but you can also take my wishes that your success slides downhill in every way possible from now on.'

'You shouldn't be so bitter, Alec,' Ben said in a low and dangerous voice. 'You'll have a clear road to get at the one thing you've been skulking after for ages. You know what – who – I'm talking about. It's why you wanted me at Tremore in the first place, isn't it?'

'Who else would I have placed there, you young fool? It's your actions, not mine, that have been born out of malice and jealousy. You thought it all out, didn't you, Ben? How you could cause me the most insult, and perhaps get back at Emilia in some way too. No doubt, you'll be taking the Trewins with you, leaving me badly understaffed again.'

'Why shouldn't I take them with me? I was the one who offered them some dignity, they're loyal to me. You'll soon have your workhouse brats. It's what you want, see how you get on with them.'

'You and the Trewins can go first thing tomorrow. I won't have deceitful men on my property.'

'So be it. In due course, when I need to ask for your consent to marry, I hope you'll not be petty for Honor's sake.'

'If it wasn't for that foolish girl, I'd tell you to go to hell!'

'As you did Lucy, brother? I overheard you wish that on her when she was dying. She hated you. She treated you just exactly as you deserved. You're a loser, Alec. A nobody. Lucy felt demeaned to have a husband who could do nothing more for her than sign his name on the marriage lines.'

'Shut up, Ben!' Emilia screamed, then she rushed to Lottie, sorry to have raised her voice, for the old lady was getting agitated. 'It doesn't matter what someone can or can't do, only the way they are. You deserve every word of the description Alec's given you.'

'Do you think she'll mind?' Ben indicated Emilia to Alec with a jerk of his head. 'The clever, efficient little country girl you want so much? She'll ask for a lot less than Lucy, but will she mind being stuck with someone who's so stupid he has to get his four-year-old nephew to write to his wounded brother for him?'

'God in heaven, what ever have I done to you?' Alec smashed his fist across Ben's jaw. Ben was plunged backwards, his arm striking the table and sending crockery and cutlery hurtling to the floor. 'Get out from under my roof! Go to your grander friends or sleep the night with your workmen, but never, ever, set foot in my house again. I won't have you back here even for Tristan's sake.'

Lottie was shrieking and drumming her heels. Emilia motioned to Tilda to help her take Lottie towards the larder – her intention to shelter in it, for Ben never walked away from a fight. Thankfully, the distraction of the goods on the shelves distracted Lottie from her hysteria.

'He deserved that wallop,' Tilda said, her nervousness replaced by indignation.

Emilia watched, horrified, as Ben emerged from the breakages, wiping blood from a cut lip, his sight boring into Alec. Alec balled his fists, and Emilia could see he was ready for his brother, welcoming a battle.

Ben took a deep breath; then, letting out a mighty roar, he hurled himself at Alec.

It surprised Emilia that Alec should be faster than Ben. He nipped aside and punched Ben in the gut, sending him reeling to his knees, his head bent over nearly to the tiles. 'The bullies never got the better of me at school, little brother. No one ever has.' Then he added in slow, deliberate stings. 'Now here's a shock for you. Emilia's mine already.'

The breath crushed out of him, it was several seconds before Ben was able to look up. Panting, gasping, he struggled to his feet. His eyes burned into Emilia, then Alec. 'I might have known you'd waste no time. There's one thing you should know about her, brother.'

Emilia waited, without caring, for him to turn their time together in Tristan's house into something sordid.

'I know what it is and I don't care.' Alec went to Emilia, laid possessive hands on her.

Ben gazed at Emilia with a conflict of expressions. Disbelief, regret, sorrow, anger. Then in a hard and fixed way, something which Emilia knew he would never forsake. Unforgivingness.

Chapter Twenty

Passchendaele had been taken and British tanks had defeated the Germans with little resistance at Cambrai. The Allies were concerned that Russia was about to pull out of the war. All this seemed to Tristan to have happened in another world, another lifetime. Here in the countryside of his birth, where the air was so fresh he could taste its purity, only the khaki on his wasted limbs told him he had lived through the deepest depths of a hellish nightmare. A nightmare that was continuing for others with a persistence far beyond the call of honour and bravery.

His house seemed smaller, as if it had never been his. A quick glance through the rooms convinced Tristan that Ursula was never coming back to him. She had left most of her clothes, many of her personal things, even her childhood toys, but there wasn't anything of *her* here. Someone had been in recently and given the house a methodical clean – the smell of polish lingered but the air was stale.

Easing the stiffness cramping around his ankle, he went to his dressing table to see if he was crying. He felt so numb he wasn't sure. He took off his cap. No, he wasn't crying.

Dear God, is this how I really look?

Away from the hospital and a hundred variations of unhealthy pallor, he saw just how pale and thin and grey he was. He had scars and furrows, pits and dents all over his body, but his face bore deeper affliction. Aberrant – that was the only way he could describe himself, with his pronounced cheekbones, colourless lips, sunken staring mad eyes and withered skin, all bordered by his startling hair of dull blackness.

No wonder Jonathan had hidden behind Alec throughout their first visit and had still been unsure of him on the next. No wonder the medics were adamant that it might be months yet before he was fit again for active service. He looked more in the next world than this one, hardly good for morale for those he'd take into battle. But, by God, he was determined to get back in the show again, and to do something more useful next time.

His mind given to lapses of concentration, Tristan forgot why he was looking in the mirror. Tears were dripping off his chin. Pulling open the top drawer, he searched for a handkerchief. Out with it came an envelope; Ursula's writing was on it. He gripped the furniture. He couldn't face her 'Dear John' now and stuffed it in a pocket.

'Right, right.' He cleared his throat, made to comb his hair but his toiletry things were missing. 'Where . . . ? Oh, yes, the farm. Get along there then, got a son to see. At least I've got my son.'

Emilia was teaching the girl from the workhouse the secrets of butter making. The butter was sold at sixpence a pound locally and outside the county and made a good income for the farm. 'Now we press the butter with damp muslin to wash off the buttermilk. This is when we add the salt . . .' Fourteen-year-old Sara Killigrew usually paid attention but she was peering out of the window. 'Sara?'

'Sorry, Miss Em, only there's a soldier, an important looking one out there.'

'What? Let me see. Tristan!'

Emilia rushed out from the dairy, telling herself she wouldn't cry in front of the man whose discovery of Billy's body had confirmed his death, but she did. Limping, using a walking cane, he was a shadow, a ghost of the man who had left his family over a year ago. Through his kind, informative letter about Billy's death, she felt a special connection with him.

Tristan held out his hands to her and it seemed natural to share a hug with him. A clinging, prolonged hug, for he was shaking with emotion and, while she fought to check her own feelings, she was glad to give him comfort. She reached up and dried his eyes, hiding how it disturbed her to see his decline.

'Thank you, Emilia.' His voice was a whisper. He wasn't sure if he could cope with her vibrancy or her compassion. There was a silent thought-ridden moment. 'So much has happened . . . I thought I'd never see the farm again.'

She held his hand for some moments. 'I know, Tristan. I understand. I'm so pleased you're home at last. I'm sorry about Mrs Harvey.'

Tristan could only nod.

'Jonny's gathering firewood with Jim, one of our new hands,' Emilia said brightly, hoping to raise his spirits. 'Jonny likes to trot along behind him. They should be back soon. We weren't expecting you until tomorrow. We were planning a proper homecoming for you.'

'I talked the hospital into releasing me a day early.'

'You must be tired. Come inside and rest. You'll meet Tilda, and this is Jim's twin sister.' Emilia introduced the girl who had crept out behind her.

'Good heavens!' Tristan said under his breath, before responding to Sara Killigrew's polite curtsey.

'Yes, we were taken aback on our first sight of her,' Emilia said with satisfaction, for she felt a sort of maternal pride towards the girl with stunning Nordic looks. A snowy-haired beauty with large eyes the colour of cornflowers, slender and shaped with grace. 'Her mother was a local woman, her father a sailor. She's a good worker, as is Jim, although he's a bright spark and takes a bit of handling.'

'I think I can carry on by myself, Miss Em, if you want to go in for a yarn with Cap'n Harvey,' Sara said, as if awestruck. Jonathan's account of his father, on his return from London, stretched his being a hero to a saviour.

Tristan was astonished by the sweetness of her voice.

'You should hear her sing. The rector trained her to sing part of the *Messiah* and she's performed it in church for the war fund. It's funny, but it seems like she and Jim have always been here,' Emilia said, as she and Tristan walked through the yard.

He was devouring the familiar sights. His old home, the well, the barn, the stables, the animal and store houses. The pigs, the goats, the pond, the cackling poultry bidding him a raucous welcome. It was good to see Pip chasing the cats. Tristan was striving for normality, for a little peace in his soul.

'Does it seem you were always meant to marry Alec and not Ben? To me, nothing at all seems real. And here's the other surprising-looking individual you have here now.'

Archie had come out of the washhouse, where he had been keeping the furnace fuelled for Tilda. He touched his forelock to Tristan. Tristan hastened as best he could to him and grasped his hand. 'No, no, I won't accept that from you. We have a lot in common. My brother's told me about you. I'm pleased to meet you, Mr Rothwell.'

Emilia watched, pleased, as Archie answered in quiet respect, not guarded, not pulling away. The sound of Sara's singing flowed out of the dairy. Archie's eyes drifted that way. Emilia frowned. At every opportunity Archie watched Sara.

'I don't like the look of you one bit,' Alec told Tristan at supper, which, for his homecoming, was being eaten in the dining room. Alec wouldn't hear of the table being waited on, and Tilda and the Killigrews were eating there too. 'After this, a good drenching with brandy will help set you up.'

'Thank you, but I thought I'd spend some time with Jonny.' Tristan had been adding to the jolly talk, but he wanted only to be alone with Jonathan. If not for Jonathan, he'd wish only to drift off to sleep and never wake up, now he was finally facing life as a deserted husband.

He smiled at the boy who had been allowed to stay down late for the occasion, and who, at regular intervals, slipped his hand inside Emilia's. 'You still don't know what to make of me, do you, son? I know I look little better than when you saw me in London, but it's definitely me, your daddy.'

'I know,' Jonathan said, shuffling his knife and fork.

'He'll come round,' Alec said.

'I know,' Tristan replied, but his dejection was plain.

'I think Grandma recognizes you, Tris. See how content she is? It's all due to Emilia.'

Emilia would be content now Tristan was home, presently safe, if it weren't for her concern about Honor. If Ben could change so much, would he be good to her? Honor had written to her, asking for her understanding over her and Ben's engagement, and stating that she was too busy for the moment to call at Ford Farm. Was Ben insisting she stay away? Ben's treachery, to Alec's delight, had not gone all his way. The two labourers of Tremore Farm had turned up asking for work, saying they didn't trust their new boss. Bernard Vickery was now living in Wayside Cot. Midge Roach had always lived with his wife's family in the village, but now took a different direction to work.

'Excuse me,' Tilda said self-consciously. 'Would you like some more beef pie, Captain Harvey?'

'Aha! Now there's a look of determination to build a fellow up, if ever I saw one,' Tristan grinned, as if he was suddenly his old self again – how he wanted to be. He patted his stomach, which appeared hollow even in his uniform. 'The doctors say I must take things quietly at first, Tilda.'

Jim Killigrew pushed his plate forward a fraction. Everyone heard Sara catch her breath. Raised for half their life in the workhouse in Truro, they were partly institutionalized and usually waited for permission to do even the simplest thing. The restraints were fast losing their hold on Jim.

'Feed him up, Tilda,' Alec bawled down the table. 'He's already built like an ox, but like any chap his age he can do justice to his meals. Eh, darling?'

'What? Oh, yes, Alec.' Emilia was still getting used to his public endearments. She saw to Lottie, who was intent on stirring her dessert spoon round and round in the remains of her dinner.

Tilda nodded at Sara and they began to clear the dishes.

Tristan said, 'I'll go over to see Ben and his bride-to-be

tomorrow. I'll take Jonny and Grandma with me. Now I'm home, I'm hoping you and he will make up your differences, Alec.'

Emilia shot a look at Alec. He clamped his mouth shut.

Tristan breathed heavily. He'd say no more about it for now.

'I'm glad Uncle Ben's gone. I don't like him,' Jonathan said, sharp and grumpy.

'Why's that, Jonny?' Tristan asked.

'I don't think he liked me. Can I go up to Jim's room after pudding, Daddy? Just for a minute? He's got something for me.'

'And what is that?' Tristan asked the older boy. Jim Killigrew didn't possess the same perfect quality of features as his twin, but his blond unruly hair and deep blue eyes hinted that a good face would be reached in time.

Jim shifted but looked Tristan in the eye. ''Tis a model aeroplane, sir. I carved it out of wood, copied it from a picture in a book Master Jonny showed me.'

'Just for a minute then, Jonny.' Tristan forced a smile at his son. It hurt to his soul to see how Jonathan had moved on with his life without him.

Emilia was in bed when Alec slipped in beside her. 'You can't stay tonight,' she said, sitting up in panic. 'It's too much of a risk with Tristan in the next room.'

'I know, but I hate it when I can't say goodnight to you like this.' He pulled her down, and his kisses made her forget the fear of disgrace if they were discovered.

Then she was wriggling away from him. Alec knew so many ways to make love and every way to make her respond to him. 'If we go on like this you're going to have to talk to Dad again.'

'With all my heart I hope so. Now Tris is here I'm going to try to persuade Edwin to let us marry before the six months' mourning for Billy is over. A wedding would cheer Tris up more than anything else I can think of, and I'm sure Billy wouldn't have minded.'

Emilia recalled Billy's appearance on the Newquay cliffs. 'No, he wouldn't have.' She snuggled back into Alec's warm, sensitive body. 'Sometimes, Alec Harvey, you can be so smug.'

'I'm happy at last, that's all.'

She caressed his neck and chest, knowing he liked soft fingertips there. 'Alec, I've been thinking.'

'About what to call our first child? I want at least half a dozen noisy brats tearing about the place. Think we can manage that?'

'I don't doubt it for a moment. Seriously though, considering what might happen if Tristan returns to battle, and weighing up what's really important, shouldn't you think about what he said about you and Ben making things up? I mean, it's not pleasant, us not speaking while we live in the same parish. I miss Honor so much. I'd like to go over to Tremore with the others tomorrow to see her – your gran will need me to care for her anyway. You wouldn't mind? Alec?'

He was lacing his fingers through her hair, something he always did when they were intimate. 'You may go anywhere you like at any time, Emilia darling, with or without Grandma. Of course you want to see Honor. She's still welcome here.'

'What about Ben?'

'I don't know anyone called Ben.'

She raised herself up and looked down on him in the candlelight. He had not tensed, the tone of his voice had not hardened, but there was something unyielding about him. She knew no matter how much she argued or pleaded he would not compromise. Then she had it. 'You don't forgive, do you?' Was this what Ben had meant about her not knowing what Alec was really like?

'It depends . . .'

'On what? Wouldn't you yourself have to be flawless for such harshness to be justified?'

'Is there something you wish to know, Emilia?'

She was facing the rest of her life of sharing a bed with this man, of helping to run his farm. He knew Ben had been her first lover – she had the right to his secrets. 'Well, I've always wondered why Maudie left so suddenly. And this is a bit delicate, is it true you took a mistress before Lucy died?'

Alec leaned against the bedstead and pillows. 'Someone's obviously been saying things about me. Very well, I've got nothing to hide. Lucy accused Maudie of flirting with me and she flogged her. Went up to the attics one night with a horsewhip. The rage Lucy was in, the poor girl might have lost half the flesh on her back if I hadn't intervened. The next day I escorted Maudie to the railway station, saw her off to Redruth, to a cousin's, and I had to pay her not to report Lucy to the police. As for the woman I was seeing, the widowed Eugenie Bawden, yes, I started with her before Lucy's death, but not until I'd done my best to make my marriage work. It was for company rather than sex. Someone's been trying to turn you against me, Emilia. It has to be Ben. If you still have doubts about me, ask yourself if any woman in the village, or even yourself, has ever been bothered by me.'

'If I'd thought you were a libertine, Alec, I wouldn't have stayed downstairs with you in Winifred's house.' Emilia was sorry she had brought the issues up. Ben's lies would reinforce Alec's reasons not to forgive him. She didn't like Alec to brood.

'Do you want to know about Lucy? I never loved her. At the end I think I hated her. There was nothing to admire about her, as there is you. I've wanted you for a long time, my darling angel. I intend never to be without you.'

Chapter Twenty-One

Emilia drove the trap over to Tremore Farm. While Tristan and Jonathan were helping Lottie down, she wondered how Honor, if she was here, would receive her.

Then Honor came running and waving, skirting around Sully, leaping over a startled clucking hen, out into the lane. She looked so pretty and excited, and out of place in front of the ancient, weathered, inadequate farmstead. A rescued damsel brought not to a castle, but a hovel. She shouldn't be wearing an apron over an old dress. Her glorious hair should be flowing free down her back, not restrained by a headscarf, tied gipsy-style. Then Emilia realized these were her own expectations for Honor, and she had no right to them. Her friend had endured this from others all her life. But what plans did Ben have for her?

'Em! What a lovely surprise. I saw you coming from upstairs. Aunt Florence and I are here most days helping out, although I think Eliza would prefer it if we left her to it.'

Eliza Shore, the only female living and working at Tremore Farm was putting two buckets on a yoke across her broad shoulders to fetch water inside from the well. 'S'pose you'll be wanting tea?' An insincere offer. Blunt and coarse, a tower of a woman, about forty, heavy-footed, dressed like a man, her hair chopped off at ear-length, she nodded hello to Emilia.

'I'll see to it, Eliza. You carry on,' Honor said.

'Goodness, Em, that woman scares me. She drinks and smokes and swears. Aunt Florence wants Ben to dismiss her but he won't hear of it. Mind you, she's capable and hard-working.

Makes a light loaf and delicious butter, does good work with the laundry, and fetching and carrying, but she doesn't dust a thing.' Honor added in a whisper, 'And she smells.'

Emilia took her friend in a tight hug. 'Are you going to be happy, Honor?'

'Yes, I think so. I'll make it work. We must talk, I know. I wasn't going to leave it much longer before coming over to see you, honestly. How's Tilda? And Archie?'

'They send their regards.' Emilia linked her arm through Lottie's.

'Well, well.' Lottie stared at a tuft of brownish grass growing out of the wall. 'I had one just like that.'

'That's lovely, Lottie.' Emilia patted her gloved hand.

Florence Burrows appeared at the front door. 'Captain Harvey! God be praised for your safe return. And Mrs Harvey and Mrs Harvey-to-be are here as well to visit the other Mrs Harvey-to-be, how splendid. And Master Jonathan, you must be thrilled to have your daddy home?'

'He's a hero,' Jonathan said, making faces at the poor surroundings.

Florence flushed and cleared her throat. 'We're going to be terribly busy for some time, as you can see. Has Honor told you about the renovations and extensions planned for Bracken House, Emilia? We're going to change the name to Tremore House, more in keeping, of course.'

'It means we're going to have to move in here for a few months,' Honor said. 'I can't say I'm looking forward to it, especially with the deepest of winter still to get through.'

'But the sooner it's finished, the sooner Honor and Ben can get married,' Florence broke in. 'Come along everyone, into the sitting room. Honor, you run along and fetch Ben.'

With the help of Albie Trewin, Ben had pulled down the wire netting, straw and sacking that made up the badly fitting roof of his cowhouse. Next they had emptied the inside, and while Ben lit a bonfire of the rubbish, he had sent Albie to fetch buckets of hot water, soda and antiseptic.

'We'll do this together today, but you'll know what to do

if I ask you to do something like it again, Albie.' Patiently, Ben showed the pallid-faced, skinny youth how to dip his broom into a bucket and scrub down the walls and rough stone flooring. They scrubbed until Ben was satisfied any trace of the viral pneumonia that was affecting his small herd had been eradicated. Then they washed away the filthy water with fresh bucketsful drawn from the pump.

'Mug of tea, boss?' Albie wiggled his cap, which he always wore pushed back from his broad forehead, and nodded and grinned, revealing the gap in his lower teeth, a legacy of the bullying from his greengrocer employer. He was short and stooped and seemed like a wizened old man.

'Hey, you,' Ben laughed. 'We haven't finished yet.'

'Mug of tea, five minutes, boss?' Albie repeated the nodding and grinning. 'Miss 'Onor said so.'

'Ten more, Albie.' Ben held up his fingers and thumbs.

Albie had no conception of time, but he contentedly whooshed his brush into a bucket, knowing he would get his tea in due course. His mind incapable of holding on to the knowledge of his two former positions, he believed his parents were only recently dead, and he was convinced Ben was his and Cyril's godfather, the person now responsible for their welfare. Honor, with her golden hair and her caring ways was an angel to him, and he was convinced that Florence Burrows, whom he was in awe of, was connected to royalty. He had addressed her, 'Duchess, ma'am.' She had been amused and the label had stuck.

Honor came flying across the cobbles, holding up her skirt. 'Ben! Ben!'

'You shouldn't be here, sweetheart. You'll get yourself messy,' he said.

'You've got to come. Now!' She always had a hard task to part Ben from his work. He was determined to get Tremore Farm into reasonable order before Christmas.

'If there's a crisis inside, then you and your aunt will have to cope with it on your own. I haven't got time to chase out a wandering cow, catch a mouse or unblock a sink, and nor has Albie. Ask Eliza to do whatever it is.'

'It's nothing like that, dear. It's—'

'Your older brother,' Tristan said, appearing in the yard. 'Have you got time to stop for me?'

'Tris!' Ben threw the broom down and hurried to shake Tristan's hand. Then he threw his arms around his neck. 'Did you come straight here off the train?'

'I arrived yesterday. I've brought Jonny and Grandma with me. They're inside.'

'Albie, sweep all the rinsing water out of the cowhouse, but whatever you do, don't put anything, not anything, inside. It's got to stay empty for two weeks, a long time. Understand?'

''Es, boss,' he said. 'Mug of tea, Miss 'Onor?'

'I'll send Eliza out with one for you, Albie.' Honor walked away with Ben, who wrapped his arm round her trim waist.

'Congratulations to you both,' Tristan said. 'I'm sorry I missed your engagement party.'

'It was just a quiet meal with friends at the Red Lion. Honor looked beautiful, of course,' Ben said. 'It's so good to see you, Tris, you obviously took a pasting. You'd do a fine job as a scarecrow at the moment. Listen, about Ursula. I'm glad you got my letter eventually. I didn't know what to write at first. Kept hoping she'd give him up, then when she left, I thought the plain facts were the only thing I could say. I'm sorry this homecoming isn't to be a happy one.'

'Well, it's good to be with Jonny.' Tristan said no more: it was too personal. He couldn't help feeling worried about Ursula – despite everything, he still loved her.

'I wish I knew something to say to help you.'

'Time – that's the great cure-all, isn't it? I'm sorry about your eye, Ben, but you have a new future to look forward to with your lovely bride. You're having a few problems, I see.'

'The fields are in pretty good order but Dick Buzza should have retired years ago. This latest problem could have been prevented, of course, if all the draughts had been stopped up. There's enough good waste material lying about to make a new roof, it will tidy things up at the same time. I'm looking to increase all my stock by the spring. The inspector was here yesterday and he's impressed. Going to see about getting a Land Girl or two.'

While Honor went to her guests in the sitting room, Ben pulled off his boots and washed in the back kitchen, a lean-to roofed by rusted galvanized sheeting. On the rows of haphazard shelving was an argument of cooking utensils, cleaning agents and tools. 'I've got a hundred and eighty-six acres, and there's a lot of virgin land that should have been cleared. I've managed to get hold of a builder to renovate Bracken House, he'll take a lot of what he needs from the old manor.'

'I'm happy for you, Ben. I understand how devastated you must be over missing out on a regimental career.'

'Thanks, Tris. It's good to hear someone say that. I don't think Alec cared all that much about how it affected me. He was too wrapped up in fathering Jonny, and plotting to take Emilia away from me.'

'Is that how you see it? I don't know the full details of what happened, but I can hardly believe Emilia would be so fickle.'

'She was entirely responsible for our splitting up: it's her damned fault I'm partially blind. You ought to be careful, Tris. Alec can be subtle, he might like to take over your son.'

'He wants a family of his own, not mine.' Tristan patted his brother's shoulder. 'Try not to feel bitter over what was a disastrous stroke of luck, Ben.'

In the bleak sitting room, made peculiarly distinguished by some of Florence's elaborate curtains, Emilia noticed things belonging to Ben. A tie was cast carelessly over an overstuffed chair. Among his books was the dog-eared notebook in which he'd jotted down the scores of some of their childhood games. She had written him a love poem on the flyleaf. She opened the cover. He had ripped the poem out – she felt hurt by that and strangely abandoned.

Being in an unfamiliar place, Lottie was clinging to her hand and it was several minutes before she started up her habitual humming. Jonathan, bored and restless, made actions as if using a slingshot. Jim had introduced him to the delights of a real one – which had soon caused Alec to yell at Jim when Jonathan had deliberately startled the poultry. Florence came in with the tea tray, and Honor followed her.

All went quiet when the two men arrived.

Ben and Emilia stared at each other for a full ten seconds. Then as if he was chewing something sour, he said, 'I suppose Grandma needs the services of someone for her visits to the unmentionable.'

Emilia did not lower her steady gaze at him. The atmosphere seemed to crackle with animosity and Florence quickly enquired about Captain Harvey's health.

'I'm healing slowly,' Tristan replied. 'What happens next depends on this ankle.'

'Well, all I can say is it's an honour to have such a brave officer in our midst.' Florence's voice was husky with emotion. 'So terrible, the number of our casualties, thousands and thousands lost. I feel sad for all those poor wives and mothers.'

Ben dropped his head, and Emilia guessed he was festering with the same humiliation that had caused him to unjustly accuse her of causing his blindness.

'Have you set a date for your wedding, Em?' Honor asked, self-conscious and pink, but the subject might as well be aired and done with.

'Not yet, April probably.' The wood on the fire was damp, the logs smouldering. A sudden crackle and flare of anaemic flame took her eyes to the fireplace. The tiles were cracked and soot-stained; the carpet didn't meet the edge of the dented brass fender, and was frayed and grubby from generations of slumbering dogs and cats.

'Well,' Florence said, as if she had been criticized. 'We've all got what we wanted, now it's up to us to make the best of it.'

Florence had brought in some savoury patties, and while Emilia passed one on a plate to Lottie, the sudden greasy smell made her feel nauseous. As the tea was drunk and the patties eaten by the others, she was growing hotter and hotter, and feeling dizzy and strange. Her stomach heaved and she shot to her feet. 'I'm sorry, I feel faint. I'll have to go outside.'

Nearest to the door, Tristan opened it for her as she picked her way past feet and the various encumbered spaces. The crisp late November air revived her, but on her apologetic return she found herself almost at once in the same predicament.

As she hastened for the door again, Ben stationed himself in front of her. 'It would appear the next local wedding will have to brought forward.' He raised a sardonic eyebrow. 'It is safe to assume that?'

Emilia dashed a hand to her mouth and pushed past him. She stayed outside. If the sickness hadn't prevented re-entry, her embarrassment would have done.

'I've brought you a glass of water. Can I get you anything else?' Honor joined her at the side of the house, which looked over some of Ben's under-harvested fields.

'No, thanks.' Emilia sipped the water and took a deep breath. 'I'm sorry it's ruined our visit. I so wanted to talk to you alone, but it's not going to be possible with your aunt's constant tittle-tattle.'

'I'm sorry about Ben's lack of tact. Are you pregnant, Em?'

'I think so. I'm always regular and now I'm several days late.'

'Could it be Ben's? I've guessed that you and he . . .'

'It's definitely Alec's. You must think me loose.'

'We women submit either out of love or because we must. Ben hasn't made advances to me.' Honor's voice grew winsome. 'But then he's always seen you and I in a different light. I know he doesn't love me, Em, but he's good to me. He says I'm everything he wants in a wife. I'm content with that. My future was looking horribly dim before.'

'But if Ben hadn't played his dirty trick, Alec would be your landlord now. Is this life better for you? One half of a loveless marriage?'

'Whatever you think of him, he's still the same old Ben inside. Now it's my turn to be frank, Em. Ben's right about one thing. Alec hankered after you for a long time, he might not be above manipulating things for his own ends too.'

'Oh, I think I know all about Alec. I didn't go into our relationship with my eyes closed. Setting him and Ben aside, let's agree we'll always be friends, Honor. I'm going to need your support. My dad's going to be furious and disappointed with me.'

'He won't take it so hard after losing Billy, I'm sure. He'll come round when it sinks in he has a grandchild to look forward to.'

Chapter Twenty-Two

'Well, Edwin, have you got over the shock of looking forward to becoming a grandfather yet?'

Outside the church, where the Christmas Eve wedding party were posing for photographs, all eyes of both families, guests and villagers, turned on Edwin Rowse to see how he answered Ben's question.

Emilia glanced anxiously at her father. He had not spoken to her or Alec since being informed of her disgrace, and had walked her up the aisle, pursed-lipped and staring ahead. Dolly, in a hat loaned her by the rector's wife, dewy-eyed and hoping for a grandson, peeped round Edwin and slipped Emilia an encouraging smile.

Edwin stuck out his chest, seeming to grow several inches in stature. 'The answer's yes, to you in partic'lar, seeing as how I approve of who the father is.'

Alec studied Ben's burning face with pious nonchalance, then ignored him. Emilia was sad to see Honor pinched and self-conscious. Before she and Alec climbed up on the trap for the journey to the farm for the reception, Ben and Honor were gone – in Julian Andrews' motor car, she was later to learn from Tilda.

Tristan allowed Jonathan to go on to the farm with Winifred, Great-Aunt Clarissa and Vera Rose. He stayed in the churchyard to pay his respects to his parents' grave. Henry's name was inscribed under theirs on the headstone. Not far away Billy Rowse's name was remembered on a simple wooden cross, of Edwin's making. At least Alec and Emilia were salvaging something out of the insanity. A child was to be born. New life. Nothing gave greater hope. The merest touch of innocent spring in this God-forsaken world of winter.

On his way out he looked in the area of more recent burials but couldn't find a grave belonging to Lucy. Then he remembered the letter informing him that the Pollards had taken her body away from the farm as well as all her things.

His mind turned to Ursula, he couldn't keep her out of it. Worrying and fretting about her. She was to have a child, another man's child. *Don't think about that. Imagine she's dead. It's the only way.* But if she was abandoned, all alone, with no money and no honest way to make a living. *Dear, God, not that for her.* She might even be dead. He couldn't bear that thought.

He limped on over the gravel path, trying to keep his mind on his next duty, a speech for the reception, not seeing the woman on the other side of the lychgate until he had climbed down the steps outside. He made to lift his cap but solidified on the spot. She was even more pale and drawn than himself. Her clothes were soiled, her hair was in tangles, fading bruises mottled her face. She was big in pregnancy and about to faint.

'Ursula!' He hurried the small distance to her and caught her before she hit the ground.

Jim Killigrew had his eye on the wedding fare, a good spread despite the ever-tightening rationing, set around tall candles encircled by holly. Used to scant workhouse food, he was savouring a dip into the meat pies, while flicking over the wines with dishonest intent.

'Don't you dare,' Sara, in ribbons and her one good dress, warned him. She was waiting to entertain the gathering with a song or two, but the proceedings were being held up by Captain Harvey's absence.

'Master wouldn't mind.' Jim received a disapproving frown from Tilda, intimating he should move away from the dining table and stop slouching with his hands in his pockets. Jim blew her a kiss and she tut-tutted and he blew her another. Of the few things he took seriously, one was outsmarting those who thought themselves superior, another was his duty to protect his twin, and her extraordinary beauty meant he was having to watch out for her more and more.

From the window he saw Archie Rothwell in the garden. There could only be one reason the strange-eyed cripple was this close to the house and so many people. Sara. He never missed an opportunity to ogle her. Mr Harvey may respect him, but Jim thought the same as some of the villagers, that there was something 'not quite right' about him.

'What are you doing here?' Jim confronted Archie on the lawn.

Archie had his smarter Red Cross donated clothes on. He was using two walking sticks, the second once belonging to an ancestral Harvey; Alec had persuaded him he'd keep his balance better with a second aid. He regarded Jim with mutual distrust. 'It's none of your business, boy. Go away.'

Jim leaned towards Archie's face. 'I know your game, mister, but don't think for a moment I'd let you get your hands on my sister. What're you always hanging around her for? You're old enough to be her father. Disgusting, that's what it is. You're one of those perverts, aren't you? I've heard you at night, all those weird noises you make, it's not bad dreams, like Mr Harvey reckons. I learned all about your sort in the workhouse. Your mind's either gone west or you've been like it all your life. It's why you want to keep everything about yourself a secret, ain't it?' Jim produced some shocking swear words. 'Don't forget, I'm watching you. Upset Sara and I'll have you. Get all that?'

A tiny muscle worked in Archie's cheek, his fair complexion was suffused with blood. 'You're accusing me of something so unspeakable? That I'm . . . it's so unfair, so cruel.' Keeping his eyes on the ground, he stumbled out of the garden.

Satisfied, Jim's thoughts returned to the food waiting to be eaten inside. If Captain Harvey didn't come soon he'd have to go back to his jobs, and even though Tilda would put something aside for him, he'd miss the best stuff.

Then he saw the captain hobbling up the front path, carrying a burden. He raced towards him, shouting, 'Miss Em – Mrs Em, it's the Captain at last and something's up!'

'Your fiancée's a sweet little thing, Ben,' Polly Hetherton said. It was long past dinner, Honor had gone up to her room for the overnight stay, and Julian was asleep in his chair.

'Yes, she is, very sweet,' he replied. He was taking in the modish simplicity of Polly's small drawing room. Christmas decorations were kept to the minimum, but few houses had the heart for the festivities. There was nothing fussy or dull or packed in. Pristine white paint and light colours; smooth lines to furnishings; paintings of shapes and abstract figures, and the occasional eye-catching bronze figure or glass ornament; all as if Polly had something new to say. He might have a similar approach in his new house. Honor had said she liked it. She shared none of her aunt's stuffiness.

Yes, Polly had flair and originality. There was a lot he admired about her. She was well travelled, intelligent and witty. Now he was a landowner, the difference in their ages and experiences seemed less marked. Not that she had ever made him feel patronized. They had talked a lot when Julian drifted off into his often and necessary sleeps, and she had understood, as a friend would, how he felt, even now, about the things he had lost, and why and how he had won his property.

'I can still hardly believe you're thinking of getting married, you're so young, Ben.' Polly brought him a brandy for which he was grateful. Before this, alcohol had not been drunk because of Julian's necessary abstention. 'Are you going to be happy with Honor? She's a different prospect to the other girl. That one's got spirit, an earthy beauty, which I believe you prefer.'

'It will be a long engagement, Polly. May I ask if you were happy with your husband?'

'We were a good match, but there was no spark, that something special, if you know what I mean.'

'I thought Emilia was someone special. Well, that's in the past, dead and gone.' Ben looked fondly at Julian, his skin was almost translucent, veins visible in thin rivers, his lips blue. 'I suppose I'd better get his nibs up to his room.'

'I'd be grateful if you would. I'll come with you.'

Ben carried Julian's light weight up the stairs, then he and Polly undressed him and laid him in bed. 'He looks even more of a boy than when I knew him at school,' Ben observed.

Polly slipped her hand inside Ben's, her voice a tremulous whisper: 'I'm so afraid of losing him. I know it's inevitable, but I'm hoping it won't be for many years yet. Help me to look after him, Ben. Promise me you will?'

'I'd do anything for him, I owe him more than he'll ever know. Did you know he had a notion to marry Honor? But he accepted that I'd asked her first with all his charm and grace. Perhaps I should have stepped out of his way.'

'No, Ben, they would have made each other miserable. She adores you, and Julian couldn't have been a husband to her at all, you understand? He fools around, but his heart isn't strong enough to make a proper bedfellow. He's got me and you as the friends he's always wanted. It's enough, God bless him. Enough for him, while for some of us . . .' Polly pressed the palm of her other hand on Ben's chest. 'We expect, we hope for something more.'

Ben found Honor waiting for him in his room. 'Darling, is something the matter?' There was a disapproving knot in her brow, an agitation in her delicate hands. Obviously she wasn't here to share his bed, uninhibited away from her suffocating aunt. Hell, how that overbearing woman annoyed him – he'd have to find a little cottage for her before his marriage, far enough away where she couldn't interfere.

Like a shadow Honor moved up close to him, sweetly gorgeous in demure white silk, smelling divine. 'Where have you been all this time? I want to speak to you.'

'I was talking to Julian, he's going to help put a bit of business my way. It's the chance . . . well, never mind. Then he dropped off and I carried him up to bed.'

There was something schoolmarmish in Honor's expression. 'Ben, you shouldn't have said what you did to Mr Rowse.'

He loosened his tie. 'What? Why are you bringing that up now?'

'It was Emilia's wedding day. It was a horrible thing to say in front of her family, with practically the whole village there and Alec's business friends.'

'You've been waiting all day to say this to me? Is *she* more important to you than I am? Are you angry because I embarrassed you? Is appearances all that matter?' Ben was irritated by her displeasure. Few people allowed him to lead his life without advice and recriminations. Polly was one of those few.

'I'm not trying to be quarrelsome, dear. I don't think there's a need for all this continuing unpleasantness. Emilia's been my friend all my life. The village children didn't want to mix with me because of Aunt Florence's attitude, and I had no one except for her, Billy and you. We all used to mean so much to each other. Why can't we let bygones rest and try to lead a happy life?'

'Because life's not a game, Honor.'

He turned from her, wanting her to go. Just now Polly's touch and sympathy had invoked desire in him, but Honor had no effect on him in that way. She was lovely, but she could never make him want her just by thinking about her; as Emilia had done. She was insubstantial, a child, incompatible with a man who had a man's needs.

Since leaving his brother's wedding, he had been thinking about how he had got himself engaged to a creature of fairytale, a doll, while the bride today was a woman in body, soul and spirit. Emilia's kisses had been filled with passion, and passion had been in her every touch. Through his eagerness and inexperience he had hurt her that time in Tristan's bed, but she had still given him all she could, and just at the end she had discovered the same joys, which in subsequent times would have been exciting and fulfilling for both of them. Alec, damn him, would be receiving her woman's love tonight, while all he was likely to get, if he seduced Honor, was a little chaste reaction and half pleasure. He felt cheated all over again.

He turned back, kissed Honor's forehead. 'Look, darling,

you run along and enjoy a good night's sleep in the sort of surroundings your aunt's always wanted for you. I'm not tired. Think I'll pop down to the study and go over those figures Julian and I were looking at. See you at breakfast.'

'What figures, Ben? What business? By your reaction just now you must think I'm not capable of understanding such matters.'

He would never tell her the business was illegal, hiding black-market goods in his farm buildings. He was going to build his own little empire, and for that he wanted to make a lot of money fast. 'Not now, Honor. I just want you to enjoy yourself.'

He escorted her to her bedroom door. Then instead of going downstairs, he lingered at the other end of the landing, outside Polly's bedroom. Had he read her signals right? If he tapped on her door would he make a terrible fool of himself? He wished he had the sophistication to know about these sorts of things.

The door opened. Her hair loose, in an exotic nightdress that exposed one long leg to the thigh, Polly beckoned him in.

Emilia came out from behind the screen of the master bedroom. 'Alec . . .'

He was staring into nothing, still dressed, the champagne he had brought upstairs unopened.

She swished the filmy folds of her nightgown, the only one she had ever worn with a décolletage and leaving her arms bare. 'Alec, what do you think?' This was her wedding night, the union she was expecting to share with him need not be quick or furtive, and she was feeling a little shy.

At last she gained his attention. He came to her. 'I think you're the most beautiful bride a man could ever have. Sit down, darling. I'll brush your hair.'

He employed the hairbrush with gentle devotion, gliding, smoothing with his hands, but his reflection in her mirror was set tight. She turned round to him. 'I know what's on your mind. Please don't let Ursula being here spoil this night for us.'

'I'm worried she'll upset Tris and Jonny again. I don't understand why Tris was so eager to give her succour after all she's done to him.'

'He still loves her.' Emilia caressed his face, hoping to ease away his stern expression. 'Darling, I wish you didn't brood so.'

He moved to the champagne, dithered with it. 'I suppose I've got into the habit of building up my defences, for myself and those I feel responsible for.'

She followed him. 'Do you think Tris needs to lay down defences against Ursula? She's been beaten and abandoned, has had to beg for food and has practically walked all the way back here from Bristol. Anything terrible could have happened to her, perhaps did. Don't you find some sympathy for her?'

'None, and I'll never trust her.' He thumped the bottle down on the tray, making her blink. 'She chose to go off with a man I hate and she knows the reason why – that shows me what sort of character Ursula is. And do you want to know why I hate Ashley? It's because he helped Lucy to kill my baby!'

As suddenly as he'd flown into a fury, he was swiping at the tears flooding down his face. 'I'm sorry, I should have told you before, not now, when a woman's got the right to be at her happiest. Forgive me, Emilia. But Lucy did it to spite me. We'd agreed, you see, that once she'd given birth I'd release her from the marriage. She had suddenly declared that she'd never wanted children, that she only married me because she didn't want Eugenie to have me. I was even going to allow her to divorce me as the guilty party. Then she saw Maudie larking about in front of me and she got rid of my baby, even though it was a dangerous thing to do in the later months. The botched-up affair cost her her life, but rather than dying in fear or making peace with her Maker, she taunted me to her last breath. I can't forgive and forget that, Emilia, please don't ask me to.'

Emilia took hold of his hands. 'All I ask, Alec, is that you look forward to our baby. I want it with all my heart and lots more children too, and I want you in the same way. I'm glad I know how Lucy really died, even on our wedding night. It means we can look forward to the future with no secrets, only our hopes and dreams. I love you, Alec. You can trust me. Say you'll try.'

It seemed as if heavy scales of despair fell away from him and he visibly relaxed. 'I love you, Emilia, and of course, I trust you. You and Tris are the only two people I really trust in the world, and I'd do anything, absolutely anything, to protect you both and his and our children.'

He kissed her, finally opened the champagne and the wedding night began. Long after he had fallen asleep in her arms, blissfully replete from their passionate lovemaking and their new empathy, Emilia lay thinking about this complex man she had married. She had told Honor she thought she knew all about Alec. Now she was sure she did not, and she was glad. She did not want someone boring and easy to read, whom she could take for granted.

Alec stirred and his hand came to rest over where their baby was growing inside her. Emilia was consumed with love and joy. Ursula was back because she had made a mistake. Honor was definitely making a mistake with her future. She, herself, knew that whatever lay ahead, she had done the right thing.

Chapter Twenty-Three

'You did it, Daddy. You found Mummy and brought her back. It's better than anything Father Christmas will bring me.' All night long Jonathan's excited, trusting words echoed inside Tristan's head in the same way the ghosts of the bombardments still did.

'My dear boy,' Tristan whispered through the bleak lonely hours, watching Jonathan lying asleep in perfect ease next to his mother, unaware of what the bump protruding from her body was, or what it meant to his father.

'Please, Tristan, let me stay,' Ursula had begged him after coming round in this room, shortly after Alec and Jim had carried her upstairs. 'I went to my parents but they turned me away. I was so relieved when the maid called after me that you were alive, and home and well. I didn't know where else to go.'

She had wept and hugged Jonathan until he had cried out. 'Oh, Jonny, Jonny, I've missed you so much. It's been unbearable. I should never have gone. Let me stay, Tris,' she had whispered. 'Please don't tear me away from my boy again.'

How could he dismiss her pleas? Leaving Jonny behind must have been the hardest decision of her life, and Jonny loved and needed his mother. She was ill and hurt and almost starved. She and her lover had been forced to hide from the successive troubles he had brought on them from the law, various landlords and crooked associates. Tristan hated Bruce Ashley for that.

Tristan was so close to the bed that Ursula's dull, lifeless black hair was only an inch from his arm. She was thinner.

Her skin, where not bruised from a violent beating, was parchment white. He could smell her. That wonderful, exquisite sweetness was still the same. He couldn't bring himself to touch her, and didn't know if he ever could again. She was contaminated. Bruce Ashley was on her and in her, and Tristan wished him dead. He wanted Ashley to suffer. At that moment, he felt he would not hesitate to try to kill him.

Ursula moaned in her sleep, as if in fear, in anguish. She snapped her eyes open as if sensing menace. Gasping, she tugged Jonathan to her as if seeking protection from his little body. Her chest heaving, she expelled a frightened breath.

'You're quite safe,' Tristan said, and he was mystified at how soft and calm his voice sounded. He wanted to comfort her. He couldn't help himself.

'Th-thank you, Tris. Thank you for taking me in. I'm sorry, I'm so sorry.' She was weeping in full flood, at times incoherent, but he was able to cipher her pleadings. 'I made a dreadful mistake. Please don't think too badly of me. Did you read my letter?'

'No, I couldn't bring myself to. What does it say?'

She reached out a hand. Tristan flinched inside but outwardly it seemed he had merely ignored it. He had touched the dead many times, bodies of men and animals, some horribly corrupted, but he couldn't touch her.

'It asks you to forgive me, and begging you that if I made a good life for myself to allow me to see Jonny three or four times a year. It all went wrong, Tris. I was so ashamed, I didn't want Jonny to know my humiliation, so I never wrote to him, although I wanted to so much. You won't send me away, will you?'

'No, of course not, Ursula.'

'Thank you. I knew you wouldn't really, although you have no reason to be kind to me.' She used the hem of the sheet to dry her eyes. 'What happens now?'

A sudden wave of weariness came over Tristan. His head felt as if it had taken a battering. His nerves were shredded, his bones ached. He had suffered enough of thinking and wishing and hoping. He felt abused. All used up. 'The district nurse says you must have bed rest for the next few weeks, and Alec is prepared to let you stay here for your – for your confinement.'

'And then?' she went on, anxious again.

'I can't think that far ahead now. You must excuse me, I'm so tired.'

If he didn't get out of the room he would suffocate, lose his mind. Ursula was back and had brought a whole lot of new problems with her, not least what to do about her baby. He didn't want to think about that. He staggered to the door, stumbled blindly to Henry's room, recently vacated by the bride. He fell down on the bed, wanting only to sleep and sleep.

Chapter Twenty-Four

'Ben, have you seen Sully?' Honor had slipped outside after breakfast to feed the old dog some scraps, becoming puzzled, and then worried at not finding him in any of his usual places near the house. Half an hour had passed and there was still no sign of him.

Ben was on his way to the office with the plans, and the builder who had made them, for Tremore House. 'I've got more important things to see to, Honor,' he replied, giving her brief eye contact. 'He'll turn up.'

'But it's so cold today. I don't think Sully usually goes off for as long as this.' Hearing Ben's impatient sigh, she answered with one of her own, marched away, wrapped herself up against the biting weather, and set out across the fields to look for Sully.

She was glad to get away from the shabby, draught-ridden farmhouse, where her opinions did not seem to matter. Where she was excluded in the discussion today over the extensions, including two more bedrooms, a conservatory and a balcony, of the house where she was to spend her married life. The improvements, during a time when such work was rare because of the war, was invoking unwelcome comments. Ben was impervious to them, declaring jealousy the cause. He was out to impress and he wasn't going to let anyone stand in his way. Granted, he had brought her catalogues and swatches of material to choose the new drapes and colours for Tremore House, but that was causing strife. Aunt Florence disagreed with her and Ben's simplistic choices and was demanding tradition and ostentation. Ben had muttered something like, 'You won't be living there anyway.' Did he have other plans for her aunt? Honor wouldn't see her pushed out.

If I can just get through the winter, Honor told herself, perhaps everything will be better. The house would be ready to move back into then, but she would happily forego its new luxuries if she could gain Ben's attention. Was it too much to ask to be courted a little? He drove himself hard and any spare time he gave to Julian Andrews and their business associates. He wouldn't say what the business was but it had to be dishonest. From time to time he and Cyril would disappear after dark with the workhorses and cart. With his plans for the house and the farm growing increasingly adventurous, how he was funding it was causing speculation, equal to that of why his brother had taken back his trollop of a wife, and why, on the other brother's wedding day, Archie Rothwell had suddenly disappeared.

Honor would never believe Jim Killigrew's vile assumptions about Archie. She had seen him at his gentlest. He was just an ordinary man who had been dealt a terrible fate, again and again. Where was he now? Damn that stupid workhouse boy.

Archie was lurching across a field on Tremore property. There had been a light fall of snow in the night, but he didn't hear the crunching noises his boots were making on the frozen tufts of grass. He was dreadfully thirsty. Just ahead was a well, where he assumed the farmhouse had got its original water supply. His throat was burning and his head was throbbing so much he could hardly focus to see. The fever that had afflicted his every sense during nearly all the four weeks he had slept rough was remorseless.

Hitching a ride on a cart on the outskirts of Hennaford on the afternoon of the wedding had been easy due to his smart appearance. The carter, an old, weather-grimaced, chattering smallholder, had been on his way to nearby Zelah. From there, travelling by foot or the kindness of others, Archie had moved on, taking pot luck in the destinations of St Newlyn East, Mitchell, Indian Queens, Holywell Bay and St Agnes, hoping always to be rid of his persistent cold. There had been no need to work for food – Alec Harvey had paid him a fair wage and he had saved it all. He'd washed in streams and rested in places away from humanity. Lonely every minute. So utterly lonely. Loneliness that had shredded his soul. But he couldn't have stayed on where someone had planned to cause such dreadful mindless trouble for him.

Yesterday, at Perranporth, while on the sea front, shivering with cold, the salty mist chapping his lips, believing, as he so often did since his ship had been sunk, that he'd be better off dead, he was startled when a woman in a formidable overcoat and no-nonsense hat, wearing a steely pince-nez clipped to a redoubtable nose, had thrust something into his hand. She had nearly unsettled his precarious balance, buffeted as he was by the cruel winds. 'You've done your bit, haven't you? Take this with my blessing.'

She'd walked away before he could gather his wits to respond. Her compassion made his thoughts sweep towards the gentle young woman who had earned his trust, his admiration. He had been disappointed to see so little of Honor Burrows since the time he had allowed her to get physically close to him, to ease away a little of his detachment. She was an amazing young woman. Others, not even Emilia Harvey, saw her strengths, recognized her needs. He couldn't go back to Ford Farm, but he'd likely find a welcome of a sort from Honor Burrows and her fiancé – Ben Harvey had always treated him with respect.

He had caught a horse-bus to Hennaford, eating the food the angel-in-disguise had given him. He could have been taken right into the village, for such was the horse-bus's route, but he got off at Henna Lane, where he had hitched his first lift, and walked the rest of the way via the back lanes until, forced by fever and dizziness and an unrelenting shower of rain, he had taken shelter in the manor ruins. He was tantalizingly close to his goal, but his crippled feet and steadily growing weakness prevented him making the last part of his journey.

He hadn't wanted to stay huddled in a corner of the stripped building, leaning against cold hostile stone where the panelling had been ripped away, under a scrap of ceiling. Comfortless, desolate – needing people, needing friends. But when the rain had eased, it had immediately turned to snow, then the darkness had fallen as if some mighty hand had dropped a heavy black curtain. He had tried to stay awake but his frailty had won. Woken by the screams of his own nightmares, he had panicked, not knowing where he was.

Then he had remembered Honor. She would be living at the farm now that work was being done on the former Bracken House. Next had been an agonizing wait for daylight, the struggle to get up and walk, and then the rampant thirst that urgently needed to be assuaged. Through a five-barred gate he had seen the well. From there it was only a short walk across the field to the farmhouse, and hopefully warmth and acceptance again. If not, he would find it impossible to bear out until the end of this day.

His feet never more painful, his breath coming in anguished gulps he was finally closing in on the well. And then he was going down, his sticks hurtling out of his hands, his hat tumbling to the iron-hard ground. He tried to fight the fall, but the moment after his knees struck the frozen sod his head hit something solid. He knew nothing more.

Honor was so deep in thought she didn't see the obstruction close to the well until she fell over it. A scream built up in her throat. She was half sprawled across a man's body. There was blood on his temple and matted in his hair. It was Archie Rothwell. He was dead.

Honor took her weight off him, pressed her hands either side off his stiff face, his beard frosted, his eyelids closed tight, as if frozen to his dramatic sad eyes. 'Oh, no, Archie. How did you come to this?'

Then he moaned and her nerves leapt in relief. He tried to raise his hand. She took it. 'Archie, can you hear me? It's Honor.' His eyelids flickered. She sought the farmyard but she could see no one about outside. 'Ben! Eliza!' It was unlikely anyone would hear her above the wailings of the wind.

'Ohh . . .' Archie was squinting up at her. 'Help me.'

This was the first time he had asked for anything and it made her want to cry for him. 'Don't worry, Archie, I'm going to look after you. Do you think you could get up?'

'Don't know. I came here to get a drink. Dizzy, fell, think I passed out.'

On the rim of the well she saw blood. She pressed her hanky to where he was bleeding. His rolled-up belongings were lying inches away and Honor reached for them and placed them under his head. 'Archie, I'm not strong enough to help you up on my own, but you couldn't walk far anyway. I'm going to get Ben. I promise I won't be long.'

The eyes that were usually piercing glazed over, and Honor tore back the way she had come.

Moments later she returned with Ben and Eliza. Archie was still unconscious.

Ben shook him, then more forcefully, but he didn't stir. He put his ear to his chest. 'His breathing's harsh. If we don't do something quick he'll die of pneumonia.'

'He might well have died if I hadn't gone looking for Sully,' Honor said. Someone else would have to look for the collie – Archie needed nursing.

'That bleddy old mutt come back just after you went out,' Eliza guffawed, before helping to heft Archie up and off to the farm.

'Aunt! What on earth do you think you're doing? You can't go through his things.'

'Don't be foolish, Honor. We've a stranger, with the most terrible rumours circulating about him, lying on the sitting-room couch, and we've the right to know more about him than his name.' Florence Burrows was gingerly rifling through Archie's bedroll, which had been dropped on the kitchen floor. She paused. 'But Ben knows something about him, doesn't he? He was eager to take care of him, and obviously doesn't believe he's an ungrateful wastrel or worse.'

'Alec Harvey trusted him. So does Ben.' Honor placed her hands over Archie's things. 'That's all we need to know.'

Florence set sharp eyes on her. 'You know something too, don't you? What is it?'

'Emilia told me that Archie's a man of honour and that's good enough for me.'

'Well, it isn't for me.' Florence tried to wrest Honor away so she could resume her search.

Ben came back from seeing the builder to his bicycle; on his way back to Truro he was going to inform Dr Holloway his services were required at the farm. 'What's going on? I thought someone would be sitting with Archie.'

'Archie's still not come round but his breathing seems to have eased a little,' Honor replied. Her tone turned confrontational. 'I was on my way back to him when I caught Aunt Florence going through his things.'

Florence pushed Honor, none too gently, away from the bedroll. 'I resent your accusation that I'm doing something wrong.'

'He must have been making his way back to Ford Farm. When he's up to it I'll drive him over on the jingle. Well, Mrs Burrows, have you found anything interesting?' He nodded at the source of her investigation.

'Ben!'

'Your aunt's right, Honor. That workhouse brat's been spreading lies about Archie – you can never trust his sort, but I think it's time we knew more about Archie.'

Florence produced a faded brown paper packet tied up with string. 'What shall we find in here, I wonder?'

Honor didn't like it, but she joined Ben to watch. The knots of the string were tight and damp and aged, staining the brown paper, difficult to undo. With eager fingers, Florence opened the packet flaps and pulled out a collection of papers and photographs. She spread them out on the table. And grew excited. 'He's Commander Archibald Stevenson Rothwell. These photographs are proof of his identity. It's easy to see it's him even with his beard and untidy hair.'

'I already know that,' said Ben. 'What else is there?'

'He looks older than these photographs suggest he really is – rough living, I suppose,' Florence's tone was one of awe now. 'One of these places seems familiar to me, and so does one of these women. I've probably seen them in the society pages.'

'There's a newspaper cutting about his torpedoed ship. There were few survivors. It's how his feet got deformed.' Ben shuddered. He had not allowed Honor to settle Archie as she'd wished to do. He had taken off his boots and socks, to be reviled at the sight of his shrivelled, blackened, toe-less feet, bloodied by his trekking. 'Is there a clue to his home address or a family?'

'There's some letters and poems, but any addresses have been torn off,' Honor said, full of sorrow for the quiet unassuming drifter. She was sure his reason to keep his past a secret was an honest one. 'This one's signed "Mummy and Daddy". He has, or did have parents. I think we've seen enough, and should respect his wishes to remain anonymous.'

'Yes, I agree. I believe he's genuine. Put this all back, Mrs Burrows.' The words were hardly out of Ben's mouth when a terrible howling started up from the sitting room. He rushed there, with Honor close after him. Florence joined them after she had secreted one of the photographs into her handbag.

They found Archie sitting up, rigid and sweating, his hands reaching out for something unseen, his eyes huge and staring, his lips moving in babble, but he wasn't awake. Ben shook him hard, it took an effort to bring him out of his nightmare. He was convulsing and gagging. Honor passed Ben the glass of water left in attendance.

'Archie, take a deep breath. Calm yourself. That's better. Drink this.'

Archie clutched the glass and gulped, shaking water over himself and the horsehair blankets placed over him. He snorted and made a guzzling noise before falling back on the cushions, staring up at the beams and ceiling.

Ben said in a soft voice. 'Old memories?'

'The worst.' Archie's voice was a rasp. 'You couldn't imagine . . .'

'Your ship went down, I understand.' Ben had not felt emotional since the day he had cried in Julian Andrews's motor car, now he could cry a river for this man. Archie had lost his ship, his men, his feet, and one of man's prized possessions, his dignity.

'Men were burning. Screaming. The sense of fear. The smell . . .'

'I'm so very sorry. Archie, forgive me, but before we talk more I must ask you this. Would you tell me why you suddenly left my brother's farm? You see, I want to put things right for you, Jim Killigrew's been saying things about you. Vile things.'

Archie wiped a sweaty hand across his brow. The shaking started all over again. 'I swear I had no wrongful intentions towards his sister. Jim threatened me. Staying at Ford Farm would have been intolerable. Mr Harvey would have had to choose between us, and I didn't want any distress caused to Sara.'

'Why were you in the garden that day, Archie? You always keep away from people.'

'I was waiting to hear Sara sing. I had a sister . . . she too sang like a nightingale . . .'

'It's outrageous, you being treated like that, Archie.' Honor edged Ben aside and dabbed gently at Archie's wet brow. 'You shall stay with us and when you're well again you can do the same jobs here as you did for Alec.' There was a pleading in her eyes. 'You will stay?' Then to Ben. 'You won't let him go?'

'Indeed not. There's no spare room in the house with us living here at present, but I'm sure you won't mind the barn. I've made it clean and watertight. You shall stay in here until your cold's gone.'

'I'm grateful to you both. What about you, Mrs Burrows?' Exhausted, he was desperate for sleep. 'I'd rather move on if my presence was to breed resentment.'

'I might be called a duchess round here because of my grand ways, but I'm not a termagant, Mr Rothwell,' Florence said, in a voice unusually steeped with compassion and humour. 'Forgive me for being inquisitive. Why have you chosen your way of life? I felt I had to look through your things, you see. In your photographs there are people, children, a dog, one of you on horseback. You have a family somewhere, haven't you?'

'Not any more. I have no one. I spent months in a nursing home after I was brought back to England. I left, after terrifying a patient with a din like the one you've just heard. I keep myself to myself because I don't want others subjected to it.'

'But surely the Navy has an obligation towards you?'

'Yes, they have, ma'am, but the only option they gave me was to be stowed away in an ex-serviceman's institution for the rest of my life. I didn't want that.'

Honor caught hold of Ben's arm. 'We can't let him sleep in the barn when he's well. Archie's suffered so much. He deserves better than that.'

Ben held out his hand to Archie. 'I'm asking you to stay, Archie. I'll need a manager. I'll rearrange the office, make a cosy room for you to work and sleep in. And I'll scotch those despicable rumours that damned boy has spread about. I swear, you'll live here in peace.'

Archie gazed up at Honor. Her golden loveliness, her soft scent was soothing. She smiled at him, nodded at him to accept Ben's offer.

Mustering up the energy, Archie shook on it. Breathless, he closed his eyes. 'God bless you, Ben Harvey, you're a man of honour. One gets so weary of trailing about. I don't think I could have started all over again.'

Chapter Twenty-Five

Tristan went into the den and raised his brows at seeing Emilia behind the desk, while Alec, ambling about with his hands in his trouser pockets, dictated facts and figures to her. 'Oh, I came in to offer my services but I see you have everything under control.'

'We do everything together,' Alec said, smiling with pride and affection at his wife. 'You rest, spend time with Jonny.'

'I think my son's beginning to feel I'm stifling him. He's just roped in Jim to help him build a snowman, during his crib break. Sorry about the hall mirror, I've spanked Jonny's leg and warned him not to bring that blessed slingshot into the house again.'

'Well, he's a damned good shot.' Alec included Emilia in his grin. He settled in his chair to enjoy Tristan's quiet, unchallenging company. 'Nearly on par with Jim himself. Jim can hit a rabbit and kill it stone dead at over a hundred paces, you know. We had a particularly tender rabbit pie soon after he arrived, didn't we, darling? He hasn't said so, but I'm sure when his father was in dock he took him poaching. Don't worry about Jim's influence on Jonny, I'll keep him in line.'

'Oh, I'm not. Jim's got an unfortunate imagination, but I've commanded enough men to know a solid character when I see one.'

'Shall I get us some tea?' Emilia said. She wished Tristan showed signs of putting on weight, of losing his gauntness, but she guessed he had a lot on his mind concerning his wife, who never ventured out of Jonathan's room, which she shared with him.

'No, thanks, Emilia. I'm about to go up to Ursula. I popped over to see Ben this morning. Archie Rothwell's recovering well.'

Alec elected not to answer. He'd seen Archie's defection as a lack of trust in him, a break of friendship. From his uninterested expression, he hadn't changed his mind.

'He's written to say that he'd thought it best he moved on over the misunderstanding with Jim,' Emilia replied. 'I hope you've explained to Archie and Ben that we've taken Jim to task over what happened – it was a particularly nasty accusation. He's got a suspicious streak in his nature, and he can be as stubborn as others I know.' She glanced at Alec, who merely smiled back. 'I miss Archie being here.'

Tristan settled his gaze on Emilia. The bloom of pregnancy made her captivating, everything about her glowed and stated promise. A pity, though, that the child inside his wife's belly appeared to be flourishing.

Emilia noticed him looking. Such sadness he had, and insightfulness. How sensitively he had spoken to her and her parents about Billy. On turning out his tunic pockets to send it to the cleaners, she had come across some words scribbled on a grimy scrap of paper.

> Moments of time, it's all we have.
> One moment alive, then forever silent.
> For the silent, no hearing, no seeing, no touching.
> Forever denied their share of moments of time.
> We're all just moments of time.

Such a pity he had married an unfaithful woman and was still facing the consequences of her affair. Tristan had not discussed his feelings with Alec about Ursula or her baby, and because of Ben's age he had probably not confided in him either. An awful burden to carry alone.

Mentally, Emilia reached out to Tristan, hoping he sensed her concern, her consolation. He nodded, as if he had.

* * *

Tristan put his head round Jonathan's bedroom door. 'All right if I come in?'

Ursula was reclining by the window overlooking the front garden, where she was watching Jonathan and Jim build the snowman. 'Of course, Tris. Sit down, please stay. Jonny's having fun.'

'It's good to see him doing a few of the usual boyhood things. I suppose Jim never got the chance to play before, he's like another child out there. You look a little better again today.' He stood beside the fire, not wanting to be too close to her, his hands clasped behind his back. He saw her every day, but only stayed a few minutes. He knew they should talk, about Bruce Ashley, about her child, but he'd shunted his feelings into a sort of no man's land, and wanted to keep them there.

She gave a self-conscious smile. 'I'm feeling quite strong again. I'm being well looked after, thanks to you and Emilia.'

'She's a good sort.' An amazing sort, he thought, grateful for her soothing presence at the farm. 'Can't say how glad I am for Alec after what Lucy put him through.' His eyes darted off. He might have been conversing with a mere acquaintance. At times he wished she had not come back, yet he knew his worrying about her would have eaten him up. He didn't care what outsiders thought of the situation. The scandal was unimportant. When his thoughts returned to the trenches, he despised the small-mindedness and false values held by all walks of life.

Wearing the clothes of her first pregnancy, Ursula angled her dark head to try to win eye contact with him. 'It's hard to believe Emilia's so young. I'd like to make a friend of her, but I can't expect her to feel the same way about me.'

'Try to get to know her, I'm sure she'd be reasonable. I'm off in a minute to see the medics.' He indicated his wounded ankle.

'You still limp, Tris.' She peered down at his boot. 'How does it feel?'

'Stiff and sore, it aches. The rest of me is in pretty good order now.'

'It doesn't appear so and I hope the doctors will agree. I mean, I hope you never have to go back there. Men are still dying in droves. I don't want that for you, Tris.' She reached out a nervous hand, retracted it. He had ignored it. 'You don't deserve anything else bad happening to you. You're such a good man, you've always been good to me. I don't deserve your goodness now.'

'I've never stopped loving you, Ursula,' he found himself blurting out. 'It's as simple as that.' The simple truth, and it made him sick to his guts. Her gulp of relief made his insides coil into a tight painful ball. She was probably only here to be with Jonny. If she told him she still loved him, just to keep him on side, to exploit this goodness she reckoned he had, he'd shock her and tell her how he really felt. That like every other mortal soul in this world he was capable of hate and the desire for revenge.

'That makes me feel humble and even more ashamed of what I've done.' She was talking rapidly, as if afraid of losing his attention. 'But things will soon get . . . difficult. Tris, about—'

'Be careful what you say, Ursula.'

Ursula paled and shook. She had never heard this tone from him before, harsh, discordant. Hurt. An immeasurable volume of hurt. She was becoming aware of how much she had wounded him. She had hoped for forgiveness, if anyone was capable of forgiving so much, it was Tristan. She was suddenly afraid he would send her and her baby away.

She wet her lips, her lovely, velvety brown eyes darting with nerves. 'We've never spoken about . . . about Bruce Ashley, the fact that I'm carrying his child and soon to give birth to it. Oh, Tris, I made a terrible mistake. I'll never stop telling you how sorry I am and I'll never stop praying you'll forgive me, but whether or not you'll let me stay with you and Jonny, a decision will have to be made soon about this baby.'

Tristan was petrified with disgust at her lover's name. The thought of her being with another man – how could she have done this to him? He thought his head would split open with all the loathing and anger. He made himself think as an officer: cool, detached, in control. Jonny's future, that was what mattered. This odious mess must be sorted out somehow. 'Let's face facts then. First, do you want to keep it?'

Ursula hung her head, unable to meet his burning eyes. 'No. I'm finding it hard to feel anything for it. It couldn't be hidden from Jonny – my disgrace – he's too clever, and unfortunately he's excited over the prospect of a new brother or sister. I've thought a lot about what to do if you'd take me back, Tris.' She looked up at him now, with tears. She seemed like a small girl, pathetic, near panic. 'It's complicating matters between us, isn't it? I should go away for the confinement. Some people are looking for a child to adopt. If it's a boy, perhaps a lost son could be replaced.'

'What would you tell Jonny then?'

'That the child was stillborn. He'd soon forget all about it. Then . . . then you could see how you feel about me. I thought we could move away, where nobody knows us. We could start over again if you want, Tris. Be a family again.'

Be a family again. The notion milled round inside his head. It was all he had wanted each time he had left home to fight. And now? Why couldn't he come to a decision? He still loved Ursula. Why couldn't he go near her, let her reach out to him? He glanced at her bulging middle. It was that damned child. When it was out of the way, perhaps he'd be able to think differently. He was silent a long time.

'Will you at least think about it? Please, Tris?' Ursula was sobbing.

Part of him wanted to go to her, but the reviled part kept him distant. 'Yes, I'll do that, Ursula. We'll talk, about Ashley, about what exactly led you to betray me – that I have to know. If you'll excuse me, I must go, don't want to be late for my appointment.'

Emilia and Alec left the den. He put his arms round her and his smile told her he had something good to say. 'I've been thinking. I'm going to make Edwin up as manager. And why don't we ask him and your mother to come here to live when there's a room free? You're going to need help with the baby, and we're all family now.'

'Mum and Dad have been lost since I moved out, and more so since knowing Billy's never coming home. It's a wonderful idea. Thanks Alec – ' she kissed him – 'for being so thoughtful.'

They moved along the passage and saw Ursula on her way down the stairs. She went rigid. Her eyes were puffy and red from weeping. 'I-I . . .'

'I'll leave you to see to this, darling.' Alec strode away.

'What are you doing, Mrs Harvey?' Emilia said politely, though not with friendliness, towards Ursula. 'You should be resting.'

'I wanted . . . I'm sorry, I'll go back up.'

Emilia noted the same lost misery of Tristan's and Archie's. She guessed the other woman was lonely, but no one here wanted her company. 'Can I fetch you something?'

'Well, I thought – ' Ursula eyes shone in a sort of desperation – 'perhaps I could be doing something useful. It's not fair that you or the servants should have to wait on me, you've all got enough to do. I could sit and sew.'

So that was it, she was trying to act like a good wife. 'I'll bring some mending up to you.'

Ursula couldn't stand the reproach in Emilia's face. 'Emilia, you have to believe me,' she cried. 'It was the worst day of my life when I had to leave Jonny behind, and I'm sorry for what I've done to Tristan. I'm trying to put things right and it means I'm having to give this baby away!'

Ursula collapsed sobbing, clinging to the banisters. Emilia rushed up to her. 'Let me help you back up. You'd better lie down.'

'No, please.' Ursula leaned against her, seeking comfort. 'I don't need any more rest. I want to go outside. I want to see Jonny's snowman.'

It was such a plaintive, childlike plea that Emilia felt the stirrings of sympathy for her. 'Come down to the sitting room. When you're calm I'll take you outside for a little while.'

Ursula searched her sleeves until she found a hanky. 'Would you? It sounds silly but I've always loved snow. For a moment, while watching Jonny finishing his snowman, I felt like a girl again, then I remembered what a mess I've made of my life, and Tristan's, and I thought I'd go mad.'

In the sitting room, Emilia watched Ursula until she was satisfied there was to be no fainting or early labour. 'You must have had a hard time travelling all the way back here alone.'

'Yes, but no more than I deserved. The whole experience proved to me how fortunate I had been with my life, and how stupid I was to throw it all away, and for what? A handsome face, a smooth talker. I actually believed Bruce Ashley was in love with me. He'd promised he'd had a job and a house ready for us to go to in Bristol. It was all lies, of course. He took me to places frequented by shady types. I was to learn that they close ranks and only look after their own. He only knows how to live on his wits, by lying and cheating, it's not surprising he's always moving on.

'I've told my share of lies too, of course, but actually it wasn't Bruce who hit me, he was always gentle. I was desperate and thought Tristan was more likely to take me back if he thought Bruce was responsible for my bruises. The landlord of our last lodgings discovered we were about to slip off without paying the rent. Bruce ran off. I couldn't get away and the brute beat me. He took the last of my jewellery – otherwise I don't know what would have happened. I'd hoped Tristan would let me explain all this to him; now he's finally agreed that we'll talk.'

'It sounded just now that you want to keep your baby. Are you hoping Tristan will agree to become its father?'

'There's no chance of that. I'll just have to accept it. Could we go outside now, please? I've been cooped up hiding from people for so long I'm beginning to feel I'll suffocate.'

In coats, hats and boots, the two women gazed at the snowman, innocently built and appealing. Its dimensions were small, for not a lot of snow had fallen, its adornments an old scarf, stones for buttons, twigs for a face.

Emilia glanced at Ursula, she seemed less tense. 'I'll let you have a few minutes alone. Promise you'll soon go back in by the fire?'

'I promise.' Ursula gave a soft sigh. 'Thank you, Emilia, for being so understanding.'

Ursula took a turn round the garden, enjoying the feel of the snow under her boots. The snow was already thawing. If only her problems could melt away as quickly. She heard a noise. It was so odd and unexpected she paused to listen. It came again, like a hiss, behind the tall privet hedge, where the garden shed was. She smiled. Jonny was playing a game with her. He enjoyed hide and seek.

She crept round there. Gasped in disbelief and horror. From round the side of the shed a man appeared. He was dressed in clothes fitting for a labourer, but she had instantly recognized Bruce Ashley. She spun round, skidded on the slippery path and nearly fell. Her lover clamped his hands on her. 'Don't go, old girl. We need to talk.'

Ursula fought him off, but she couldn't get away. He faced her. 'Keep away from me. How dare you come here. If you're seen, you'll ruin everything for me.'

'Look, Ursula, darling. I know I was a swine to run out on you like that but I thought you were right behind me. I've had to keep my head down for ages, but I'd guess you'd come back here, be safe. I couldn't write to you, the Harveys would have been on to me. You've got to believe me when I say I really do love you.'

'How can you expect me to believe anything you say? I want you to leave, Bruce. I never want to see you again.'

'I knew you'd need proof of my feelings. Look at this.' He pulled something out of his coarse coat. 'It took me a while to get the money together but I've bought your necklace back. Sorry about the rest, Sidney Matlock had already sold it. I know I was a coward, but I've plucked up the courage and paid off the rent. Sidney was impressed. He's says we can go back anytime. He'll give me work. We'll soon have that house I'd promised you, we can always be together, Ursula, just like we wanted.'

'You're just a dreamer, Bruce. Sidney Matlock could only give you something dishonest to do. Go away, take that wretched necklace with you. Leave me to try to salvage my life.'

She made to walk round him but he held on to her again. 'I'm not a dreamer any more. I promise I've changed. I've finally fallen in love, properly, for keeps. You're having my baby, Ursula. I want you both.'

'Oh God,' Ursula groaned in misery. She had made the mistake of looking into his beautiful face, of allowing her love and passion for him to sweep through her once more. There had always been something more than reckless charm about Bruce. He was good-humoured, generous, fun, clever rather than cunning. And here he was, giving her a terrible choice. She could have a future with him, a man who was irresponsible and weak, and their baby. Or she could opt for an uncertain future with her husband who might never forgive her, but she would have Jonny.

'Listen, darling, I've got it all worked out. We'll take your boy with us this time. Nothing will make me leave him behind. Above all things I want you to be happy. Think about it.' He pressed a piece of paper into her hand. 'Write to this address. It's where I'm staying. I'll be doing nothing until I hear from you. I love you.' He kissed her lips and was gone.

For long moments Ursula stared at the paper in her hand. Bruce had not had to come here. He could be working his charm on other women, women with money, position, with no complications. He had said he loved her. She believed he truly did.

There was too much at risk. She must rip the address he had given her into shreds. But she could not bring herself to do it yet and slipped it inside her glove.

Chapter Twenty-Six

Hennaford was holding an auction for the war effort, and Emilia found herself, as wife of the principal landowner, plunged into a major role of the proceedings.

She was in the Wesleyan hall, which was attached to the chapel, situated at the bottom of a lazily sloping hill. With Florence Burrows and Elena Rawley, the Methodist minister's daughter, and Harriet Frayne, the schoolmaster's wife, she was supervising the laying out of the trestle tables and teacups, and the spreading out of Union flags.

Florence had almost put her nose into the boxes to see what Ford Farm had contributed; it was a generous supply of produce, half a dozen bottles of wine – French, since the formerly favoured German wines were now shunned, and some crocheted work of Tilda's.

There was a steady coming and going as the villagers brought in anything from a child's poem to a prized collection of disciple spoons, all to be brought under a hammer wielded by Alec. The pub was in frowning distance of the chapel, and the landlady of the Ploughshare arrived with a box of knick-knacks and a treadle sewing machine, carried in by one of her elderly patrons and Jim, whom Emilia had brought with her to help.

Florence viewed the newcomer as she would an insect that should be stepped on. 'That woman should close her establishment for the evening.'

'She is.' Emilia shook out a large white tablecloth with noisy gusto. Ruby Brokenshaw had only just received word that her husband was 'missing presumed dead', a victim of the sunk hospital ship *Glenart Castle* in the Bristol Channel. A particularly tragic blow for Ruby, who had nearly got him back, and it angered Emilia to hear her spoken of with disrespect.

'How do you know this?'

'When I was approached by Miss Rawley to help with the occasion, I went round the whole village to encourage people to get involved in ways not thought of before. Mrs Brokenshaw told me then.'

'Oh? I'd have thought she would have come to me, as usual.' Florence showed her hurt and jealousy by giving Elena Rawley an 'Emilia's going to ruin everything, and it's all your fault' look. 'I hope you haven't come up with anything undignified, Emilia.'

'Why should I?' Emilia reached to pin up a list of the men and women from Hennaford lost or serving in the war. Billy's name was there, and Albert Brokenshaw's would soon be added by Elena Rawley's artistic pen.

'Oh, my dear Emilia – ' Harriet Frayne hurried to her, edging her aside from the task – 'you mustn't stretch like that in your condition.' Mrs Frayne, rosy-cheeked and rosy-hearted, dropped her voice. 'You risk hurting yourself and causing the cord to twist around the baby's neck.'

Both amused and frustrated by the frequency of this sort of remark, Emilia was about to gently mock the warning given her by the woman who had once warmed her schoolday pasties, then she noticed the horror on Florence's face of 'her condition' being mentioned in front of a young unmarried woman and a boy. Florence disapproved of Jim's every manner and circumstance, and Jim, who showed an untimely interest in the fairer sex, was presently ogling Miss Rawley. 'Thank you for your advice, Mrs Frayne. Jim, come here, you're more able to put this up at a good height.'

'Yes, Mrs Em.' His voice had been described as an insolent drawl by Florence.

'Stop it,' Emilia said, while she transferred the tacks into his meaty open palm.

'What?' He smiled a warm, indolent smile.

'Keep your mind only on why we're here, and what was all that whispering to old Mr Quick about?'

'Nothing.'

'Don't think for a minute you're slipping away to try to charm a drink out of Mrs Brokenshaw.'

Jim gazed back with feigned hurt innocence, then gave the broadest grin. In between pushing in the tacks he kept glancing at Elena Rawley. Emilia was thankful that Elena, who, in Florence's opinion, was 'exactly what one expects her to be', was oblivious to his admiration. Not yet twenty, not tall or elegant, not pretty, but demurely appealing, she dutifully kept house for her widowed father. Emilia thought it would be good to invite her to the farm for afternoon tea. If she could get Honor to come, it would make a pleasant occasion. She was still waiting for Honor's promised visit.

'Mrs Harvey has come up with a wonderful idea, Mrs Burrows.' Elena's voice was clear and uninvasive. She was tying a numbered piece of card to each item to be auctioned from Ruby Brokenshaw's box. 'She's suggested people might like to auction their talents.'

'I beg your pardon?' Florence squinted to see if Jim had pinned the roll call up straight.

'Like my sister singing,' Jim chipped in, amused at his rudeness. 'It's what gave Mrs Em the idea. If someone pays a shilling say, then Sara'll get up on the platform and sing a song.'

'Or someone could make an offer to do some gardening or something like that,' Elena said.

Before Florence could comment, Jim said, 'What about you, Miss Elena? What can you do?' He was there beside her, passing her a small brass Toby jug.

'Hasn't that boy got something more useful to do?' Florence cried.

Emilia smiled to herself.

Clinging to the top of a hedge in Back Lane, Emilia studied

the piles of stone and timber being used for the renovations and extensions of Tremore House, then the house itself. The chimneys were currently being rebuilt and a pole-thin boy, thankfully well below the damnable age of conscription, was mounting a ladder. It appeared that the house was to retain its solid, square look. But, 'something's modern going on inside it' was Hennaford's general, unsure opinion.

'Have you brought Grandma with you?'

Startled by the sudden voice, she turned too quickly and lost her footing. Ben caught her, settled her balance, then let her go. Emilia straightened her ruffled hat. 'Of all the stupid things to do!'

'Don't you know it's unwise to be climbing about in your condition?'

'I was just taking a look. It's going to be a fine house.'

'I don't need your approval.'

He was staring at her middle. She was beginning to show, and Emilia could see he didn't approve of that either. 'A fine house for Honor is what I meant. No, I haven't brought your grandmother today. I've come from the Wesleyan hall – the auction. Florence Burrows is taking tea with Mrs Frayne, and I thought I'd call on Honor without her aunt's presence to stop us enjoying ourselves. Excuse me.' She sprung off along the lane.

Ben walked at her side. He was in his work clothes, should have been busy with a hundred other tasks, but every day he couldn't resist taking a studied look at the progress on his house. 'Is Grandma well?'

'She's fighting fit.'

'As you always are, Emilia.'

'As you would have been to fight the Germans, eh, Ben, if I hadn't deliberately blinded you? Is that what the sour look on your face means?'

He shook his head. 'I never realized how much of a bitch you could be.'

'Nor I how unforgiving you can be.'

'Isn't that Alec's forte?'

'Alec's got nothing to do with this. I'm not to blame for what happened to your eye. It's time you accepted it.'

'Did you always want Alec? The farm?'

'Ben, I wanted you, but now I'm glad I married Alec and I'm looking forward to bearing his child.' She stopped directly in front of him. 'Look, Ben, for Honor's sake, I'd like to clear things up between us. I shouldn't have been so cold towards you after Billy died. I was going to tell you this after our quarrel in Wayside Cot, about how much I regretted it, but then your gran broke the window and you were furious with me, *cruel* to me, and things got even worse. I am truly sorry about your eye, whether you believe me or not.'

He took his time weighing up her words. 'You were hoping for us to go on being engaged?'

'Yes, at the time. Can we not be friends now, Ben? Leave all that's happened in the past?'

He saw the perfect colour in her face, her passion, her energy. She would give Alec fine, healthy babies. A perfect helpmate for a farmer. He despised her then, over her deliberate cold-heartedness that had made him act in ways that had led to him losing her. 'You didn't grieve over me for long. You went straight into Alec's bed.'

Her compassion turned into scorn. 'I can see I'm wasting my time. If you're going on to the farm, please be good enough to tell Honor that I'll not stop now but I'll seek her company this evening.'

'I've got work to do!' He strode off, scaling a field gate in one foolhardy leap.

Emilia watched his tall, athletic form. There was nothing defeated about him now. She marvelled at how easily they had come to detest each other.

A sharp pain in her stomach caught her unawares. Followed by another. It was as if her insides were being squeezed. 'Ben! Ben!'

She had her arms wrapped around her middle when she heard his voice. 'Em! What is it?' His hands were supporting her.

'I don't know. Ow! Oh, help me, Ben. It's my baby.'

Chapter Twenty-Seven

'What do you think you're doing, Emilia? Get back into bed at once!' Alec put an arm round her waist, took her hand and led her towards their bedroom as if leading an invalid.

'Alec, I was on my way to the bathroom.'

'There's a commode in the bedroom for that. Come along.' He carried her the rest of the way, saw to what was necessary with tenderness, then tucked her, sitting up, in the bed. He held her gently.

'It was just a fright, darling. The district nurse says I can get up again tomorrow.' She nestled against his warmth and his strength, needing his care, his closeness. 'But I admit I've never been so frightened in my life. I love our baby so much already – something tells me it's a boy. Sometimes I hear his voice, sometimes I see him about the house and yard, like a ghost of the future. I'll keep him safe for you, Alec, I promise.'

'I know, darling. The baby means everything to me too, but I'm even more concerned about you. You're so much a part of my life now, nothing would make sense without you.'

'I feel the same about you.' She kissed his hand, kissed it until she hoped she had left an everlasting impression on it. Ben had asked her earlier if she had always wanted Alec. Perhaps she had.

'Ben was good to me.' He had carried her into his sitting room. While he had run to the dairy to fetch Eliza, Honor had held her hand, asking if there was any more pain. There wasn't, or any loss of blood, and Eliza had judged she should be taken home to bed. ''Tisn't uncommon for a woman to have a pain or two anywhere along a pregnancy,' the Amazon of a woman had deliberated. 'Or 'twas just the baby pressing on a nerve. Fittest pregnant woman I've ever seen, anyhow.'

Honor had accompanied her home on the Tremore jingle and helped her into her nightdress, and sat with her while Alec had been fetched from the fields and her mother sent for. 'Knowing you, Em, you're probably overdoing it. You haven't been lugging bales of hay about, I hope.'

'I wouldn't do anything foolish to harm my child, Honor.' Emilia had kept her hands spread over her swell, as if to protect the tiny human forming inside her. 'It's such a powerful feeling, the desire to keep this little one safe.'

Honor's smile of understanding had turned serious. 'I hope I don't have more than one baby. In fact, I'll make sure I won't. I know about the proper medical ways to make sure of it.'

Emilia was speechless at her friend's uncharacteristic remarks. It struck her how much Honor had grown in confidence.

'I thought you'd be shocked. Well, I've read these books. They're frowned on, of course. There's a new woman at the Red Cross meetings, she's involved with the Suffrage Movement. She was horrified at learning I was engaged. She gave me quite a lecture. She brought me the books the next time I saw her. I was mystified at first, but they explain ways to prevent conception, so married women don't have to go on producing a baby year after year. And, even more controversial, that side of life isn't only for men to enjoy, you know, Em.'

'I know that, Honor,' Emilia had said, feeling silly to be the one to blush. 'Gosh, if your aunt knew you held these views she'd die in a blue funk.' Like Alec, Ben had always said he wanted a large family, so he and Honor had entirely different outlooks. 'You are doing the right thing by marrying Ben, aren't you?'

'Oh, I think so, but I do envy you, Em. Your marriage is

more of a partnership. Alec relies on you, while Ben thinks he has to protect me, no, I think he *needs* to be in that role. We still have no love life. I get the feeling that when it does happen, he'll think it's something for me to endure, while he'll be jolly sorry about it. I know that's what would generally be considered a wife's duty, but, well, I'm not planning on settling for that. Ben might take me more seriously if we were closer in that way. Don't you agree, Em?'

Emilia had squeezed her friend's hand. 'Yes, good for you. Show him you're every bit a real woman.'

'I'm grateful to Ben for bringing you home,' Alec had said when he'd arrived.

'Good.' Emilia had wound her arms round Alec's neck and kissed his mouth, kissed him long and hard.

'Wow, what was that for?'

'Just showing you how much I'm looking forward to being completely well again.'

That evening in the Wesleyan hall, Tristan handed Ben a bottle of brandy. 'With Alec's compliments. He's also asked me to pass on his gratitude for your care of Emilia today.'

Pleased with the offering, Ben dismissed the sentiment that went with it. 'Is that why his lordship isn't here? People are getting concerned, he had a duty to perform.'

'He said he wouldn't leave Emilia if the Kaiser himself turned up on the doorstep, so he talked me into coming in his place.' Aware of the sidelong glances aimed his way, Tristan braced himself. He was in for a hell of a time warding off underhand remarks about Ursula, and he would have to keep an eye on the boisterous Jim. He felt guilty about leaving Ursula, with only Jonathan to run to Alec for help if she needed anything urgently. Alec had insisted Tilda and Sara should not miss this rare social event.

'You'll give us an equally fine performance, Captain Harvey,' Florence Burrows pontificated when she learned of his deputization.

'What do you mean?' Tristan felt himself burning all over.

Although there was no heating in the modest, bleak hall, it had already grown warm and stuffy with so many bodies packed inside it, all determined to show their patriotism. There were other uniformed men, but his superior rank meant he was receiving more attention from their salutes. 'What do I have to do?'

'You're the auctioneer, of course.' Florence tried to usher him towards the platform.

Tristan's eyes widened in panic. 'I couldn't! I thought I was only here to present Alec's cheque. No, it's out of the question. I'm not up to it.' He clutched hold of Ben's smartly overcoated arm. 'Ben, you've got to help me.'

'It's all right, Tris.' Ben caught his trembling hand. 'I'll do it. If Alec wasn't so bloody damned selfish he'd have known you're not up to this sort of thing.'

The first part of the evening proceeded well under Ben's charge, the goods had all been cleared and he announced an interval before the auction of the 'talents', saying that over seventy pounds had been raised, a sum already way beyond the total of a previous similar occasion.

Finding it hard to concentrate, Tristan had sat rigidly next to Honor. 'Thanks for that, Ben,' he said, wiping the sweat off his brow. 'Everything still seems strange, some things even more alien than when I was over there. Normal life – but it doesn't seem normal to be living a normal life.'

'Life isn't normal for any of us, Tris. Some of us die, some of us are changed beyond recognition, some of us do things that would have been unthinkable before the war. The war, the war, we all live, think and eat it every moment of every day. Now, here am I only eighteen and already planning to marry. Tris, have you made any plans yourself yet?'

'With Ursula, you mean? I'm prepared to give our marriage another chance.' He had come back from seeing the medics about his ankle to find Ursula crying. Not the soft, sorrowing sniffing she had employed most days since her return, but pitiable, body-wrenching moaning. He had gone to her, where she had been lying on her side on the bed, facing away from the door.

'Ursula, what is it?' His hand had hovered over her. 'Are you in pain?'

The blubbering had stopped, she shook her head.

'What then?'

She had buried her head in the pillow, and he had walked round the bed, sat close beside her, then, after a moment's waver, had touched her hair and kept his hand lightly on her head. 'Tell me, don't be afraid.'

Slowly, she had revealed her face, red and swollen and pathetic. 'I don't know what to do, Tris.'

He'd had to lower his head to hear her ragged words. And she had reached up and grabbed him, pulling him down to her, clinging to him. 'It would be better if I was dead, wouldn't it?'

'Don't say that!' He had eased her away from him, but only so he could lay down at her side and hold her to him. 'We'll make it right somehow.' He wanted to. God help him, he still loved her, and because of that, despite his revulsion at feeling the movements of another man's child inside her, he had forced himself to stay and talk, to listen to the terrible truths of her infidelity, and to make plans for the future.

He went on talking to Ben, marvelling at how he made it sound like ordinary conversation. 'The CO's been understanding. I'm transferring to the 3rd, at Freshwater, the Isle of Wight, as soon as Ursula's complication is out of the way. I'll be tied down to an office while this ankle makes up its mind. Eventually, we'll have to settle somewhere where, I hope, current events won't ever catch up with us, for Jonny's sake.'

'It's not right that you and Jonny should be exiled from your family.'

'Fate has us in its hands, I'm afraid, Ben.'

Jim, scrubbed and presentable in his suit and stiff collar, had been trying to get close to Elena Rawley, and was staring, open-mouthed, because her father had hissed, 'Bugger off!' at him. He prodded his sister's arm. 'Sara, aren't men of the cloth forbidden to swear?'

'Course, they are. What on earth are you talking about? You better not be upsetting anyone. You promised Cap'n Harvey you'd behave.'

'Don't nag. I'm going to get myself something to eat.'

Whispering broke out when a latecomer arrived, but Sara was unaware of it. Nervous about the possibility of singing in front of so many people – there seemed to be a lot more here than when she'd sung in the church – she was trying to view herself in a mirror, bargained for and won for two shillings by Mrs Frayne. Tilda had arranged her hair in the same style Mrs Em wore hers, the front part sweeping up in generous folds, the long length in a single fat plait. She hoped it made her look more grown up. She caught a man's reflection smiling at hers.

'Miss Sara,' he said. 'I hope you'll be given the chance to sing often tonight.'

She turned to the man. He was like a pale, thin tower. She could hear a little gasp at the end of each of his breaths. His walking sticks seemed inadequate to the task of supporting him. 'Archie, how did you get here?'

'Eliza has a donkey and cart of her own. She talked me into coming. If you'll excuse me, I'll find myself a seat.'

Tristan was also staring at Archie. 'Good heavens, Ben. Never thought to see him turn up for this. He's changed under your care. His peculiar eyes have taken on a less stark appearance.'

'That's because Honor fusses over him like a mother hen. I'll get her to fetch him a cup of tea.'

'Get away from her!' Jim had pushed his way back to his sister. He prodded Archie's shoulder before he could move towards a chair.

'I was only—'

'I've told you before,' Jim threatened, hurling himself in front of Sara. 'Go near her again and I'd knock your bleddy block off.'

'There's no need for that young man. I—'

'You just don't listen, do you?' Jim pushed Archie again. With a cry, he toppled to the floor.

Ben had been making his way towards them. 'How dare you lay a hand on an elder and better, you workhouse brat!'

Smarting at the insult, Jim's resentment bubbled up over the opinion of his character Ben Harvey had put about when defending Archie Rothwell. Jim scowled under his breath, 'Mr Harvey, the dead-eyed nothing.'

Ben's hands were on Jim's lapels before he'd finished muttering his disrespect. He butted Jim in the face, making blood gush from his nose. 'You scum-ridden bastard! Get out of here.'

'No one treats me like that!' Jim was nearly as tall and as broad as Ben. While people gasped, he used his brawn to rip Ben's hands off him, then smashed his fist into Ben's guts. Ben doubled over, but his sparring hands grabbed the hem of Jim's jacket and he ploughed into him, taking them both down on to the planked floor, near to where Archie was sprawled. They hit a trestle, denying some of the glass and china new ownership as pieces fell off and broke.

Women screamed and men protested, and those nearest the falling brawlers staggered into others. Children wailed as their feet were accidentally stepped on, their faces cuffed. The gathering scattered, cramped as it was, to a safer distance. Honor was struggling to get through to Archie.

Furious with Ben for furthering the violence, Tristan tried to wrench him away from Jim; likewise, Edwin Rowse tried to get Jim under control. All pleas for order were ignored as Ben and Jim grappled on the floor, until Ben, afraid Tristan would get hurt, released the lock he had on Jim's neck and gave him a contemptuous push.

There was a fresh outbreak of indignant mutterings and children's whimperings. Here and there, insidious remarks began to circulate about Archie.

'Please, listen to me,' Archie implored. Somehow his voice rang out above the exclamations and shufflings. 'I didn't mean to cause any trouble. I didn't mean any harm to Miss Sara. I only wanted—'

'I know what your sort wants, whatever others choose to

believe about you,' Jim bawled in the manner of stubborn adolescence, spitting blood out of his mouth. 'You're a living disgrace, you should be dead. We've got no reason to trust you. You should be run out of the village, dumped in the sea.'

'I wish I was dead,' Archie whispered, sinking further down. 'Dead in the sea.'

While Honor finally reached Archie, her aunt got to Jim. Florence smashed her hand across his face, the sound was bone-crunching. 'You viper! You wretch. I'll have you know that poor man is an officer and a gentleman. He's crippled because he fought in the Battle of Jutland for the likes of you. No one but those he's lived with knows that, because he's too humble to boast of his sacrifice. I'm going to demand that Alec Harvey either throws you out or thrashes you for your vile assumptions. Shame should weigh down your shoulders for the rest of your life, Jim Killigrew.'

Jim stared at the man he had insulted and humiliated, the man now coughing and paler than ever before, who seemed to have shrunk to half his height and was clinging to the young woman who had gone to his aid, as if he wanted to hide away for ever. The boy hung his head. Silence drifted down like a heavy layer of dishonour in the hall.

Barely holding back her sobs, Sara bundled Jim outside. Tristan, after mumbling his apologies to the people, followed them. He felt he was choking on a throatful of bile.

Ben reached down to Honor. 'We'll go as well and take Archie with us. May God never forgive that boy!'

'The ignorant little wretch! Jim will feel more than the back of my hand round his ear for this.' Alec's agitated paces were threatening to wear away the carpet in the sitting room, where he was sharing a nightcap with Tristan. 'But tomorrow I'll tell Ben to keep his damned hands off my staff. It was his egotistical actions that made the situation get out of hand.'

'You will not, I forbid it.' Tristan tossed back his whisky. 'I know Ben's upset you but he's just a boy, a boy you were a father figure to until a short time ago. He's your flesh and blood.'

'All the more reason for him not betraying me.'

'For goodness sake, what do you think this evening's been all about? War! Because men of one country have no respect for the rights of men of another and would rather live in suspicion and hatred, and choose to send their countrymen to die on their behalf. It's no wonder the world's in such a state when two brothers are too bloody damned selfish and too pigheaded to let bygones rest.'

Alec allowed a period of silence for his brother to fume. 'Jonny fell asleep at eight o'clock, haven't heard a squeak out of him since.'

'So Ursula's been left without attendance since then? I'll go up and see if she wants some cocoa or something.'

'I'm not that unfeeling, Tris. I took her up some hot milk and biscuits an hour ago. She's resting comfortably.'

Tristan helped himself to another large whisky. He would take the bottle up with him. He couldn't face another sleepless night.

'I thought we'd have a farewell family dinner before you take up your new posting, Tris,' Alec said.

'It would mean a lot to me if you invited Ben and Honor too,' Tristan replied. Now he waited while his brother stewed in a moody silence. 'You could at least think about it.'

Ursula was wringing her hands beside the banked-in fire in the bedroom. Alec's sudden appearance with a tray had unnerved her.

'You haven't come out of concern for me. What do you want?'

He'd put a hand either side of her chair, bringing his face close. 'You're soon to leave my house and good riddance. I want you to dwell on these words, Ursula. You've broken Tris's heart once, don't think to do it again. He's not going to the Front again, thank God, and I want him to have a contented future, if that's ever possible with you. Never forget what you owe him. You treat him right, you honour and cherish him, or, I swear on God's holy name, I'll come after you. Understand?'

Leaning away, she'd nodded. 'Tristan wouldn't approve of you treating me like this.'

'I'm looking out for my brother, that's all. I don't trust you, Ursula. And I'm sure Tris won't ever really trust you again.'

Now, she heard two sets of footsteps on the stairs, then Alec going into his room. She looked hopefully at the door. Tristan's tread had stopped outside. 'Come in,' she whispered. 'Oh, please come in.'

He moved away to Henry's room.

Getting up on awkward limbs, she shuffled to the door. She would go after him, ask him how the evening went, show an interest, make an effort, prove she would be a good wife from now on.

She let her hand fall off the handle. Alec had been right about Tristan showing no trust in her. He was still aloof. On edge. He had changed. Because of her adultery, his battle experiences, or both, he was no longer completely selfless and compassionate. How could he be? Why should he be?

In a week or two she would give birth and only see her baby for a few minutes. Then she would go away with her son, whom she'd have to lie to about a dead brother or sister, and her husband, who might regret his decision to take her back. Apart from having Jonny, it was a miserable prospect.

'Mummy, can't you sleep?' Jonathan was sitting up in bed. 'Shall I fetch Daddy for you?'

'No, darling.' She got into the bed with him and cuddled him against her. 'Let's try to settle down.'

Bruce Ashley came into her thoughts. Since his sudden appearance in the garden he had shadowed them every part of every day and night. She had destroyed the paper with his address on it, but not before she had memorized it. His appeal to run away with him, that he'd ensure they took Jonny with them this time, became more enticing. She would have everything then. Her son, her baby, and the man she still loved. Could Bruce pull it off? He was a master at schemes. But would he still be lying low at this inn in Chacewater after three weeks of silence from her? Bruce got bored quickly. He may have gone back to Bristol, or somewhere else.

If he was still there, it meant he really did love her. And that she could trust him, and all he had planned for their future this time would actually happen. Jonny would be upset for a while, but he would soon settle down with a new brother or sister and an exciting and charming stepfather.

It was a huge risk to take. She might lose everything if it went wrong. Was it worth it? Was Bruce worth it?

'Jonny, darling, if I asked you to do something for me in secret, would you promise not to tell anyone? Not even Daddy?'

'Are you planning a surprise for him?'

'Yes, that's right. Promise you'll keep it a secret? It's a terrible thing to ruin a surprise.'

'I promise.'

'Mummy's going to write a letter. You usually see the postman first. All you have to do is pass it to him without anyone knowing, then in a day or two, if Mummy gets a reply, bring me the letter in the same way.'

When Jonathan drifted off to sleep, Ursula pressed a hand over where she could feel her baby moving. 'Please be there, Bruce,' she whispered. 'Or I'll have to give our child away.'

Chapter Twenty-Eight

On the platform of Truro railway station, Ben gave Florence Burrows a wad of money, which she secreted into her handbag.

'It's so good of you to understand about this, Ben. I don't like leaving you and Honor to cope alone, but, well, I'd heard about the spa, you see, always wanted to go there.' Although she had never looked and acted as chirpy before this, Florence brought a gloved hand up to her brow as if she was feeble and faint. 'If I don't get a little break soon . . . You will make sure Eliza doesn't leave too much for Honor to do? It's time you stopped that woman slipping off to the pub. Ruby Brokenshaw shouldn't allow women patronage.'

'Don't you worry about us, Mrs Burrows,' Ben said, a sparkle in his eye at being rid of her demands and nit-picking for a while. 'I hope you'll find the hotel you've chosen a perfect place to rest. Write to us as soon as you're settled, and send a telegram when you want me to meet the return train.'

When the steam engine chugged in, he helped her into a first-class carriage and delighted her by kissing her goodbye.

Shortly afterwards he was kissing Polly Hetherton. After a frantic coupling on her bed, he lit them both a cigarette, took a puff of his, then started to dress. Polly dragged him back to her.

'It was a lovely surprise to see you this early in the day, darling, but I'm not going to allow you to leave me yet,' she crooned in his ear, nibbling the lobe.

Ben enjoyed the shivers it gave him, but he checked his fresh desire. 'Sorry, Pol, I've got too much to do at home.

Then there's Eugenie Bawden's officers' party tonight. Can't let the guests down, they need every bit of support. I'll see you and Julian there.'

The lovers' thoughts turned to prayers. The officers would not long be on home soil. The British had far extended their lines, but the Germans, with reinforcements released from the Eastern Front, were preparing a massive new offensive.

'Is Honor attending the party?'

'Yes.'

Polly drew in on her cigarette then stubbed it out. Apart from social occasions like tonight, life had been boring until she and Julian had happened on Ben. She adored his body and enjoyed his energy. She liked his gentle side, but his betraying the young dairy maid had turned him on fire, and she was thrilled by the festering, dangerous part of him. It had been a succession of treats to teach him the arts of sensuality. He was inventive, an eager pioneer, and she longed for him when he wasn't with her.

Before he could pull on his shirt she snatched it away and tossed it far from the four-poster. 'Busy, busy, busy.' She tapped the words down his well-formed chest. 'You've got a couple of Land Girls now. You'll be able to get on a lot better without Honor's nightmare of an aunt to hold you up. Wonder why she chose Lincolnshire to take a holiday? I'd have thought Bath would have been more suitable. Let your dear little Honor put on a pair of overalls and spoil her hands. Oh, let's forget them. Think about us instead.'

'I don't care what the aunt's reasons were, I hope she stays away for months. I can afford to fund her and I've told her so. Pol, stop that, it's not fair. Heaven though. Look here, darling, I really do have to go.' He gave her one last deep kiss.

'Heaven?'

'I'm going, Pol. Right now. Move.'

'You're not going anywhere.'

'Oh, yes, I am.'

'No, you're not.'

'I am.'
'No . . . Oh, yes, Ben.'

Honor had never put her hair up without her aunt's aid. While getting ready for the evening at Eugenie Bawden's, she asked Eliza to do it for her.

'Sorry, Miss,' Eliza replied, hiding her umpteenth cigarette of the day behind her back. 'I can put me hand up a cow and pull out a calf, and empty the privy bucket without spilling a drop of slops, but as for anything fancy like that, you'd best ask the boss. Or what about Archie? He's got nice long hands, think he could do the job for 'ee right enough.'

'Thank you, Eliza,' Honor said, wondering what had provoked her to ask the woman, who wore her own hair in matted tats, to take part in anything refined and feminine. 'I'll manage. At least could you manage the hooks on my dress before you scuttle off somewhere?'

Honor was glad when Eliza left her cheerless, basically furnished bedroom and took her earthy smell with her. In her new dinner dress, of midnight-blue ninon over dove-grey satin, with silk red roses pinned just above the waist, she was trailing her waist-length hair through her fingers, deciding how to arrange it so she looked mature.

She heard Eliza stamping back up the stairs. Eliza burst through the door. 'Miss! Miss!'

Honor swung round. 'What is it, Eliza?'

''Tis Archie. He's outside in a bad way, coughing his guts up! Don't like the look of him this time. You'd better send for the rector – reckons if Archie's anything, he's church.'

Honor interrupted Ben's preparations for the evening out. They decided Archie didn't need the services of the rector, but definitely the doctor. Eliza was despatched to fetch him.

Before the doctor arrived, Ben, with Cyril Trewin's assistance, got Archie inside his room and on to his bed. 'You need looking after. And stop apologizing, we don't mind.' Ben stilled Archie's protests.

'You shouldn't have gone outside, Archie,' Honor chided,

having fetched a bowl of tepid water and a cloth for his fevered brow. 'I'll leave the men to undress you. I'll make a hot-water bottle in case you get the shivers.'

'Such a bother to you all,' Archie said, puffing and gasping. 'This will make you late for your evening out, Ben.'

'Sit up against them pillows and let us do the worrying,' came Cyril's rough voice. 'Dammit, mate, your politeness do get on my bleddy nerves at times.'

Ben pressed his hand to Archie's shoulder. 'Being late's all the rage in some circles. Dr Holloway should be here soon.'

'You saw his handkerchiefs?' Dr Holloway whispered to Ben, after listening to Archie's chest and prodding him in the appropriate places. He was aged about fifty, heavy of body and droopy of jowl, which made people surprised at how nimbly he could think and move. 'Not good, not good at all, really. This fellow's going to need some attentive nursing. Have you got someone who's capable of that? Cleaning out spit basins? He'll need plenty of fluids. A steamy atmosphere will help and there must be absolutely no smoking in this room. Take this, rub it on his back and chest morning and night. I've something in my bag that will help bring up the phlegm. I'll come back tomorrow morning, if there's no improvement I'll see he's admitted to the infirmary. Naval man, you say? Spent time in the drink? In my opinion his lungs haven't been clear since swallowing a vast quantity of sea water.'

The doctor repeated his deliberations to Honor, and most of them to Archie, then he took his leave, his fee topped up with a hunk of ham.

'Right then,' Ben said. He was supporting Archie while he coughed and retched into one of his own handkerchiefs. 'Cyril, you fetch the primus stove and a kettle, and a pan of water to hang from the fireplace. We'll keep a steady flow of steam in here all night. Honor, fetch some basins, small bowls, that sort of thing, and lots of rags, which we'll burn. Where's Eliza? She can sit with Archie. Are you willing to take a turn, Cyril? I need to attend this party tonight, there will be some important contacts there who I need to see.'

'I'll stay,' Cyril agreed. 'And I'll give him a whack or two on the back when he needs it, which looks like it's going to be often. Just let me nip out and tell Albie where I'll be.'

'Ben, we can't leave Archie to Eliza's dubious mercies. I don't trust her to be clean or not to smoke.' Honor looked anxiously at the sick man wheezing on the bed. It saddened her to see burn scars on his exposed chest. 'We should have carried him up to my room. There's hardly space to turn round in here and it's dark and gloomy.'

'Never mind the room, it's warm and dry, that's all that matters. Who else do you suggest? We can hardly ask the Land Girls. There's only Albie, he hasn't got the sort of intelligence for this.'

'I'll stay, I haven't got anyone important to see tonight.' Honor had a suspicion Ben would spend more time with these 'contacts' he was expecting to see than with her. It would be humiliating and boring to be ushered into the company of a maidenly-aunt type, sitting about like one too many flowers in a garden verge. Emilia, now back to full health, would be there, but Honor didn't fancy watching Ben ignoring her and Alec, causing an atmosphere. Suddenly, Honor wasn't sure she liked Ben any more, and she wished she wasn't wearing his half-hoop diamond ring.

'But sweetheart, you were looking forward to your first proper social event in ages.' He lifted up handfuls of her glorious hair. 'You look beautiful, by the way, a nymph of the meadows. I'd be proud to introduce you as my fiancée. Your Aunt Florence is enjoying herself, it's time you did too.' And if Alec was going to show off Emilia, he wanted the same people to see he had done even better in that respect. Emilia was lovely in her own way, but she was lower class.

Honor wasn't swayed. 'I wouldn't enjoy myself worrying about Archie. You go, Ben. There will be other occasions I can attend.'

'Well, if you insist, darling.' Ben was thinking about all the unrestricted fun he could have without her there. 'Promise me you won't overdo it? It's hard work, caring for an invalid.'

'If Em can manage with your grandmother and her pregnant sister-in-law, while being pregnant herself, I'm sure I can rise to the challenge.' Honor's voice had risen syllable by syllable, as if in answer to a criticism. 'It will be worth it if Archie's brought to lasting health. It's no more than he deserves. Say hello to Em for me, *properly*. She'll be nervous, her first time mixing in a different circle.'

'As if she'd let anything like that faze her,' Ben snorted. He didn't bother to ask Honor why she was suddenly so touchy. She had called on Emilia the day after the fund-raising auction and stayed for hours. If Honor missed the old days, it was regrettable, but also . . . too bad.

Emilia also had a new dress for the occasion. Similar in colour and style to Honor's, it was parted and layered cleverly at the front to accommodate her impending motherhood. Alec handed her fur-trimmed cloak to the maid, then wrapped his arms around her from behind, his hands over her bump. 'Wonder if he knows what's going on in there, all this noise and excitement?'

'Of course, he does. Our baby's the cleverest in the world. I think he'll enjoy this rag-time music.'

'Alec, dear heart, at last! You've been very naughty keeping away from me for so long.'

Emilia knew that the woman who had spoken, her long-gloved arm outstretched in a dramatic manner, had to be her husband's old flame, Mrs Eugenie Bawden. Her hair, dyed black, as glossy as a raven's wing, was parted in the centre, gently waved, with a chignon. She was painted like a moving picture star; diamonds and rubies flashed on her neck and wrists and swung from her ears. Healthy country looks and overstated elegance gazed at each other, but there was no instant dislike, no competitiveness.

Eugenie Bawden waved her jet cigarette holder in an exaggerated spiral. 'Now I can see why. Good God, so this is your angel? Welcome to my house, m'dear. And your brother's got himself engaged to a fairy doll. Couldn't believe my eyes when I saw her at the Hetherton gel's house recently. She's a child, so *sweet.*

'Aha! A Harvey in uniform. Well, come along in, Captain, don't hide behind your brother and sister-in-law. Tristan, my dear, I'm honoured. Can't say how delighted I am to see you again in one piece.' Walking by placing her feet directly in front of each other, she wiggled up to Tristan and placed a loud kiss on his lips.

Emilia glanced at Alec, bemused. The woman was a riot, not Alec's sort at all. She wasn't young and she wasn't beautiful.

'She's fun,' he explained, putting his war fund contribution into a huge glass dish that already contained notes and cheques. 'A woman who lifts the spirit. There's nothing else to say about Eugenie. All you have to do tonight, angel, is to enjoy yourself. You won't find anyone stuffy invited here.'

'Drink up. Emilia, isn't it?' Polly Hetherton swept a glass of white wine into Emilia's hand. 'Good evening, Alec. You look good with all the farmyard muck scrubbed off. And you, Emilia, look positively gorgeous. Who did your hair? But, of course, you've got the services of the Rules's former maid. She's a gem. I was about to snap her up myself but Alec got to her first. Did you know he can be ruthless when he wants something? Of course, you do. You don't look the sort who'd want a cissy.'

'Are you keeping well, Mrs Hetherton?' Emilia enquired, as if she didn't care whether she received an answer. She had only seen the woman the day she and her brother had brought Ben home, and there had been too many distractions then to consider her. Emilia sensed her welcome wasn't genuine. She glanced about for sign of Honor, and spotted Julian Andrews, sitting with a group of older men wearing natty suits and flamboyant bow ties. He bowed his head to her and she raised her hand in a polite wave.

'Oh, I'm very well indeed.' Polly's eyes danced about the

room, as if to convey she was already bored and would soon move on. 'But I keep good company these days. Ben's at my house every chance he gets.'

'If you'll excuse me, ladies,' Alec smiled at Polly, but his eyes were widened in mulish irritation at the mention of his youngest brother. 'I'll keep Tris company.' Tristan was talking to a stand of men in uniform.

'Still not made it up, he and Ben?' Polly asked, eyes shining in mischief.

'You must know that if you see a lot of Ben,' Emilia replied in a tone that told she would not be made fun of.

'Well, I do. Everything, in fact.' Polly sashayed away, leaving Emilia in no doubt as to her meaning.

Emilia was waiting for Ben when he arrived. She hardly gave him time to dispense with his overcoat and scarf before dragging him into a quiet corner.

He brushed at the place where her hand had been, looked down on her glittering eyes. 'What's got you seeing red?'

'Where's Honor?'

'At home, her decision. Archie's sick, she's sitting with him. Well?'

'You've been sleeping with that Hetherton woman, haven't you?'

Ben laughed aloud, pulled his strong brows together and bent close enough for Emilia to feel his breath on her face. 'Have I?'

'Don't play games, you rotten, two-faced, cheating piece of, of—'

'Horse shit? How Billy and I used to laugh when you got angry like this. I still admire your passion.' He brought his body close. 'I enjoyed the time I had you. I think I'll always rate it as one of the best experiences of my life. No one can ever wipe out the fact that it happened. Do you ever think about it, Emilia? I do, a lot. I'll sleep with you any time you care to mention.'

His face was horrible, lecherous. Emilia felt he would soon be suffocating her, but she took in a slow easy breath. 'I'll tell Honor. I won't let her spend the rest of her life with a lying, thoroughgoing bastard!'

'And what would that achieve? She'd feel compelled to leave her only home. Where could she go? She's got nothing. I promised to look after her and I will. She'll have wealth and position one day, I'll see to that. At least I respect Honor enough not to expect her to drop her drawers for me.'

At the same time Emilia slapped her hand across his face, she brought her knee up in his groin. As Ben groaned in agony, clutching his delicate parts, he was hauled away from her. She was afraid it was Alec and there would be a fight, but it was the natty suit brigade, including Julian.

A thick-bodied, middle-aged man with slick hair, smoking a fat cigar, flashed large white teeth at her. 'You've not got the experience yet to know when a lady doesn't desire your attention, Ben, my son. You have my word, miss – ' he looked from Emilia's swollen middle to her wedding ring – 'I beg your pardon, Mrs, that he won't bother you again.'

'He certainly won't!' Emilia glared at Ben, still doubled over. 'You listen to me, Ben Harvey. If you hurt Honor, I swear I'll make you suffer.' She stalked away.

'Who was she?' the man asked Ben, when he was able to stand up straight.

Ben wiped the tears from his eyes, tried and failed to make his voice sound normal. 'My brother's wife, the bitch!'

'Best looking piece I've seen in a long, long time,' the man drawled, licking his lips, which appeared perpetually greasy. 'Poison on her tongue, a sting in her tail. I like a challenge. Might find myself in your little backwater one of these days. Speaking of which, now that whoring sister-in-law of yours is back, have you seen any sign of Bruce Ashley?'

'Don't be daft, Dougie.' Ben used a cushion-framed mirror to straighten his tie. 'When his sort ditches a woman they're never seen again.'

Dougie clapped a hand on Ben's shoulder. 'I didn't build up my little empire by being daft, Ben, my son. Ashley was hoping your brother would be killed in action, making Ursula a well-off widow. She's back, and everything looks as one expects it to be, but Ashley was unusually attracted to the lovely Ursula. He might sniff round her again. If you get wind of him, let me know at once. He owes me and I want to collect.' Dougie stuffed a stash of notes into Ben's breast pocket. 'Now, my son, I'm expecting a consignment two nights from now. Arrange for your man to meet mine, same place. Best cover I've got, your little farm. Come on, you can forget about having jollities with Mrs P. H. tonight. We're having an all-nighter at cards.'

Hoping for Honor's sake that the men Ben was mixing with – a shady lot, by appearances – wouldn't lead him into trouble, Emilia joined Alec and Tristan, who were now on their own. Tristan was trying to sound cheery, but Emilia knew the only reason he was here was the hope of reconciling his brothers on neutral ground. She felt awful: there would be less hope of that after her clash with Ben.

Ben and his friends were on the way to another room.

'Ben!' Tristan beckoned him to join the group.

Ben excused himself and came forth. 'Good evening, Tris.'

Alec stared across the room.

Tristan sighed in frustration at his brothers' obdurate faces. 'Ben? Alec? Speak, damn you. For my sake?'

Ben suddenly muttered, 'I'm willing, for your sake, Tris.' But he would not remain civil to his eldest brother after Tristan had joined his new unit. 'Good evening, Alec.'

Emilia nudged Alec. He rolled his eyes at her, glared at Ben, then glanced at Tristan. The forlorn, vulnerable expression he received, as if Tristan was looking for something good and normal to cling to, wrenched at his heart. 'Me too. Good evening, Ben.'

'At last. Now the ice has finally been broken, before my family and I leave, I'm going to arrange for us to have a farewell supper.' Tristan felt Emilia touch his hand. He wrapped his fingers around hers for a moment, taking comfort from their warmth and capable roughness. Coming home and finding his brothers estranged meant that he had felt unable to share his feelings and experiences about his time in the trenches. Emilia was the only one he felt would fully understand.

Chapter Twenty-Nine

Emilia drove the trap over to Tremore Farm the next day, taking Lottie with her. While waiting for Eliza to clump off to fetch Honor, she began tidying up the neglected kitchen. On Florence and Honor's first inspection here, they had asked Eliza to give the room and its contents a proper clean, but grime still clung to edges and choked corners. Dust was layered on the mantelshelf over the open fireplace, which hadn't been swept for days. The curtains had dirty marks, as if used for wiping unclean hands. The new copper cooking pans had lost their shine. The lamp wicks, usually one of the first jobs each morning of a housekeeper, had not yet been trimmed. However, the windows were open and the fresh spring air mingled pleasantly with the smell of cooked breakfasts.

Moments later, Honor appeared, weary-eyed but smiling. She was wearing trousers, at which Florence would have been outraged. Eliza came in next with an uncovered chamber pot, and after announcing something indelicate about Archie's functions, she went outside to empty it and catch up on her jobs in the yard.

'Thanks so much for coming, Em.' Honor sunk down at the table. 'I knew you would. I think Dr Holloway's going to be pleased – Archie had a rough night but he seems reasonably comfortable now, able to sleep at last.'

'You need some sleep yourself, Honor. Lottie's amusing herself with your knitting bag. While she's content, I'll make you some breakfast, then I'll give this place a birthday. I'm sure you'd rather have the carthorse busy outside.'

Emilia's light-hearted reference to Eliza made Honor's eyes mist over. 'Oh, I miss you so much, Em. How was last night? I still think you were brave to go to Alec's former mistress's place.'

'Hasn't Ben told you about it?'

'I think he came in to check on Archie, but I was dozing at the time.' Honor yawned.

'The party was quite entertaining.' Emilia put on the apron she'd brought and got busy with the kettle. 'And Eugenie Bawden was surprising.'

'In what way?'

'I thought she would be more like the Hetherton woman – and now I've got to know *her*, I think she's a right cow – but I liked Eugenie. She's scatty and, I should think, kind. She probably saved Alec from sinking into a deep depression, and I'm grateful for that.' Emilia became serious. 'You've got to get out and about yourself, Honor. You haven't done any proper courting with Ben yet, you need to build up a relationship with him.'

Honor kicked off her slippers, pulled open a cupboard door of the dresser and put her feet up on its edge. 'There's no need to worry about me, Em, dear. I know what Ben's expecting from me, and I've accepted that I'll get no more than a kindly concern from him. He'll probably take a mistress, if he hasn't got one already.'

'Are you willing to settle for that? Surely not, Honor?'

Honor pushed her hair, unaccustomedly loose and awry, back from her shoulders. 'Em, I've considered all my options. Aunt Florence is my responsibility now, rather than I hers, but if it wasn't for her I'd ask Ben to release me and I'd seek a live-in job and somehow get some more education, then set myself up as a secretary or something. But due to my limitations, there's no other choice but to marry Ben. I'll be a good wife to him, and use my position to help those less fortunate. Right now, I wish people would stop treating me as if I'm a little girl.' She was suddenly sitting on the edge of her chair. 'That's it!'

'What?' Emilia replied, alarmed, although she was pleased Honor had a firm grip on reality.

'Scissors. See those scissors hanging up there?'

Emilia scanned a line of kitchen implements, hanging up precariously from hooks on a low beam. 'Yes. What about them?'

'I'm going to get liberated and you can help me. Mabel at the Red Cross will be proud of me.'

'Honor, what are you talking about?' Emilia stared, puzzled, at the big pair of steel scissors she had taken down.

'I want you to cut my hair into a bob, about the length of my chin will be just right.'

Emilia's mouth gaped open. 'Don't you think that's a bit extreme? What will Ben say?'

'I don't care. Em, haven't you taken in what I've just said? It's my hair and I'll do what I like with it. Why don't you have yours cut too? Or are you afraid of what Alec will say? Do you see him as your lord and master?'

'Honor Burrows, whatever's come over you? Your aunt will have a fit!' Then Emilia was laughing. 'Right then, if that's what you want. Turn round. You can trim mine next, but only to shoulder length because that's how I want it. It will be wonderful to get rid of some of this weight. As for Alec, I think I'd talk about anything that would be a dramatic change with him first.'

Emilia combed Honor's long beautiful hair with her fingers. 'Ready? Are you sure?'

Honor was trembling with excitement. 'This is going to be a turning point for me. Today I become a woman and a person in my own right.'

Emilia took a deep breath and opened the scissors. 'Well, here goes.'

'Get on with it!' Lottie suddenly shrieked, pursing up her face like an ugly baby's and tossing tangled skeins of wool on to the flagstoned floor.

The two young woman burst into laughter.

Chapter Thirty

Tasteful in furs, a rolled-up umbrella hanging from her wrist, Florence was viewing a building known as The Jungle. Never had there been a more triumphant expression on her sedate face. She had a photograph of this curious dwelling that was covered with a mass of vegetation and had a sham-castle folly façade, its centre formed into two circular corners, with window frames and doors made from oak branches that were shaped into Gothic arches. Its name, according to Florence's research, came from the builder's passion, in the previous century, for keeping exotic animals.

Florence wasn't particularly interested in the building, but in the people photographed in front of it, about a decade ago. One was Archie Rothwell.

A man, mature, distinguished and straight-limbed, of amiable smile, came out of the front door before Florence could knock and ask for information. After spending a pleasant half-hour drinking sherry inside with him and his amusing little wife, and receiving a local history lesson about the picturesque parish of Eagle, she walked to the parish church, a building only ten years old.

She went inside and here, trimming candles near the altar, was the woman her kind informants had said was likely to be found here at this time of day.

Aged in her mid-twenties, in a simple hat and well-cut suit, the woman approached Florence on graceful feet. Her hair was fair, a mix of corn and golden sand, her eyes a vivid green. 'Good morning. Are you new to the parish or are you taking a look around? There are many splendid things to see locally, the windmills and The Jungle.'

'I also believe your house, Oak Tree Warren, is worth taking a look at, Miss Rothwell.'

'You've been talking to someone hereabouts?'

Florence introduced herself then held out the photograph to the young woman, who, from a short while ago, she knew to be Miss Edith Rothwell. 'I've come up from Cornwall about your brother, Archie, and I bring you good news. He's not dead or gone mad or become even more crippled, as I've been told you've been fearing for several months. He's well and is living on the property owned by my niece's fiancé.'

'God be praised!' Edith Rothwell grasped both of Florence's hands and was no longer careful to keep her voice down in the solemn surroundings. 'God bless you, Mrs Burrows. You must come home with me without delay and meet my parents.'

Honor carried a bowl of hot water, a flannel and fresh towels into Archie's room. He was sleeping with his arms outside the covers and they were lying flat and relaxed, his eyelids the same. Last night had been the first he'd gone without nightmares, or groaning and twitching, or breathing with a harsh rasp. It was a shame to disturb him but he needed to take his medication.

Archie opened his eyes and watched her pull back the curtains, go to the cupboard that doubled as a washstand, and prepare the liquids and pills he was to take.

After she poured a glass of water, she found him looking at her with a soft, grateful smile. 'Good morning. I'm sure all nurses wish their patients were as cooperative as you.'

'Not all patients have such a tender-hearted nurse,' he replied.

She sat on the bed and passed him all he had to swallow. He glanced at her throughout. 'You like my hair like this, don't you?'

He studied the glossy frame around her perfect heart-shaped face. 'It's stunning.'

'Ben doesn't approve. He won't believe that it was my idea

and not Em's. He says she's a bad influence on me. Oh, well, it's my hair, my life.' She rubbed the edge of his pyjama jacket. 'You're sticky. Let's get this off and make you comfortable.'

'I don't want to keep putting you to so much trouble, Honor. I can manage.'

He had given up the habit of dropping his eyes, and as she undid his top button and started on the next, his gaze was locked to hers.

'Archie, it's no trouble at all. When you've freshened up, Eliza will bring you a hearty breakfast. You might as well make the most of being in the country, where it's not hit so hard by the food shortages.'

'You won't be happy until you see some flesh on these stick-thin bones of mine. But I really must get up and do some work. Ben's insisted on taking all the paperwork away so he won't disturb me. Please persuade him that I'm sure I can manage to get to the desk now. I owe you and Ben, Cyril and Eliza so much. Even Albie's been sitting with me, concern written over his dear little face.'

'The last thing we want is for all our hard work to be undone by you wearing yourself out. You must look after your chest, Archie. You could have died. Dr Holloway is sending Nurse Roberts to redress your feet tomorrow. They're to be kept dressed until they're completely healed, and then we must make sure they're always dry and padded in the right places. It's important to keep them comfortable. You're easily at risk from gangrene, you know.'

'I know. Don't worry, I won't neglect myself again.'

She soaped the flannel. Archie dropped the hand that was about to reach for it.

She smiled as she set to work. She enjoyed nursing him more than anything she had ever done. She carefully dried his skin and helped him into a clean pyjama jacket, sitting close while she fastened each button and turned back the collar and smoothed down the lapels.

He did not lean back against the pillows as before. She did not want him to move away.

Archie suddenly took her hand. 'You sang to me during the times I was delirious. I heard you, you pulled me through. Thank you, Honor.'

'Shall I sing now? What did your sister sing for you?

'"The Distant Shore", it was my favourite.'

In her clear, gentle voice, Honor sang the tale of Victorian pathos, in which a maiden tragically died. Tears watered Archie's eyes. 'When did your sister die, Archie?'

He tightened the hold on her hand. 'She didn't.'

Honor had suspected he was still keeping secrets, and she knew she must be careful. 'You mean she's out there somewhere, probably worrying about you and missing you as much as you're missing her?'

'Yes, that's the truth. You must be appalled.'

'Have you any more family?'

'A mother, father, aunts, uncles, cousins, even a grandmother, not unlike old Mrs Harvey.'

'Have you a wife and children? I've often wondered about that.' She was praying he would say no – not that it should directly concern her.

'I never found the time. I always seemed to be at sea, but then, I never fell in love. Honor, please don't despise me, my current life is a fraud from start to finish. I've never needed to beg for work or take clothes from charity. My family are wealthy, and I have money in my own right. To have drawn on my bank would have alerted them to where I was.'

'But why live like you have all this time? Enduring rejection and risking your health?'

He fell back against the pillows, letting Honor's hands slip free. 'I heard the men on my ship begging for help. I saw others burning like torches. My own boots had burnt through and I was trying to batter my way through to some of those who were trapped, but either someone pushed me or I fell overboard. There were lots of us in the water. But the cries grew fainter as they drowned or died from their wounds. I clung to a body in a life jacket. I don't remember being picked up, everything was a haze until I woke up, as if from a nightmare, and Edith, my sister, was there. I was in a nursing home. I had no right to be there while all those others had perished, there with my lovely sister. I felt such pain for Emilia when she heard her brother had died. It's what those of us who go to war are expected to do, die, and not come home and taunt the living that their loved ones will never come back. When my ravings frightened one of the patients in the nursing home I felt so ashamed. I didn't want my parents to see me, to know what I'd become. They're genteel and simple. How could I put them through that?'

'But my dear Archie, you've been seeing this all wrong. That's the tragedy, not your injuries or how your terrible experiences have affected you.' Honor grabbed his balled-up fists, and after spreading out his taut fingers, she kissed them. 'Oh, you poor, dear, mistaken man. All this time you could have been cared for by those who love you, who must be longing to hear that you are alive and well, instead of letting yourself suffer all this alone.'

Archie sat forward. 'Not alone, Honor. The Harvey brothers have been good to me, and then there's you. I'd go through it all again just to be with you.' He kissed her hands as she had his. They gazed at each other for a moment. Then leaned closer and closer until their lips touched. They closed their eyes and allowed the kiss to go and on. It was the most sensuous moment of her life: the sweetest sense of adoration for him.

Ben was devouring his breakfast when she went downstairs. 'Sorry to be in a rush, got lots to do before I go into Truro.'

'I think I'll come with you,' she said.

'Why?'

'To spend some time with you. I've got something to tell you about Archie.'

'You'll have to make it another time, sweetheart.' He planted a kiss on top of her head. 'I've got people to see, I can't have you getting in my way.'

'Oh, I promise I'll never, ever do that, Ben.'

When Ben had gone, and with the workforce busy away from the farmstead, she returned to Archie and latched the door behind her.

'Time for more medicine already, is it?' he asked, meeting her eyes. 'Look, Honor, I want to apologize about what happened. I shouldn't have kissed you, you belong to Ben.'

She took off her engagement ring and dropped it beside Archie's medicines. 'No, I don't. It was never really on for us. It's such a relief to take this off, I only had years of monotony ahead. Ben meant well towards me, but it's not enough, is it? I think he will be relieved too. One day he'll find someone more like Emilia, it's what he wants and what he needs.'

'What will you do?'

'Oh, I'll think of something, and Aunt Florence will just have to come to terms with it. Happiness doesn't lie in settling for something less than one deserves. And Archie, you deserve to be with your family. Don't you think you should get in touch with them? It's the right thing to do.'

'It is, but I don't think there will be any need for that.' He beckoned her to him and she went. 'Your aunt's holidaying in Lincolnshire, and by strange coincidence, that's where my family lives.'

'What? So that's why she chose a place so far away to rest. And you were content to let her find you out? Aunt Florence, the canny old fox! That's the best news ever. I suppose someone will be down to fetch you soon. I'll miss you, Archie, but I'm pleased for you at the same time.' Honor tried and failed to put on a brave face. This was one sudden change too many. The best thing for Archie, but a dreadful, unwelcome change for her. In one awful moment, she realized what it would mean no longer to be near him. She had never loved Ben, but she loved this man who had once been a lonely stranger.

Archie raised her downcast chin. 'Honor, I wouldn't have come between you and Ben, that's not my way. But now you've taken off his ring, may I suggest I telegram your aunt to stay where she is, and that we join her and Edith and my parents instead?'

'You mean you'd find somewhere for Aunt Florence and me to live? Would you want a housekeeper? I'd very much like to go on looking after you, Archie.'

'I thought we could look after each other,' he whispered, putting his long gentle hands on her. 'You see, Honor, I love you. It's what brought me back to you.'

'Oh, Archie . . .' She threw her arms around his neck. 'And I love you.'

When they kissed, Honor learned what it was like to be kissed by a man who showered real love and passion on a woman.

She undid the buttons of her blouse. 'We'll be alone for hours, Archie, and I've a woman's love to give you.'

Chapter Thirty-One

For the second time in a week Ben was waiting to see someone off at the railway station. He jigged about with his hands rammed in his overcoat pockets, his face drawn, aloof. A youth, obviously a recruit into the services, saluted him. Ben returned a curt nod. It rankled to be considered invalided out of the fighting because of his damaged eye, when, in fact, he'd never lifted a gun except to shoot a pheasant or a rabbit.

'Ben . . .' Honor said. She was sitting next to Archie in the waiting room.

'I've told you both I'm not angry, not really. It's the best thing all round.' He couldn't bear to receive her explanations again, definitely not her sympathy. He lit a cigarette. 'A new start for you and your aunt. The best of luck to you both, and you, Archie.' He was welcome to Florence Burrows's daily presence. 'Keep in touch.'

The sound of fast tapping heels brought Emilia to them. Honor jumped up and they embraced.

Ben watched the two young women who, each for a brief time, had been his. One a brunette, strong and determined, who had forgotten him as quickly as a crop withers in stony ground. She wasn't his Em any more, she had got what she was best suited for and had acquired a ruthless streak to protect it. And the blonde beauty, not destined to stay his little princess. He had misread them both. Emilia had never been his soul mate, and Honor had never been totally vulnerable. Neither had needed *him*, to live, to be, to find happiness in this world rent by darkness and tragedy.

A wretchedness was invading his soul and, in a wash of fear, he recognized what loneliness was like, more frightening than facing death. He acknowledged the completion of one of life's purposes. He, like his two childhood friends, had grown up.

'I was so afraid I'd miss you.' Emilia kissed Honor. 'The village is agog at your news. I wish I could be there at your wedding, but you must send me a snap.' She wasn't surprised Ben was ignoring her after their clash at Eugenie Bawden's, but because he was looking downhearted – a contrast to Honor's joy and confidence – she felt compelled to speak to him. 'Hello, Ben.'

'Hello, Emilia,' he replied, able to look at her now, and the couple.

'God willing, we'll be down often for holidays, what better place?' Honor said to her. 'You take care of yourself, Em, and your little one, you hear me?'

'I promise.' Emilia went to Archie. 'It's hard to believe you're the same man who came to the farm just a few months ago. And to think I sent you away.'

'You did the right thing, Mrs Harvey. I could have been a violent criminal for all you knew,' Archie replied. At last, his tall frame seemed fleshed out a bit, his skin promising a healthy pink would come. The haunted aspect of his eyes was not so apparent, but Emilia knew, as for so many others, that his dreadful memories, his unnecessary guilt at surviving, would never fully vanish.

'Here's the train,' Ben said. He'd heard enough slushy talk for one day.

Emilia followed the train until there was no platform left. When she walked back, Ben had not moved. The other passengers, and those greeting or seeing them off had all dispersed.

Now Honor had gone, they were both feeling a little lost.

'How did you get in?' he said.

'The trap. You?'

'A cab. There wasn't enough room for the three of us and the luggage on the jingle. I'm going to get a motor car.'

'Good for you. Want a ride back?'

He would rather go for a drink, or to Polly or Dougie. Home would be empty and bare without the feminine variety of female company. But he would not run from his fears and loneliness, and not waste a precious moment on pleasure. At a farmers' meeting in Truro last month, the gravity of the grain and meat shortages had been a shock. With a hot spring promised, he would graft in his fields from sunrise till sundown to get his crops planted.

'I'd better take the reins. You should have got someone to drive you over in your condition.'

'Hardly necessary. Anyway, no one could be spared.'

'Tell me about it.'

'Of course, you're going to be shorthanded without Honor, Archie and Florence.'

Ben handed her up on the trap. 'Don't suppose it'll make much difference. Florence didn't work in the same way she did at Ford Farm, and these last few days Archie was laid up and Honor was too besotted with him to do much else but nurse him.'

When he was sitting beside her, Emilia said, 'You're not bitter about Honor breaking off with you then?'

'Not at all. I feel a bit of a fool. People will say I can't keep my women.' Ben steered the nag down Richmond Hill. 'It's a lucky escape for us both. Honor and I were already beginning to make each other miserable. I wish her everything. Archie too, he's a good bloke.'

'You're learning, Ben.'

'What does that mean?'

'Nothing belittling, I swear. Our lives have changed a lot recently, we've had to learn how to deal with different sorts of relationships.'

Another sideways glance. 'Is that a hint for us to become friends?'

She gave him a level look. 'It could be.'

'Emilia, I want to ask you something. Don't take this wrong, don't get angry about my curiosity. I mean, you can hardly blame me for wondering . . .'

'What is it, Ben?'

'The baby, your baby. There was very little time between you and me, and you and Alec. You're sure it's his? I couldn't bear the thought of Alec bringing up my child.'

'I swear on Billy's memory that this child is Alec's. I wouldn't have got involved with him if I'd become pregnant by you, Ben. This business with you and Alec is silly. You never fell out before, it's time you made things up. Will you make an effort at the farewell supper for Tris and Ursula? Think about it, for your sake as much as Tris's, or you'll be all alone.'

'I don't believe Alec really wants me back in his house.'

'If you apologized for your sneakiness, he might come round. Don't forget, Ben, you've a grandmother there. You shouldn't stay away from her.'

Ben took his eyes off the road and met her frank gaze. 'And you shouldn't be so bossy. During the supper, you be sure to keep that workhouse brat out of my way.'

'You're two of a kind, you and Jim. Adventurous, reckless.'

'That boy hasn't a trace of honour in him.'

'Let's not fall out about him.'

Ben looked forward again. 'Do you love Alec?'

'Yes.'

'I didn't want to hear you say that.'

'You'll find someone who you'll really love one day. Someone better than that Hetherton woman to keep you warm at night.'

They were going past a newsagent's at Hendra and Ben brought the trap to a halt. He bought a copy of *The Western Morning News* and *The Times*.

'Things are looking a bit sticky for us, aren't they?' She used one of his phrases. The Germans were unleashing a fearsome offensive in France, with town after town falling, with the wounded, after only the minimum of attendance, being despatched within hours to England, and the dead receiving a hasty burial.

He did not reply. He folded the newspaper and stuffed it inside his overcoat.

She glanced at his blinded eye. He noticed and his handsome features tightened. She wanted to say something, but she knew he would always blame her for the horrifying result of the incident that had denied him his treasured career. She would never accept his unfairness. Friendship between them was impossible. A cool silence divided them as he drove the trap on to Ford Farm.

Sara was carrying a bucket of household scraps to the piggery. Ben had taken little notice of her during the evening he had fought with her twin. He pulled in his bottom lip while eyeing her. After helping Emilia down, he said, 'She's a glorious little creature. You want to watch Alec doesn't start flirting with her.'

'Oh, Ben! Just go home.' Missing Honor already, Emilia marched indoors, wanting to forget he existed.

'Sara Killigrew, isn't it?' Ben said in his most gracious voice, casually lighting a cigarette while ambling at her side. Her skin was the softest shade of primrose, she smelled of sweetness and promise. Her plaits, her plain smock dress and sacking apron, added to her maidenly charm.

'Yes, sir,' Sara replied awkwardly, turning a pretty shade of pink – her workhouse training always to be polite to her betters slowed her to his pace.

He left her at the small doors where she would tip the pigs' feast into granite troughs. Before striding off to his own property, Ben smiled to himself. He punched the tantalizing fresh warm air in jubilation. He was free! Free to court and bed any woman he chose. In a couple of years, it would be a breeze to show an interest in a certain girl here. It would upset her upstart brother and Alec. And Emilia.

Chapter Thirty-Two

Emilia was in the boxroom, setting aside the nursery items of former Harvey babies for her own. The cot, highchair and pram were all in good order. In a few months she would be the mother of the next generation to grow up on the farm.

It made her feel sad that Jonathan was leaving – being forced to leave the place where he was settled in. Last night he had confided in her and Alec that he would miss them, and his great-grandma, and Jim, Sara and Tilda, and that he was frightened of going far away to a strange place. How would he cope with the lie that his brother or sister had died at birth?

There was a tap on the door and Ursula joined her. She looked fidgety. 'I'm sorry to bother you. If Tris comes back from the lambing in Long Meadow, will you tell him Jonny and I are taking a nap together?'

'Of course. He and Alec probably won't be back for ages. There's nothing wrong, is there? You look uncomfortable.'

'That's exactly the way I'm feeling. You'll find out for yourself when you're nearing the end of your pregnancy.' Ursula gave a small smile. 'I want to thank you for being good to me, Emilia. For allowing me to stay under your roof. Well, Jonny and I are going to take five minutes of fresh air first. We'll be down for afternoon tea. It's exciting, isn't it, preparing for a baby? Be careful you don't lift anything heavy.'

'Be careful you don't walk too far,' Emilia said, opening the door for Ursula, then watching her descend the stairs in slow, laborious steps. Poor woman, she thought, it's going to be hard to give her baby away.

*   *   *

'It's time we went back, Mummy.' Jonathan tugged on Ursula's hand. 'We're nearly at the ford. I heard the nurse say you should stay off your feet.'

'Just a few more steps won't hurt, darling. We're going to have a little adventure today, but first we need to go home.'

'To our old home? Is it about Daddy's surprise? You keep saying it will happen soon. Has the letter I brought you the other day something to do with it?'

'Can't hide anything from you, can I?' Ursula laughed, but her insides were aching with worry. She had been overjoyed at Bruce's letter. He loved her and she was sure she could trust him. All she had to do was to get herself and Jonathan to Ford House, where Bruce would be waiting with a horse-cab, which would take them to an inn at St Austell. From there a carrier cart was to take them on to Bristol. Pray God, it was taken for granted by now that she and Jonny had come back from their little walk and were napping. When it was discovered they had disappeared it would be thought she had made for the railway station with him, and this time a clean escape would be made.

Her ankles were badly swollen and every step over the bridge and up the next hill was painful and jarring her back. There was no sign of Bruce yet, and in the event of this, she had taken the back door key to the house from Tristan's room.

She fell down on her chair in the parlour, out of breath. Her back, legs, stomach and chest hurting. She had a blinding headache. 'Jonny, could you fetch me a drink of water, please?'

'But what about the surprise!' He was hopping about in excitement.

'We'll have to wait a while.' She prayed it was no longer than a few minutes.

'Daddy's been here.'

'What?' She sat up suddenly, causing a sharp pain to cut through her body. 'Oh, you mean the packing chests.' Thank goodness, Tristan had finished the preparations for the removal men yesterday.

Bruce, where are you? she pleaded silently. There was no clock now to tell the time by but she was sure he was at least ten minutes late.

Emilia was interrupted again in the boxroom. 'Hello, Tris. I didn't expect you back yet.'

'There's another ewe about to lamb. I thought I'd fetch Jonny. Jim told me he'd been keen to witness a birthing but he thought he'd better stay close to his mother. Noble of him, but he shouldn't have to miss out on other things. Where is he, Em?'

'With Ursula, taking a nap together by now.'

'He doesn't need a nap. I won't have him namby-pambied.' He noticed Emilia was dusting the rocking cradle. 'Promise you won't you do anything silly, like carrying furniture to another room?'

'I promise. Tris, I think Ursula just wants company, that's all. I hope you don't mind me saying this, she's got an ordeal ahead of her.'

'I suppose she has.' He hesitated at the door. 'Do you think I'm being too harsh with her?'

'That's for you to say, Tris.'

'If I want to make a proper go of it, I should be more understanding. I intend to be, I will, it's just this baby. When it's finally out of the way . . . not easy for Ursula though.'

'She's bound to be downhearted afterwards. I think you should be prepared for that.'

'Yes, you're right. Good advice. I'll try to make things easier for her from now on. Thanks, Em.'

Emilia smiled to herself after he had gone. She was Em to Tristan now. She liked that.

She became alarmed to hear him banging in and out of Jonathan's room and charging down and then back up the stairs. She came out on the landing. 'They're nowhere to be found, their outdoor things aren't hanging up,' he cried. 'I think she's gone, and taken Jonny with her.'

Reasoning that Ursula and Jonathan had not passed him on

his approach to the farm, and that she would avoid the village, Tristan hurried down the hill to the ford. Emilia had suggested that Ursula might have gone to Ford House for some reason, it was the obvious first place to look. The garden gate was closed, the house looked as deserted as when he had left it the day before. Frightened and furious, he peered through the front window and gasped in relief to see Jonny in the parlour. Ursula was huddled in her old chair, and it looked as if Jonny was encouraging her to take a drink of water. It seemed they had walked too far and Ursula had been taken ill.

Tristan entered by the back door and made his way down the passage.

'Bruce? At last, I was getting worried.'

Ursula's voice and the loving, longing way she had said those words, *his* name, made Tristan recoil in anguish and fury.

'Bruce, why are you taking so long to come in?'

'Mummy, who's Bruce? Is he bringing Daddy's surprise?' Tristan heard his son say.

Tristan found his feet and made the last of the short distance into the parlour. 'No, Jonny. Daddy's brought his own surprise.'

'Tris! Oh, my God!' Ursula sank deeper into the chair, her hands hiding her face.

'Daddy, you're not supposed to be here. You'll ruin everything.' Jonathan pouted.

'You don't know how right you are, son.' The desperate rush had weakened Tristan's ankle and he hobbled to Jonathan and picked him up. 'There's no need for any more lies, Ursula. We'll leave now and let you go with your lover. I— no, there will be no more words between us. Jonny, say goodbye to Mummy.'

'But he's not coming,' Ursula said, her teeth chattering with the shock at Tristan's discovery of her treachery. 'I'm sorry, but I'll need your shelter a little longer.'

'No, you don't, darling. Sorry, I'm late, got unavoidably detained.'

The suddenness of the roguish cultured voice made the breath lock in Tristan's lungs. Its owner had a good deportment, was tall, well-honed, with healthy fair looks. He was giving Ursula a boyish white-toothed smile. And the insolent swine was not the least bit concerned that her husband was there. 'Ashley!'

'And you are the good Captain Harvey.' Bruce Ashley turned a supercilious gaze on Tristan. 'Pity things aren't quite going to plan, but never mind. We'll soon be out of your hair. I slipped on ahead to see if the coast was clear. The horse-cab's just pulling up. Very sporting of you to allow Ursula to leave without any bother.'

'Get out of my house, you unspeakable viper – ' Tristan shook with rage and disgust – 'before I forget my son is here and give you what you deserve.'

'Daddy, what's wrong?' Jonny whimpered, hiding his face in his father's neck. 'Why are you so angry?'

'It'll be all right, Jonny. No one's going to hurt you.'

'Sorry about all this, Harvey. Look, there's no need for any fisticuffs.' Ashley shrugged his well-clad shoulders. 'Come along, darling. God, how I've missed you.'

Ursula struggled to her feet and Tristan stepped back from her, as if she was something tainted. Facing him now was more nerve-wracking than when she had faced Alec's bitterness. 'I'm truly sorry about this, Tristan. I wanted my baby, you see, and I'm still in love with Bruce. I couldn't bear to leave Jonny behind, try to understand. You must forget all about me, make a new start for yourself and Jonny. Will you let me write to him?'

'I don't know. Perhaps it would be better if you go out of his life for good.'

'Afraid you've got no say in the matter, old boy.' Ashley whipped back his coat and pulled a small pistol out of the waistband pocket.

'Bruce, what are you doing?' Ursula demanded nervously.

'I promised you we'd take the boy with us this time, Ursula, and I'm going to keep my word. You know the drill, Harvey.

Put the boy down. Hands up. Move slowly over to the fireplace. Don't be fool enough to try anything, I'm quite nifty with a gun.'

'Why did you stay with me so long?' Tristan hurled the question at Ursula, keeping a firm grip on Jonathan. 'Why lie to me all these weeks? That man's corrupted you.'

'I did want us to try again, Tristan. I only decided to go with Bruce a few days ago.'

'And are you going to let that scum take my son away from me?'

Ursula glanced at her lover. Torn between her love for him and her desire to keep her son, and the terrible hurt she would cause her husband, she hung her head. Feeling dizzy and in pain, she said to Bruce Ashley, 'We should go. I can't stand up much longer.'

Tristan backed away with Jonathan. 'I'll never let you take him.'

'You should have let the Hun finish you off, Harvey, then Ursula could have claimed everything you had,' Ashley jeered.

'That's where you're wrong, Ashley.' Tristan's voice was saturated with hate and hostility. 'I changed my will in Jonathan's favour in the trenches, everything in my name would have been put in trust for him, and my brother Alec his guardian. Neither you or her would have got your hands on a single penny.'

Ashley had made a bead form on Tristan's forehead. 'Put the boy down.'

'Bruce, for heaven's sake, lower the gun,' Ursula cried. 'You could hurt Jonny, and I don't want Tristan to be hurt. He doesn't deserve this.'

'If you're so concerned for your son, Harvey, you won't put him at any risk, will you?' Ashley brought his other hand up to steady the gun. 'Well, what's it to be?'

Chapter Thirty-Three

After despatching Sara to alert Alec of Ursula and Jonathan's disappearance, Emilia followed Tristan. She realized now that part of Ursula's speech in the boxroom had been a goodbye. She was puzzled by a horse-cab waiting near the gate of Ford House.

'Are you delivering something?' she asked the driver.

'No, miss, I'm waiting for the people inside. If you've come to see them off, tell them to get a move on, will you?

'Is it a lady and a boy?'

'And a gentleman. Tell them I haven't got all day to waste.'

A gentleman too? Emilia felt the cold fingers of apprehension. There could only be one gentleman Ursula would go away with. Bruce Ashley must be inside and the couple were about to act out their original plan. Ursula had been playing Tristan for a fool all these weeks. Tristan must be in there too. What was happening? She climbed over the wall and stole up to the same window Tristan had looked through. What she saw made her leap back against the wall. Tristan, in the act of lowering Jonny down from his arms, was being threatened by a stranger – Bruce Ashley – with a gun.

The cab driver was staring at her. 'Hey, miss, if there's something strange going on, I'll be off.'

'Shush!' Emilia hissed, waving her hands frantically at him. 'Please, I need your help.'

'Don't know what's going on, but I'm not getting involved.' The cab driver lashed his whip above his pony's back.

Emilia prayed he would change his mind and get help. All

she could do now was slip away to a safe distance and wait for Alec.

The front door of the house was thrust open and an unfamiliar voice boomed out. 'Hold fast!' The stranger pointed his gun at her. 'Cabbie! Come back! We're ready to go.'

The cab driver did not stop.

Howling in rage, the stranger seized Emilia's arm. He was livid in attitude and colour and was visibly shaking. Like a cornered rat, he was dangerous. In fear for her life, her thoughts turned to Alec, her baby and all she held dear. 'You must be Bruce Ashley.'

'The boy saw you and mentioned you were out here. You, Mrs Emilia Harvey, will be sorry you sent the cabbie away.'

'I didn't. He knew something was wrong and left. Look, whatever's going on, it needn't get more out of hand.'

'Shut up! Let me think. Inside!'

The instant Bruce Ashley had dashed out of the parlour, Tristan had pulled out the heavy sideboard and placed Jonathan behind it, then he had dragged two of the packing trunks in front of it to barricade Jonathan in. 'Stay hidden, Jonny, what ever happens,' he ordered.

To Ursula, who had sunk down on the settee and had both hands on her back, he hissed, 'The man's mad. If you value your own and Jonny's safety, take shelter and don't make a sound.'

'What are you going to do?' she asked, anxious and fearful, as he stalked out of the room. 'Tristan, be careful for all our sakes.' Left alone with Jonathan, she was about to try to still his fears, but she became doubled over in pain.

Tristan crept along the passage and squeezed himself in behind the open front door. A cowardly, desperate man with a gun was dangerous, and Tristan wasn't going to allow the hostage situation to continue. He heard sounds, assumed Ashley was pushing Emilia through the doorway.

As Tristan had hoped, Ashley lacked a soldier's perception, and without checking if the passage was clear, he pushed Emilia along in front of him. The moment she was past the door, Tristan shoved it hard and there was a satisfying clunk as it collided with the gun in Ashley's outstretched hand. Ashley yelled in shock and pain as the gun was knocked out of his hand. Tristan immediately swung the door back, ready to make a grab for the gun and smash a fist into Ashley's body.

Ashley was sent staggering back over the front steps.

Tristan picked up the gun, bolted outside and tossed the weapon far away where it landed in a flower border.

Stunned by the sudden scuffles, it took a moment before Emilia registered what was happening. She saw Tristan clutch Ashley by the collars, yank him to his feet and disappear from her sight with him.

Tristan drove Ashley back against the wall of the house. 'Now it's just you and I, man to man, although no one could describe you as a man.' Tristan's hands crept up and formed a circle around the other man's neck.

'Steady on, H-Harvey . . .' Ashley gagged and choked, his eyes swollen in fear, his body sagging over buckling knees. 'I meant you no harm. The-the gun's not loaded. Ch-check it and see. No one was going to get hurt. Just a precaution. Let me go!'

Tristan's face was a hideous red and purple. He began to squeeze his hands on his captive's neck. Everything became strangely grey and then dark. There were sounds, voices, but they were distorted. He felt tugging on his arms, his waist, his shirt, as if hands were reaching out from the quagmires of mud and slime he'd left behind in another time and land and were trying to drag him down to hell. He didn't care. The only sense he had was the burning desire to kill this despicable coward who, for the second time, had sought to destroy his life, leech his soul and leave him utterly abandoned.

A heavy crack on the head sent Tristan into blackness.

When he came round a moment or two later, he was sprawled on the floor and Emilia was supporting him by the shoulders, rubbing his temple, which was sore and painful. 'I'm sorry, Tris. I had to do something or you would have killed him, and he's not worth hanging for.' For minutes, it seemed, Emilia, joined by Ursula, had begged Tristan, in vain, to let Ashley go. Emilia had struck Tristan with a two-handed blow.

Tristan's head cleared and he saw Ashley in a heap, where he had slid down the wall after his hands had fallen away. Ursula was on her knees close beside Ashley, and he was gingerly holding his bruised throat. His face was horribly discoloured and streaming with tears. Ursula took out his pocket handkerchief, but he pushed it away. His voice emerged as a raw rasp. 'You tried to murder me, Harvey. I'll get the law on you.'

'You threatened us with a gun. Loaded or not, the law would put you away for a long time,' Emilia snapped back. 'I'm going to take Tristan and Jonny to the farm. My husband will see to it that you and Ursula leave here, for good this time.'

'I'm afraid I can't go.' Ursula groaned and leaned against the wall. 'I'm unwell and I'm getting pains. I think my labour's started.'

Tristan's expression was blank. He saw her distress, but felt nothing.

Bruce Ashley seemed to have nothing to say, and Emilia went to her. 'Alec should be here any moment. We'll get you back to the farm, Ursula, and send for the district nurse. You must go, Ashley. Where are you staying? We'll send word to you after the birth. In due course, arrangements will be made for Ursula and your child to join you.'

'Ahhh!' Ursula suddenly yelled out. 'There's no time to get to the farm. The baby's coming soon.'

'What's happening?' The small, nervous voice came from Jonny, who crept out of his hiding place.

Tristan scrambled to his feet and took Jonny's hand. 'There's nothing to worry about, son. There was a quarrel, a silly grown-ups' quarrel, but it's all over now. Mummy's poorly. Run inside and fetch her coat, there's a good boy.' When Jonathan had left, he glanced at Emilia. 'I suppose she'd better be taken upstairs. First, I'll make sure the gun's safe, then I'll send this . . . person on his way.'

Ashley clambered to his feet. Still holding his throat, he stared down at Ursula. 'No need to do anything on my account, Harvey. I'm off and I'm never coming back.'

'Bruce!' Ursula wailed, reaching out to him.

'Sorry, old girl.' Ashley skirted round her, now talking in jolly lounge-lizard style, although he was obviously scared. 'I gave it a fair go. Too many complications for me. Not used to so much drama. All this has made me see just how much responsibility I'd have taken on. I wouldn't have made much of a father anyway, not cut out for that sort of thing. When Harvey's not trying to polish off a lover, I'm sure he's a decent sort – you always said yourself that he was. He'll set you and your baby up in some nice little cottage or something, I'm sure. So all's not lost, eh? You go ahead, Harvey, and get the gun. It'll show you I'm harmless and I'll say cheerio.'

'Bruce! Bruce!'

Emilia had to prevent Ursula from struggling after him. 'I'm sorry, he's gone.'

Chapter Thirty-Four

Ben arrived at Ford Farm an hour later. Tristan was watching over Jonathan, after coaxing him to sleep.

'How are you, Tris?' Ben whispered. 'Edwin arrived at Tremore and told me what happened. Julian was there, and he brought me over. He's downstairs. Is there anything we can do?'

Tristan was perched on the edge of a chair, rocking himself, his arms wrapped round his body. He kept his sight on his son. 'Have you heard how things are at the house?'

'Tilda says Emilia's still there. Alec too.' Ben tried looking up under Tristan's face.

Tristan refused to budge. 'I couldn't stay, not after all her lies. She wanted to take everything away from me again.'

'Tris, look at me.' Ben put a hand on him.

'Can't.' There was a tremble in Tristan's voice. He sounded younger than Jonathan. 'Best leave me. I'll be fine . . .'

'I'll ask Tilda to bring you up a brandy. Have you eaten? Look, I'll ask Julian to drive me to the house. You stay up here with Jonny, he's going to need you. I'm so sorry, Tris. You didn't deserve this.'

When Ben reached the door, Tristan looked up. 'Ben, I tried to kill Bruce Ashley with my bare hands. I hated him, but I never thought I was capable of such a terrible thing.'

'It's understandable, Tris. Don't fret about it. We all do things we'd never thought possible.'

'Did you say you're going to the house? Yes, see how Ursula is. She'll have to go away. I never want to see her again.'

* * *

Emilia had been encouraging Ursula throughout her labour, holding her hand, sponging her face.

The district nurse, Gertrude Roberts, a competent, middle-aged spinster, was shaking her head at the lack of progress. She passed her hand over Ursula' stomach. 'Come along, Mrs Harvey, you're not trying at all. That was a strong contraction and you've wasted it. If you'd only push, we'd soon have this baby out.'

She passed Emilia a worried look and lowered her voice. 'Do you think your husband would fetch Dr Holloway? I think it's the wisest course.'

'Yes, I'll ask him.' Emilia tried to relinquish Ursula's hand, but hers was being held in a desperate grip. 'Ursula, listen to me, I need to step out of the room, just for a minute. I promise I'll come straight back.'

'No, no.' Ursula rolled her head.

Another contraction came, and Nurse Roberts shouted, 'Push! Push, Mrs Harvey!' But Ursula closed her eyes and suffered the pain for nothing.

'Oh no!' For an instant, Nurse Roberts's quick efficient movements solidified.

'What's wrong?' Emilia cried, although she could see for herself. Ursula was haemorrhaging, the bedding beneath her was rapidly being stained red. 'Alec!'

It had been obvious that Ursula's labour was going to be difficult, and Alec had been sitting on the top stair, ready for any urgent instructions. His nag was saddled outside. He stubbed a cigarette out between his finger and thumb and raced into the bedroom. He froze while taking in the situation.

'Fetch Dr Holloway, hurry!' Nurse Roberts shouted to him.

'Right.' Anxious too for Emilia, before he pelted down the stairs, he said, 'Be strong, darling, I'll be back as soon as possible.'

With deft hands, Nurse Roberts spread out some instruments.

'What are you going to do?' Emilia asked, trying to ignore the warm coppery smell invading the air.

'If the baby's to survive I've got to pull it out now. Emilia, you're not to worry. Mrs Harvey's unconscious and won't feel a thing. I want you to watch her and not to look this way.' Her voice was steady, but Emilia sensed anxiety in it.

Emilia concentrated on the mother, horribly aware of the nurse's frantic efforts and Ursula's growing danger. Ursula's face grew whiter and whiter, her lips waxen. Her breathing shallow. A steady drip, drip started on the floor. Emilia prayed as she never had before.

The sounds changed, still quick but gentler. There was a peculiar gurgle. Emilia held her breath. She couldn't resist glancing round, keeping her eyes averted above the bed, yet unable to avoid seeing the crimson stain spreading on the sheets. Nurse Roberts had the baby in a towel and was wiping its nose and mouth. 'Come along, come along,' she was whispering. The baby gave a loud wail. Emilia's heart leapt, a rush of emotion making her eyes fill with tears.

'Thank God!' Nurse Roberts blew out her relief. She saw to the umbilical cord. 'You take the baby, Emilia. She feels a good weight. Keep her wrapped up.'

Letting go of Ursula's limp hand, Emilia encircled the baby in her arms, and appealed to Nurse Roberts. 'Ursula?'

The nurse shook her head, set to work again. 'I'm afraid it's only a matter of time. I can only try to make Mrs Harvey comfortable.'

The baby's cries brought Ursula to wakefulness. She was too weak to finish the smile that was forming on her bloodless lips. Her voice was barely audible. 'What is it?'

Ben arrived that moment at the open bedroom door. He heard Emilia say, 'It's a girl, Ursula. Would you like to hold her?' He watched, horrified at the reason behind the new mother's drained complexion and the nurse's losing battle, as Emilia placed the baby on Ursula's chest and brought her hands up to hold her.

'My God!' Ben hissed. 'She's not going to pull through, is she?'

'This is no place for you.' Nurse Roberts's voice was brisk

but not without understanding. 'I know there are certain circumstances, but your brother should be summoned here. I know Captain Harvey for a gentle, caring man. I think he'd like to say goodbye to her.'

'Right, yes, he probably would. I'll ask Julian to fetch Tris – as if he hasn't suffered enough.'

Ben knocked on the door minutes later. He had been thinking about Emilia, eighteen years old, holding a baby soon to be motherless, pregnant herself, in a scene similar to what it must be like in a field hospital. 'Can I come in now? I think someone else in the family should be there.'

Nurse Roberts appeared in front of him. 'There's nothing more I can do for her now. Yes, keep Emilia company until Mr Harvey arrives with the doctor or the captain gets here.'

Ben went to Emilia's side. They exchanged sorrowful looks, united, for the moment at least, by tragedy. Ursula found the strength to touch her daughter's face. She looked at Emilia and Ben. 'You two . . . were to marry . . . funny . . . how things work out . . . promise me . . . you'll look after her . . . promise . . .'

'I promise.' Emilia swallowed hard. 'I'll see she goes to a really good home.'

'Promise me?' It was as if the dying woman's eyes bored into him and Ben shuddered.

'I promise, Ursula. I swear.'

'Take her . . . she'll never know me . . . but if you can, tell her . . . that I loved her.'

'We promise,' Emilia vowed, glancing at Ben before she took the baby back into her own arms.

Ben placed one hand on Emilia's shoulder, the other over the tiny girl's form. 'We promise.'

The doctor arrived and ordered Emilia and Ben downstairs. 'Nurse Roberts will attend to the baby in the kitchen. In view of her intended adoption there's no need for either of you to see her again, although, of course, the final decision will rest with Captain Harvey. It was brave of you to stay throughout,

Emilia, but you must rest now. Please be sensible, I don't want to find myself at your bedside.'

They joined Alec, Tristan and Julian in the parlour. Tristan looked more haggard and desolate than on the day he had hobbled into the farmyard.

'Tris, the doctor said to give him a short while, then you can go up,' Emilia said. She touched his hand. It was marble cold.

'Are you going to be all right, Tris?' Ben said.

'I'll go up with you,' Alec said.

Tristan ran a hand down his face. 'No, I'll be fine alone. I, uh, didn't want this for her. Has she suffered much, poor thing?'

'She wasn't aware of anything really,' Emilia said.

'Not even the baby?'

'She knows she has a daughter.'

'Thank you, thank you, Emilia. I'll go up and wait outside the bedroom door.'

Emilia went straight into Alec's arms. She needed him to stop her from shivering, to soothe her from the horrors, but she did nothing to stem her tears. 'I don't think she wanted to live.'

'I shouldn't have let you stay.' Alec hugged her tight. 'You've been through so much today. If I'd been here I'd have been tempted to finish Bruce Ashley off just for frightening you.'

Ben turned away from them. He did not want Emilia any more, but it didn't rest easy to see his brother giving her comfort, to witness their closeness.

Alone at the bedside, Tristan held Ursula's cold clammy hand. Her hair, so black and fine, was spread out on the pillow, her terrible paleness made her seem dead already. Her eyes had been closed for some time.

'If only you'd written to me about Ashley.' He rubbed her icy fingers, which he held a breath away from his lips. He wasn't tearful, he felt nothing, as if he had died inside. 'I'd have released you. We could have made some arrangement about money, about Jonny. I was never heartless, was I? We could have worked something out, Ursula. It didn't have to end this way.'

Her lips parted and her almost white tongue wetted the lower one. 'Forgive me, Tris. And live, live for Jonny and live for yourself.'

'I'll try.'

Her eyelashes flickered. She tried to form a last smile. Then, with a sighing that was low and dreadful, she fell into everlasting silence.

Tristan kissed her lifeless fingers and closed her eyes. 'Goodbye, Ursula.' He laid her hand down on her body and crossed it over with the other.

He stayed in that silence. And suddenly he was weeping without sound. Not knowing if he could stand any more loss.

Those in the parlour heard the nurse and doctor in the kitchen. Prepared beforehand for the details of this birth, Nurse Roberts was lighting the primus to heat milk for the baby.

'She'll soon be taking the little mite away,' Emilia said, feeling strangely bereft, remembering the soft warmth of the baby in her arms.

'My God, this is awful,' Alec lamented, shaking his head. 'I couldn't wait for that child to be taken away, but now I've heard her cry, knowing what her birth meant for her mother, a woman I'd been so unkind to . . . The baby's going to suffer.'

'If I may say so,' Julian said in his feather-soft voice, 'not if she goes to a good family, where she won't know the circumstances of her birth.'

'That her father was a treacherous coward, her mother the unfaithful wife of a war veteran,' Ben said. He glanced at Emilia. 'Adoption would be for the best, but . . .'

'But what, Ben?' Alec demanded.

'Well, Emilia and I promised Ursula we'd look after her baby. It was one of her dying wishes.'

'It seems so cold just to give her away,' Emilia said sadly. 'But Julian's right, it's the best thing for her. People round here have long memories.'

'Well, whatever the state of affairs, she is Jonny's little sister,' Alec observed.

'Part of the family,' Ben confirmed. For the first time in months the two brothers looked at each other in agreement.

'She shouldn't be relegated to the kitchen, as if she's something insignificant. I know what that feels like,' Alec said. 'Perhaps we should bring her in here with us until it's time for her to go. Nurse Roberts is exhausted, she can make herself some tea. She's got another family to visit tonight, probably a long journey to make.' He went to the door. 'Anyone object?'

No one did, but Julian gave a curious sigh.

No one spoke, each lost in their own mournful thoughts, until Alec returned with the baby, now in a gown, bonnet and shawl. Emilia held out her arms for her. 'Had a hell of a job to get Nurse Roberts to let me take her. No, I'll do this, darling. I haven't held a baby since Jonny was tiny.'

Emilia exchanged a sad smile with Julian. Ben moved close to where Alec sat, next to Emilia on the settee. Alec pulled back the shawl from the baby's face. 'Oh, heavens above!'

Ben gasped.

'What is it?' Emilia leaned over to take a look. She gently touched the dark pink stain spread over half of the baby's cheek. 'Poor little soul, I didn't notice this before.'

'She'll have to carry this mark for the rest of her life,' Alec said, appalled. 'Nurse Roberts was muttering something ominous. I understand why now. No one's going to want to adopt a child with an imperfection like this.'

'People are superstitious about that sort of thing, aren't they?' Julian said, sitting forward from his armchair, craning his long pale neck to see.

'They'll say she's tainted with the sins of her father and mother,' Ben said, angry on the baby's behalf. His desire to protect her outweighed any other promise he had made.

Emilia caressed the baby's downy hair, thick and fair like her father's. 'What will happen to her? Not an orphanage? They're terrible places. We can't let that happen to her, Alec.'

'She'd be condemned to ridicule for the rest of her life,

over something that's not her fault. I know what that's like too,' Alec said, with feeling. 'No, I won't have that for her. To be pushed out into the world without a name, to be doomed to never know any sort of family. I couldn't do that to an innocent child.'

Ben placed a fingertip into the baby's fist. 'Are you saying we should keep her? She hasn't got anyone in all the world except us, and as you said, she is Jonny's sister. I'm willing to keep the vow I made to Ursula.'

'Not you,' Alec said in a none too friendly tone. 'I don't take any vow you make seriously. Emilia and I will take her in.' Gently, he pressed on the baby's bottom lip with the teat of the bottle until she searched for it and started to suckle. He had fed many a sick or orphaned animal in this manner, but giving life-saving nourishment to this baby girl, pledging to give her a home, bonded her to him in his heart. 'All we need now is for Tris to agree.'

'It was Emilia and I who agreed to look after her,' Ben bit back. 'Like it or not, I'm included in this decision.'

Tristan was met with another silence when he came downstairs.

'I'm so sorry, Tris. I don't know what else to say,' Alec said.

Ben placed his arm round Tristan's shoulders.

'Thank you for staying.' Tristan addressed all there in officer's formality, but they could see, and almost feel, the depths of his anguish. 'I've seen a lot of death, one never gets used to it. Can we go back to the farm? After the events of today, I never want to set foot inside this house again.'

'Of course.' Emilia knew Tristan was pretending not to notice the baby, now asleep, in Alec's arms. She rose, took the baby, but before starting the exodus, glanced from brother to brother, ending with Tristan.

'Well, it looks as if you all have something to say?' Tristan squared his body and braced himself – by the string of serious expressions he was sure he needed to.

Emilia approached him. 'Tristan, I know this is asking a

lot of you, but would you take a look at the baby? There's a particular reason for asking.'

Tristan swept his head to the side. If the child looked like Bruce Ashley he would not be able to bear it, if she looked like Ursula, even less so. 'I can't. I don't see any point. Tell me what you'd have me know.'

'She has a birthmark, Tris, over a large part of her face. The people who were to adopt her won't want her now, the nurse has confirmed it. She's innocent in all that's happened. If we send her away she'll be taken to an orphanage, almost certainly destined for a wretched life. I know this will be hard for you to accept, but we, and that includes Ben, want to give her a home, a chance. Even though you're not her father, as Ursula's husband, we need your permission.'

'If you're all so set on it, let the nurse take her away and then you can adopt her from the institution.' Tristan swore shockingly. When he'd left his wife's deathbed, he had counted on his family to shelter him and his son in their grief. He saw this latest episode as a betrayal and felt as if his insides were being physically shredded. He felt that the people who should care for him the most were mocking him. 'God in heaven, how can you all be so heartless as to involve me in this sordid scheme? You're actually asking me to sign my name on her birth certificate?'

'The baby's conception and birth were sordid, but she, herself, is not, Tris,' Alec said in a quiet, soothing voice. 'And I'm prepared to put my name on her birth certificate.'

With a toss of his head Tristan stared at the baby. She was as hateful to him as any enemy he had faced, as hateful as the mud and blood of the barbarous trenches he had survived. 'That's the sort of birthmark that will lessen in time. You're all being melodramatic.'

'The thing is, Tris,' Ben said, 'it's at its worst now, when it matters the most in her life and future well-being. Yes, we could adopt her from the orphanage, but that could take months. Why let her suffer one day without the care and attention from those who want her? Alec and Emilia are having their own baby, let me take her to Tremore and you'd never have to see her again. Eliza and I will manage until I can appoint a nurse.'

'No!' Alec cut in. 'Emilia and I can offer her a proper family home.'

Tristan rubbed the back of his neck, pressed taut fingers over his eyes. 'This is the most pathetic thing I've ever heard. A happy future for this child? With the pair of you arguing over her less than an hour after her birth? How would it help if you were to bring her up, Ben? What would Jonny think about his half-sister being reared on the other side of the village? And you, Alec and Emilia? The villagers would know her true origins and she'd be shunned and ridiculed anyway.'

'But at least she'd have a family,' Emilia said, feeling awful to be badgering Tristan while he was at his most distressed.

'A family who would shield her from most of the hurt,' Alec persisted.

'Taking on Ursula's child isn't going to replace the one you lost partly through her actions. Why can't I make you all see sense?' Tristan's words blasted through the room like an explosion. 'Nothing on earth would make me allow any of the family to adopt her. There is no way I'd allow Jonny to endure the consequences of her parents' offences.'

There was a dreadful pause, as if the foundations of the house had been shaken and were being allowed to settle.

It was broken by the smallest voice in the room. 'I could take her.'

Emilia and the Harvey brothers all stared at Julian.

'It might be the perfect solution. Polly and I could do a lot for the little girl. If Polly and I were to adopt her, our friendship with the Harveys would mean those who want to could have a protective influence on her life. I agree with Captain Harvey, that young Jonny should never know the truth about her. The answer as to what should go on the birth certificate is father unknown, surely? The child need never see it, or ever find out who her mother was.' Julian was ashen-faced and puffing when he finished, having given way to an unusual and undesirable amount of passion. 'Well, that's all I wanted to say. Perhaps you'd like to think about it.'

There were several moments of fraught quietness as the others thought through his suggestion.

Tristan spoke first – Emilia, Alec and Ben felt it was his right. He took centre-stage, straight-backed, by the mantelpiece. 'In light of what's happened, I think it's best Jonny stay on at the farm until I complete my service. Somehow I've got to tell him he's lost both his mother and sister. I'd rather this child was taken far away, where there would be no risk of contact with him or myself in the future. But I'm not heartless. I agree she's an innocent child. Take her if you must, Andrews, or she goes to the orphanage. I never want to see her again.' Turning his back on the room, he fumbled for a cigarette.

Alec was beside Emilia. His face was pinched. Like Emilia and Ben, he was shocked by Tristan's outburst, feeling guilty about his insensitivity. 'Give her to Julian, darling. She's his now. You, I and Ben can watch her grow up, look out for her interests if it's necessary. You agree with this, Ben?'

Ben nodded.

Feeling she could cry every sort of tear, Emilia kissed the baby. The tiny face looked lost, somehow tossed about. Her heart wrenched in pieces, she handed her over to Julian.

He smiled wanly at her, then gazed dotingly at the child he would be legal guardian to in the years he had left. 'I'll ask the nurse to travel with us to Truro. I'd better be off. Ben, I'll call on you in a few days.'

'Tris, I'm sorry about all you've suffered today,' Ben said, then left too. Outside, he gazed up at the twilight sky, slashed with pinks and purples, a beautiful sight but it reminded him of bruises. His emotions felt bruised. For a while he had fancied himself as someone's saviour and shield again, only to be rebuffed once more.

He started the trudge home. Then he heard small animals rustling in the hedges, busy about their usual affairs. Even the war had not stopped them. And nothing must stop him. Fate had dictated that he kept his life. He would make something of it. His weary steps turned into purposeful strides.

Alec glanced uncertainly at Tristan. 'Do you want to walk back with us?'

He turned round. 'I couldn't bear to be alone.' He glanced overhead. 'Dr Holloway's going to arrange for Ursula's body to be removed at dawn. I think if she could choose, it would be to stay here alone, just her and the silence.'

Chapter Thirty-Five

From the dairy, Emilia saw Jonathan running through the yard, Pip barking madly at his side, the pair scattering the hens, ducks and geese and disturbing the larger animals. She went outside to meet him.

'There's heaps of letters today,' he shouted, before reaching her. 'One from Daddy, and one from Honor, and one from cousin Winifred, probably saying she'll come to Uncle Alec's victory party, and I've got one from Vera Rose.'

They perched on the steps of the goat house. Pip ran off to torment the cats. Jonny waited for Emilia to rip open the envelope bearing his father's plain writing and hand over the expected enclosed letter for him. With his head resting against her arm, they read quietly under the pale mid-November sky. It was a soft grey sky, not murky, not gloomy, with light dashes of clouds, and there was a languid warm wind stirring the dry autumn leaves.

Emilia read Honor's letter first. She was well. Archie's health was improving steadily, but because of the Spanish influenza epidemic, which had annihilated further millions across Europe, Honor was playing safe and keeping him isolated. There was good news. Honor was expecting a baby. Her one and only baby, the letter stressed. Emilia smiled. What would Honor say when she replied with the news that she, herself, was already starting on her second child?

Tristan's letter *was* good news. In the first months after his new posting, his communication had been short and informative. This time it seemed friendly, a little cheerful even.

She would never forget the day he left, three weeks after

Ursula's harrowing funeral, a daughter supposedly buried with her; there had been an unexpectedly large attendance from Hennaford; sympathy for Tristan and Jonny.

Jonny, inconsolable for days, had clung to Tristan at the farm entrance, where Tristan had insisted he say goodbye to the family. 'I'm afraid you won't come back, Daddy.'

'I wish I could take you with me, but the farm's the best place for you. Hopefully, the war will soon end and we can all be together.' Tristan had kissed Lottie, said goodbye to Tilda, Jim and Sara, Bernard Vickery and Midge Roach, and Edwin and Dolly, who had taken over Henry's room.

Grave and thoughtful, Tristan had shaken Ben's hand. 'Make me proud of you.'

To Alec. 'You've got everything you need now. I'm pleased for you. Don't be too hard on others.'

He had left Emilia to last. He had kissed her, given her a sentimental line or two, then suddenly crushed her against his body. She had felt his thin, bony form, and his trembling and despair. He had whispered in her ear, 'I want to thank you for all you did for Ursula. I was selfish at the end. I wish I'd stayed with her too. I'm glad you'll be here for Jonny, he's going to need you so much.'

'You're not the least bit selfish, Tris. Don't be hard on yourself,' she had implored him.

She had felt his lips and his tears on her cheek, then he had pulled away. Tristan had wanted someone to hold him, not just for a while, but for hours, to give him comfort and companionship. He had left it too late. He'd had to go – leaving her to pray he would find the solace he so badly needed.

Another thing he had said: 'We never did bother with that farewell supper. Perhaps we'll make it a celebration when I next come home.'

There had been no demurrals from Alec and Ben. Ursula's tragic death, and their continuing interest in Julian's adopted ward, the birth-marked, but otherwise thriving Louisa May Hetherton-Andrews, had softened their stubbornness. Since then Ben had called at the farm occasionally to see Lottie and Jonathan, and Emilia was hopeful the two brothers would one day be on old terms again. Ben was civil and non-confrontational towards her, and she treated him in the same manner, wanting nothing more.

'Daddy sounds quite happy, although he says he's going to have to stay on a bit longer in the Army. Why isn't he coming home yet?' Jonny suddenly asked.

'It will take time to demobilize the troops. I'm afraid there's going to be a lot for all of us to do to put the world right, Jonny. Your daddy is serving the country where he thinks it's best.' And it's best for him, she thought, until he can face life again as his old self, quietly content and optimistic. Somehow he had found the beginning to a new purpose and self-respect, and hope and a measure of peace, all of which he so richly deserved. 'I'm sure you won't have much longer to wait.'

Satisfied with the answer, Jonathan grew exited. 'They're coming to the party. Vera Rose and the others. Will I have to dress up, Em?'

'Everyone's going to dress up.' She ruffled the boy's hair. Jonny was at his happiest when scuffed and scruffy.

'Ohhh-ah.' He scowled, a habit he had picked up from Jim, to show his toughness.

'You should be proud to wear your suit, the Armistice was hard won, you'll understand one day. Cheer up, I'm sure I'll be sending you up to get changed before you end up in your usual mess.'

'I've got some brilliant games planned.' He gave her a sideways grin. 'We're going to have a flipping good time.'

'Nothing too rough, I hope. The village children don't play as wildly as you do, and don't forget little Vera Rose is a young lady.'

'Uh, uh, there's nothing prissy about her.' Jonathan pressed the healing edges of a cut together on the back of his hand, caused by his high jinks. 'Uncle Ben says I'm just like him when he was a boy.'

Emilia studied his untidy black hair, the broadness of his body, his shooting height and sturdy limbs, the stubborn but affectionate stamp of him. 'Oh, you're a lot like your Uncle Ben, and your Uncle Alec, but most of all like your dad.'

'And William's just like me, and here he comes with his granny.'

Emilia looked up and saw Dolly carrying her four-month-old son towards them. Dolly was tickling his chin and receiving a lusty chuckle in reply. Emilia was always chiding her mother for spoiling William, and chiding Alec too, but she didn't really mind. Her labour had been quick and easy, but it had not prevented Alec from being a mess of nerves throughout, fearing, understandably after the tragic event in Ford House, he might lose them both.

'I wish William was old enough to play with me now.' Jonathan pursed his lips and frowned in the manner of an ancient sage. 'He won't really know about the end of the war, will he? That we finally beat the Kaiser? And the party we're having?'

'We must make sure we have a wonderful time, then we can tell him all about it when he's older. Despite the rationing, we'll make a feast.' She reached out her arms for William, and Dolly, knowing she would get him back when Emilia continued her work, gaily handed him over.

'He blows bubbles just like Billy did,' Dolly said proudly.

William Henry Harvey knew his mother and contentedly snuggled into her neck. Emilia kissed him. 'Billy knows he's here. He watches over all of us.'

With a sad intake of breath, Jonathan pressed his face against Emilia, and she gathered him in to the comfort of a shared hug with William. 'Does my mummy watch over me?'

'I'm sure she does.'

The boy lapsed into a thoughtful silence, reminiscent of Tristan. 'My sister never really was, was she? Tilda says she went straight back to heaven.' He was suddenly all rough and playful again. 'I bet they have brilliant games up there.'

Alec trotted into the yard on the nag, greeted everyone, but his eyes were on Emilia.

Jonny jumped down from the steps, ran to him, and both

laughing, they shadow-boxed for a while.

Dolly watched her daughter's eyes widen in joy and appreciation and love as Alec advanced on her and their son. Emilia hadn't been expecting him home for hours, but he had a habit of turning up unannounced.

Dolly grabbed Jonny's hand and tugged him towards the hay house. 'Let's go see the new kittens.'

'What new kittens? There aren't any.'

'Let's pretend there are.'

'Why?'

Dolly glanced back. Alec and Emilia had their arms round each other, William cuddled in between them, and they were kissing.

'Just because, Jonny.'

'Because of what? No, don't tell me. It's another thing I'll understand when I grow up, isn't it?'